KENORA REINVENTED

...SHE'S STARTING OVER, HER WAY

HYACINTHE M. MILLER

WRITE IN PLAIN SIGHT PRESS

This novel is dedicated to the women who have had the courage to be change-makers, but especially to my forever friend Jessie, one of the most fearless people I've ever known. She inspires me, makes me laugh and has always been there for me.

Courage is the most important of all the virtues because without courage, you can't practice any other virtue consistently.
~ Maya Angelou ~

I believe that one defines themselves by reinvention.
~ Henry Rollins ~

Copyright © 2019 by Hyacinthe M. Miller. All rights reserved.

No part of this publication may be reproduced, distributed, converted or transmitted in any form or by any means, including photocopying, recording, or other electronic or mechanical methods without the prior written permission of the publisher, except in the case of brief quotations used in critical reviews and certain other noncommercial uses permitted by copyright law. For permission requests, write to the publisher at the email address below.

Write in Plain Sight Press/Hyacinthe Miller Books - permissions@writeinplainsight.com

Publisher's Note:

This is a work of fiction. Names, characters, places, and incidents are a product of the author's imagination. Locales and public names are sometimes used for atmospheric purposes. Any resemblance to actual people, living or dead, or to businesses, companies, events or institutions is coincidental.

Kenora Reinvented / Hyacinthe M. Miller -- 1st ed.

ISBN 978-0-9936132-1-0

ACKNOWLEDGMENTS

You can't go back and change the beginning, but you can start where you are and change the ending.
~ C. S. Lewis ~

Many thanks to:

My esteemed editor and writing mentor, author Barbara Kyle.

My sharp-eyed beta readers, Catherine B., Germaine H. and Lenore H.

My talented cover designer, Melanie Moor of Melli M DESIGNS. https://mellimoor.wixsite.com/faeries

Photo credits: *Woman* - BigStockPhoto. *Brick wall* – Shon Ejai. *Man walking* – Umberto Shaw (pexels.com).

1

The free world wouldn't topple into chaos if I didn't conquer my performance anxiety but damn it, my carefully reconstructed life might.

Two years ago, if the Magic 8-Ball had predicted my forty-two-year-old self would willingly return to the place where I'd lurched into unemployment, I'd have tossed it into the garbage. But as I'd learned the hard way, life was unpredictable. Sometimes though, the irony was delicious.

Cheviot University College, the second-largest educational institution in Toronto, Ontario, was my unlamented former employer. Their coffers had been ripped off to the tune of almost $300,000. Understandably, their insurer wanted to know whodunit and how. I was the newbie private investigator who caught the case because no one else in the office thought it was exciting enough.

My head-held-high arrival at the marble-clad Administration Tower had caused shock, awe then enough grudging cooperation for me to get my job done.

The investigation had been long but simple enough. The magnetic north of guilt pointed to Baljinder Mehran, an IT consultant who went by the name of Mitch. Working part-time on one of those automatically renewing contracts endemic to public sector institutions, he'd hopscotched through the alphabet and populated the clerical roster of the Registrar's Office with electronic poltergeists like Bonnie Baker and Donna Davis.

Mehran was twenty minutes late for the *j'accuse* interview. My minder–a junior manager from the insurance company– was a no-show, too. Not an auspicious beginning. After taking another turn around the squeeze-box excuse for an office they'd assigned me, I straightened the sleeves of my navy sincere suit and scrubbed my damp palms across my thighs. My phone binged with a text message.

'Kenora, you've got this.'

The message was from Jake Barclay, my boss. Jake was sophisticated, serenely professional and ruggedly handsome. He was also the first man in decades who made my knees go wobbly. God, if I could close this case successfully—no, *when* I pulled it off—I'd prove he'd made the right decision to hire me instead of some beefy twenty-something dude with a Criminal Justice certificate.

The door handle rattled. I straightened my business card on the desk in front of the suspect's—no, interviewee's—chair.

Showtime.

I'd prepped for days for this get-tough conversation with Mr. Mehran. I needn't have bothered.

Mitch swaggered in on a waft of funky aftershave flaunting a dark half-zipped Lululemon Knock-Out hoodie and Seawall pants. In one hand, he was swinging a clunky blue leather Mad Men briefcase with brassy fittings. His longish black hair was gelled and sculpted, no doubt to conceal his too-high forehead. The oversized timepiece peeking from his jacket cuff was worth more than my car. Apparently, crime paid better than being a salaried employee.

We'd worked in the same building on campus for a while and he hadn't taken it well when I'd fended off his amorous advances. Sticking out my hand, I launched into my prepared script.

"Kenora Tedesco, Barclay, Benford & Friday Risk Management."

"Hey there. I've missed seeing you around." He gave me an exaggerated once-over. "You lost weight? You're looking fine."

He pronounced it *foine*, like he was from the west side of somewhere tougher than Brampton.

"Traffic sucked large," he said, squeezing my hand and giving me a meaningful look. I tugged my fingers from his moist grasp.

"Why don't you have a seat, Mr. Mehran?"

"Why so formal? You and me go back a ways. Here's an update for you," he said, fluffing his wedge of chest hair. "I'm thinking of changing my name to Zed. Mitch sounds too, uh, British Empire, ya know?" He winked. "Zed's the last letter of the alphabet. Like, last guy in."

I didn't want to get his meaning, but the leer made it clear. "I'll call you Mitch."

"You can call me any *thing* or any *time*. Number's right here."

He whipped out his smartphone and flashed the lock screen in my face. The background photo was of a bare-chested Mitch in a body-hugging shiny grey suit, smirking-cool behind decks of DJ turntables and sound mixers. A garter-snake sized gold chain hung from his neck. He was surrounded by a posse of tousle-haired club rats in dresses not much longer than my workout t-shirt.

I suppressed a grimace. He flashed a naughty-little-boy smirk. My hand itched to wipe it off his face. Where the hell was the guy from the insurance company?

"Why don't you put your device away? This will take a while."

"Anything for you Kenora. Although, I'd say you'd suit a

softer name." He posed with an index finger under his chin. "Rose. No, Rosie. Sweet, soft and—"

Damn. I noisily rearranged my piles of papers. "Have a seat. Let's focus on this meeting. I'll be recording our conversation."

"Not a problem," he said, adding, "May I say, for someone your age you're a bit of a babe?"

"No, you may not." I suppressed a groan. Our interaction was not going the way I'd planned.

"We should go for coffee sometime. You know, I've had my eye on you for some time."

Lounging with one arm slung over the back of the plastic chair, he adjusted the designer sunglasses tucked in his hair. His smile was all teeth and too much gums. Dampness prickled my armpits.

"Knock it off. Mitch, this is serious."

"Really?"

There was a tentative rap on the door and a balding young man in a pink polo shirt, chinos and rumpled blazer eased inside. Seriously, this was the hard-nosed insurance adjudicator the client had assigned as my co-interviewer? The man looked beaten up.

He spoke in a rush. "Ms. Tedesco? Sorry I'm late. My wife's having a baby and...."

"That's wonderful. I'll try to move the interview along." I pointed at the chair to my left. "I'm ready to go when you are."

He started to sit but before his bum hit the seat he bounced up and thrust his hand at Mitch. "Ferris Galley, Carnet Lesage Commercial Insurers."

Mitch shot Ferris a pitying look. After a pause, he gripped the other man's fingers in a quick up and down shake then dropped back in his chair in full man-spread. I silently counted to ten and fixed my gaze on Mitch's collar.

"Mr. Galley represents the interests of the University's

insurer. We're here to discuss the twelve ghost staff you created. Remember Mindy Glass?"

Mindy was the only non-ghost. She'd worked for me in the Registrar's Office, replacing a staffer on maternity leave. During our phone interview four months ago, her comment about having stayed in one of Mitch's condos had been a fruitful clue.

"Hold up, Rosie. I think you're on the wrong track. We dated, sure." He adopted a sorrowful grimace. "Mindy and I are just Facebook friends. A while back, she messaged to say someone had been asking about her techno-genius former boyfriend. That would be *moi*." He high-fived himself. "When I got your call I put two and two together."

Damn! Little Miss Over-share couldn't keep a secret if it was tattooed on her ass.

"Let me explain something, techno-genius. The day after Mindy resigned suddenly, her email passed through the University's mail server. Interestingly, her master personnel file was updated with new login credentials that same day. The resignation letter disappeared. Instead, her records showed a transfer to another department, a new financial institution and a rural Ontario home address."

"So?" He was flicking glances at his watch like he was late for a spin class.

"So, I remember Mindy because she was very conscientious. I'd kept a copy of her email with the detailed header info." I opened my investigation report to a highlighted page and slid it across the desk. He sighed heavily. "Here's what caught my eye when I checked the HR files after the salary irregularities were discovered. For another year, Payroll continued to deposit $889.58 bi-weekly for her work as a mail room assistant. But when I checked with Mindy, she said she'd moved to Timmins with her new hubby to raise emu. Not East Garafraxa. You redirected those deposits. Fraudulently. We're here to talk about the money."

He snorted. "Money? I thought you brought me in 'cause someone ratted me out about the porn stash."

Now *that* was news. Ferris smothered a cough then busied himself scribbling in his notebook. Mitch opened his jaws in a yawn so wide I glimpsed the silver fillings in his back teeth.

"Probably that dweeb, Sandor. I can explain. I found 'em on the server during maintenance. Homemade stuff. Fascinating story lines. Uploaded by various profs. Friggin' intellectual perverts. My personal favorites are *Buttman of La Muncha* and *Pulling Pork*. I'll send you copies."

The pen slipped out of Ferris' hand.

"Don't bother," I said. "Mr. Galley, would you please describe your role?"

While Ferris was speaking, Mitch examined the laces of his leather high tops. Afterwards, he gave an exaggerated sigh and said, "I have no idea what you're talking about."

"There's no record of a Bonnie Baker or Donna Davis or any of the other alphabet staff being hired," I said. "You made them up. We figured it out. Let me show you."

After months of poring over a wagonload of material, I'd connected the dots. The bank transit numbers and account information for Mindy and the phantoms matched a slew of Canadian and offshore accounts Mitch controlled. At first he pouted, but as I flipped through my reports, his scowl grew fierce. When I wrapped up, documents littered the desk top. It looked like we'd been playing a Pai Gow Poker game. I slid a copy of my final report and cover letter to Ferris, indicated where he was to initial them to confirm receipt then gave him a quick thumb's up.

I let Mitch see my satisfied grin. "Anything to add?"

"To what? That bullshit?" His savage stare made the hairs on my forearms stand up.

"Hey man," Ferris sputtered. "That's uncalled for."

"Screw you. I built the University a payroll system according to their specs. They wouldn't pay me enough to make it perfect. No one asked questions because it worked. Sort of. Not my fault it developed glitches."

"Glitches? Please."

He jabbed his finger at me. "You were a manager here. You know how crappy the University's record-keeping is. So what if you couldn't find hiring reports for a handful of people? There's thousands of employees. Margin of error."

Ferris piped up. "There're no benefits sign-ups. Everybody working longer than six months gets benefits. You overlooked that."

Mitch's eyes darted from Ferris to me then back. The acrid scent of his anger crowded the too-small space.

Picking up my business card, he said, "You're feeling pretty good right now, aren't you, Rosie? You sure you want to put your new job on the line for this crap?"

I smacked my palms on the desk and snapped, "Enough, you arrogant douche. Stop talking rubbish and stop calling me Rosie. Crooks get caught because they make stupid mistakes." For a moment, I didn't care if I was being recorded. Maybe I could edit out the almost-losing-my-shit parts. "I uncovered your criminal activities, smart guy."

Nodding, Ferris said, "Yeah, she did."

Mitch jerked to his feet and hammered the stacks of reports with his fist, sending them slithering to the floor.

"I'm outta here."

No. If he walked, my months of hard work would go for naught.

"Not so fast. There's a lot of money involved. It's called embezzlement."

"That's harsh."

"Stealing's harsh. Sit."

"What's up with the mom voice?" he whined but sat down.

I rounded on my desk mate. "Ferris. That's the third time

your pants have buzzed. Are you going to answer the damned thing?"

He glanced at the screen of his cell phone, stammering, "I gotta go, I gotta go," then leaped up, sending his chair skidding against the wall.

"Wait. We're almost done."

"Sorry, sorry." He bolted for the door.

Mitch made a rude noise with his mouth, slapped his hands on his thighs, levered up and snarled, "I guess we're done now that your sidekick's gone."

I remembered Jake's encouraging text. "What about restitution?"

Mitch growled, punched the stop button on my digital recorder then leaned in. Our faces were a hand span apart. His oniony breath turned my stomach. I clasped my fingers in my lap to hide their shaking and held his gaze even though I wanted to bolt after Ferris.

"No can do, Rosie. Money's gone. Invested, snorted, bet, spent, *excedera*. Nothin' you can do." He stepped back and cracked his knuckles. When he noticed me wincing, he smirked and did them again, one joint at a time. "Even if you call the cops, they don't care about white-collar crime. I may be a brown guy but I'm about as white collar as you can get. My sources tell me no one cares much about some entrepreneurial fiscal real-location."

His cockiness pissed me off. That helped me refocus. "Who, your posse of guys known to police? Your sources are wrong."

"Careful, Rosie. I got friends. You have no clue, do you? You know nothing about me. I got responsibilities."

"Pffft. That's all you've got to say?"

Swatting my question away, he jiggled one leg then the other. With a contented sigh, he slid his hands into his pockets. I held my breath. His grin widened. The thieving little degenerate wasn't just rearranging his package, he was stroking himself. But I wasn't done.

"By my calculations, you walked away with almost three hundred thousand dollars. Did you report your income?"

"Dude, why would I do that?" He looked genuinely puzzled.

"Because it's the law. Even drug dealers declare income and pay taxes."

"Because drug dealing's illegal."

"And theft over $5000 isn't?" I flipped open a fat file of property listings. "Let's not forget your impressive condo portfolio. And proceeds of crime are just as taxable as employment income."

He slouched back in the chair again.

"I got no income to garnish."

"Garnishee, you mean? Do the terms asset forfeiture and repossessed mean anything to you?"

A sheen of sweat gleamed on his upper lip. Looking everywhere but at me, he muttered, "Bring it on, Rosie."

With a flourish, I handed him a copy of the letter of transmittal I'd sent to the Canada Revenue Agency.

"I've got friends, too, Mitch. The Informant Leads Centre in St. Catharines has an initiative they call Project Trident."

"Yeah, so?"

"See paragraph three? The Criminal Investigations section has assigned you a file number. They're serious and so am I."

He grabbed his briefcase and tossed the paper at me. "By the time they find me, I'll…."

I tapped the intercom button on the desk telephone console. "You got that, Jerry?"

"All of it," came the muffled reply. "Good job. Be right there."

"Mitch, that's an agent from the CRA Enforcement Bureau. You're done."

Snarling like a pit bull, he gripped the back of his chair as if he wanted to smash it into my head. I fought the urge to roll my seat closer to the wall but got ready to drop and roll under the desk if he lunged. His lurid cursing and gesticulating might have been funny if they hadn't been aimed at me.

"It's over," I said.

"It's not over, you stupid twat. I got resources. I'll be fine."

"Calm down."

"Oh, trust me. I'll be calm in about three hours when my lawyer and I have dealt with this. You think you got me? Wrong. I'm gonna make your pathetic divorcee life a living hell. Then I'll get your middle-aged brown ass fired from your fancy detective agency job."

I choked back a gasp and glanced down at the phone: the red button still glowed. The CRA guys were just down the hall. What was taking them so long?

"Yeah, Rosie," he crooned. "You think those two dopes you work for can protect you 24/7? You'd be surprised how much I've found out. Maggie, Lilly and Anderson ring a bell?"

My best friend and my children. I wanted to hurl myself across the desk and throttle him.

"The recorder's off so it's your word against mine, bitch."

"The CRA agents are still monitoring." I hooked a thumb at the desk console. "I told you, Mitch, you keep forgetting the little things."

"You think you're so clever? Not!" He flung the chair aside, grabbed his crotch then threw me a two-fingered, I-see-you, you-see-me salute. "We could have been good together. I told you, I know stuff. For you, I'll plan something special."

The office door banged open. A surge of relief made me light-headed. Hoshi (aka Jerry) Nakano hustled in wearing a somber suit and polished Euro style boots. Jerry was a Special Enforcement Investigator in the Taxation Section. He also happened to be the coach of my recreational hockey team.

"Game's over, Mitch. We've got warrants for your bank

accounts and safety deposit boxes." Jerry didn't try to hide his grin as he reached for Mitch's arm. "Let's go, 'Dude'."

"The bitch and I are not done." Leering, Mitch flipped me a fingers-under-the-chin *non m'importa*, then a stiffly jabbed sign of the horns. "I'll beat this, you know." As Mitch struggled, Jerry tugged harder. "Ouch, you dick."

"Jerry, the briefcase. Might be some incriminating stuff inside."

Mitch, his face screwed into a bitter mask said, "Don't forget, Rosie. You'll be hearing from me."

"Sure, sure," Jerry said, dragging him into the hallway.

I dropped into the chair and rested my forehead on my knees. My pulse gradually slowed to a trot. I'd done it. My first big case, closed. Well, closing.

As much I wanted the cocky bugger sent away for long enough not to be a threat to me or my family, I couldn't ignore the nagging suspicion that I might have made a misstep. Surely the venal weasel hadn't meant what he said.

2

While I was bracing Mitch, Jake and an executive from the insurance company had been debriefing Cheviot's senior managers about my investigation. Jake had promised to text when they'd made their decision. I powered on my phone. No message.

There was one more thing to do—formally notify the insurance company who hired us, Cheviot's auditor and the CRA. I touched my hairline. The flop sweat had dried. I opened the three draft emails I'd composed in the office, updated my list of observations from the interview, attached a copy of the final investigation report and fired everything off.

I was stacking reports when the screen lit up with a notification for my next meeting. I speed-dialed Jake, eager to brag about my accomplishments.

"Hey, there. How's your meeting? I just finished my interview with Mitch."

"Hi," he whispered. "Meeting's not over. We need to talk."

"About what?"

"Hold off on your follow-ups."

"What?" The word came out as a squeak. "But why?" I slumped against the desk.

"Later, Kenora. I have to go."

"Wait, I...." Dead air.

'Hold off'?

Pain cramped my gut. The previous Friday, after we'd rehearsed the interview for the umpteenth time, Jake had said to use my judgment about next steps. I'd just done that. Taken the initiative and informed the stakeholders. If there was damage, it was done. I couldn't recall my email messages. Damn. The reminder alarm on my phone jangled. I jammed the mess of papers into my messenger bag and raced up two flights of stairs.

Wind-whipped rain sheeted across the glass walls and ceiling of the third-floor faculty lounge, turning the dim space into a smeary, echoing bowl. The last time I'd experienced a similar downpour had been two years ago, after my mother's funeral.

Ravi, my soon-to-be ex-husband, had cornered me in our kitchen and berated me for moping. I'd remained silent, stirring my omelet instead of flinging it onto the front of the shirt I'd ironed for him the night before. As I was buttering an English muffin, he stepped closer and with a sly smile on his lips, announced he'd met his soul mate at Bible study class. While I'd been playing recreational hockey, he'd found a traditional woman who knew her place. I'd burst out laughing.

"Didn't you hear what I said?" he huffed, giving my shoulder a shove. I slapped at his hand.

"Don't ever do that again," I said. "I heard. You just told me you're freeing up my future." I'd wiped the spatula down his tie. "Your bride can do your domestic maintenance now."

After he stomped off, I'd hunched over the sink sobbing until my chest hurt. I wasn't crying about being dumped—our marriage had descended into tedium long before the children left home—as much as for the abrupt end to my familiar way of life. In my daydreams, I'd always been the one who would choose to declare my independence in some flamboyant way.

I wandered to the tall windows overlooking the front entrance of the administration building and pressed my hot forehead against the cool glass. The rain was subsiding to mist. A trio of men stepped from under the awning. In the middle was one of the University big-wigs, Dr. Marvin Something. To his right, the man checking his Blackberry gave off a cop vibe. To the left was Jake, shortening his stride so the others could keep up. Tall and robust, he wore a cream shirt, maroon silk tie and a blue-black bespoke suit that fit him so well it made my pulse race. My boss was a trifecta of shrewd, sensual, and witty. *An off-limits trifecta.*

The lounge door banged open. Dan Hordiyenko, the University Budget Director, hustled in, apologizing for being late. Round tortoiseshell glasses perched on his snub nose between close-set eyes, making him look like a pleased Pekingese. His fleeting handshake was clammy as a cold boiled potato.

"Thanks for coming, Dan. It's been a while."

He plunked himself onto the couch. "I heard what happened about you, um, retiring."

So, that scurrilous story hadn't died.

"Dan, do I look old enough to retire? My former boss detested me because I objected to her overseer management style and draconian cost-cutting for years. That insubordination charge was a crock."

"We sort of knew that. But you got your payout. Two months after you left, they fired her."

'Her' was the former Madame Provost who'd orchestrated my push out the door. She hated that my staff supported me. Over three years, I'd been reassigned to progressively more isolated and low-power positions but none of the moves was so egregious my faculty association would champion my grievances. It was alleged Madame had the ear (and possibly some other body parts) of several senior administrators. Mitch's thefts from the Finance portfolio had occurred under her negligent watch. She'd since moved on to other opportunities.

"I heard. Listen, I've interviewed Mitch Mehran and advised him of my findings."

Dan's Joker smile disappeared. "I was in that meeting with Mr. Barclay and the Standing Committee on Finances." Brow furrowed, he said, "Your reports put the University's decision-makers in a ticklish situation. They're, um, loath to proceed with the filing charges route."

'Loath?' The first decade of the twenty-first century was almost over. Who talked like that?

"It's not like let's pick road A or road B, Dan. Mitch is a criminal." I bit my lips to stop from blurting 'fucking criminal'.

When I stood up he leaned forward, seemingly finding my footwear fascinating. "But Kenora—"

"The insurers are my clients. They may be liable for the stolen money. They'll want to press charges and go after restitution."

"Our legal advisers are not happy."

"Too late, Dan. I was duty bound to refer the matter to Metro Police and the tax authorities. In fact, based on my investigation a CRA agent apprehended Mitch when my interview was done."

He blanched when I said apprehended.

"Mr. Barclay, your boss, indicated there was no rush to file your final report. There are options. That maybe we could...."

'No rush'. 'Options'. A trickle of sweat snailed down my spine. That's what Jake meant by 'hold off'? Damn it, I wasn't a mind reader. Why hadn't he been more explicit *before* the damned interview?

"But the evidence is overwhelming." A thought occurred to me. "Do you know what the University's liability ceiling is?"

Head tilted to one side, Dan watched me wring my hands then jam them into my pockets. His Adam's apple bobbed.

"We have an annual aggregate deductible of four hundred thousand dollars."

He gestured for me to sit down. Although I wanted to squeeze my head between my palms and scream, I pasted on an artificial smile and parked one hip on the arm of the sofa. He had to twist his neck to make eye contact.

"Subtracting the other claims settled this year, that means Cheviot is on the hook?"

"The Standing Committee voted to book the funds as Other Expenses."

I couldn't get a full breath. "No."

"Yes."

"You mean to say my carefully constructed case built on months of checking and double-checking is circling the drain because a roomful of faint-hearted academic administrators didn't have the stones to make a tough decision?" He tapped the side of his forefinger against his lips. I lowered my voice. "They're going to bury the loss? And Mitch might walk?"

"It has nothing to do with your work. That's top-notch, as always. Mr. Barclay said...."

Pain thrummed against my temples. I'd been so sure.

"Just so you know, Dan, it's not over. Mitch threatened me with personal harm."

Dan shifted from cheek to cheek as if the couch was burning his rump. "That's awful." His expressions ping-ponged between concern and resignation. "You have to appreciate how the potentially negative press, I mean...coming on the heels of that other incident...could cause a great deal of, um, angst."

While investigating Mitch's escapades, I'd discovered that the organization was a financial sieve. A ten-year old with a lemonade stand had better control systems. The gatekeepers had gone careless with a constant inflow of donor cash.

The 'other incident' involved a former vice president who'd constructed a mega-mansion in the Caledon Hills with money he'd redirected from the University's coffers several years before. He'd been convicted of four criminal charges and sentenced to custodial time. The debacle had rattled the academic community like croup. Media had a field day. Donors bailed. Alumni donations took a big hit.

By comparison, Mitch's haul was small, bury-able cheese.

"Well, I guess that's it."

"It's too bad. Personally, I'd have pursued the matter. It's just..."

I stuck out my palm to forestall another apology. Dan grabbed his papers and fled.

As weak sunlight brightened the lounge, I closed my eyes and contemplated the thin limb I was perched on. Had I put my new job in jeopardy? And no matter what I thought of Mitch, I'd interrupted his fruitful enterprise. Could he get to me? Perhaps. But that was the least of my worries.

My phone binged with a text from Jake.

'At the office. Picked up sandwiches. Let's debrief over lunch.'

If Jake was going to feed me, he likely wouldn't be firing me. I still had a chance to convince him that sending out those three reports wasn't irreparable. As much as I wanted today to be over, I'd have to tough it out and not throw up from an attack of nerves.

If I lost my job, I'd lose my house. I couldn't let that happen.

* * *

*I*n the visitors' parking lot I miscalculated the depth of a puddle by the driver's side door, twisting my ankle and soaking the bottoms of my trouser legs. *Great, just great.* I examined the wet Notice of Infraction plastered to the windshield under the wiper blade. 'Exceeded permitted time/meter expired'. I recited a litany of swear words and climbed inside.

Instead of me toasting success, I was hunched behind the wheel of my barely road-worthy Altima, fighting to get the twelve-year-old starter motor to turn over and trying not to cry. My stomach ached. I wrenched my pinkie when I twisted the key in the ignition for the fifth time. Finally, the engine coughed into life. Hot damp wind blasted from the air vents. I called my mentor, Bosco, switched to hands-free and put the car in gear.

"Farad's Deluxe Taxidermy and Wing Shack," he said. "Yell-o. I'm on the move. What's up?"

"Mitch didn't outright deny anything. Jerry took him into custody."

"Good job. Hold on. I gotta pull over."

Ingraham (Bosco) Poon had retired as a Detective Superintendent in charge of Central Investigation and Support Command after thirty years of exemplary service with Metro Police. The thing is, once he was behind the wheel he couldn't multi-task worth shit. He'd run Intelligence Services and Joint Forces Counter-Terrorism operations but maneuvering a vehicle through city streets while talking—even hands-free—was a skill that eluded him. His company car was a dun-colored mini-van festooned with a rear window decal of a family (including dog and cat) in Star Wars gear. Still, he drove as if he was in a marked police SUV with a full emergency package of flashing LED light bars, dash cams and a take-down strobe.

Horns blared in the background. Bosco mumbled a curse. The outside sounds faded as he rolled up his window.

"We didn't expect they'd be happy."

"Mitch put the moves on me."

"You serious?"

"Yeah."

"Did you control the interview?"

"Eventually."

"What the…."

"I got most of it on tape. The insurance company guy left early because his wife went into labor."

"Most of it? Guess that's better than nothing." He chuckled. "Listen, shit happens but it all comes out in the end." I didn't laugh.

"The more I think about it, I'm not sure I did all that well." I couldn't mask the plaintive quaver in my voice.

"Cut that out. What did I tell you about doubting yourself? Kenora, we've had this conversation before and I'd be damn happy never to have it again. Wait. One. Minute." He drew the three words out into a paragraph. Picturing his deep frown, I held my breath. "What are you not telling me?"

"The University wants to bail."

"And?"

Dodging an idling courier truck, I merged into the middle lane. "And the Budget Director said Jake told the Standing Committee we could delay notifying the police."

"And?"

"As soon as my interview with Mitch was over but before I spoke with Jake, I emailed a summary and my report to the three stakeholders. I was supposed to, right?"

He whistled. "Oh boy. Did you tell Jake?"

"He didn't give me a chance. You're coming to the debrief?"

"Uh-uh. On a case. You sweating?"

"Buckets."

"You'd better get your story straight."

"I know, I know. Um, when Jerry the CRA agent took him

away, Mitch threw me a *malocchio* and a *cornuto*. Said it wasn't over between us."

"The evil eye and the horns? I thought he was Southeast Asian."

"He was acting like a thug because I'm half Italian."

"Probably. But watch your back."

I crossed my fingers.

"He's just blowing smoke, Bos."

3

I bolted through the parking lot and up the back stairs to the buildings housing Barclay, Benford & Friday, arriving sweaty and breathless.

Jake was lounging with one hip against the counter in the office kitchen, chatting with one of the staff lawyers. He'd changed from his designer duds. Now he wore a cream knit shirt with the sleeves pushed halfway up his thick muscled forearms, pleated navy dress trousers and black penny loafers. I stared at the swirl of reddish-blonde hair around his chronograph wristwatch, wondering what his skin felt like, imagining his chest without a shirt. Was he furry or smooth?

I snapped out of my reverie when he said, "I figured you'd need something stronger than San Pellegrino."

He motioned to the half glasses of Belgian Trappist beer beside a plate of deli sandwiches on the refectory table.

"Excellent."

"Nice outfit."

Suddenly, I felt like I was glowing. Was it Jake or perimenopause? "Uh, thanks," I said.

"Check these out."

He pulled up his pant leg to reveal black socks patterned with a collage of Modigliani-style portraits of long-faced women. What stopped my pulse was the expanse of muscular hairy flesh above the top of the socks. Flustered, I hiked up the right hem of my suit pants to display my baroque patterned purple, grey and turquoise Pucci style knee-highs.

"You win."

"Dunno," he said. "Might need Bosco to adjudicate."

Ah, Bosco, my assigned mentor. On my second day on the job he'd handed me a sheaf of densely-printed foolscap pages, insisting I follow along as he read aloud.

"No skirts while on active duty. Start wearing long pants–dark ones, nothing fancy. No faded jeans. Washable wool would be good 'cause it breathes. Microfiber doesn't wrinkle and it's easier to clean stuff off. Plain tops, a blazer, comfortable dark rubber-soled shoes or lace-up boots. Socks'll be more durable than pantyhose. You can go nuts with your socks and underwear."

I'd taken him at his word about the socks. Jake, Bosco, and I jumped into a friendly but fierce weekly competition. The winner received a six-pack of craft beer and got to stick a Dollarama red ribbon on their office door. I spent hours scouring the Internet for new finds, the wilder and crazier the better.

"No sneakers. They don't look professional. Learn to carry valuables anywhere but in a purse. One of those multi-pocket vests would work. Find a plain navy-blue or black back-pack without reflecting tape. There's some compact slash-proof stuff that CAA sells. Get a plain messenger bag or briefcase."

"Plain? How plain? Can it be leather?"

He'd given me another once-over.

"Sure. No shiny accessories, no fancy jewelry. Keep it simple. A nondescript dark coat, not too long in case you have to run."

"Geez. Run? Where? Why? You said I was starting as a researcher."

"We'll issue you a flashlight, digital camera and voice recorder. If you're assigned to a special project we have some equipment you can put to good use. You'll get a smartphone that's encrypted and GPS enabled. We'll always know where you are. Make sure your personal electronics are all secure."

"Okay."

He finished with, "Your hair's good; not too long, not too short, no weird colors. Makeup's optional unless you're one of those ladies feel naked without eyeliner and blush."

Mumbling, he'd half turned away, but I had mom ears and heard what he'd said. Confront or let it pass?

"What do you mean, too good-looking?"

"Nothing."

"Don't fib," I said. "Wolfette is attractive."

"She was a cop."

"Amber and Clutch are beautiful."

"Cop, lawyer." His cool gaze was unwavering.

"I'll dress down. I promise I can handle myself, Bosco."

"Yeah, well. You'd better. You'll be hard to camouflage."

It was no hardship to comply. In fact, I liked keeping things simple. Learning from Bosco, as crusty as he tried to be, would be a welcome change from the toxic hen house atmosphere in the university's administration office. I'd done all right until Mitch, but he'd been my first interview. Did he really have the hots for me or was I just easy pickings?

I was suddenly starving; the sandwiches were warm and delicious and chewing gave me time to format my story. Jake poured another beer. We kibitzed with the staff coming and going from the kitchen as they grabbed food from the fridge or heated up lunch. The former cops and lawyers shared an easy familiarity I'd come to enjoy. They hadn't given me a nickname yet but Bosco promised I'd earn one in time.

We retired to Jake's expansive office for the formal debrief. The room smelled of leather, hot coffee and an elusive scent that was Jake. He arranged himself on the couch. I took the armchair, covertly admiring his thick, neatly barbered hair lit with grey at the temples. He wasn't classically handsome but all the parts made an attractive whole. Facing him across the coffee table, I flipped the pages of my reports and breezily delivered a précis of my interview with Mitch.

"What do you mean he turned on you?"

My buzz evaporated. I was immediately sorry I'd let that comment slip. The beer and brownie chaser had made me relax my guard. Jake's cop instincts were too sharp to take for granted. I wasn't going to lie because I was a forgetful liar.

"He talked about having friends and a lawyer who'd spring him. Heat-of-the-moment remarks. I mean, I'd just buried him under a ton of evidence."

"Uh huh. Bosco mentioned he came on to you."

I glanced at my fresh manicure and swore under my breath. I'd already chipped the Va-Va Vixen red polish on my thumbnails. "It got me off script for a while. No problem."

"Anything else?"

I made myself look up and maintain eye contact. "Not really. I handled it."

Jake's frown eased. I let my breath out slowly.

"I'll listen to the interview recording later. Dictate your notes. Next time, be clear on my instructions and the limits of your authority. *Capisci?*" I nodded. "What saved you is that Metro initiated a criminal investigation based on the information you laid weeks ago."

He slid a file labelled Magasin Bernards/Martin Bernard across the table.

"Who or what is Martin Bernard?"

"Your next case. Martin owns Bernards, a high-end clothing store catering to big-money folks and those who wished they were. I've heard rumors about his past but nothing I can confirm. He reports that sales are up but net income is down. Inventory is coming in and being sold, but the money's not getting to the counting room. The other thing is, their cash deposits have been wonky."

"Wonky. Is that a police term?"

"Yeah. Make a note of it." He grinned. My temperature rose. "Couple of times, the bank courier picked up the day's deposits. The store's accounting printout read $496,980 but the bag actually contained $469,980. The bank made the corrections and notified Bernards of the cash shortfall."

"Ninety-six, sixty-nine. A transposition error?"

"It happened three times. Before anyone could mount a formal investigation, it stopped. I've talked to the Metro detectives who caught the case. They concluded it's probably an inside job. Someone on a hatch-a-scam trial run. You know by now that in their world this is not top-of-mind. That's why Martin came to us."

"No suspect, private property, no one's been hurt and the thefts were covered by insurance." He smiled like I was a bright student. "What about the in-house security detail?"

"They don't have our kind of expertise. Besides, the staff know them so they're burned for undercover."

"Surveillance cameras?"

"Video only works if you know what you're looking for. They've tried to follow the money but there are too many people involved. No smoking ledgers, no mail room clerk driving a Porsche."

"What does Martin Bernard really want?"

"He wants us to catch the thief or thieves."

I rubbed my palms together. "I can do that."

"Your cover is that you're an external auditor looking for weak spots in the new data tracking systems. Hang out, get to know people, detect by walking around. Martin will be very grateful when you clear this up. And at fifteen hundred a day plus expenses...."

"Does he want to know why the thefts are happening?"

"Not really, which surprised me. He's more fussed about being taken advantage of."

"I expect I'm not to make a fuss or cause a disturbance?"

Jake smiled. Oh my. The man had a dimple. "That would be advisable."

"When do I start?"

He got to his feet and flexed his shoulders. I dropped my eyes to avoid staring at his intriguing midriff.

"Now. Read the files. Check out the police report, skimpy though it is. Draft a work plan. Call his assistant Eleanor to schedule an appointment. I'll go with you. Check my schedule on the Intranet."

"This is bigger than the university. Why me?"

"They need someone who's definitely un-cop-like. Meticulous. Dogged. Crooks are crooks in academia or in business. And just so you know, Bosco's praise for your abilities has been almost embarrassing."

The telephone on his desk burbled. He peered at the call display then snatched up the receiver, growling, "Can't it wait?" He cupped the mouthpiece against his shoulder. "Sorry but I have to take this. Sit tight for a few minutes."

He murmured into the handset, not glancing at my walking-away profile. I sat at an inlaid walnut desk set into the corner between a window and floor-to-ceiling bookcases beside a display of law enforcement service medals and framed Canadian and international diplomas bearing the name John Francis Xavier Barclay, M.A., LL.B., M.O.M.

Instead of reading the Bernards file, I angled my chair and admired Jake's muscled back. He'd probably played football and hockey when he was younger. Maybe still did. Many kilos of red meat had smudged the sharpness from his frame but with those broad shoulders, long thick legs and narrow hips, he still looked like an athlete. The self-confidence he radiated made what he did and what he wore seem right. Maybe it wasn't just confidence but competence.

I distracted myself by calling Martin's assistant. In a clipped British accent, she scheduled a meeting in three weeks. Blocking out the sound of Jake's rising voice, I speed-read financial statements and background reports on Bernards' managers.

I jumped when Jake slammed down the phone. He was leaning with his fists on the desk, breathing like he'd just finished a triathlon.

"You okay?"

He pushed himself upright and gestured to the visitor's chair. His lips curled but the smile wasn't warming his eyes.

"Yeah. My ex." I wanted to commiserate but his grim expression made me reconsider. "Please have a seat. Let's continue."

When we adjourned thirty minutes later he still hadn't mentioned what his ex-wife had said that rattled him so badly.

By the time I'd churned through the teetering stack of papers in my in-basket, it was after six o'clock. The opening bars of Bill Haley's 'Rock Around the Clock' rattled my cell phone signaling another distraction, this one a text from Maggie.

'Hey Girlfriend. Thinking of you. Hard to believe Bernice is gone and tomorrow would have been her 65th b'day. Said a prayer at St. Peter's.'

My breath punched out of my chest. I'd been deliberately focusing on work so as not to think about my gone-too-soon mother and the questions I wish I'd asked long before she died. The weight of being half-an-orphan was sometimes unbearable. I didn't want to break down, especially not in the office, but thinking of my mother swamped me with sorrow so fierce my muscles quivered like I'd been electro-shocked.

There was a sharp knock on my office door. I grabbed a handful of tissues and scrubbed at my cheeks.

"Yes?"

Jake paused on the threshold then strode in and squatted beside my chair. He stretched out his hand but didn't touch me. "What's wrong?"

"Nothing. I'll be okay."

"Hey now." His face had a worried-puzzled expression. "You can tell me."

I blew my nose. "I... I was thinking about my mother. Tomorrow would have been her birthday. It was an aneurysm. I never got to say goodbye."

Jake gave a muffled groan, stood then massaged his knee. "I'm sorry, Kenora. Doesn't change anything, but I understand."

* * *

Oddly enough, getting stuck in northbound commuter traffic on the way home helped dispel the painful loop of remembering my dad's middle-of-the-night phone call and the aftermath of mom's death. In her memory, I cooked a big dinner of anchovy and roasted red pepper salad, *pasta alla Norma* and ricotta crostini, washing it all down with red wine. My belly full, I soothed myself even more with the monotony of household chores and yard work.

Later that night, my daughter Lilly called to talk about her Nana and how much she missed her. We shared a little cry. Before Lilly rang off, she told me she was off to New Zealand for a sabbatical from teaching English at Chulalongkorn University in Bangkok. Lord, but my life was boring.

The highlight of my week was to be another private investigator training assignment with my mentor. I laid out my clothes on the bedroom armchair. I'd sewed the dark hooded jacket and stain-resistant pants of many pockets myself. I was proud of the neat Hong Kong seams I'd constructed using a funky-patterned bias binding. Bosco said I had to wear subdued colors on the outside; he hadn't mentioned restrictions on inside finishes. I liked the notion of getting away with bending the rules. After I showered, I flat-ironed my sprongs of curls into submission and set two alarm clocks. I'd only been late once, but Bosco's lecture and cold looks made me paranoid about keeping cop time and being punctual.

Just as I was sinking into a fantasy of a sandy beach, cold drinks and a candlelight dinner with a sexy man I didn't recognize, the phone rang. I glanced at the clock. Midnight. The only calls after midnight were bad ones. I stabbed the answer button and whispered hello. My heart was pounding so hard I felt it in my throat.

"Aw, Mom, why does life have to be so awful?"

I jolted upright. "Andy?" Envisioning industrial accidents, kidnappings and buses overturned in unreachable mountain passes, I clamped my fingers around the receiver until they went numb. "What's wrong, Sweetie?"

"Relationships suck."

I took a shuddering breath. My baby Anderson, all six foot two of him, was calling from a mining camp in Peru to wail about heartbreak and not a broken femur. His project teammate/girlfriend from Queen's University had ditched him for an American heavy equipment company executive. I spent fifteen minutes trying to talk him up from the depths of despair. When that didn't change his outlook, I reminded him that I'd walked the rejection road not that long ago.

"Yeah. Sorry, Mom." He switched to chatting about the people he'd met on the job sites then about how much he missed his grandmother. I was heartened that my children remembered her so fondly. "Could you send me some wool work socks, a new iPod Touch and a case of the granola bars I like? And another subscription for Audible books? We have a lot of downtime. Love you." My sweet boy.

I rang off. Unable to sink back into dreamland, I got up and drank a mug of chamomile tea. That was a mistake because I awoke three times to go to the bathroom, in between disturbing chase dreams and hot/cold sweat cycles.

I left for the office before dawn, riding the first wave of commuter traffic clutter. When I pulled into the back lot Bosco, outfitted in cargo pants, crew neck shirt and a matching forest green plaid jacket, was leaning against the loading dock platform sipping from an insulated Tim Horton's mug. He looked me up and down, nodding at my ensemble.

"I got you a tall coffee. Black. Cream and sugar are bad for your stomach. This week I buy: next week you buy." The man knew how to treat a lady. He swung up behind the wheel. "What happened to your eyes?"

I flipped down the visor and flinched. My eyes looked like they'd been simmered in beet sauce. When I'd dressed in the near-dark ninety minutes before, I hadn't turned on the bathroom lights or looked at my face because I didn't apply any makeup. I sucked in a breath then blew my nose for the tenth time that morning.

"Today would have been my mom's sixty-fifth birthday. She's been gone for two years but I ache like its fresh."

He patted the back of my hand. "You seem to be managing okay."

"Most of the time. Some days the memories creep up and...."

"I know what losing a parent is like. It'll take a while." He shifted in his seat. "Look in the paper bag. I got you a frosted apple cruller from the bakery. Sugary carbs are medicinal, you know."

4

The tightness in my shoulders eased as he drove the Bosco-mobile around Toronto in no discernible pattern. He regaled me with stories about places where he'd made arrests or gotten into mud-wrestling bouts, which is what he called fights. There had been a lot of those during his career.

Jake may have been the strong silent type but Bosco loved to talk about being a cop. I soaked up his stories like a thirsty plant, knowing that what was revealed in the van stayed in the van. I finally understood what it meant to laugh so hard you thought you'd pee your pants.

Sometimes we got so caught up he'd have to pull over. He spoke matter-of-factly of his years with Jake on patrol and as a senior officer dealing with discipline and PTSD and too many cop funerals but I knew there was more to their shared histories. When I quizzed him about the calls that still bothered him, he'd change the subject, deliver a Twitter version of an incident, or grill me about my investigation plan for Bernards. I was learning patience, so I didn't push too hard.

He trained me to keep a road diary to record weather conditions, what I saw and did, who I spoke with, what they were wearing and the investigative value of what we learned from them. He'd grill me on what the old guy in the newspaper kiosk at Bay and King Streets was wearing or how many condiments were hanging from the side of the dirty-water hot dog wagon on Front Street. He reviewed my notes and marked them up with a red pen just like in high school, except there was never a gold star.

His favorite places to teach me about being undercover were Toronto's less gentrified neighborhoods. He opened my eyes to a parallel world that wasn't so much shocking as sad. I thought I'd seen a lot of life's weirdness working at Cheviot University but I was wrong. As we toiled through late spring and the steamy weeks of summer, Bosco pushed me hard to toughen up.

We'd usually park the vehicle at the Eaton Centre garage then meander through Ryerson University campus or south along Jarvis Street and west along Front Street or the Esplanade. Bosco knew most of the more unique pedestrians by name. They'd give me a dispassionate once-over when he introduced me. Then, as if I was invisible, they'd pick up a conversational thread with him and we'd walk away with a name or nugget of information that might prove useful.

On Queen Street west, I got the weepies every time the gent with the Santa beard waved as we cruised by his permanent spot on a grate by City Hall. Union Station and the nearby taxi stands were a bonanza of partially consumed cigarettes and the occasional half-eaten hot dogs tossed by commuters rushing to board the five-fourteen GO train on the Lakeshore line. Neither they nor I could have survived away from hearth and home for long.

I broke some unknown P.I. rule late one afternoon when my sciatica was acting up and I was tired of my partner grousing because I didn't answer him fast enough or use the terminology he demanded. He grew tight-lipped. I'd retreated to my fallback of fuming silence.

We were idling at a red light on University Avenue by Osgoode Hall. At the sight of a limping, white-haired woman as bent as a boomerang dodging construction pylons on the sidewalk, I began to sniffle. My sniffles turned to sobs before she'd tottered across the intersection—she looked too frail to be shunting a cart overflowing with shopping bags.

Snapping his gaze in my direction, Bosco growled, "What now?"

"She's probably younger than my mother."

"It's called living rough for a reason." When I pointed to the jeweled leash attached to her three-legged dog and the jaunty yellow bow between its ears, he'd shrugged. "Everybody needs somebody, sometime."

After several more episodes like that, Bosco remarked that if reading about abused children in the newspaper or meeting sick homeless people made me too sad to function, I'd better rethink my chosen field of work.

"Do you enjoy your job? Yes? I'll give you three weeks. You'd better learn not to wear your emotions on your sleeve or you'll be of no use to anyone."

His tough-love remedy was to arrange a month of weekend ride-alongs with patrol officers in Toronto and with Peel, York, and Durham Regional Police.

My exposure to the slurry of indignities humanity served up after too much booze, drugs, rage and despair was brief but brutal. I wouldn't have lasted long as a cop because I'd have ended up lecturing, pimp-slapping or Tasering people behaving badly. What I saw, heard, and smelled would stay with me forever but Bosco's strategy worked. The sensory overload knocked the edges from my sensibilities. I told him I could deal with it, which was a fib at the time, but I got better at wearing a neutral mask and crying at home in the shower.

A few weeks later after buying a new pair of work shoes, I was crossing Nathan Phillips Square and spotted the old woman sitting with her pooch on a bench. I sat at the far end and said hello, then tried to talk about the weather. She drew in on herself, mumbling in monosyllables, worried I was a social worker or after her stuff.

After a while she relaxed. I found out her name was Belle and that she liked peanut butter cookies. She'd been on the streets off and on since her husband died and left her destitute. Decades ago. She'd lost touch with her children. She said she'd never spoken with a 'colored girl' who wasn't a do-gooder or peddling sex. That left me momentarily speechless.

When she shyly asked if she could touch my hand I nodded. She stroked the back of my wrist then turned her fingers over to see if any of me had rubbed off. I wept on the subway ride home, not just for Belle and her doggie but because in different circumstances I could have become a Belle. No one paid me any mind.

I recognized—after getting to know the names and habitats of dozens more hollow-eyed men and women with questionable grooming, untended injuries and fewer teeth than the letters in their names—that universal health care was a cruel hoax. Most of the people I met had untreated intestinal problems, mental health or substance abuse issues. Their pets received better care because the well-to-do would whip out their credit cards for veterinary treatments before they'd give the pet owner ten bucks for a hot meal.

Many of the street citizens went by only one name. Some wore all their possessions no matter what the weather. Others could have been migrants from another uglier universe. But as they pushed their spavined shopping carts along, they heard and saw things we did not. Who notices folks who are down and out? A homeless person on a sidewalk or in an alley is invisible unless they cause a disturbance or you get close enough to smell their world. That's why they were great informants. Eavesdropping was their entertainment. Information was their currency.

They marked me for a soft-hearted sucker right away. Following Bosco's lead, I'd spot them for a daily special at the local diner or swing into Shoppers Drug Mart to buy them personal care items instead of doling out cash. I knew it wouldn't make much of a difference in the long run but then again, I had a good job and no one was holding telethons for them. Those small purchases made me feel I was being useful.

Whenever we parked, I was allowed to open the limo-tint van windows only enough to let in fresh air.

"To prevent someone punching you in the side of the head or throwing shit on your shoulder," Bosco said when I asked why. "Back in the day, a copper in York Region got stabbed one summer while he was sitting by a tennis court with his cruiser windows down writing reports."

He'd drill me on laws of evidence, the Criminal Code, forensics lite and how to assemble an investigation brief. During our twelve-hour coffee-fueled days, I was alternately giddy and overloaded but I did learn how to control my urge to pee regularly.

While we sat in the van waiting for something to happen, I'd read from the Martin Bernard file, ask him questions and jot down his answers. He made me dress up or down and practice blending into a crowd which, given my perma-tan, wasn't always easy in some neighborhoods. I learned to disguise my height, wear a do-rag or cheap wig to change my appearance, 'walk weak' and avoid eye contact. Want to figure out if the sports car you're suspicious about was parked recently? Bend over as if to tie your shoe then press your hand on the hood for support when you rise. If the metal was warm or the engine still crackling because it was cooling, the vehicle hadn't been there for long.

Bosco and I had our first domestic one afternoon when my personal phone wouldn't stop ringing, buzzing or making unfamiliar beeping sounds.

"I thought I told you to turn that damned thing off when we're on the road."

"I put it on vibrate. I swear, Bosco, I've turned it off fifteen times."

"Doesn't it have a shut-the-fuck-up switch?"

I scrabbled in my pants pocket for a dime. As I pried off the back of the device, the thin plastic cracked. I tossed the pieces onto the floor and yanked out the battery.

"Ow. Damn it. Shit, shit, shit." I flapped my fingers back and forth.

"What?"

"Battery's hot as a charcoal briquette."

"Told you those things were tools of Satan. I need a break. Let's go to Cusimano's for gelato."

He cut a hard U-turn across Lowther Street. Cusimano's, an institution in downtown Little Italy, was Bosco's cure for everything. Gelato was code for carb loading. It was the end of our work day—close enough to call it dinner time.

As I swung the heavy glass door open, the scent of hot tomato pie made my stomach rumble. The lineup for the takeout counter snaked onto the sidewalk but my partner was well known and we were waved to a table right away. While Bosco worked his way through a basin of baked ziti with hot Italian sausage, I downed two slices of pizza Napolitano with pepperoncino and a Peroni beer chaser, a side of grilled vegetables then a cannolo followed by a cereal bowl of lemon gelato as a palate cleanser.

"I don't know how you can put all that food in your belly and not be the size of a...a...."

"A *botte di vino*? Great metabolism. It's the Italian in me."

He burped, grabbed the sports section then ambled off in the direction of the library—the men's room.

What I didn't admit was that in the months following my

divorce/grad school/house renovations, I'd fretted off twenty-three pounds.

For most of my married life I couldn't wait to be truly independent. On my own. But being single again wasn't all the lifestyle magazines cracked it up to be. On-line dating was the shits, with too many poseurs posting high-school era headshots or scary-looking dudes seeking prey rather than social companions. Now that I had stability again, I wanted to get my curves back rather than worry about another crisis.

I pulled out my cell phone and slipped in the battery. Message notifications flashed like strobe lights at a rave. A disembodied voice said, "You have one hundred and twenty-nine messages."

The first was a reply to the ad I'd posted on a buy-and-sell website. I'd offered a good deal on hobby equipment that had belonged to my mother. The potential buyer, Ash-Leigh Trivet, sent a link to her Facebook page. Lots of photos of a dark-haired shyly smiling young woman holding a toddler who looked like her, cute knitted children's sweaters on colorful tiny hangers and before-and-after shots of re-purposed furniture. I checked my calendar then texted back, giving her a few date options.

There was a slew of newsletters from cat-lover web sites, looking-for-love guys and gals asking me for personal information and daily scripture readings. Obviously, someone was playing a joke. A not-funny joke. The last three messages were confirmations that my passwords had been reset. What the hell?

I clicked on the settings button for my first email account. Incorrect username or password. I did the same for the second account. Incorrect username and password. I hit the forgot password link but was stymied at the pop-up that said, enter old password. I tried the one I used for most of my accounts. Error. Damn it. Hands shaking, I tried again. Error, error, error. Too many failed login attempts. Your account has been locked. Fuck.

I pressed the power button and tossed the handset into my backpack.

Later that evening, as I hunched over my laptop checking reviews for new smartphones, the land line in the kitchen shrilled. I checked the call display. It was my lawyer.

A lanky, sharp-eyed redhead who loved NASCAR and loved NASCAR drivers even more, she was a sole practitioner as tenacious as a rare-earth magnet. A few months after my ex-husband and I had signed the divorce papers, she'd forwarded me a cheque for $55,000. The accompanying note said: 'It seems your ex-husband did not declare property he bought on the sly fifteen years ago. He sold it on the sly. I found out. Enjoy!' That cash bonanza had funded most of my top-tier home renovations.

"Hey, Lynette. Working late?"

"Hi. Yeah. Listen." Papers rustled in the background. Lynette didn't like to be interrupted so I waited. "I've received correspondence from counsel for the couple who purchased your former matrimonial home. It says they've received packages addressed to you from sex shops."

"I got a note from them forwarded to my post office box. When I spoke to the lady of the house, I said to throw the stuff away."

"They're complaining about being harassed because it hasn't stopped."

My stomach sank.

"Harassed? Uh, by whom?"

"Parcels containing kinky products. Unsavory looking men and two women knocking on their door insisting they have an appointment with you for erotic interludes paid for online."

"You know it's not me doing that."

"Yes, but someone who knows you is. You don't sound surprised."

"Oh, hell." I rubbed my temples to shove back the stab of a

fresh headache. "Yeah. I know who it is. Fucking Mitch."

"Excuse me?"

"Ah man. Are we on the clock?"

"No."

I stretched the phone cord and began to pace between the table and the sink as I delivered an abridged version of recent events.

"Christ on a crutch." She sighed. "You've locked horns with a computer wizard who's hacked into the university's open-source payroll system and ripped off a couple hundred thousand dollars?"

"That was because of my job. I investigated him. Now the CRA have him in their sights."

"To top that off, you think he might be sweet on you but you rejected him with extreme prejudice?"

"I suspect he harvested my personal information. And hacked my cell phone."

"No shit." She grumbled for a few minutes. I could hear Lynette drumming her acrylic nails on her teak desk.

"What should I do?"

"OK. Listen. It's a bad situation with the home buyers but they haven't called the cops. Yet. I'll express abject horror at the invasion of their privacy and apologize profusely. You pay the post office for mail forwarding for another six months so at least they won't be getting kinky deliveries. Not much we can do about couriers or the folks who show up at the door, though. By the way, did you get any feedback from Lot and his bride?"

I choked back a laugh at her nickname for my ex.

"I'm not sure that's the right couple, but no. I'm going to call and let Ravi know about the harassment... in general terms."

I didn't say when, though.

"We have to make sure you don't become collateral damage. As your counsel, I'm going to contact Cheviot's legal department. I'll huff then lay it on thick about negligence and liability, how your personnel records may have been compromised and express grave concerns for your safety."

"All right."

"In any event, my call might tighten up their sphincters enough to do something besides wring their hands." She sounded far too happy. Lynette, my legal Amazon, loved a fight. "If anyone calls, refer them to me. If Mitch gets in touch, record the conversation."

"Don't I have to tell him I'm doing that?"

She groaned. I visualized her tugging her hair with one hand while she glared at the telephone.

"Are you joking? The man's stalking you. He's an alleged criminal. Why the hell would you tell him anything but fuck off? Oh, and file a report with the police, pronto. You gotta be cold as ice on this even though your guts may be turning to water. I'll get back to you."

Lynette knew I'd be as scared as I was angry so she'd given me tasks but damn it, I couldn't control the situation. First the deliveries and the skeevy visitors to my old house, and now I was sure Mitch had hacked my phone. Who could I talk to about my IT issues? We had technical wizards at work but if I said anything about my Mitch problems, they'd tell Jake and Bosco. I had to deal with it myself.

I popped a bottle of Leffe beer and leaned on the deck railing contemplating the rotted dock and reedy shoreline of my lakefront, calculating how much I'd have to spend to get it cleaned up. My job at BB&F was the best I'd ever had but my drive to succeed wasn't making it easy. Plus, if I messed up and the bi-weekly Paycheck Fairy stopped coming, I'd be in big trouble.

I locked the patio door and called Maggie. Her profane, anatomically impractical advice about Mitch made me laugh. The laughter died when she reminded me what had happened when she's been stalked a few years before by a former client. She repeated Lynette's advice to contact the police.

5

When Maggie texted that she was at the intersection of Sumac and Main, I was on the porch, shifting from foot to foot like I was waiting for my turn on Santa's lap. I'd tried to burn off some energy touring my back yard, but the soothing lap of Lake Simcoe waves against the boulders at the edge of my property couldn't compensate for what looked more like a cow pasture than flower gardens. Another clean-up chore to add to my to-do book.

According to my flighty former real estate agent, my vintage ranch-style bungalow now had 'super curb appeal'. Of course, if you'd spent enough coin on architects, designers, handy-persons, shingles, windows, doors and hardscaping, an ice hut could look good. I'd had the poop-brown stucco covered with lap siding in a warm taupe and the trim painted a darker shade. Despite how much I'd invested in updating the place, every time I pulled into the cobbled driveway I got a shiver of satisfaction —it was all mine. And if I didn't perform well enough to justify my fat salary, I'd be unemployed again and my refuge would belong to the bank.

Enough with the negative thoughts. Things were moving

along. I was due for a chunk of R&R time with Maggie, my sister from another mother.

With more stories than a fat couch has loose change, she'd been my steadfast friend since we almost knocked each other out chasing a fly ball in grade ten gym class. A day in her company was like a week of binging gourmet food and beverages at an adult theme park.

Her Range Rover squealed to a stop in the driveway. I shrieked, "Maggie," and raced down the steps.

We collided on the front path, kissing and hopping around in a dancing hug. Anyone watching would have thought we were two drunken sweethearts. When we finally paused for breath I started to sob. She held me at arm's length.

"What?"

"I'm just so happy you're here."

"Me too. Help me carry these goodies inside. Oh, and I brought a box of old stuff your mother left at my condo. Photos, too. Maybe you know what they are."

"That's my job. Kenora Tedesco, Private Investigator. Solver of mysteries."

On my third trip, she handed me a cluster of bright shopping bags stuffed with bright tissue.

"Maggie? Presents? You're too good to me."

"Someone has to be. I'm going to change then I want a cold beer."

"But I love you just the way you are."

"I'm glad." She headed for the guest room, bouncing back a short while later dressed for the country in a white t-shirt printed with 'Good Girl Gone Bad' in pink glitter over burgundy cargo pants. "Ta-da." She posed in the doorway.

"Good grief. Your shorts match your hair and mani-pedi," I said.

"Check this out," she said with a sly grin, unzipping and pointing to her bikini line. "Touch it."

"Geez, Maggie. Your skin's smoother than a baby's ass. It feels peculiar."

She zipped up. "I had it done in Vienna. Have you heard of vajacials?"

"Get out. You're pulling my leg."

"Nope. Cleanser, decongestant scrub, exfoliator wand and a steam-clean of my lady-cave."

"Sounds awfully complicated. For you and the poor woman who has to examine you with a magnifying glass."

"Yeah. All that was missing was the happy ending. Matteo hated it, though. Said he felt like a pervert when he touched me. Ergo, never again." She gestured over my shoulder. "Did you know the message waiting light's flashing on your phone?"

I whirled around. "Guess someone called when we were outside."

"You're jumpier than a pastor in a peeler bar," she said as I dithered between her and the phone. "What's bugging you?"

Mitch, the bastard. But I didn't want to talk about him.

The receiver was cold against my ear. I punched in the access code.

"Bosco here." I sagged with relief. "Sorry to call you at home but I never know if that frigging cell phone of yours is working. Listen, something's come up. I need you to go to a meeting. I've asked Seta to leave you the file. Call the client to schedule. Sorry for the late notice, Partner. Have a good one."

Maggie pressed against my elbow. Her breath was warm against my cheek. "What was that about?"

"Guy I work with wants me to go to a meeting in his place."

"You acted like someone plugged your foot into a socket."

"I've told you a million times you exaggerate."

She harrumphed and pulled two pilsner glasses out of the cupboard while I penciled the appointment onto the wall calendar by the phone. Avoiding her gaze, I opened the oven door then remembered I'd put the fish to cook on the barbecue.

"What's going on, Kenny?" Maggie opened a can of Wellington County Stout and poured it slowly.

"Nothing. What did mom leave you?"

"Deflecting my questions, eh? Letters I'd written to her that year my mother and I were on the outs. A pastel drawing I did of her in art class and a stack of yellowing yearbooks."

"Oh."

She scrubbed at her nose and smiled weakly. I'd secretly resented sharing my mother's affections with Maggie. Now, I felt like a jerk.

"I found someone who wants to buy some of mom's old handicraft equipment."

"You still have that storage locker after all this time?"

"Yeah, but there's not much left. Woman named Ash-Leigh agreed to meet me there so I don't have to schlep the stuff here."

"Good. That's safe in case she's a nutter. Tell me about your new job while we eat lunch."

I was relieved she'd changed the subject. We ate grilled salmon and *fattoush* salad under the pergola on the deck and killed a bottle of Chilean white wine. Under a sky crowded with fluffy clouds and wheeling birds, the breeze pleated the sparkling surface of the lake at the south end of my property.

She was curious about my colleagues at Barclay, Benford & Friday and couldn't wait to meet Bosco.

"I wanna hang with you guys. Kenora Tedesco plays Pam Grier as Foxy Brown. Bitchin'."

"Honey," I drawled, "I may have a whole lotta hair but I can't hide no pistol in it. Honestly, I'd rather be like Olivia Pope."

"Wear fabulous clothes and sleep with a head of state?"

"No, you idiot. Be chillingly competent and solve big problems without breaking a sweat."

"You can do that. I have no doubts whatsoever. Remember you were so scared you'd lose your house if you didn't get a decent job? And voila, here you are."

"That was my un-confident inner child. Sometimes I can't get that damned negative voice in my head to shut up. What makes it worse is coming home to an empty house."

"But you used to say you were lonely being married to Ravi."

"I was, but at least sometimes I could talk in his direction and get a grunt in response, even if it wasn't a genuine conversation."

She threw me a sidelong glance. "Maybe it's time you had a guy who liked to get his freak on? Someone un-safe."

"I'm too old for wild monkey sex in odd places. Having to wax my peach to resemble a ten-year-old girl's? Ugh. Getting all scratched up and sweaty with some guy who thinks foreplay is a golf term? No. I want someone who's attentive and gentle and gives me regular orgasms."

She pursed her lips and stared at me through narrowed eyes. After a minute, she said slowly, "Sounds like you need a woman."

I stared back. We'd had variations of this conversation many times over the last twenty-five years. "No, my friend. I need this job or I'll go over the financial edge. Having a hunk around who was hot for me wouldn't be bad but I've got enough drama in my life right now."

She turned to the lake where a pair of teen-aged boys in a stubby sailboat were running before the wind. Their laughter carried through the fragrant summer air, pure and unself-conscious.

"Doesn't sound like it to me. You have any luck on the meet market?"

"A couple coffee dates. Most of the men have enough baggage for a U-Haul. I don't have the patience. Maybe I'm becoming one of those do-it-yourself types."

"Oh, shoot. I almost forgot!" She jumped up and returned with a gift bag.

I peeled green foil gift wrap from the heavy rectangular package. The tasteful label on the box read: 'The Throbber. No need to stroke him before he'll stroke you. Soft and pliable with a firm core for a life-like experience. 100% skin safe. Cleans up with soap and warm water or can be sterilized by boiling. Satisfaction guaranteed.'

The vibrator sported an impressive scrotum, life-like veining and a cleft-plum head. BoB, Battery-Operated Boyfriend, was stamped into the base. Maggie held The Throbber aloft and flipped a switch under the testicles. The device writhed from side to side with an intermittent rhythm.

"Thanks, I think. And here I thought a bob was a hairstyle."

"There's a twelve-pack of extra batteries, too. Touch it."

I wrapped my fingers around the girth.

"It's getting warm! Another first. Good grief."

She covered my fingers with hers and stroked up and down on the firm silicone shaft.

"Mark my words. You'll use it."

Her mouth was smiling but her eyes were serious. Heat flushed up my neck. I withdrew my fingers, turned off the toy and returned it to the box. Maggie burped then pushed herself away from the table.

"I thought you'd be more excited. I'll wait if you want to go try him out."

"Not right now."

"Suit yourself, Ms. Born-Again Virgin."

"For now. I'm going to take my time this time."

"I told you way back when you didn't have to marry Ravi because you'd had sex with him. So did your mother."

"Maggie, stop beating that dead horse. I know. I paid for my impetuousness. Once bitten...."

"This is depressing the shit outta me. A gorgeous, accomplished woman like you and no man in her life."

"Damned right I'm accomplished. Have you seen my power tool collection? But I need intimacy, Maggie. Someone who'll listen. Respect me as an equal. Make me laugh in bed. I won't settle just to get laid."

There was no way I'd tell her how I ached for a simple hug from a man I liked. Maggie had a husband who was mad about her, something else I'd always wanted.

A small aluminum boat carrying an older couple clad in long-sleeved shirts and Tilley hats puttered by about twenty feet from shore. They looked like awkward birds with their arms propped up on the wings of their yellow life jackets. Casting rods hung over the gunwales. The man was holding the trolling motor with one hand and a pair of big binoculars with the other. He steadied the motor with his knee and waved. The woman spoke to him. He handed her the binoculars. Maggie and I waved back.

"Who was that?"

"Neighbors, I guess."

She poked me on the arm. "That'll be you in a couple years if you don't get off your ass. Speaking of ass, what about this Jake character?"

"What do you mean?"

"Don't be coy. Your new boss. Does he have potential?"

"Hadn't crossed my mind."

"You were always a terrible liar, Kenny."

To distract her, I opened a second bottle of wine. The sun flared hot in the flawless late afternoon sky, baking the scent of heated flower beds into every breath. We lounged in the shade, listlessly swatting away flying insects as we sipped and chatted about safer topics like our four children. She kvetched about having too many clients and how hard it was to find loyal employees who could follow the rules and keep their mouths shut. I had no rebuttal. I was trying hard to become one of those employees for BB&F. We quieted, listening to the distant drone of lawn mowers and the chirping rasps of cicadas.

"Something's going on in that big brain of yours," Maggie said without turning her head.

I swung my feet to the deck. "I'm—I'm being stalked."

She twisted to face me, her eyes and her mouth opened wide. "What? I thought your job wasn't dangerous."

"It's not. I'm basically a trainee P.I., for god's sake. This guy I was investigating—Mitch—flipped out, which was not part of the plan. Threw me *l'ombrello* and a *si t'ancagliu*."

"Holy shit. You worried?"

"Yes. Everyone at work keeps saying I shouldn't be."

"But they've had self-defense training."

"Exactly. I got a taste but not enough to do anyone much damage. Maggie, Mitch mentioned your name and the kids."

She sat up and gave me a hard look. "What?"

"He's a hacker and he had access to my personnel files."

"Jesus, Kenora. What if his threats were serious?"

"I know, I know. Except for a blip with my bank he's been quiet lately. I'm hoping maybe he's forgotten about me."

"You wish. What do the cops say?" She poked her index finger into my forearm, hard. "You have gone to the police, right?"

"Not yet but I will. I mean, I'm surrounded by ex-cops every day. What could go wrong?"

I didn't mention that Mitch had cast aspersions on their ability to protect me.

She fell silent. When I asked what was bothering her, she fidgeted with her diamond crucifix then erupted into a disjointed story of a discussion she'd had with her mother-in-law, the Contessa.

"She's pressuring me to give up what she calls my 'nomadic life' and be a 'real wife' to Matteo," she said, stabbing the air with her fingers hooked into brackets.

A surge of annoyance made my neck hot. Maggie had an unconventional marriage with a genuine prince of a man who managed his family's businesses in Italy and raced ocean-class yachts. Their twin children attended university in Switzerland while she ran a wildly successful lifestyle management company in Toronto and organized her rich clients' lives for huge sums of money. There I was, having been dumped by my philandering ex-spouse and struggling to keep an intact roof over my head while Maggie, who had the wealth, lifestyle, and relationship I envied, chafed at the prospect of living full time under the same roof as her husband.

She dabbed at her eyes with the hem of her shirt. "I'm afraid of the boring normal life," she said, twisting her rings, "But when the kids left for school, I felt like the passion was waning. I don't want our relationship to dwindle...."

"Like mine did?" I pressed her hand between mine. "Maggie, Matteo thinks the sun shines out of your bum. His family owns a palazzo, for chrissake."

"I know, I know." She had the grace to look embarrassed. "At least now that Ravi's not controlling your life, it's been better, hasn't it?"

"Sure. Getting shoved out of my job for a bullshit reason, temping at a so-called waste haulage firm for a boss whose nickname was Vinnie the Camel, going into debt to renovate this place, sleeping alone, being stalked by a hairy punk with low self-esteem. I'm living the dream."

"I'm sorry, Kenny." She left and returned a few minutes later carrying a crumpled brown envelope. "I've been cleaning out my closets, getting rid of stuff. Decluttering." She untied the brown cord securing the envelope flap. "I came across this stuff."

On top was my grade seven class photo. Lanky and gap-toothed, I was resplendent in an orange tie-died blouse, grape-fruit-sized afro puffs and butterfly barrettes. We looked at each other and burst out laughing.

"This is too much."

"Thought you'd like it. Use it for your Facebook profile shot." She sobered. "Then there's these."

She handed me a trio of faded Polaroids. One was of a handsome blond man holding a fat, smiling baby in pink rompers and floppy sun hat. The second shot was of my much younger mother in a flowered sun dress and wide straw boater. She was cradling the same baby and laughing with her head thrown back. One hand was outstretched to the photographer, her index finger crooked in a come-here pose. In the third, a solemn toddler in overalls hung from the hand of a short, square-faced woman with a tenuous smile. The sign in the background of the photos read, Fort William Park. The initials: BT, ML, ET and JT, were printed on the white border of one picture, but there was no date.

Maggie fanned the pictures out like a poker hand. "Do you know any of them?"

"The woman is my mother. God, she was lovely. But the others? No."

"What about the baby?"

I peered closer. "The baby looks like me." A skitter of memory gave me a chill. "Hold on."

I hustled to my home office and searched the bookshelves until I located a photo album dating back to my toddler years.

"See, I've got the same silver bangle on."

Maggie drained her wine then stared into the glass a few moments. "Ever wonder why there are so few pictures of you when you were a baby? And they're mostly of you and your mother. Mysterious, no?"

"Not really. Leo was probably the photographer."

She flipped me a photo of five young men posed behind stacks of tools and of what looked like camping equipment.

"Who are these dudes? Looks like they're on the hunt for buried treasure."

"No idea."

"There's names and a date on the back." I glanced at the back of the group shot then gave it to her. She said, "Aren't you interested in family mysteries?"

"We don't have any. You're trying to make a mountain out of a mole hill. Besides, I've got enough on my plate right now, thank you very much."

Muttering under her breath, she stuffed the photos back into the envelope.

6

Maggie and I shared a hearty breakfast before she left. Afterwards, I putzed around a bit then skimmed the snail mail from my community mailbox. An envelope had been forwarded from an old Shoppers Drug Mart post office box to my new address. That surprised me because I hadn't yet renewed the box rental contract.

Inside was a scrawled note from the couple who'd bought our matrimonial home.

Several questionable parcels have arrived for you. We are not prepared to incur any expense with forwarding. Collect them immediately or we will contact the authorities.

I ran a Canada 4-1-1 check of my old address and got the new occupants' phone number. The woman of the house answered. Her voice turned frosty when I introduced myself.

"Could you tell me who the senders were?"

"Mistress Sally's Pleasure Apparel and," she took a deep breath, "Horny House. What am we supposed to do with such filth?" The words fell from her mouth like ball bearings.

It had to be Mitch, damn him. He'd hinted he knew things about my personal life. Luckily, my trail seemed to have ended at the house I'd shared with my ex. Bosco's lesson about what to do when accused popped into my mind: express concern; show surprise; deny, deny, deny.

"I am so sorry you had to be bothered. I can't believe someone I know would pull such a tasteless practical joke. There must be a mistake."

Using my most conciliatory tone, I asked if she would please throw the packages in the garbage. I was tempted to suggest her hubby might be interested but I wanted her to think well of me in case something else untoward occurred. I ended by telling her what a wonderful neighborhood they'd moved into.

* * *

Monday morning, Jake and I had arranged to meet at the Tundra Building where Martin Bernard's offices were located. I'd ditched my plain-Jane work outfit and dressed to impress in dark pumps and a tailored business suit that was snug in the right places. It was odd to be wearing pearls and makeup again but I felt good.

When I caught sight of my boss leaning nonchalantly against the marble wall at the end of the vestibule I jerked to a halt, oblivious of the tide of bodies surging around me. I swallowed hard. Expert tailoring had shaped the sooty pinstripe suit fabric to his big body like a glove. His white shirt gleamed under the overhead pot light. Holding a newspaper in one hand, he radiated power. I wanted to unbutton and unzip and run my hands over his bare skin until we were both short of breath.

A burly guy in a too-tight checkered suit elbowed me. "You're in the way, lady."

I shook my head and walked up to Jake. "That is one snazzy suit."

"Thank you." He smiled, tucked away his paper then pressed his fingers lightly against my back to steer me toward the elevator to the penthouse floor. My flesh sizzled under his touch. "Ready to meet Mr. Bernard? What's wrong?"

The express car arrived. I wiped my palms against the seams of my skirt as the doors whispered open.

"I hate this," I muttered.

"Nervous about the meeting?"

"No. I hate crowds but I hate tight spaces and heights more."

"What do you mean?"

"We're going to the fiftieth floor, Jake. I don't like being more than five floors up."

My tastefully shod feet moved me in slow motion over the metal threshold. I pressed into a corner, clutching my designer satchel. Jake touched the button for fifty and the doors sighed shut.

His eyebrows rose. "You do have a flaw?"

Oh, if you only knew, Mr. Barclay.

We were mirrored to infinity in the smoked glass walls. Muted Weather Network music enveloped us. Knowing he was watching me, I stared at the floor indicator buttons and concentrated on pranayama breathing.

A synthesized female voice murmured, Going up. Four, five.

"You look great," he said. I was warmed by the compliment and his attempt at distraction. "More freckles than before. From working in the garden?"

Eighteen, nineteen.

"Bushwhacking before my dad arrives to do his handyman thing."

Twenty-five, twenty-six.

"I'm past my comfort zone." I tried to joke, but my voice came out flat.

"Hey." When I glanced up his steady indigo gaze met mine. "Not to worry. I've got your back."

You can have my back, my front, whatever you want. I felt my cheeks grow hot. Where did that thought come from?

Thirty, thirty-one.

Suddenly, the elevator skipped like an old man hitching up his pants. My breath caught in my throat. What if we got trapped? I peered for the help button on the control panel and jumped when Jake tapped my forearm with his leather portfolio.

"Can you hold this for a minute?"

"Pardon?"

"My shoelace is untied."

I glanced at his cordovan brogues then reached for his case. He bent one knee to the floor. His dark hair, shot with silver, curled softly at the temples. I wondered what it would feel like under my fingers. The elevator slowed then lurched again. I reset my feet into a wider stance, unsure if it was his proximity or the rapidly ascending metal box triggering the electric current arcing along my spine. I casually touched my ears; they were on fire.

When Jake straightened he was close enough for me to smell his citrus aftershave. The scent made my mouth water. God, but he took up a lot of space. There was a tiny cut on his chin where he'd nicked himself shaving. I wanted to stroke it with my thumb.

"You look a little green. You okay?"

Sweat prickled along my shoulder blades. "I don't need Gravol, if that's what you mean," I said.

"You'll be all right. Just a little performance anxiety I imagine."

He snaked one arm around my shoulder and pulled me into a quick hug, the impersonal kind guys give each other after they've scored a goal. I kept my eyes averted and didn't press closer, even though his brief touch had addled my brain and sent hot dragging throbs to my groin. Talk about awkward. With me, the man had always been the epitome of cool professionalism. He was trying to keep me from being nervous and I was getting hot and bothered. Understandable perhaps, given my long dry spell without intimacy but inappropriate. I silently repeated the mantra, 'The man is my boss, the man is my boss', and shoved the portfolio into his hand.

Forty-five, forty-six.

"Still nervous?" He was staring at the flashing floor indicator numbers.

"About what?"

He chuckled. The doors whooshed open.

We stepped into a reception area fragrant with the essence of cultivated wealth. Light from a wall of tall windows shimmered across jewel-toned Oriental rugs. Arranged across the expanse of marble floors, they glowed with the muted beauty of precious antiques.

The woman seated at a glass-topped deck-sized desk off to the right watched impassively as we approached. A triple strand of pearls circled her well-maintained neck. That couturier suit she wore was worth at least three of my mortgage payments. Age fifty may have been a distant blur in her rear-view mirror but Ms. Eleanor Fitzgerald had mounted a heavy-duty counter-attack. Her hands gave her away, though.

Eleanor nodded at Jake, relocating her perfect lips into a version of a smile. She pressed a button on her phone console. Three minutes later, the pair of carved mahogany doors I'd thought were purely decorative were flung open and a compact man strode over with his arms outstretched. His smile was very wide and showed too many perfect teeth. I took half a step back, bumping into Jake. He clasped my elbow briefly then released it and stepped forward. I knew the man's face from somewhere. The newspaper? A [Toronto Life](#) magazine piece?

"Martin," Jake said.

Half a foot shorter than Jake, Martin Bernard was bright-eyed, crisply barbered and Caribbean bronzed. He was wearing a skillfully tailored double-breasted deep mulberry suit, a butter-colored shirt and cocoa striped tie. Despite his barrel-chested fighter's body he had a finished look, as if he'd stepped straight out of a Men's Vogue photo shoot. The only anomaly was his too-black slicked-back hair.

"Good to see you again, my friend." He pumped Jake's hand then fingered his lapels. "Fine charcoal wool. Italian. Very nice."

"I took your advice about the tailor in Kensington Market," Jake said. "This is my associate, Kenora Tedesco."

"Pleased to meet you, Mr. Bernard."

"Call me Martin, lovely lady," he said. "After all, we will be working closely together."

There was something about Martin that sent a shiver up my neck but I murmured enough pleasantries to pass muster. He gave my arm a gentle squeeze, tucked my hand into the crook of his elbow and swept me into his showroom-sized office that was more opulent than the foyer.

The steel and black marble slab that was his desk was backed by a stunning view of Lake Ontario glittering in the distance. He toured us around the mini art and photo gallery lining pale silk-covered walls. As he described the price and provenance of each piece, I listened not so much to his words but to his accent. Austrian, French, Swiss? Before I could ask, the phone on his desk burbled.

"Excuse me. It must be important or Eleanor would not have interrupted. Enjoy the rest of the exhibits."

Jake pulled up a chair in front of the windows while I strolled the installation of framed prints featuring sweeping landscapes, prosperous-looking men in rain gear on racing yachts and Martin with assorted celebrities. A modest low-hanging photo in the corner caught my eye. I slipped my reading glasses on and leaned closer.

"Jake. Would you come here for a minute?"

"What is it?"

"That looks like a young Martin, doesn't it?"

He pulled his glasses out of his breast pocket and squatted, steadying himself with one hand on the arm of a nearby chair. "Seems so." He tapped another face and said, "That guy looks like him, too."

According to Bosco, there was no such thing as coincidence. How did Martin Bernard, bon vivant and successful international entrepreneur, end up with the same photo Maggie had found among the mementos my mother had tucked away? Was she right about there being a mystery in my past?

"Where was it taken, I wonder?"

"In Peru." I jumped. We'd been so intent on examining the photographs we hadn't heard Martin crossing the plush carpet to stand beside us. "Do you know anything about mining?"

I shook my head. "The setting reminds me of the Klondike gold rush."

"It was a rush of sorts," he smiled thinly. "My gang and I were looking for copper and gold. Those were wild times. Political, economic. Dangerous and very competitive." His voice trailed off, then he recovered. "We had an interesting journey."

Jake pushed himself upright. One of his knee joints popped. "Did you find what you were looking for?"

Martin stared into the middle distance. "In a manner of speaking, yes."

"When was the picture taken?" I held my breath.

He unhooked the photograph and flipped it over. I peered over Martin's shoulder at the penciled notation and read aloud, "July 1976." In the upper right corner was the photographer's name and a number in a circle. A shiver raced up my arms. The same name and date were on the print Maggie had found.

I asked in a steady voice, "Who were the men?"

"My dear, it was so long ago." He sighed dramatically. "They are forgotten. Unimportant then; even more so now."

His offhandedness intrigued me. He rubbed his palms briskly, as if trying to loosen something sticky.

"Let's get back to business, shall we?"

We sat in a quartet of deep chairs around a free-form glass coffee table. I opened a blank Word document on my iPad. He flashed a too-bright smile and launched into his narrative. Concentrating on my keyboarding, I was only half paying attention. I glanced up when he paused to pour us more tea from an antique bone China pot.

I took a sip and sat back. That's when I recognized what Bosco called the 'tell'. Martin's facial expressions didn't jibe with the flamboyant hand movements that punctuated his speech. He wasn't being truthful. When he began speaking again, he was repeating himself.

"It must be quite troubling," I said.

"Yes." For a moment, he worked on a frown that didn't quite form. Hell's bells, I thought. The man's been botoxed. "I am affronted that someone would steal from me."

"What do your auditors say?"

"The auditors? On paper, everything is in order." He made a dismissive motion. "I don't care what the reports say. All of the cash that should be there, is not there."

"How long have you worked with that particular firm of auditors?"

He narrowed his eyes at me. "Why is that important?"

"I'm wondering if they've become complacent." He nodded slowly. I continued in a neutral tone. "You're a valued client. Perhaps they don't want to upset the status quo."

Or whoever is skimming the cash is very good at concealing their tracks.

He waggled his finger in my direction and said to Jake, "You were correct. She is a clever one!"

7

I'd confirmed the identity of the buyer for the knitting machines and picture frames I'd stored after mom died. Having read Marie Kondo's book about the joys of decluttering and organizing, I'd finally accepted that nostalgia was not my friend and became ruthless about disposing of emotionally charged clutter.

Mindful of Bosco's advice about stakeouts, I arrived thirty minutes before the scheduled meeting. I parked my car in a sliver of shade close to the chain link entry fence, wondering where Claude the office manager was. He was usually good for ten minutes of gossip over a lukewarm cup of gritty percolated coffee. After locking my work phone in the center console, I strapped on my fanny pack and tucked in my car keys.

Three bays down, a chubby young woman was leaning against the hood of a bronze Honda Civic with ultra-low-profile tires and limo-tint windows. Awfully small car to carry two long knitting machine boxes, I mused. She'd been watching me but seemed startled when I called her name. She rushed over. A ball cap was pulled low over her forehead.

"You Ash-Leigh?"

"Yes. I've got the cash." She was squeezing a wad of twenty-dollar bills between her fingers and appeared overly flushed.

"What, no haggling?"

Frowning, she said, "Oh, no, no. Your price is reasonable. Can I see the merchandise?"

"Sure. The knitting machines are stacked against the back wall."

I pulled on work gloves then knelt to struggle with the stubborn bicycle lock, finally kicking the hasp to loosen it. She grabbed the flaking chrome handle and flung open the metal sectional door. We cringed at the squeal of rusted wheels on the steel railing. I stepped inside. It was dim and hot and reeked of dust, rodents and damp concrete. Entering the small enclosure always gave me the creeps but the monthly rental was cheap. She glanced over her shoulder. I turned to follow her gaze but she stepped into my line of sight.

"It's just that my little girl is asleep in the back seat. If she wakes up, she'll freak out. Can we hurry?" The woman pressed her fingers to my bicep then snatched them away and clutched her hands against her midriff. "Sorry, I... I don't get out much. I work at home."

Not an unbelievable explanation but something wasn't quite right. She was shifting from one foot to the other like she had to pee. Maybe she was agoraphobic? I leaned around her shoulder and poked my head out the door. Just her vehicle and mine and the loud hum of cars speeding by a few meters away on Holland Street.

Shrugging, I switched on my flashlight. The upper reaches of the slanted corrugated metal ceiling were veiled with thick cobwebs. I swatted them away with the handle of an old umbrella and retrieved a box of cartoon character baking pans and a wrapped bundle tied with twine.

"Rip off the plastic and look at the picture frames. Your daughter might get a kick out of the cake pans."

She backed out of the locker, tilted the frames back and forth in the sunlight then leaned them against the exterior wall. The aluminum pans made tinny music, shifting as she tried to pile them on the asphalt. I picked my way past an old hibachi, a stack of vintage phonograph records and a carton of my kids' dusty soccer and hockey trophies. Trickles of sweat dampened my forehead and underarms.

"The knitting machines are at the back." I steadied my torch on the lid of a rusted cooler chest. "They're heavy so I'll need you to give me a hand."

"Okay. Be right there."

A male voice snarled, "Move out of the way, stupid."

I dropped the box I'd been holding and whipped around, knocking my flashlight to the ground. The light flickered then winked out. It took a few seconds for my eyes to adjust from the gloom at the back of the locker to the slash of brilliant sunlight outside. Her palms outstretched chest high in a blocking motion, Ash was backing away.

I yelled, "What the hell are you doing?"

A large arm appeared off to one side and slammed the door to the ground, plunging me into stifling twilight. Instead of bouncing up as it usually did, the door stopped and the latches held. Damnation. Someone was scrabbling with the lock I'd left open on the ground. Cursing and swearing, I stumbled in the semi-dark and pounded on the metal door but it was sturdy. Dust and bug corpses rained on my upper torso. Choking, I stopped banging, brushed at the debris and tried to catch my breath.

"This isn't funny. Open the damned door?"

There was a muffled, "I'm sorry."

"There's no reason for you to do this."

What I heard next made my blood run cold.

"Hey, Rosie. You're not so fucking smart, are you?" He made exaggerated 'mwa-ha-ha' noises. "Didn't I say those two bozos you work with couldn't protect you? Enjoy your hotbox. It's supposed to get up to thirty-three degrees this afternoon."

"Don't do this, Mitch."

"Hey, Rosie. Your phone's ringing. Can you take a call? Oh, sorry, it's locked in your beater car."

Ash was whimpering, "Don't, don't."

"I told you to shut your mouth." There was a scuffle, a slap then a brief cry. "Get back to the car and mind the kid. I told you to keep your nose out of my business."

Was he talking to me or her? The pulse hammering in my ears was blocking out sound. I leaned close to the door then jolted back. Thin plumes of smoke oozed between a gap in the frame at eye level. Was the bastard going to set the place on fire? I shouted and pounded on the metal until I got a stitch in my side. Mitch began laughing even louder. When he wound down, I eased myself upright then took a few assessing breaths. Cigarette smoke with an undertone of weed. Not a conflagration.

I slammed my boot into the base of the door but it had been reinforced with plywood to prevent break-ins. All I managed was to jam my toes and torque my bad knee again. Pain radiated down my shin. I wanted to scream with fear and rage but that would probably egg him on. The chain rattled. Stifling a whimper, I stumbled back then remembered I'd slipped the key into my pocket. At least he couldn't get inside.

"Please, Mitch."

"Please, Mitch", he repeated in a falsetto. He blew a few more gusts of smoke. "I could burn this dump down, Rosie, but then the fire guys'd come rescue you. Where's the fun in that?"

"There's no need for this."

"You should have been nicer to me. No one can hear you. Buh-bye."

After tooting his horn twice, he peeled out of the parking lot.

Jesus, I was in trouble. I was dressed in long work pants,

thick-soled leather shoes and a long-sleeved cotton shirt. It was dirty, musty and sweltering in my cement-block prison. Even though the locker was much bigger than the closet my dad used to lock me in, I couldn't shove away my seven-year-old kid memories. *Stop thinking. You're not helpless. Do something.*

Pressing my mouth close to the crack between the door frame and the wall, I yelled for help until my throat burned. Either Claude had gone down the street for a sandwich or he'd left for the day. A distant phone was ringing. My work cell. Damn it. I yanked on the door handle so hard I bent it off its bolt and sliced the web of my left hand.

"Shit, that hurts."

Fighting back tears, I sucked at the wound. A headache bloomed at the base of my skull. My heart was beating so hard it turned my vision to semaphore-like blinks. I sank onto a plastic tub and hunched over, intending to drop my head between my knees but jerked upright at another stab of pain. The forgotten fanny pack was digging into my stomach. I unbuckled the pack then opened the largest compartment. My shoulders sagged.

Inside was a half-empty water bottle, crunched almost flat. I sipped slowly, letting the tepid liquid slide across my tongue to clear the parch from my throat. I unzipped the rest of the bag's pockets and tipped the contents onto an old TV table. The handle of my Leatherman Multi-tool and the diamond-knurled barrel of a mini MagLite gleamed in the dim light.

"Thank you, Bosco," I whispered. He was constantly nagging me to be prepared and I was. Accidentally, perhaps, but what the hell.

I poked around the chain and cables but they were too thick to use the wire cutters or the saw blade on. Even if I could unscrew the door mechanism, I couldn't push it off the guide rails. For sure I wouldn't be able to lift it. The corrugated metal ceiling was too high to reach. No way could I MacGyver my way out.

The bright beam of the flashlight illuminated cardboard cartons and plastic boxes holding Anderson's Lionel train set, Lilly's Girl Guide uniforms and my yellowing wedding album. I drop-kicked the album into a corner. Three mice raced across my feet then squeezed through a gap between the cinder block wall and the cement floor. The cut on my hand burned. Sweat stung my eyes. Or maybe it was tears. Why the hell was I paying to store stuff I should have thrown out or sold long ago? No one cared anymore. What stupid amateur would let herself get duped like this? Me, me, me.

I stripped off my shirt and picked up the last item from the fanny pack. My old cell phone. I pressed the 'on' button. The screen remained dark then flickered as the device rebooted. A pair of sullen green lights pulsed: two bars of signal. Twenty one percent battery remaining. Who the hell was I going to call? Bosco? Never. My mentor was worse than a harpy. I'd never hear the end of it. Jake was in the office but how was I going to explain what had happened and not look like an idiot? Eighteen percent. Sixteen percent. The damned thing was draining before my eyes. Swell. Just swell.

Was Maggie in town or on one of her jaunts? I called her number and got voice mail. I talked fast and left a detailed message. Sweating like a racehorse, I paced three steps up and three steps back trying to figure out another option.

Nine percent. In the superheated silence, I caught the incessant ring tone of my unreachable work phone. I could call 9-1-1 but as I'd learned, cops and firefighters were avid gossips; they loved sharing intelligence, the juicier the better. Undoubtedly, someone who knew Jake and/or Bosco would broadcast a version of my escapade before I could massage the truth.

Just as I was about to admit defeat and call the office my cell rang. Maggie's words tumbled together, she was so excited. It would take her an hour to arrive from downtown Toronto but I could manage the wait. Rescue was on the way.

I stuck the lock key into a plastic photo sleeve ripped from my wedding album. Maggie was able to lift the door up enough to create a decent-sized gap, giving me room to slide the package underneath. When I stumbled out blinking and mumbling thanks, she grabbed me in a bear hug.

After I'd finished my abridged version of what had happened, she was ready to dash off to a police station and file a report. She believed me when I explained I'd look incompetent and maybe lose my job. Still, she'd tailgated me as I took the long back route to the office.

* * *

When I snuck in the back entrance and tip-toed past Jake's closed door, I met no one.

I washed off the stink of fear and perspiration then bandaged my hand and overdressed in a frilly white blouse, summery trousers and low-heeled sandals. I artfully tousled my hair, adding dangling earrings and a strand of bright beads, figuring if I looked cool, calm and snazzy I'd be able to tough out the rest of the afternoon.

No sooner had I eased into my chair than the intercom buzzed. My heart sank. What did Jake want? The man had more acute hearing than a wolf. He'd have heard the water running in our shared bathroom so I couldn't ignore the call.

I snatched a folder from my credenza and breezed into his office. The drapes were closed against the glare of sunlight. Jake was seated at his desk with his hands folded on the blotter. The green stone in his FBI ring glinted in the glow of the desk lamp. The wide stripes in his dress shirt matched his eyes. He surveyed my outfit. His right eyebrow quirked up then he dipped his chin.

"Have a seat."

I sat, plastered on a too-bright smile and knotted my fingers in my lap. "What's up? I was on my way out the door to Bernards."

His eyes focused on me like a tractor beam. "I've been trying to call you for the last couple of hours."

"Sorry I didn't pick up."

"When you didn't respond, I had one of the IT guys run the phone locater program." He rustled a sheet of blue paper. "What were you doing at a storage facility in Bradford for three hours?" Sweat erupted under my arms. "I don't see that location on the assignment roster. You're not trained to do solo stakeout. Where was your phone?"

"Locked in my car. I—I can explain, Jake."

"Try."

Gripping the arms of the chair so hard my fingers went numb, I told the truth, speaking quickly and trying to sound authoritative.

"How did you confirm Ash's *bona fides*?"

"I did a Google search, checked out her Facebook profile and...."

"Facebook? Google? I said confirm." His tone blistered like acid.

"Why would I suspect that some young woman from Georgina would be Mitch's girlfriend?"

A muscle jumped along the edge of his clenched jaw.

"Mitch's girlfriend, you say? Did you actually think using consumer search engines and social media would get you reliable information?" He glanced away, took a few deep breaths then said, "You're trained to suspect everyone. To think dirty."

His voice had a teeth-clenching control that reminded me of a leashed bear. There was nothing more to say that wouldn't dig me in deeper. I shrugged. Circles of rage burnishing his cheeks, he erupted from his chair and smacked the desk. I pressed my palm to my chest to keep my heart from bursting through.

"Jesus Christ, Kenora. That was dumb. Amateurish. When

were you going to tell us what happened? You're not taking this seriously."

"I am. I am. It wasn't—"

"Why didn't you call Bosco?"

"I didn't want him to think—"

"Think. Right. You didn't think." He sat down slowly, examining me with a narrow-eyed stare. "Do you want this job?"

My body was frozen in place. "Pardon me?"

"Do you want this job?"

"Of course. Yes. I love my work."

"Well, then?"

My lungs seized. I struggled to take in enough air. He waited. The only sounds were the ticking wall clock and pinging email notifications on his computer. Random scenarios—all disastrous—cycled through my brain. Finally, I fixed my gaze on his chin and tried not to blink like a trapped rabbit.

"It was a little mistake. Nothing bad happened," I said.

His eyes flared wide. My tone had been off, more defiant than contrite. "Excuse me?"

The temperature in the office chilled by ten degrees.

"Nothing." My body ached; my head ached. I stood, aiming to face off on a more equal footing. I'd had my day's quota of scared. Clutching my hands to my belly nullified that. "Will there be—"

"I listened to the recording of your interview with Mitch Mehran."

"Y... Yes?"

"During our briefing, you glossed over his threats."

"I didn't think—"

"Obviously."

"I can explain."

"No. You can't. You're terrible at trying to rationalize. How about you stop getting into situations where you have to?"

"Sure. I can do that." Perhaps he wasn't as pissed off as I'd thought. I stretched out my hand for the chair and perched on the edge of the seat.

"Today is...? Ah, Wednesday." He swiveled to the computer monitor and tapped his keyboard. "Bosco's almost done his project. Not much on your sched that can't wait." Jake's voice was conversational, pleasant almost, but the undertone chilled me. "I'm sending you home, Kenora."

"What? No."

"Yes."

The locomotive of terror tracking through my skull was deafening. How was I going to get out this intact? I had to. If he'd berated or belittled me the way my ex used to do during a disagreement, I could have stuck it out, but Jake's demeanor had thrown me off. It took me a few moments to clear my throat.

"You're firing me?" Willing myself to stop shaking, I unclenched my cramped fingers one by one.

"No."

I jumped up, hope swelling. "I realize I made a dumb mistake. I'll do better next time."

"Kenora, stop."

"Please, I need...."

Jake slashed his hand through the air. "Stop. Talking. Now." He stalked to the door, threw it open and stood to one side. "I'm suspending you. Over the weekend, I'll talk with Bosco about your performance to date. Revisit your assignments."

"Weekend? My performance? You mean to take me off the Bernards investigation?"

"Perhaps." He extended his palm. "Give me your security equipment. Leave all your files."

Squeezing back tears, I unclipped the lanyards holding my proximity cards and access control fobs, photo badge and biometric ID credentials from around my neck. They clattered together when I held them out.

"Jake, please."

"Goodnight, Kenora."

I trudged from his office to mine, packed my personal belongings then stumbled to the parking lot without falling over. I slumped behind the wheel of my vehicle and sobbed, not caring if anyone saw me.

What the hell was I going to do?

8

When my mother died, I ate. When Ravi kicked me to the matrimonial curb, I ate. When I had to quit the job I'd hated for decades and bills threatened to snow me under, I ate. Now, all I could keep down was mint tea with honey. I'd drunk so much I seriously considered putting on an adult diaper to keep from having to drag myself off the couch so often.

Twenty-four hours after my dressing down by Jake I'd cried so hard and for so long my gut was cramped solid. My face looked like someone had massaged it with a meat tenderizer. I was almost forty-three years old, embarking on my best second chance and I'd set myself up for failure by acting like I knew better than the experts. But that approach had worked for so long. Why not now?

I already missed being a P.I. Hanging out with the ex-cops and lawyers who treated me like one of the gang. Having something useful to contribute about research and HR. Being suspended or having one foot on the path to getting fired—was terrifying. What if Jake decided to let me go? I had enough cash to last for three months but where would I find another job like the one I already had? Just in case I got a chance to defend myself, I dutifully cataloged what happened at the locker. Once that task was finished, so was my motivation.

How many times had I reached for the phone to call Jake or Bosco and throw myself on their mercy? I lost count of how many scenarios I'd concocted to get my job back. I schlumped around getting familiar with the mechanical echoes of my house expanding and contracting around me, fretting that I'd end up living in a dingy basement apartment with my new vibrator and three neurotic cats with people names.

By dawn on Saturday morning I was red-eyed, red-nosed and faint from lack of protein. I microwaved a carton of curried squash soup and ate it standing at the kitchen counter. The back yard needed an intervention from a crew of HGTV landscapers. Maybe I should fill out a casting call form? Maybe later.

I showered, dressed in old jeans and a t-shirt sans bra and sought refuge in a routine that reminded me of happier times and my mother—working with flour, sugar, and a hot oven. I lost myself by baking a dozen lemon blueberry cupcakes and an applesauce ginger Bundt cake. I could always use them as a peace offering at work. The measuring, stirring and buttering were temporarily therapeutic. Before I bagged everything, I Instagrammed the bounty and sent photos to my children, hoping their responses would lift my spirits. *Crickets.* They were probably busy. Offline. Living fulfilling lives.

I called and caught Maggie on her way to the airport to visit her children in Switzerland. She didn't understand why I was so upset. After all, she'd reminded me, we'd pulled dumber stunts in high school.

"But this is work," I wailed. "My new career. I'm this close to fucking up starting my life over and being successful at something of my choosing. I can't fail now. Ravi will never let me hear the end of it."

At least she'd agreed with that.

"Get a job in a bakery. You took classes at George Brown College."

"That was a year of night school, Maggie. And I gained eight pounds. Dreams don't pay the bills. Except for some people."

She ignored the jibe. "Why don't you put on a revealing outfit, sit on your boss's lap and convince him to let you come back to work? 'Come' being the operative word, my friend."

"You're not taking this seriously."

"And you're being a drama queen."

"My life is shit." My nose felt thick with unshed tears. "Why did I buy this bloody money pit? I'm alone, my line of credit is coming due and the renovations aren't finished. Now you're suggesting I sex Jake? With my luck he'd dump me on the floor and laugh. And still give me the heave-ho. Never mind, Mags. I can stand on my own two feet. I'll figure something out."

"Kenora? Don't cry, sweetie. I'm sorry you're feeling so down."

"Thanks for understanding. Bye. Enjoy your trip."

Before she could say anything else, I hit the end button and banged the receiver down. She didn't call back. I didn't call her, either.

I peeked outside, cursing the grimy clouds scudding across the gunmetal sky. The gusting wind was fierce. In my office, I propped the old snapshots of my mother and me with the unknown man and the unknown man with his four buddies on the credenza.

Why did my mother keep those photos? Did the handwritten notations mean anything significant? Why had she stashed them in an old high school yearbook where they might never have been found?

I was an investigator, dammit. I liked solving mysteries but tackling a personal one would be something new. And scary. There wasn't much to go on. How the hell did things connect to Martin Bernard? I flipped on the photocopier and ran off half a dozen enlargements. Asking my dad was my best bet. I'd put on my good daughter hat and entice him over to do yard work in exchange for home-cooked meals and mending.

On Sunday the sun was shining, coaxing scent from the damp earth. A thin haze hung above the wet rocks along the shoreline. Forest flotsam littered the yard. The patio furniture on the back deck had been shoved against the railing as if by a giant hand.

I was hungry again. My mother had always made me boiled eggs with toast when I was sick. Recuperative food, she called it. Thinking of my mom made me think of my dad. As ambivalent as I still felt about how he'd treated me, I called. Got his voice mail. I waited five minutes and called again.

He picked up, sounding surprised to hear my voice. We chatted about my brothers and the Italian ladies who still dropped by with food to tide him over. Over what, I wasn't sure. I teased him about being a catch—a sensible man with his own hair, good teeth, and a nice pension. He wasn't amused. When I tried to talk about my mom he changed the subject. But I persisted with my invitation. He finally agreed to drop by to help with the landscaping and stake the perimeter of the summer house he wanted to build between my back garden and the lake. I consoled myself that although he wasn't warmly affectionate, we were progressing to a new normal of civility.

The timer sounded. My eggs were perfect—soft, runny yolks with tender but not snotty whites. The twelve-grain toast slathered with butter tasted fantastic.

Before I could talk myself out of it, I swallowed the remainder of my pride and crafted a long email to Bosco, hoping he'd read it before work Monday morning. I had nothing to lose. Without my job at BB&F, where would I be? I needed to know if I should report to work or freshen my resume.

Rain had soaked into the plastic bag holding the morning

papers. I was halfway through the sodden help wanted ads when the doorbell rang. I froze. An image of Mitch's sneering stubbled face popped into my head. The bell rang again. My fingers trembled so hard the newspaper flapped like a fan. What the hell? I made sure the patio door and windows were locked. Armed with a wooden rolling pin, I tucked the telephone handset into my pocket and peeked through the curtained side windows in the front hall. Two thin shadows. Not Mitch-sized. I silently twisted the deadbolt then flung the door open, startling a pair of maroon-haired ladies with crepe paper complexions.

"Oh hi." I stepped onto the porch, in no mood to invite them in. "Sorry to startle you."

I'd met them at the community mailbox. What were their names? Flower and opera. Dahlia? Rose? No, Iris. And Sydney. From the green stucco cottage at the end of the lane. They were dressed alike in pastel shirtwaist dresses, white walking shoes and straw hats. Sisters, friends, partners? They wrangled their leg-humping Yorkies away from my calves. I glanced over their shoulders. No strange brown guy was lurking on the wet lawn but a fresh mound of dog crap had been deposited by the decorative planter flanking the pathway.

Iris stammered, "Sidney and I thought we'd pop by and say hello."

Sydney warbled "hello" and waggled her fingers.

Iris was a flutterer. Whenever she moved, she gave off the scent of lavender talcum powder. Her spasmodic nodding reminded me of her pooch. She stared at my t-shirt then at the gauze swaddling my hand. I swiped at the glob of egg yolk over my left breast.

Sidney said, "Do you play bridge? Euchre? Line dance?"

"No, I don't."

"Are you a feminist?" Iris said.

Before I could answer, Sidney thrust a pot containing an

African violet sporting wilted pink blooms in my direction. She said they'd heard I was a gardener and reckoned keeping busy outdoors would distract me from being a single lady again. *Lovely.* That intrusive tidbit must have come via my blabby real estate agent. If Mitch ever found out where I lived and canvassed the neighborhood, he'd hit the chatterbox jackpot with these two. I realized the telephone was ringing.

"That's very thoughtful. I have to get the phone."

"It needs a little watering," said Sydney.

"Right away." The phone went quiet then rang again. What if it was Jake calling to say he'd changed his mind? "I have to get that," I muttered. "Thanks. Bye."

Clutching the cracked plastic pot, I threw the bolt and sprinted for the phone. No one was there. Call display showed 'unknown number'. I counted to forty but the message waiting light didn't blink on. I stuck the plant pot on the kitchen windowsill. I was no good with indoor vegetation and had no intention of getting better. The violet would dry an easy death.

There was still a lot of yard work to do. Physical activity always helped clear my mind. The bark mulch on the flower beds was littered with ruined blooms but the damp soil made digging easy. If I got fired, maybe I could work as a landscaper or in the garden center at Lowes? They were always hiring. Half an hour later, rain began to pelt down, dousing me with cold reality. As I loped towards the back steps, I tripped over a tree limb impaled in the lawn and tumbled head-first into a dripping tangle of fallen branches. Perfect. Just perfect.

A term from grade twelve English class popped into my head as I rolled to my knees with a groan: pathetic fallacy. Yes, I was pathetic. My dreams of making my mark as a private investigator were in shambles. I hated to admit that it was nobody's fault but my own.

I stumbled into the enclosed back porch, leaving a trail of wet clods on the floor and a footprint on the door panel.

Sobbing, I wrestled out of my wet clothing, wrapped myself in an old quilt and curled up on the wicker daybed to consider why it was the men in my life kept rejecting me no matter what I did or how hard I tried to do what they wanted. I'd been a good girl all my life. Where had that got me? I drifted off, knowing I could never be that girl again.

I awoke with a start. The phone was ringing. Call display read, J. I. Poon. I pressed the handset to my ear.

"Oh, Bosco, I've made such a mess of things."

* * *

I was scheduled for a debriefing at eleven o'clock. Of course I was over-thinking and what-iffing, but this job meant the world to me. I sighed. Wasn't that what every contestant on every talent show said about winning?

My fingers were so unsteady my eyeliner looked more like rick-rack. I had to wipe it off three times to get a straight line. I deeply regretted my new short haircut—another questionable impulsive decision. The outfit I chose made me look I was going for a job interview at a nunnery: navy trouser suit, high-collared white blouse, pearl studs with a matching circle brooch in my lapel. I glammed up with bright galaxy socks and red leather dress boots.

Jake wasn't going to fire me, but Bosco had said I couldn't take anything for granted. I was truly penitent and knew I'd dodged a bullet. The suspension had put me on multiple ropes. Good as I was—Bosco's words, not mine—the company and clients had to come first. His advocacy with Jake had helped but my get-out-of-purgatory pass had been validated by Martin Bernard. Jake had done such a stellar job selling my services to Martin, he'd inadvertently painted himself into my corner. For Martin, no other investigator would do. That puzzled me momentarily but his insistence—a gift horse I'd look squarely in the mouth when the time came—made me giddy.

First, I had to survive my meeting with Jake. He gazed impassively as I strode in with my head held high. My back was straight and I didn't shrink under his frosty gaze.

"Morning," I said cheerily.

"Have a seat."

He flipped open my blue personnel file then picked up an expensive-looking fountain pen. He shifted it from palm to palm for a moment. I stared at the play of muscles in his thick hands and forced my fingers to be still, resisting filling the silence with chatter.

"Care to tell me what happened to your face?"

Crap. He'd noticed the weal running from below my lip and across my cheek to my temple. I'd tried but obviously failed to hide it with layers of foundation.

"I was in the yard after the storm yesterday, surveying the damage. Stumbled over a fallen tree limb. When I stood up, a branch whipped across my face."

"That's gotta hurt. Lucky it missed your eye."

My spirits rose. Was he thawing? He picked up his phone on the second ring, listened for a minute then said yes. There was a commotion in the hallway. Buck Tooey, our technology specialist, strode in murmuring greetings. He dropped into the second visitor's chair. When his gaze slid from me to the floor I began to perspire. What now?

He flipped his notebook open. "Some black hat's been doing network reconnaissance on BB&F's corporate systems. The perimeter LAN/WAN devices alerted us to the scanning attempts. The guy's persistent but he's using a crowbar approach."

Jake murmured, "Any intel on that, Kenora?"

Both men turned their blood-chilling cop stares on me. "It might be Mitch, the guy I...." My voice sounded small.

"The intrusion detection and prevention walls blocked him," Buck said. "Then he tried to social engineer through the generic info@ email address and use our domain name registration lookups but no joy there. They dead-end to a secure server in northern Sweden."

Jake closed my folder with a snap. I managed not to jump out of my seat but it was a near thing. He said coolly, "Kenora, why don't you brief Buck on the Mitch incidents?"

I opened my own notebook. Buck's eyes grew wide as I described Mitch's threats and his shenanigans with the university payroll system. I'd never seen anyone so gleeful about hacking attempts.

"Now we're cooking with gas," he said.

He rubbed his hands together and practically ran out the door. Back to his techie bunker, no doubt. Jake reached into a drawer then tossed my security credentials across the polished surface of his desk. I looped the lanyards around my neck with an audible sigh.

He said, "What's on your agenda this week? You haven't updated the schedule."

I chose not to remind him that my access had been revoked and I'd been shut out.

Paging through my notes, I read, "My first meeting with the Bernards people. A chat with a client Bosco asked me to see. Revising my investigation plan. Surveillance training."

"Fine. We'll chat Friday afternoon and you can catch me up."

My pulse pounded so hard in my throat I could barely squeeze the words out. "Jake. About that other thing?"

"Later. I have to leave for another meeting." His expression was grim. "I suggest you get back to work."

9

Thank goodness I was a fast healer. Except for the occasional twinge, I felt all right. I hopped off the crammed Queen West streetcar in front of Magasin Martin Bernard.

The store, a red-brick pile lacking only a moat to qualify as a castle keep, dominated a commercial block where rental costs per square foot exceeded what some folks paid each month to rent their condos. Beneath a majestic facade of carved marble that might have been looted from some doge's palace in Italy, an enormous white and blue striped canopy shaded the soaring entrance. A doorman who, despite the hothouse weather conditions was wearing a jacket and forage cap heavily laden with gold braid, jumped to open the gleaming brass door. He offered directions and snapped a salute. I popped the collar of my jacket and put on my I'm-in-charge face.

A tasteful chime sounded as I pushed through the smoked glass doors to the Human Resources Department. A person with skim milk skin and pomaded hair that matched their tight pale jacket sat in an office chair. The name plate read: Andrew. A hint of beard shadowed his chin. He gave my fashionably wrinkled linen blend pantsuit and white silk t-shirt a judgmental once-over, glanced at the envelope I handed him then slipped a long black-polished pinkie nail under the flap. Plucked brows rose as he read Martin's letter of introduction.

"The Director isn't in yet. Wait here. I'll get the Office Manager."

He dashed down a short hallway, his leather trousers shushing with each stride. He returned in a few minutes with a well-dressed middle-aged man.

"I'm Gavin, the Office Manager's assistant. How may I help you?"

Before I could answer, a gruff voice called out, "Never mind, I'll handle this," and a rotund, sawed-off man in a grey houndstooth suit bustled in. "Doug Decarie." He waved his hand dismissively to the two men. "That'll be all."

"I'm Kenora Tedesco from...."

"Identification?"

Luckily, he didn't snap his fingers or I'd have smacked his hand. He, too, looked me up and down before snatching away the letter. Had I left my buttons undone?

"Follow me."

The chorus of Run DMCs "Walk This Way" popped into my head. I snickered to myself. Doug shoved my business card into his pocket and stalked down the hall to an office furnished with a nondescript desk and computer. An unadorned window overlooked two cardboard recycling bins in the rear parking lot. Obviously, Doug was not that high up on the management food chain. He shouldered the door shut and dropped into a chair that emitted cat-like squeaks as he shifted his bulk.

I made a production out of positioning the guest chair then slipped on my reading glasses and pulled a file folder from my briefcase.

"Now Doug–you don't mind if I call you Doug, do you?"

I launched into my prepared story. He began swiveling in

slow arcs, humming tunelessly as he rolled a pinch of his cheek between finger and thumb. In the confined space his cloying aftershave made my eyes water.

According to Bosco, Rule 1 was to tell them what you were going to do. Even if they've fucked up, he said, they wouldn't be smart enough to hide everything.

Rule 2 – leave them a little anxious. I faked a bright smile, then a thoughtful frown.

"Bernards installed new inventory management technology and refreshed the financial systems last year. I'm here to validate their effectiveness. Nothing for you to worry about, I'm sure."

Doug suddenly became interested in scraping a blob of something from his keyboard tray.

Rule 3 – exert your authority.

"Mr. Bernard said I'd have top level security clearance." I stood up and, placing my palms on his desk blotter, leaned into his space. He stopped gnawing on his thumbnail and gazed up at me. His lips parted. "What I need from you is a set of full-access ID. Next, you can assign me a competent assistant. I'm going to do a walk around the store now. When I return, I'd appreciate someone showing me to my temporary office."

"Uh, sure. I'll have Gavin escort you."

Rule 4 – be gracious and confuse them. I opened my eyes wide and reached across the desk to shake his hand, thankful he rubbed his fingers across his left sleeve beforehand.

"I'll be collecting a lot of documentation. Whoever's working with me will set up an interview schedule with the senior managers and staff."

"That won't be easy. Most of the managers take a couple weeks off during the summer," he said with a sly smile.

"You're here, so you'll be first up. Besides, as my research plan unfolds I'm sure I'll have lots of questions you can help me with. Hold that thought for now."

"You asked for an assistant?" He twisted his face like he smelled something unpleasant.

"Competent assistant, Doug."

"Except for Merchandising and Receiving, we're short staffed. I doubt...."

"Then I'd appreciate if you'd let your fingers do some walking. I'm sure you can free someone up fairly quickly," I said and turned on my heel.

Gavin was waiting in the reception area when I returned from my tour. He held out a pair of chunky plastic security cards attached to a blue lanyard.

"When you swipe the card, it'll register your card ID, location and the time. Tracks every move."

I filed that factoid in the back of my mind. Gavin led me down a hallway littered with office detritus up a flight of concrete stairs past a dusty alcove and into my new office on the mezzanine level.

"It's like a discarded fishbowl."

A thick film of dust covered every surface. Dead bug carcasses littered the corners. The Venetian blinds over the plate glass overlooking the main floor sagged between yellowed tapes. A dead mouse lay belly-up by a broken file cabinet in one corner. It struck me that Doug might be having a chuckle at my expense.

"They didn't offer any other workspace," Gavin said. "Sorry."

"Could you get a guy from maintenance in to clean up and find some usable furniture? Someone from my office will come in and set up an encrypted communications line for my phone and broadband connection."

"You know," he said hesitantly, "I have a friend in Fine Interiors. If you don't mind, I can ask if he could make this more habitable."

I pointed to the black plastic rodent bait containers scattered around the room.

"Habitable would be good. Make a list of what we need. If there's any flak from Doug I'll go directly to Eleanor." I swear I saw him shudder. "Did Mr. Decarie mention who they've assigned as my assistant?"

"No." He looked away. "It may take a while."

That sounded more like never. I leaned against a clean spot on the wall and scrutinized the man as he made lists on a smartphone app. His tanned face carried worry lines around his eyes but he had an honest smile and a firm handshake. He was sharply fashionable and came off as polite but skittish as a kid used to being bullied. I'd read the dossiers of all the managers and senior staff. Two had stood out as racehorses in a stable of dray-pullers—Gavin and a woman named Pilar. I'd run a background check and they'd both come back clean.

"How long have you been with Bernards?"

"Thirteen years," he said cautiously. "Why?"

"Lucky thirteen?" He grimaced. "The audit I'm doing will take a couple of months. I need a self-starter with a solid business background. Someone who's not afraid to get his hands dirty."

"Like this, you mean?" He picked up the dead mouse by the tail, dropped it into a rusty waste basket then wiped his fingers on a square of spotless handkerchief. "Would you consider me?" His smile was tentative.

"There could be blow back if, when I finish my investigation, there's...."

"No doubt about that."

So, Gavin knew something. That was a good thing. He reached for my hands then realized he'd probably crossed some etiquette boundary and jerked away.

"How would taking on a temporary assignment affect your career?"

"Career?" He scoffed, "Mine withered a long time ago. Doug won't approve a transfer. He's punishing me but I'm not sure what for. He's not happy with you doing an audit, as you call it."

"That was clear. I think he could be persuaded."

"Why are you really here? And what do you want of me?"

His gaze didn't waver as I took my time scrutinizing his face. "I've been assigned an investigation into inventory fraud. That's all I can tell you right now."

"I'm right about it being something more?"

"Perhaps." I liked that he was quick but it was too soon to be too trusting. "What I can disclose is that there are several complex issues."

What I wanted to say was that this was my second investigation assignment and that I needed to prove myself.

Instead I said, "You should also know that I'm tenacious. And thorough. I'd expect you to be the same. I'll be working at Bernards three days a week starting next Wednesday. Will that give you enough time to get set up?"

"Yes." He was blinking so fast I could hardly see his brown eyes.

"I've got another interview in a few minutes but," I said, giving him my business card, "call me at the end of the week once you've made your decision and I'll brief you on the project."

"My decision is made. I know this place inside and out and I want to help clean up whatever mess there is."

"Good. Drop by my employer's offices tomorrow. Ask for Seta, the Senior Administrator/Office Manager. You'll have to sign a confidentiality agreement and waivers for disclosure of personal information. There'll be background checks—criminal records, credit and a driving monograph as well. You okay with that?"

"Absolutely. Just so you know, Ms. Tedesco. I'm tenacious, too. And obsessively organized. I'll be loyal."

I held out my hand again. "We'll get along well, Gavin."

10

The date for my meeting with Bosco's client had been changed three times. I was determined to get it over with and move on to more pressing business. For some reason, he was avoiding the woman but I was working my way back into his good graces and wasn't about to ask why.

Back door or front? We were supposed to use the rear entrance but I was running late. I'd save a minute by going out the front entrance, avoiding the double-coded rear security doors and the construction equipment that had churned the back lane into a muddy trail. I snatched up the client files and took the front steps two at a time. At the corner, I almost collided with a bicycle courier who cussed me out. I changed direction and gave Ms. Sidewalk Warrior a thumbs-up as I hot-footed it south to Lawrence subway station.

Sweating and panting from my ill-advised sprint, I grabbed the escalator handrail then snatched my hand away when I touched a moist lump of what I hoped was industrial lubricant and not sputum. I flipped through client documents while the long escalator jerked down to track level. Shop theft at an Eaton Centre boutique. I'd probably have to dress down as a secret shopper and lurk among the clothing racks. Could be fun. As I stepped off the metal stairs onto the tiles of the concourse, someone jostled me hard from behind. I clutched at the strap of my bag, trying not to trip or crash into someone else.

"Oh, for the love of—" When I looked up, whoever it was had moved on. "Screw public transit; next time, I'll take a cab."

No one was looking; folks in Toronto muttered to themselves in public all the time. I tapped my Presto payment card and pushed through the station turnstile. I checked out my surroundings. A janitor emerged from a grey metal door at the far end of the platform, pushing a mop in a yellow bucket on wheels. Three guys wearing safety hats equipped with blue flashing headlamps were poking around at track level. Two yummy mummies pushing twin racing strollers stepped out of the elevator, deep in conversation. A white-haired gentleman in a jaunty striped tie and blue blazer nodded as he tapped by. A few feet away, a man swathed in a long dark coat with a flat cap pulled low over his forehead slouched against the tiled column by the pay phone, staring at his scuffed Doc Marten boots. A coat? In June? That's taking Goth too far, I thought. A stray impression skittered through my consciousness then was gone. I moved behind the tactile hazard line about halfway down the platform and buried my head in the file.

Startled by a burst of noise, I turned to watch a gaggle of girls wearing t-shirts and low-slung skinny jeans clattering down the stairs. They gathered at the south end of the platform squealing and chattering like foul-mouthed magpies. A short distance away, a trio of young men in skateboard gear and baseball caps jostled side by side, thumbing their smartphones.

A rush of oily cool air and the squeal of brakes signaled the train's arrival. I turned toward the bright white and yellow eyes on the snout of the lead car in the tunnel. Ah, one of the gleaming new models. Maybe I'd get a seat. The maintenance guys swung red lanterns then pressed themselves against the walls. The train slowed to a crawl.

My habit of backing two paces closer to the station wall saved me.

I was snapping the clips on my bag when someone behind me shouted, "Hey, watch out."

I swung around and glimpsed a wedge of unshaven brown cheek between the folds of a dark hoodie. The man shoved hard against my right hip. I was propelled forward, arms wind-milling, fighting to plant my feet on the bumpy yellow warning strip at the edge of the platform.

My upper body twisted, I smashed into the second car of the train, knocking the air from my lungs and sending pain ricocheting from my head down my sides. My left cheek stuck to the chilly glass door like a bug on a windshield. I lurched into an awkward bent-over running stumble, terrified of being pulled under the moving carriage. The edge of my left boot slipped into the crack between the train and the platform, the thick rubber sole dragging along the gap. My ears were ringing from the squeal of brakes and the shouting at my back. My eyes filled with grit and tears. I was slowly being pulled into a painful cheerleader split.

Dear god, I don't want to die.

My knee joint wrenched with a familiar pop. My vision filled with ugly pinwheels. Fighting for balance and hopping on my other foot, knowing that if I fell my limbs would be ground to chuck, I forced my fingers between the rubber seals of the door. My body weight was wrenching my arms like wrung laundry. There was a slight rocking as the subway car settled to a halt. Sucking air, I released my death grip and as I began to slump, met the wide eyes of a pair of women passengers wearing nurses' scrubs. The doors hissed open. I collapsed on top of my messenger bag with my upper body splayed on the grimy floor. My ankle was still trapped.

Behind me, a woman yelled, "He's getting away."

I didn't care. I knew who he was.

The taste of metal filled my mouth. Ping pongs of confused voices smacked my ears like fists. I half rolled onto my back and groaned. Everything hurt. Two legs covered with grey flannel trousers above pointy black shoes stepped between my head and my outstretched arms. I leaned forward and discretely spit into the gap by the platform. Blood. I must have bitten my tongue when my chin hit the train.

When the robotic voice intoned, "stand clear the doors, the doors are closing", I surged upright, whimpering and trying to regain my senses along with my balance.

One of the nurses shrieked "no" and yanked the red emergency stop handle to alert the driver at the front of the train. Bells started to clang. The other nurse pounded the yellow passenger assistance strip.

Half a dozen more people muttered "sorry" and brushed by.

Rough hands gripped my shoulders and tugged. A young man with blond dreadlocks jammed his booted foot against the door jamb, hooked his forearms under my armpits and tried to lift me up.

"My leg, my leg, my leg."

"Wait, guys," the nurse in the red scrubs said sharply.

She gripped the ankle of my boot, wiggling it gently until she could twist it free. I thought I was going to be sick. The grating agony of a re-injured meniscus rendered my left leg almost useless. The two ladies half-carried me from the train, propping my hip against the wall beside the recycling containers. The old man stood slightly behind and to one side, gripping me around the waist and muttering soothing words in what sounded like Italian.

"I'll be okay," I gasped.

Most of the passengers who hadn't disembarked were staring. Several citizen journalists were taking pictures with their phones. Just what I needed: my photo on a screen crawl under breaking news.

Manhandling the mop and bucket like an overweight teenager with a skinny dance partner, the janitor trudged up and asked if there was anything he could do. We all said, "no", in unison.

He unclipped a walkie-talkie from his belt. I bent at the waist with my palms on my knees, trying to catch my breath. Someone coughed. I glanced over my shoulder. My bum was pressing against the old man's groin. He flashed me a big smile and waggled his furry eyebrows. I straightened. Pain rocketed from my neck to my hips but at least I was upright.

"Thank you."

The old gent reached into his jacket pocket and asked if I needed a little toot to stiffen my joints. When I said no, he gave me a rueful shrug and stepped aside.

A voice said, "You need some help?" One of the male students leaned close. "I know first aid."

He held his hands out like a surgeon who'd just finished his pre-op scrubbing. Before I could answer, the train driver jogged over from his control booth.

"You okay, lady?"

I nodded. He checked his watch then blew out a breath. An angular woman in a ticket-taker's uniform and a peaked cap puffed up and repeated the question. The three transit employees huddled for a quick conversation. I heard the woman hiss to the driver, "damned cameras are in maintenance mode."

He looked around then asked, "Anyone see what happened?"

An elderly lady said, "Someone in a long coat pushed her. It wasn't an accident."

A jolt of hot rage raced from my belly to my scalp, replacing the clammy terror.

"Yeah. Dude had this really weird look on his face," added

one of the gum-snapping girls. "Mad and sorta whacko." That would be Mitch, the bastard.

I took a step to test my ankle. Not broken. "It's okay, I..."

I lurched to the janitor's bucket, clutched the crusty lip and bent low over the soapy water to upchuck the bacon, cheddar cheese and marmalade croissant I'd gobbled for breakfast. I wiped my mouth on a crumpled tissue I found in my pocket. When I turned around the crowd had shrunk back a few meters, leaving me in a wide circle of barf-smelling solitude.

"I should call it in," the driver said without conviction. "Get the cops." He shifted from side to side, glancing at me then at the ticket taker and the janitor. They shrugged and went about their business.

"Please don't," I said. "Really, it's okay." The next-to-last thing I wanted was to become part of a police file and add another smudge on my capability ledger. He shrugged and walked away. I raised my voice. "Sorry to make you all late." I turned to the nurses and clasped their hands. "Thanks again."

My foot was swollen and hot in my boot. From ankle to thigh, my legs throbbed like drums. There was a tear in one pant leg. I straightened my jacket, adjusted my bag then limped to a hastily vacated seat inside the car. The automated announcement came on again. The subway doors hissed shut. Trying to act unconcerned by the furtive glances from my fellow passengers, I began to neaten myself up. I gingerly stroked the lump on the side of my skull. I'd have a massive migraine in a little while.

I rooted around in my bag, found a plastic tube of pain relievers and dry-swallowed two. As the rush of relief about the near miss subsided, my muscles began twitching uncontrollably. By the time the train entered the next station, I'd decided I was done for the day. Sitting down had been a bad idea. My body had seized up. I stifled a groan as I struggled to my feet and pushed through the on-boarding crowd onto the platform at the Bloor Station interchange.

11

Toughing it out would be stupid. I could walk, but everything hurt so much I wanted to shriek.

I texted Bosco. 'Couldn't make the meeting. Something came up. Advised client.'

He texted back, 'What's your 20?'

I couldn't say, slumped against the entrance of the subway, shaking so hard I could barely type, so I wrote: 'Incident. Halfway to the client meeting you sent me to!!!'

'WTF?', he replied.

'Where are YOU?' If he was nearby, perhaps he could pick me up.

'Forensics lab. Your 20?'

'On my way back.' I had to get to the office before I fell over.

I glanced at my watch—lunch hour. Activity at BB&F paused for two reasons— food and staff meetings. I hailed a taxi and had him drop me at the back door so I could scuttle in unobserved. He grumbled about getting his car dirty in the muddy laneway but his mood changed when I gave him a big cash tip.

Jake's office was dark, thank goodness. I eased my door shut, dropped my jacket and bag on the floor and after tapping in,

'Give me 10', tossed the phone onto my desk blotter and collapsed into a chair.

I thought I'd faint when I eased the boot from my left foot. The swollen flesh above my ankle was already reddish-blue. There was a bloodstain on my pink Dora the Explorer sock. The adrenaline-dump had left me drained and grumpy. I wanted to punch Mitch's smirking face into mush. Where was he? Off somewhere laughing, no doubt.

My cell phone buzzed again.

'Hey!! What's going on?' It was Bosco. Even his text sounded bad-tempered.

Swallowing hard, I tapped in: 'Can we chat for a bit? Stealth mode.'

He texted back, 'WTF?'

Too weary to explain more, I answered, 'Please. 10-7 my office.'

Yeah, I certainly was out of service. Hopefully I wouldn't be out of a job. My screw-ups were piling up. I'd been a fool not to take Mitch seriously.

In the Jack and Jill closet/bathroom I shared with Jake, I swished toothpaste in my mouth, scrubbed my hands and the sections of my face that hadn't been abraded. In the cupboard under the sink, I'd stashed an old knee stabilizer I'd had to wear years before. It was bulky and my spare trousers wouldn't fit over the buckles and straps so I had to put on a skirt. Thank goodness it was mid-calf. If I walked slowly and kept my legs to one side when I sat down, I might be able to hide the black neoprene contraption. I closed the connecting door on my side and shambled to the couch.

I must have dozed off because the next thing I knew, Bosco was tapping me on the shoulder. He leaned over with his palms on his thighs and stuck his face a nose-length from mine.

"What the hell happened?"

"Can you sit down? My neck hurts when I turn it."

"You look like shit. What's that thing on your leg?"

Oh, no. My skirt had ridden up when I'd rested my feet on the coffee table. "Flexible knee brace. I got it after I tore my ACL lunging during fencing class."

"Fencing? Figures." He picked up my wrist like a nurse taking a pulse and stared at the second hand of his watch. I didn't pull away.

"Bosco, I…."

"Don't talk."

Bosco's touch, like his voice, was at odds with his appearance —surprisingly soft and warm. He had a lean muscular body, big hands, a high smooth forehead and a thick mullet of steel and dark auburn hair that straggled over the collar of his white denim shirt. Dark lashes framed stainless steel eyes set deep above cheeks as sharp as an axe blade. The man could grow a beard like no one else I knew.

"Fell off your stilettos and banged your head?"

"No. Yes."

Whistling soundlessly, he cupped his hands around the crown of my skull and danced his fingers lightly across my scalp, palpating the contours of my goose egg. To my dismay I began to blubber.

"That's a nasty bump," he mumbled. "Talk to me."

I'd been trying to gin up a story but my head throbbed so much I gave up. "Accident in the subway."

Leaning back in an armchair, he crossed his right ankle over his left knee. "No shit. What kind of accident?"

My eyes locked on the silver toe-tips of his gleaming black-cherry western boots. A cobbler in Chicago sent him a new pair every Christmas. A thank you gift, Jake had told me, for something that happened back when Bosco was Officer-in-Charge of Vice & Drugs.

He snapped his fingers. "Excuse me. Over here. Is my mouth forming words? Are you concussed?"

"No." I sat up without jostling my body. "Sorry."

Halfway through my version of events he banged his feet to the floor and began to pace. Like a sheep tethered in a lion's cage I swiveled my head to watch him prowl the perimeter of my office.

"Why did I agree to taking on another rookie?" He was talking to himself, gesturing at the ceiling. "Even after the previous cock-up, I told Jake you could take care of yourself. But no-o-o."

"You said yourself shit happens."

Growling, he wheeled around and stood so close his leg pressed against mine. "I've taught you to investigate. This is not supposed to be dangerous work, Kenora." His voice became almost soothing. I dropped my eyes. "You messed up, my dear." He jiggled my left foot with the toe of his boot. "Right?"

"Ow. Right." My ears were ringing again. Maybe I did have a concussion. "Let me finish."

My cell phone chimed then stopped. The desk phone rang three times before voice mail kicked in. I lost my train of thought.

Bosco rapped his knuckles on the end table. "Why didn't you call me to come get you?"

"You were busy." He snorted. "I was scared of what you'd say. Tried to tough it out but I ached so much I took a cab. I managed. Someone saw a man in a long coat and hat push me. I'd done a perimeter check but Bosco there was nothing unusual. My Spidey senses didn't tingle."

"A long coat. In fucking summer? You didn't think it strange?"

"Well, I sort of did. But people wear all sorts of weird shit all the time." My chest ached. The words scraped my throat like paper clips.

"After what happened at the storage locker, you blithely go about your day as if nothing bad could happen?"

"That's not fair. I paid attention."

Silence pulsed between us like a living thing. All I wanted to do was lie down. I dropped my chin to my chest and squeezed my eyes shut so as not to cry. He nudged my leg again.

"Fair is for hopscotch. The guy's got a hard-on for you, literally and figuratively. He's a wild card. Look at me." His face was a mask. "I believed you had promise."

"I do." Damn it, my voice sounded like a fourteen-year-old who'd failed the rope climb in gym class.

He grunted.

"I've spent months coaching you. You've been to the Ontario Police College for crying out loud. Didn't anything you learned stick?"

A shaft of rage powered me to my feet, forcing him to step back. I jammed my fingers into his chest.

"Oh, it stuck all right," I hissed, knowing I was out of control but this time I didn't care. "And it was such bloody memorable fun, too. I had to wear that damned twelve-pound duty belt and a tight sweaty Kevlar vest and run frigging obstacle courses for two days under the burning sun and smell cow shit from the farmers' fields the whole time. Loved that. Then I had to endure use of force training with a bunch of recruits as young as my own kids. They banged me around like a bloody dressmaker's dummy."

Bosco held his hands palms-up as if to stop me launching myself at him. But he couldn't suppress the upward tilt of his lips. "Chill out, Partner."

That set me off again.

"I amuse you, do I?" I hiccupped. "Aylmer in summer? Flailing away with a collapsible baton at some giant bearded guy in a red rubber defensive tactics suit until my fingers blistered and I pulled a tendon? Don't you dare laugh, Bosco."

I thrust out my right hand and jabbed at a ragged fading scar.

"Look at this. I had to fire off two hundred rounds with a

fucking heavy Sig Sauer semi-automatic and caught the web of my hand in the s-s-slide three times. I bled like a pig. I was so frigging embarrassed. Th-thr-three times. It hurt like hell. I showed you the center-mass cluster sheets from the range didn't I? I'm a damned good marksman. But for what? I'll never carry a damned gun...f-f-firearm."

"Sit down before you fall down," he said gently.

I swiped tears from my cheeks and took a shaky inhale. He blew out a long breath, dug his hand into his front pants pocket and handed me a starched handkerchief.

"Kenora, look at me. Rant time is over. Listen." He was looming over me, his palms flat on the arm of the couch. "That orientation at OPC gave you a tiny dose of what it's like to train to be a cop. It was only three weeks for Christ's sake. Recruit training extra lite. You did okay. Better than okay in fact." He made a rude noise with his lips. "It's because you'll never carry a restricted weapon that you had to learn about self-defense. And vigilance."

"Vigilance? I wasn't careless. You know what?" A slap of realization stoked my fury. "You sound as bitchy and judgmental as my ex-husband. Or...or...or my father. I was never good enough for them, either."

My mentor reared back, dropping into a nearby chair like I'd gut-punched him. Muscles in his jaw pulsed like he was masticating a giant gum ball. I took loud shallow breaths. As my thudding heart slowed down, it dawned on me that I'd just killed two burdens with one outburst. He scrubbed at his ears as if something was stuck inside. When he spoke, his voice was low and strained.

"That's some emotional bullshit baggage, my girl."

"I'm not your bloody girl. I'm a grown woman. A competent woman. Your so-called Partner."

"Hey now."

My vision kept blurring then clearing. I tapped two fingers against my diaphragm.

"Oh. Wait. Are my lips moving? How could I have anticipated being lured into a hot-box storage locker or nearly pushed into the path of an oncoming subway train by a pissed-off reject like Mitch? But I didn't crumple or have a fit of the vapors. I saved myself. Bosco, I told you I checked my surroundings. Didn't do me any damned good, did it? Why? Because I don't have x-ray vision nor can I intuit other people's nefarious motives. Yet. I *am* a good investigator, damn you."

"All right. Stop yelling," he muttered through clenched teeth.

I'd forgotten about Jake's office next door. With the hankie pressed tight against my lips, I muffled another outburst of sobs.

"Pardon?"

He chuckled. "Couple of the old guys had a bet you'd flop outta here in six months. They pegged you for being too book-smart and delicate."

"'What? Book-smart? They didn't."

"Yes. Jake and I didn't bite."

"Delicate? No. I play hockey, for chrissake." I fell back, trying to catch my breath. So much for camaraderie.

"But now?" He shook his head like he'd just found a puppy in a ditch. "I'd never have figured you for quitter. You're going on like...like a wimp."

I threw the handkerchief at him. "Don't you dare. I'm not a coward. Or a quitter. You know better."

"Okay, okay. I shouldn't have said that."

"It was Lawrence subway station not some dark alley."

He hung his head blew out a breath then murmured, "Shit, woman. You scared the crap out of me."

"I'm really sorry."

He dropped into a squat and cradled my chin in his right hand, forcing me to meet his gaze. He shook his head very slowly. I turned mine in the same direction, side to side, my eyes fixed on his mouth.

"How can I explain to Jake how you allowed some jerk to lay his filthy hands on your person and assault you in a public place?"

I hated the controlled hush in his voice.

"It wasn't just any jerk. It was Mitch. He shoved me from behind—that's cowardly. Bosco, I didn't let it happen." A hot liquid pressure pushed from under my lids again. "I noticed him but didn't recognize him."

"That's very scary, Kenora." He dropped his hand. "Don't be sorry. Be really pissed off," he said. "And careful. You realize Mitch had to have been following you. From here. Doesn't that chill your shit?"

"Yes. A lot. And I am angry," I wheezed, trying to ignore the fatigue and soreness weighing me down. "More scared of you than of him, though."

"Oh, give me a fucking break, will you?"

He gave me a wan smile. "I thought you said you were tough. I can take it. Isn't that what you said?"

"Listen, some personal stuff is going on with my dad. And I had a fight with my best friend. I was late for the meeting I was going only because you asked me to. I..."

"I, I, I." He mimicked my tone. "Holy Mother of God, Kenora. You want crackers and cheese with that whine? This isn't about you. It's about the job. Your job."

"He got lucky," I croaked. The idiocy of me dismissing Mitch as 'blowing smoke' stung as much as my cuts and bruises.

"No, he didn't. Jesus Christ. You were lucky his aim was bad."

He turned on his heel and began pacing again, leaving in his wake a torrent of profanities about Mitch's body parts and his parentage.

"My business card." I reached for Bosco's shirt sleeve as he strode by. "That's how he found me here."

He shrugged me off and swung around. His lips were drawn into a feral grimace. "Have you been fooling me about being ready to be a real investigator? Wanna go back to the university library?"

"Of course not." I flung my hands up and whisper-yelled, "No. Don't shout." My throat burned with acid and shame. "Fuck it, Bosco. Partners, eh? What a pile of.... Just go. I don't need this. Bugger off."

He jerked as if from a slap. "Have. You. Lost. Your. Fucking. Mind."

"No. Jesus, Bosco. Shhh."

"What?" He jerked his head toward the closed door. "You're worried Jake might find out about your latest escapades? Good. We have to brief him, you know. Hear that? I said we. And get Buck and his crew to do a threat assessment. It's not just you affected, madam."

"I know, I know. Shit. Not now, okay?"

"What the fuck?"

"I'm done with your nagging. Remember, I don't take that crap from anyone anymore."

He stomped away, cursing a trail across the hardwood floor. I buried my face in my hands. After a moment's silence I heard water running. There was a whoosh of air from the cushions as he sat down in the armchair. He pressed a cold glass against my wrist.

"Drink up."

1 2

It took five minutes for me to gather my wits. When I finally looked up Bosco was leaning on the edge of my desk holding a wrapped parcel the thickness of two decks of cards. He tossed it into my lap.

"This was delivered this morning. Looks legit. That's your dad's return address, right?"

"Oh geez. What now?"

I glanced at the label affixed to the upper left corner then flinched at the sound of banging. The lock to the connecting door on my side clicked shut, then the toilet flushed. The metal holder clanged against the tiled wall as whoever it was dried their hands on the hanging towel. When the second door closed sharply, I let out my breath.

"Yeah, Jake's back. Aren't you going to open it?"

No. My brain hurt.

"Sure."

I wanted to bolt. Disappear in a puff of vapor. Anything but open the package in front of Bosco then have to explain. It was hard to control my fingers as I peeled the white wrapping away and piled the tendrils of paper on the arm of the couch.

"It's not Christmas morning," he said, waving his hand in a circle. "Hurry up."

"Could I have another glass of water?"

As soon as he was out of earshot, I ripped the package open. Inside was a red velvet bag with a gold-colored ball closure. Inside that was a jewelry box with a note taped to the bottom. The card, in Leo's tidy printing read: 'Your mother left this for you. It's time. Dad.'

I flipped the lid open then dropped the box like it was hot. The last time I'd seen that thick gold circle with the oval sapphire stones rimmed with diamonds it had been on my mother's right hand. I squinted at the worn engraving inside the band: 'My Love. Always. ML.'

"What is it?"

Bosco was standing at my elbow holding a full tumbler.

"My mother's ring."

He reached out his hand and said in a gentle tone, "May I?"

I jammed it onto my right ring finger. It was heavy and warm against my chilled skin.

"She never took it off."

"Okay then. What's the story?" When I didn't answer, he said, "Look, that dust-up with Mitch scared me, too. You know I always have your back, right?"

"Yeah, Bosco. I know. It's just—I've got a bit of family mystery going on." Eyes down, I said, "My dad might be able to explain, but he's an Italian *testa dura*. If I push too hard, I'll never get truthful answers."

"Okay, so?"

"He's always treated me differently than my brothers. I thought it was because I was a girl, but now Bosco I'm not so sure. I think…I suspect my mother had an affair."

"Whoo-boy. Now that's heavy. You need to hear his side of it. Give him a call."

"Can't. He's on a flight to Guadalajara."

He snorted. "Interesting timing."

"Indeed."

My body felt like an old rag. I regretted disappointing Bosco. I'd pissed off my best friend. I was more curious than ever about my dad's behavior. Worse, I was going home to sleep in my new king-size bed alone. Not exactly the exciting single-lady life I'd envisioned. When I looked up, his eyes were fixed on my face.

"You okay?" he said in a soft voice.

I reached for his hand. "Laid out there on the subway floor. Bosco, I was so scared."

"Yeah."

"I didn't even have time for my life to flash before my eyes."

He gently cuffed the outside of my knee. "We've got work to do. When you're ready." This situation was new to me. What should I do next? As if I'd spoken, he said, "You've got to face your fear. Examine it. Strategize. Then beat it off."

"Beat it off?" I made a rude noise but he ignored me. "Sure. I'm ready."

I tucked my hands between my thighs. The ring was hard against my finger bones. He smacked his palm against his leg.

"Right. Don't you ever do that to me again."

I thumbed the thick gold circle against the base of my finger. The stones dug into the web of my flesh.

"I won't."

He pulled out his police notebook. "Tell me exactly what happened. As if you were filing a report. Don't skip anything, no matter how insignificant you think it might be. When you're done, we're going to go through it again."

I examined my raggedy cuticles while I revisited my introduction to near disaster. He made me repeat the story once, twice, three times. We sat without speaking when I finished. Muffled conversation drifted in through the closed hall door.

"Let me check with my people," he said. "I have different contacts than the cops."

I knew what kinds of contacts he was talking about. Street people with restless eyes and hard-faced guys who always sat with their backs against the wall. Swarthy men with 'the' in the middle of their names. Skittish fringe dwellers who only showed themselves after dark.

"Thank you."

"We obviously have to do more training. You need me to drive you to the hospital?"

"No, thanks."

He glanced at his watch then pulled me off the couch and leaned in for a quick hug. "You sure you don't have a concussion?"

"I'm not seeing stars or anything."

"Want me to take you to Emerg to get that knee scoped?"

"It's an old sport injury. Hurts like hell but nothing feels broken. Maybe strained a ligament."

"You okay to drive?"

"I am now. Thanks. Um, Bosco. Do we have to tell Jake?"

His look of combined pity and disgust said it all.

"Go home," he said, not unkindly. "Lock your doors. Have a hot bath. Jake's got a full schedule the rest of this week. We'll talk to him next Tuesday. Together."

* * *

Every time I braked at an intersection I scanned my surroundings, half expecting Mitch to leap off the sidewalk and grab the car door handle. My fingers cramped into claws. I'd rolled down the windows just enough to get a breeze but not enough for someone to stick their hand inside. The stench of my fear filled the over-heated air. By the time I pulled into my driveway, I was spent.

I was perched on the edge of the bed struggling into shorts and a t-shirt after my shower when the doorbell rang. An image of Mitch's sneering face popped into my head. I jumped up, wincing at the sudden contact of my feet against the cold floor. Where did I leave my purse? My car keys? Maybe I could sneak into the garage, pop open the door and back out before he realized what was happening?

Kenora, stop it. This is your house, dammit. Call the cops. Dial 9-1-1 if you're so scared shitless. This isn't the projects in Detroit. No one's going to shove a TEC-9 in your face.

The bell rang again. Even Mitch wouldn't be stupid enough to come to my house. I thumbed the controls for the recently installed portable doorbell monitor. Two elongated shadows of female bodies holding booklets materialized. Proselytizers. What, was there a sign over my house flashing, 'come bother me'? If I opened the door I might carve them a new one, as Bosco would say. I yelled "go away" into the microphone in a threatening tone. They scurried off.

Feeling like I'd been hit by a garbage truck, I stretched out on the couch and tried to snooze. Just as the noise in my head was beginning to subside, a ruckus outside jarred me wide awake. A powerful engine revved then died. Metal doors rolled up on greased tracks then slammed shut. Damn. The door monitor was on my bedside table instead of at my side.

I flicked off the lamps and grabbed my walking stick, a pair of binoculars and the telephone handset, limped into the shadows on the porch and adjusted the focus on the glasses. A heavyset man disappeared into the back of a white cube truck idling at the curb two houses down. He climbed into the driver's seat and hunched over the steering wheel, his profile highlighted in the blue-white glow of a dashboard display. Did he have brown skin? Was that ball cap pulled down to conceal his face? I pressed the talk button on the phone, ready to hit 9-1-1.

The guy banged open the sliding door, hopped out with a parcel in his hand and loped down the sidewalk to my neighbor Muriel's house. When he stepped into the pool of amber porch light I made out short dreadlocks, sloping shoulders, and long arms. Not Mitch. Crumpled against the front door, I breathed again. After Muriel answered the door and accepted the package the courier jumped into the truck and gunned away.

Falling asleep was out of the question. My mind was busy as a bingo ball tumbler. I poured myself two fingers of vodka and eased my aching leg onto a footstool. The phone shrilled, making me jump. I'd been paying for a non-published number and permanently blocking my number from call display but still, Mitch was an IT guy. What if he'd hacked someone I knew and tracked me to my house? The phone fell silent then rang again. I read the caller ID and snatched up the receiver.

"Damn it, Partner. You scared the crap out of me."

He chuckled. "I disabled caller ID blocking so you'd know it was me. How are ya?"

"Not too bad. Getting some spectacular bruises. The swelling in my knee has subsided."

"I put some feelers out. I'll let you know when I get something useful." He hung up.

Bosco and I would work out our issues. He had taught me well. I turned on the photocopier in my office, contemplating the trio of wild horses I had to wrangle successfully. They'd fouled my tidy little existence like a sewage backup, but I had to deal with them or lose my mind.

Horse number one: the mysterious photographs. Confronting my dad was Plan A, but would he disclose who M. Linden, the woman and little boy in that sun-dappled park were? Did my mother have a secret lover? Making progress on solving those personal mysteries would take my mind off Mitch tracking me like a deer during hunting season.

Horse number two: the job I loved that paid me very well. I had work assignments and major investigations not to screw up but those I could handle.

Horse number three: that bastard Mitch, messing about in

my life. Heeding all the warnings I'd received about not keeping things to myself, I'd offhandedly mentioned some of Mitch's stunts to Bosco, picking a time when he was distracted. He hadn't reacted but I knew he'd remember.

I hated not having answers, not being able to manage things. I wanted to go on a rampage and body-check someone or break something, but that wouldn't do. It sucked to be mature and responsible.

Jake was going to be the wild card. Although he gave off positive signals, there'd been no physical contact since that day in the elevator. Had he sensed the same undercurrent of sizzle when we were in close proximity? No matter what, he was cordial, arms-length and always professional and proper. I thought again of our elevator ride to Martin Bernard's office.

The bad angel on my shoulder growled, 'To hell with proper.'

The good angel whispered, 'Therein lies trouble, Kenora—the man's your employer.'

Damned angels.

13

Damn it, I wasn't a weakling with no resources. I'd find a way to stop Mitch. Do something besides locking my doors and setting the security alarm. I was tired of not being in control.

I typed York Regional Police + online reports into the search bar, navigated to the web page for Citizen Online Reporting, clicked on Identity Theft/Fraud, read the disclaimers then filled all the little boxes and hit send. A minute later the tumbling hourglass froze, the 'program not responding' dialogue appeared and the screen paled to grey. I clicked furiously and was bounced back to the original blank form. After stomping around muttering under my breath, I cooled off enough to start over.

This time, the form went through and I got an auto-respond message: *Thank you for your report. Filing time: 07/26 22:17. Please keep a copy of this form for your records. Someone will be in touch with you shortly.*

I jerked awake at four o'clock in a sweaty tangle of blankets, the jaws of a headache clamped around my skull. My brain was whirling with lists. God, I was tired. And more horny than frightened. Too lazy to do anything about that, I went to the bathroom and stumbled back to bed. An hour later, I pounded the alarm clock into silence, dressed in my Irene Investigator outfit and drove the back roads into the office.

The few days of icing and resting my elevated knee had worked wonders. I ditched the stick but wore the knee brace under wide-legged fat-pants I'd retrieved from the Salvation Army donation bag I'd forgotten to drop off.

The next few weeks were blessedly uneventful. Jake was on an extended visit with family out West. Desk-bound, I fell into a routine of delving deeper into the Bernards file and completing background checks and simple investigations. Lunch was eaten *al desko* rather than in the communal dining area. I didn't want to have to explain the limp and fading bruises to my curious colleagues. Besides, they'd have much better war wound stories involving edged weapons, fists, and firearms.

I relied on Bosco to keep me in the loop. He nagged me into making an appointment for physiotherapy then drove me to the clinic where he loitered at the front counter chatting up the receptionists. Three visits later, I was told to visit my chiropractor for regular tune-ups. After dire warnings about the crippling consequences of not taking care of my aging body and sports-injured joints, the relentlessly cheerful miracle-maker Dr. Kelly fitted me with a stretchy knee sleeve in a wild African print and counselled me to give up my circus act.

A propos of nothing, Bosco said one day as we were having brunch in a west-end hole-in-the-wall, "Jake told me you were a manager at the University for sixteen years. Same place you investigated?"

"Different area. I was careful about conflict of interest."

"How come you got unemployed?"

"I was given a choice of resigning or being fired. Um, are you allowed to ask that kind of question?"

He grinned. "Probably not. But you've already been hired so it's not as if it's a human rights thing. You offended?"

"Not especially."

"Okay then. What happened?"

"The eggs Benedict are good."

He wouldn't be diverted. "Well?"

I pushed away my plate. "A couple months after my mother died, my husband announced he'd found his soul mate at Bible study class and wanted a divorce."

"Ouch. Bible study?"

"Yeah, laugh. He was studying her lady parts and she was playing his organ, I suspect."

He didn't bother hiding an evil grin. "And?"

"Bosco, all my life I worked hard at being a good daughter then a good wife. For what? My dad has always been distant and angry no matter how well I did. I got kicked to the curb for a younger model by a man who accused me of being too competitive. Women I thought were my friends—women I'd played hockey with for years—began treating me like I was a chancre sore. My new boss at work and I hadn't been getting along. Right after the executive offices had been renovated yet another round of cost-cutting was proposed. I objected, stood up for my staff and said some things in the heat of the moment that I shouldn't have. Got documented for being insubordinate. When I asked for mediation, I was told—get this—there was no money."

"Where was the union?"

"You mean our staff association? Out to lunch. When I mentioned specifics about some of the hanky-panky-spanky I knew about, they negotiated a decent settlement with no negative entry on my employment record, full severance and the opportunity to resign."

"Sucks. What'd you do after the divorce, buy a red sports car? Start dating young guys?"

"No, Bosco. Middle-aged men do that. I put my stuff in storage, went back to grad school and bought a raised ranch with lake frontage."

"Nice. Did the fixes work?"

"Oh, yes. The man I was temping for after I graduated had a list of tradesmen to recommend. Things turned out better than I'd hoped, except most of them wanted cash. Saw a shrink for eight months. He told me I was well adjusted and that I should get on with my life."

"Huh. Don't get too cocky. Shrinks are notoriously unreliable. Either way too optimistic or they get you hooked on the couch thing for life."

I debated telling him about the photographs and the Martin connection but knew that if I did Jake would find out, which was what I did not want. Not yet, anyway. As if he read my thoughts, Bosco thumbed his half-glasses low on his nose and fixed his laser eyes on me. I hid behind my upraised mug and drained the lukewarm coffee in two gulps.

"But I've got you, Bosco."

"Yeah. Time to get back to your lessons."

As we were pulling into a slot behind the office after supper, my cell phone beeped with a voicemail notification. Bosco, too tired to kvetch, began unloading his kit from the rear hatch. I punched in my access code.

A pleasant voice said, "Ms. Tedesco. Detective Steve Mercer, York Regional Police Major Crimes. I have a copy of the report you completed online."

Clutching the phone to my chest, I whipped around. Bosco was out of earshot. I called Mercer's number and left him a whispery voice message.

"You coming or you still chatting with your new beau?" Bosco called from the back door.

"How come you're so grumpy?"

"I want to lock up. I got someone to go home to."

And I didn't. "Thanks a bunch." Instead of taking the bait, he shrugged.

Detective Mercer called while I was driving north on Highway 404. "Ms. Tedesco? Can we meet tomorrow, say around ten? Where's your office?"

Sweat prickled along my hairline. "No. Um...no. That's not convenient."

"Just trying to save us some time. When would be convenient?"

A flash of blue-red-white strobes in the rear-view mirror caught my eye. Damn, I was doing 130. I jerked my foot off the accelerator and sagged with relief when the OPP SUV blew by in the passing lane.

"I know your office is in Headquarters. I'm almost home. Can I come to your office?"

"I'm on my way back from Barrie."

"Listen, do you mind...I mean, is it okay if you stop by my house? It's on the way. I've kept notes. You can read my notes. I also have a recording of the initial interview I did with Mitch. Except for the threats. I'll make you coffee. I have fresh cookies. You like chocolate chip?"

God, my mouth was rattling like a jalopy.

"As long as the java's not instant. See you in twenty minutes." He was laughing at me for being flustered but I didn't care.

After punching the unlock code into my garage keypad, I gathered my belongings and raced through the laundry room to the bathroom. Stress was taking a toll on my bladder. The doorbell rang and I hustled to answer. The gangly red-haired man standing under the porch light was holding the fat log of plastic-wrapped weekly community newspapers. He was wearing a heather green sports jacket and matching tie, peach colored shirt and sharply pressed black slacks.

His gaze dropped to my waist. My hand groped for my belt —I'd forgotten to buckle it up and my shirt was untucked.

"Was I too fast for ya?"

"No. Well, I've been sort of discombobulated by this Mitch thing. Coffee's ready."

He handed me a business card, pumped my hand and plunked himself in a chair at the kitchen table. "I've been leaving you messages for a couple days."

"I didn't get a message until you called my cell."

"And I had to dig that one up. You left a 905 number on your report."

I smacked my forehead. "My old home number." Out of habit, I'd entered the ten digits I'd used for the last twenty years. "Sorry. My ex-husband ported the account when he moved out."

"The voice was yours though. What, he didn't change his voice mail message?"

"Guess not. Figures he wouldn't tell me about the police calling."

Lazy ass. He must have heard the detective's messages but decided to erase them. I slid a plate of cookies across the table. He waved off milk and sugar, took a few sips from his mug and grinned.

"Good stuff. You guys aren't talking?"

"It's all been said and more. The divorce was brief but unfriendly. His idea, not mine."

He made an 'I hear you' grimace, pulled out his duty notebook and gave me a rundown of his preliminary investigation. Mitch's name and several aliases appeared in the YRP Records Management System. He'd never been charged with anything more serious than speeding. He was, however, listed as an associate in a dozen general occurrence reports. Seems that the guys he hung out with—the friends he boasted of—were known to police for criminal activity involving arson, auto theft, assault, and financial misdeeds.

"That explains the quick response. Now I'm really worried."

"Until now, Mitch has been more of a hanger-on." He held up the last cookie as if to ask permission then polished it off.

"But as an insider, he planned the salary fraud and ghost staff scam. Isn't that what you call *mens rea*?"

Mercer made a face. "I talked to the Metro detective working the University fraud. We're not sure if Mehran was the mastermind or an errand boy. It'll take time to find out."

The coffee was burning a hole in my belly. "How much time?"

"Dunno. As long as it takes."

He was chatty and I was too tired from a day on the road with Bosco to get upset.

"Tell me some more about your relationship with Mitch and what got you into this identity fraud situation."

I recoiled. "Geez, Detective. We don't have a relationship. He was a contract IT guy when I worked at the University Registrar's Office. Our first encounter was three-and-a-half years ago during a feedback session about the new computer system. I'd complained it was too difficult to audit attendance and compare it with salary payouts or overtime. Mitch offered to tutor me on formulating simple queries. He dropped by my office twice. I was uncomfortable."

"Why?"

"His aftershave was too strong and his smile was creepy. He breached my personal space. Pressed against my arm when he pointed out something on my computer screen. And I could have sworn he had a woody."

Mercer stopped writing. "What did you do?"

"Dropped my pen and rolled my chair away. A few months later in a crowded hallway at the campus pub, someone bumped into me from behind but the contact lasted too long to be accidental. When I turned around, Mitch rubbed his crotch against my... hip. He was waving a beer bottle chanting, 'MILFs are hot' and 'me so horny.'"

"Over-refreshed?"

"No. His eyes weren't drunk." Remembering made me squirm. "He was, however, noticeably aroused. I accidentally thumped him in the groin with my book bag and told him to grow up and get lost."

"Other people hear you?"

"Yes. Then things began happening that made no sense. Phone calls at home or at work with no one there, suggestive emails from colleagues who energetically disavowed them, porno pop-ups on my work computer. Some minor vandalism to my personal vehicle—air let out of the tires, fake parking infractions on the windshield, glue in the door locks. When my mom passed away, someone left dead flowers on our lawn every day for a week. It never occurred to me to connect them to Mitch." I also mentioned the storage locker incident, the subway shove and bogus deliveries to my old address.

Mercer grimaced. "You keep anything?"

"Unfortunately, no. Campus security treated me like I was a nut bar. I was pissed off so I took photos. I'll email them to you. Now that I think about it, my concerns about the computer system related to the loophole he eventually used to defraud Cheviot. If only I'd known."

"Not possible. You interrupted his livelihood then made him look like a punk for getting caught. The harassment'll probably ratchet up."

"Great. What do I do? He obviously doesn't take rejection well."

Mercer slapped his notebook shut. "Watch your back. Report anything out of the ordinary. Put my number on speed dial. Send me the contact information for the real staffers like Mindy. You go to the gym?"

"Couple of times a week when I can. Why?"

"The girlfriend could access the change room."

"You're not serious? I'd recognize her."

"Do you look at other women when you're dressing or undressing?" I shook my head. "His sexual overtures worry me. Maybe he'd pressure her into taking photos of you. Not to worry."

"Easy for you to say. Now I have to eyeball the ladies in yoga class and think twice about taking a shower after a workout?"

He waved that off. "We'll get on it, but you might want to find a new place to work out. The CRA guys'll tear him a new one if they conclude he evaded paying taxes."

I unclenched my fingers. He flipped open his notebook again.

"Where did you say you worked?"

"Barclay, Benford & Friday. It's a..."

"I know who they are."

Was that good or bad? Why was he looking at me that way?

"You gonna tell them what's going on?" he said.

"I'd rather not. This Mitch thing might make me look like a liability."

"Don't go investigating on your own, hear?"

"No way. Listen, you're not going to talk to my boss?"

I had to ask, because members of the cop fraternity were more talkative than folks in a pick-up bar at happy hour.

"No." His phone buzzed. He pulled it from a belt clip, exposing a large pistol in a black holster on his left hip. He listened for a few minutes, ended the call then poked at the phone keyboard. "Great coffee. Thanks for the sugar rush." At the front door, he turned and said, "Oh, and I'll need a video statement from you."

"Sure." I scrabbled in my backpack for my personal cell phone and flicked to the calendar app.

"May I?" He took the device from me, examined it and handed it back. "I were you, I'd dump this antique piece of shit. That duct tape won't hold it together for long. Get one with a fast processor and more storage. And a new number, too."

"I've got my eye on a new iPhone."

"Do it." He opened his calendar. "Next Thursday afternoon. Four o'clock. You said you know where HQ is, just south of Wellington east of Leslie Street?"

"Yes."

14

*F*inally, finally, I'd been able to schedule my dad Leo for a visit. I'd shopped for his favorite foods and made a tiramisu for dessert. While I was rummaging in the freezer drawer for a cold pack, I found a bottle of Ice Grappa. Maybe the double whammy of ambush by tasty menu selections with a side of high-octane booze would loosen his tongue.

The dutiful daughter part of me regretted what I had to do, but I didn't feel bad. There was no way I'd give him room not to tell me what I wanted to know. I set aside the knife I'd been using to slice red peppers and sat down hard. Was this what Bosco meant when he said he sensed a ruthlessness behind my sweet lady mask? All right. I could handle that.

When dad pulled up after lunch in his vintage Alfa Romeo, I was ready.

"Good to see you, Papa. How have you been?"

He caught me in a light hug and released me right away. "Not too bad, *cara*. The time away in Mexico helps. You?"

My body was still tender from the subway incident but I wrapped my arms around him, burying my nose in his sweater, inhaling the familiar scents of Noxzema skin cream and Old

Spice shaving soap. His body was less substantial than I remembered but his posture was as unyielding as ever.

"Getting better. Let me take your bag. *Prendiamo un caffè?*"

We settled at the kitchen table in a wedge of sunlight, sipping from our tiny cups and making tiny talk. Although I couldn't put my finger on specifics, I knew something was off. I made another espresso and plated slices of lemon pound cake. He gestured to my cheek.

"What happened?"

I couldn't tell him some wacko had tried to push me under a moving train. The lie came easily. "I tripped over a rake and landed in a black currant bush. The bush won."

"You'll survive." His gaze skittered from the table to the floor, eventually fixing on the open patio door to the deck. "Your mom would like your little house."

That was the opening I needed. "Speaking of mom, I need to talk to you about something." He jumped like I'd zapped him with a cigar lighter then tossed back the rest of his coffee.

"My tools are in the Alfa. Let me check out that problem with your car then I'll measure for the gazebo."

While he hustled about doing odd jobs, my anxiety rose. The old photos Maggie had found were important but although I knew that in my gut, I didn't have enough hard information to understand why. Confronting my dad, no matter what our past relationship, wasn't going to be easy. He seldom raised his voice, preferring a passive-aggressive wall of cool silence. I'd have to gently squeeze what I wanted to learn from Leo Tedesco but he'd be a tough nut to crack.

"Something smells good," he said, rubbing his palms together. He'd showered, shaved, and changed his clothes. It looked like he was ready for mass. I prayed he'd be in the mood for confession.

I'd gone full Italian with the table—red check tablecloth, flowers, fat candles, thick glassware, rustic baskets of garlic bread and focaccia. Vintage tunes from the Four Tenors played in the background. He sat opposite me and rearranged his table setting, recited a quick blessing then grimaced when I handed him the bottle of Spanish *Heretat Mont-Rubi* white to go with the roast rosemary chicken and eggplant. He grimaced but knew this was my house and my rules. I'd grown tired of Italian wines.

We clinked a toast. I gulped: he sipped. It was obvious he was trying not to like the wine but after I refilled his plate with food and opened a second bottle, he didn't object. The alcohol didn't weaken his guardedness, though. I used the best of my private investigator tactics but he sidestepped and subject-changed so deftly my questions fell like a squirrel climbing a greased pole. Finally, I gave up on being subtle.

"I think it's time the kids had details about our family history." He kept his eyes on his plate, chewing with intense concentration.

My hand shook as I pulled the three photos from my pocket and placed them in a row beside his wine glass. His ruddy complexion blanched. After a brief glance, he flicked them face down with the point of his knife.

Tight-lipped, he murmured, "Where did you get those?"

"Maggie found them in an old yearbook she got from mom. I believe the baby is me. Who was M.L. And those other people, the women and the little boy?"

His nostrils flared. He clattered his cutlery onto his plate then snatched up the photos, stacked them together and deliberately tore them into strips before I could stop him.

"Dad, no. What's the matter?"

He shoved back his chair and disappeared down the hall into the bathroom. I dithered between following or letting him be. My brain couldn't compute what had just happened. I decided to keep busy and clear the table. When he returned ten minutes later, his color was back to normal.

Eyes averted, he said in a husky voice, "There are things better left undiscussed."

"All right. Come have dessert."

When I made a few oblique comments about families keeping secrets, he busied himself clanking his spoon around his coffee cup and pretended not to hear. I fell silent. He didn't turn aside but his lined face grew taut and more closed. The pattern was familiar but this time, instead of being wounded by his withdrawal, I was frustrated. We were both probably too set in our ways to change so I let him deflect the conversation to my three brothers, my globe-trotting children and my new job. We went to bed early, but I had a hard time sleeping, half expecting him to leave under cover of darkness.

He turned down breakfast the next morning, pleading an early appointment in Guelph. He patted my arm, gathered up his tools and left. I had no new information, but at least he hadn't stayed pissed off.

* * *

*E*arly Monday, I was annoyed out of a sweaty doze by an insistent buzzing. Not the alarm clock. A dead battery in the smoke detector? Hell of a way to start the day I thought grimly, trying to ignore the throbbing behind my eyes as I stumbled from room to room searching for the source. My old cell phone, come loudly to life, had fallen off a shelf in my office closet and landed screen down on the hardwood floor. Gingerly, I picked it up. The case was hot but the message scrolling across the cracked screen turned my guts to ice:

'Sorry I MISSED you, Rosie. LOL. I'll be IN TOUCH soon. Those pigs you work for CAN'T STOP ME. I will FUCK YOUR OREO ASS UP'.

I wanted to hurl the damned handset against the wall and

smash it to bits but had the presence of mind to open the camera app on my iPad and photograph Mitch's message.

Asshole, I'm more clever than you. You're not going to get to me. Could he track me using that old phone? I checked the network settings. Neither the wi-fi nor the telephone company's signals showed as active. How the hell did the message come in?

Identify the sender. On my iPad, a duplicate unread message sat in the inbox of an email address I hadn't checked in months. I logged into webmail, right-clicked view source, did a fist-pump then clicked off half a dozen screen shots. Mr. Too-Smart-By-Half had used a free web-to-text service. The bastard's IP address and server location were buried in an almost impenetrable list of codes and IP hops. Almost. Maybe he'd spoofed that, too, but it was a start.

Call Mercer. Of course, the police had techno-wizards who could track Mitch down. By the time I downloaded the files to my computer and attached them to an email message telling him what had happened, my headache had receded. Kenora, you are turning into a seriously competent P.I.

* * *

Instead of sitting and stewing, I'd done something concrete. Followed the rules. I patted myself on the back, finished the leftover tiramisu then texted Bosco with an update.

I desperately needed a significant something in the win column. I put Mitch and my dad out of my mind and turned my attention to Bernards.

True to his word, Gavin was a workhorse. He was also very funny. The volume of paper to get through seemed interminable and I rarely made it back to my office at Barclay, Benford & Friday before supper time. When my work phone rang later that evening, I was standing beside a chubby woman in electrical utility company coveralls waiting for the counter guy at the deli to finish assembling the smoked meat sandwich that was my lunch/dinner.

Bosco said without preamble, "I made some notes about the Mitch thing. For our meeting with Jake tomorrow." My stomach clenched. A wave of vertigo hit me. "You there?"

"Sure. Okay."

"Yeah. Be prepared. Go to bed early."

Halfway to the streetcar stop, I was debating whether to eat my sandwich or find a homeless guy to give it to when the bloody phone rang again.

"I passed the message with Mitch's threats to the supervisor of Technical Data Recovery," said Detective Mercer. "Not sure they'll be able to do much with it but our boy just added fuel to his criminal fire."

"I'm going to copy the message to the IT folks at BB&F. They're crackerjacks with this stuff."

"I've heard. Probably'll come up with something before we do. Better resources and fewer competing priorities." He cleared his throat. My heart sank.

"What, Steve?"

"I hate to be the bearer of bad news," he said. "It's Mitch. We had a good lead on his whereabouts but he's, um, in the wind."

I stuttered to a stop in the middle of the sidewalk and whipped around in a circle. A couple of guys in tight pants and Grateful Dead t-shirts jostled their way around me. One of them muttered an obscenity. "Oh, bugger yourselves you little morons."

"What's going on?"

"Never mind." Clutching the phone and the paper bag containing the sandwich in my left hand, I skittered away from the curb, pressing my back against the graffitied boards of a shuttered variety store. "What does in the wind mean?" Meat juice dripped across my wrist and down the front of my shirt. "Shit."

I tucked the handset between my ear and shoulder and dabbed at the ooze with a wad of crumpled napkins.

"It means he's slipped out of sight. For now, anyway." Mercer paused until my cursing subsided then said, "I have good news, too."

"You were joking and Mitch checked himself into the crowbar motel?"

Mercer snorted. "Ah, no. Because there are sexual elements to your case along with the criminal harassment, they've assigned another detective."

"Oh great. Now I have to start over."

"Simmer down. Her name's Ginger Kobinski. A detective sergeant in the Special Victims Unit. She'll call tomorrow. Or you can call. I'll text you her contact info."

"Do you think I'm in danger?"

"Not immediately." I wanted to shriek, when then? "There's some other stuff going on with him that I can't talk about. Let's be careful out there."

This was ridiculous. How many times were the men in my life going to tell me that?

"Yes, Sergeant Esterhaus," I snapped. "You wanna play Hill Street Blues? How about 'Let's do it to them before they do it to us'?"

"You're touchy today."

"I'm developing a crick in my neck from constantly looking over my shoulder."

"I can understand you're a bit jumpy but—"

"Never mind. I gotta go."

After a quick look around I pushed away from the wall. I could have sworn I'd glimpsed Mitch's face half a dozen times as I traveled around town but that made no sense. The police were on his trail, he was on the tax department's Special Enforcement Bureau speed-dial and he still had a crooked business to run.

Back at my desk, I chomped through the sandwich while reading and responding to a blitz of emails but my heart wasn't in it. Maggie was back from her jaunt to Europe but we'd maintained radio silence. Cutting myself off from her was dumb. My hand hovered over the keypad for a minute then I called her at home. She said nothing about our recent tiff but rattled on about her kids and her hot week with hubby in Milan. A stab of jealousy gave me pause but I rallied—my life was my own. Was I ready to change that? Not yet. We fell silent.

When I told her about getting pushed on the subway platform, she started to cry. After I consoled her—which was odd considering it was my life in danger—I recounted my conversation with Detective Mercer. That perked her up.

"You've got pent-up frustrations. Fire up your fantasies and relieve those itches tonight, my friend. You'll thank me." She instructed me to get a guard dog, a gallon of pepper spray and a body camera then announced that she wanted to accompany me the next time Mercer and I had a meeting.

"Why?"

"You know what they say about a man in a uniform. Besides, I've never been inside a police station."

"Neither have I. Mercer's plain clothes. And he came to my house."

"Ohhhh. Vixen."

"Uh, no chance. Not my type." I didn't bother reminding her that I worked with former cops all day and they were mostly as ordinary or twisted as the guys you'd run into at Canadian Tire. "I'll see if I can get you a tour."

Taking Maggie's advice, I had a long hot soak in my new tub. Come midnight I was under the covers with Obi, diverting myself with fantasies of Jake shirtless and sweaty from chainsawing fallen trees in my yard. Eventually, I sank into a dreamless sleep.

I awoke with a sore neck and dark circles under my eyes. I had no illusions that Bosco and Jake would go easy on me. Technically, I'd never been fired before. Would today be a disgraceful first?

15

My suspension was strike one. The subway thing was my second imbroglio. I was recovering quickly physically but more slowly psychologically. Job-wise, I couldn't predict how Jake would react this time.

For breakfast, I choked down two acid reducer tablets and a container of full fat yogurt. No coffee. Damned if I was going to be submissive but I certainly could appear less feisty than usual. I flat-ironed my hair into loose waves, carefully made up my face, donned a shirt in a shade of soothing pink and popped the collar. I added a glittery pendant, burgundy pinstriped trousers and a coordinating linen jacket. Coolly professional but feminine.

Bosco was already in my office when I limped in.

"Morning," I said in a bright voice that was steady and strong.

"Morning." He stopped pacing and shoved a copy of his notes at me. I handed him mine.

My desk phone rang. Without thinking, I hit the speaker button.

"Did something happen when dad was at your house?" It was

my youngest brother Gianluca. He sounded harried. I snatched up the receiver.

"Why, Luke?"

"When I called last night he sounded awful. Cut me off when I asked what you guys talked about."

"Can I call you back later? I'm sort of busy."

"No. I want to know now." He whined like I'd beat him at checkers again.

Bosco growled. His mood was palpable as a bad smell. I turned away, visualizing Luke drumming his blunt-nailed fingers on the edge of his well-organized desk. If Leo hadn't mentioned the photographs then I could give baby brother a sanitized version.

"We chatted about mom. You know, family stuff. I was sad, too."

"He's not sad, Kenny. Beaten down. Worse than when mom died. You did something."

I tipped my head back and stared at the designs on the plaster ceiling. "I'll give him a call when I'm done my meeting."

"You guys have a fight?"

"No, dear." I let him bluster. When he showed no signs of winding down, I hissed, "It not about you, Luke. My life has gotten complicated, okay? I said I'd call dad. I've got to go."

I dabbed at my eyes with a tissue and picked up Bosco's handwritten pages. They were so blurry they might as well have been written in Greek. I slipped on my reading glasses. Bosco made a hurry-up motion. The phone rang again.

"Don't answer. We've got work to do."

"Could we rehearse?"

"No. Read fast. Then let's go." He tapped the toe of his snake-skin cowboy boot against the leg of a chair while I flipped through the notes.

"Am I going to be fired, Bosco?"

He turned on his heel and marched through the door connecting my office with Jake's.

"Hey you two." Jake was seated at his desk paging through a fat binder. He swung his feet off their perch on the bottom drawer and waved us to the couch. He examined me as I tried to skulk by. "You don't look so good even with that extra makeup. And you're dragging your left leg." Bosco threw me an I-told-you-so smirk. "You all right?"

"Yes, thank you." I took the chair at the narrow end of the teak slab coffee table.

"What's up?"

"The Bernards investigation is coming along nicely," I offered.

Jake's next question was cut off by Bosco's muttered, "We have a situation. With Kenora."

"Great opening, Partner," I said under my breath.

Bosco flipped open his notebook and paused. Nobody spoke. I slid my file folder onto the table then placed my notebook exactly in the center. I lay my fountain pen across the notebook and looked up, about to launch into my defense, but I was stunned into silence.

Jake and Bosco faced each other across the table. Their postures were identical: leaning forward, elbows resting on their thighs, hands clasped loosely in the space between their knees. Unconsciously, I did the same. The only sound was our breathing. A galvanizing tension swirled between them. Eyes locked, they were engaged in a bubble of silent conversation. Without warning, Jake threw himself against the chair back and drew in a loud breath. I sucked in a breath too, because I'd been holding mine.

Bosco gestured with his chin. "This isn't Ashby Avenue, Bud," he said quietly.

I had no idea what they were talking about, but I wasn't going to ask.

Nodding grimly, Jake slapped his palms on his thighs. "I hear you." His voice was hoarse. "Still."

I tried to quietly dislodge the lump of fear in my throat but they had beastly good hearing. Four hawk eyes turned in my direction. It was hard not to shrink into the cushions or blink like a cornered rabbit. I dropped my gaze, adjusted my glasses then squeezed my fingers in my lap like I was reciting the Stations of the Cross. Jesus, help me.

Bosco read from his notebook. When he got to the part about my foot getting trapped between the subway car and the platform, Jake snapped up his right hand palm out.

In a soft, dangerous voice he said, "Someone deliberately pushed Kenora. There were witnesses. The transit people interviewed them and got signed statements, right?"

I folded my arms tight across my chest. "I said I was okay. The train was held up for like, ten minutes. I didn't want to make a fuss."

Jake snapped, "Shouldn't have mattered."

"Makes you wonder, eh?" said my mentor. Obviously, they were having a conversation only they knew how to decipher.

Jake squinted somewhere above my head, his expression unreadable but his stillness radiating fury. We waited. I tried to catch Bosco's eye but he wasn't cooperating. There was nothing I could say that wouldn't sink me into a deeper hole. Without changing position Jake said, "What, Bosco?"

Bosco shot me a side-eye glare. "I was at a cop do last night. Chatted with a guy I coached in Commercial Crime. We were talking about this and that, projects, people at work. Kenora's name came up."

"Ah shit." I'd meant to think it but I'd spoken out loud. "Detective Steve Mercer? Ginger-haired, sharp dresser?"

Bosco drummed a tune on the arm of the chair. No way would I be lulled into thinking this was going to end well. I repositioned my pen and brushed a loose thread from my shirt sleeve. I should have known I'd get busted—cop-folks gossiped all the time. On the other hand, my tongue was frozen in my mouth. Bosco cleared his throat. I'd never known anyone who could make such an innocuous gesture sound life-threatening.

A patently fake smile accompanied Jake's speculative stare. "Care to enlighten me?"

"A while back, I submitted an online report to York Regional Police about Mitch Mehran, the guy I exposed as part of the university ghost worker salary scam. Remember Bosco, when my cell phone kept turning itself on and sending arbitrary notifications? That was Mitch. He's been cyber-stalking me. Sending packages of sex toys." My face and hands were on fire. "Luckily, to my old address. I did a written and a video statement."

Bosco muttered, "She didn't share any of this with me, though."

"I was going to. Until the subway thing I thought it might go away." I tried to keep my voice low and soothing. "I, um, didn't want you to think I was a liability."

Jake frowned. "Are we that fearsome? Everyone makes mistakes."

"But I've made a few biggies. You suspended me, remember?"

"That was supposed to be a wakeup call. Teach you to trust and disclose."

"Well, I did this time even if I didn't tell you who I spoke with. I can't be running to you with every little thing. Right, Bosco?"

My mentor's frown had indeed turned fearsome. "One reason I haven't come down on you with both feet is because you did report it," he said, turning his flinty eyes on me, no doubt remembering the one-sided conversation with my brother and my comment about my life getting complicated. "You apparently still have a vestige of judgment left."

"I appreciate your confidence in me."

"Calling it confidence is an overstatement." He leaned forward until his face was about a foot from mine. "What Mehran pulled isn't a prank you can deal with, Kenora. It falls under section 264(1) of the Criminal Code. The operative word is criminal."

I recoiled, igniting pinwheels behind my eyes. Perhaps he was taking pity on me but Jake said in a slightly warmer tone, "What's happening, Kenora?"

Before I could answer, Bosco jumped in. "It ramped up after her interview with Mercer. After Metro got on his case, Mitch started going off the deep end. Escalating. Thing is, the stalking started before at the University but Kenora hadn't connected it to him."

"When did you last talk to Mitch?"

"A real conversation? When my friend Jerry, the Canada Revenue agent, frog-marched him off campus in cuffs. Remember, I told you he said some things."

I held Jake's gaze, imagining what those ocean-after-dark eyes would look like sparked by passion. Wrong time; wrong place.

"He cursed me in Italian. Could be he picked it up from the movies."

"I'm gonna do follow-up." Bosco said, tapping his palm against his thigh. "From what I can tell he's still got the hots for Kenora."

"I'm not making excuses but some personal stuff has me off balance." I shot a glance at Bosco and raised my voice to mask the tremble underlying my words. "It's not going to affect my work. I can deal with it on my own time."

Jake's expression was solemn. "Personal. Uh huh. Is that something we can help you with?" Oh Lord, he thought it was a relationship breakup or something that might turn messier than Mitch.

"No, no. It's nothing like that. It's my dad. He's been acting strangely since my mom died."

Bosco's eyes bored into mine. "Actually, she doesn't want to talk about it."

His tone was like a snowball to the neck. He expected to be the first to know. Always. I mentally rolled my eyes. Was I expected to live my life in public to make sure his intelligence was up-to-date? How long had it been since Mitch's shove had almost propelled me to serious injury or death? I'd barely had time to think through what happened. Jake peered at me then at Bosco. If I was going to be gonged there was nothing I could do to stop it, but I was fed up with being on the receiving end of scoldings when I was trying to do my best.

I leaned forward with my hands clasped. "Gentlemen, listen. You've said that I did a decent job with the Cheviot University file. How could I know Mitch'd go off his rocker? I'm collateral damage, I accept that. Beating up on me won't change that. I need you both to stop grinding my gears."

They stared. I froze. Obviously, stress was making me lose my mind. The silence stretched to snapping. Finally, Jake tapped the back of my hand.

"There's another matter."

My flesh burned where he'd touched me. I couldn't get enough air. Here it comes. I'm getting the axe.

"What is it?"

"Buck reports that your name popped up during a threat assessment check."

"What kind of popped up?"

"Chat rooms, mainly. A couple really hard-core sites." He slipped on his reading glasses then unfolded a printed note. "Freaky MILFs, Chatter-pussy and Backdoorbitches were at the top of the lists. Someone with email addresses kenorasucks@dome.com and hotktedesco@happyending.com has been posting lately."

A flaming tide of embarrassment raced up my neck. I knew my cheeks were red. Although I wanted to bolt or slide under the table, I kept my voice steady. "Jesus. Not very inventive."

"Do you even know what a MILF is?" Bosco said.

I shot him a disgusted look. "I swear those email addresses aren't mine. Obviously, Mitch has shopped my personal information. And made stuff up."

"Agreed," Jake said. "Your old cell phone number shows up on call displays from telemarketers flogging bulk freezer meat, duct cleaning services and anti-virus software. There's been complaints to the CRTC about someone using that number violating do not call listings. We'll cut you some slack this time. But from now on…."

My heart sank. This time? Recalling my panic over being suspended made my gut cramp. I had to fix this. The contractor who promised to clear my driveway next winter wanted half of his money up front. The lumberyard wouldn't order the cedar for my summer house unless I paid half in advance. I'd crunched the numbers: a part-time gig at a Big Box store would not pay the bills.

"I hear you," I said, unconsciously repeating Bosco's words. "I'll take precautions. Report everything."

Jake cleared his throat. "Have you talked with Detective Mercer?"

"Yes. They've re-assigned my file. The new detective left a voice message but I haven't had time to call her back."

"You have a name?"

"Detective Sergeant Ginger Kobinski, Special Victims Unit."

"I worked with her old man on a Criminal Intelligence project in Waterloo," Bosco said. He wore a strange look. Another blast from their cop past, no doubt.

I was getting better at interpreting their visual codes but the undercurrent was confusing the messaging. "What?" Neither of them paid me any mind.

Jake snapped his fingers. "Ginger? Is she one of the...." He cupped his fingers around his mouth so all I caught was what sounded like 'partner girls'.

"Yeah. She's good people," Bosco said.

Jake turned to me. "I'd like you to give her a call." I opened and closed my notebook. The digital clock on the desk went snick, snick, snick. Bosco was staring into the unlit fireplace. No help there. Jake said in a louder voice, "Right now, Kenora."

"I'll do that."

I managed not to shuffle through the passageway to our offices. I left both connecting doors slightly ajar.

16

While I waited for Detective Sergeant Kobinski to answer, I listened to the men's voices carrying through the half-opened doors. I was heartened that they weren't yelling. In fact, I heard laughter as Bosco's booted heels hit the hardwood floor fronting Jake's door.

Kobinski answered on the fourth ring. I explained who I was and read her the case number Mercer had assigned. She asked to record the call, stated the date and time, my name, her name and badge number, then the SVU case number and said, "Go". I recited the same details I'd given to Bosco. "Great recall. That's a big plus." Computer keys clicked in the background. "Did the transit people give you an incident number? I want to re-interview the witnesses."

"They didn't take a report."

"You've got to be kidding me," she snapped. "Hold on." There was a muffled conversation in the background. Her tone was cold when she returned to our conversation. "There are protocols."

Whether she was pissed at the transit people or at me I wasn't sure.

"I know that now."

"Steve Mercer says you work for Jake Barclay's firm?"

"Yes, why?"

"Just confirming his information. No particular reason." Her voice sounded strained. She cleared her throat. "Listen, is your home phone listing in your name?"

"No. My mother's maiden name. It's an old number I used for my fax machine before I moved. How come?"

"If it was, even a seven-year-old could locate you in two minutes. Why that number?"

"When I started my life over, I....Sentimental reasons. An extra layer of anonymity."

"Why?"

I shrugged, remembered that she couldn't see me and admitted, "Stuff. My mom died suddenly and I was a mess and...."

"Okay, never mind."

"My girlfriend told me I didn't have to use my name. The phone company didn't care. It was one of those decisions that turned out to be prescient. You know, because of the Mitch thing and my line of work."

"Great. Brilliant."

Bosco plunked himself into the visitor's chair by my desk. I said to Kobinski, "I'll call if anything else happens. Otherwise, my mentor'll kick my butt."

We chuckled. Bosco did not.

"I'd like you to come in for another interview. I'm in court next week then on holidays. How about the thirty-first?"

"Absolutely." Bosco knocked on the desktop then motioned impatiently for the receiver. "Just a minute, Detective."

I handed him the phone, miming, 'what?'

He covered the mouthpiece with his palm. "Get dressed in your work clothes. We're going on the road."

"She's recording the call," I stage-whispered.

He made a shooing motion then tucked the receiver between

his ear and shoulder. He flipped open his notebook and said something like, 'under the dome'. He looked up at me still standing by the side of the desk and waited until I turned toward the bathroom. His side of the conversation sounded like code.

After wiping my face free of makeup, I swabbed my armpits then changed into a long-sleeved linen shirt, microfiber pants and a light jacket. I snapped my newest accessory, a Leatherman bracelet Jake had ordered for me, on my right wrist. Just in case I didn't have my fanny pack with me, in case there was a next time like the storage locker. The heavy black links were very butch, but no doubt they'd be interpreted as funky rather than a set of customized hex and screw drivers, a box wrench and cutting tools. I tucked the long red MAG-TAC LED flashlight I'd bought at the Police College store into my laptop bag, re-wrapped my ankle with gauze then eased on a pair of orange and white striped Finding Nemo knee-highs. My sensible work shoes would chafe but I'd have to suck it up.

Bosco was seated behind the wheel of the van idling in the rear parking lot. The air conditioning was blasting so much cold air the inside of the windows had fogged up.

"Debrief wasn't that bad, was it?" he said. I shook my head. He handed me an extra-large espresso and a white pastry box from the bakery around the corner. "I did a walk around and checked the street. Didn't see anybody unusual but that doesn't mean he's not lurking."

I shuddered. "I never expected to get radioactive."

"Ginger's extremely diligent. Remember, it's not just you in danger."

I pulled the passenger door closed and said, "What?"

"Don't fret too much. It's happened before."

"Here?"

"Yeah. Couple of other investigators, Jake and me, once. Guy

I helped put behind bars got outta the pen and thought we should get reacquainted. Let's just say I changed his mind."

He eased west down the lane and turned south, finally pulling onto a narrow side street lined with squat brick houses. He dropped our windows a few inches and turned off the engine. The shush of passing vehicles floated up from Danforth Avenue a block away.

"Was Jake very angry?"

"No." He eased around to face me, his back against the door. "Not too happy you're caught up in this Mitch thing because of a case we put you on. Worried. How's your acid stomach?"

"Not so bad. I haven't been throwing up. My doc wrote me a new prescription."

I handed him the bakery box. He rooted around like a little kid and triumphantly held up a flaky Napoleon pastry. "Good thing for me you can't eat these," he said, biting down and showering his lap with crumbs. "Nom, nom, nom. That's better," he said when I laughed. I handed him a wad of napkins. "Everybody makes mistakes. Don't fret. We'll make it right."

"What about the threat assessment?"

"Buck's people will spelunk every electronic aspect of your life. Probably end up knowing more about you than you do yourself."

"Is that necessary?"

He rubbed a hand across his chin. "Kenora, you gotta start being more watchful. Write." I picked up my pen and notebook, wincing at a twinge that shot from my wrist to my elbow. "Notice everyone who looks out of place. Vehicles that haven't been there before. Someone who won't meet your eyes."

"Get more paranoid, you mean? I'm tired of being frightened, Bosco. This shit has got to stop."

"Absolutely. You're smart and capable. Trust your instincts. Stop reading detective novels." I laughed. "Most of that stuff's farfetched. No CSI or Cagney and Lacey. That American PI shit'll get you charged in Canada. And if I catch you wearing shades when the sun ain't glaring in your eyes...."

"I'm addicted to historical romances, actually. Three or four audiobooks a week, thanks to my long commute."

Bosco muttered something I didn't catch. I opened the Notes app on my phone.

"Here's one of my favorite quotes from Diana Gabaldon, an author I adore. Listen to this: 'And when my body shall cease, my soul will still be yours. Claire—I swear by my hope of heaven, I will not be parted from you.'" I raised my wrist to my forehead and pretended a faint. "My god, that super-heated relationship dynamic makes me melt. And the language. All her books are like that. Zowie."

Bosco clasped his head between his hands and groaned dramatically. "But they only bathed once a month. And they talked too much."

"Not at all. The men are always broad-shouldered and masterful and strong and the women are smart and courageous and equally powerful in a feminine way. And they enjoyed a surprising amount of rowdy sex."

He snorted. I shifted the pen to my left hand and stretched the cramp out of my right.

"You're ambidextrous?"

"Yeah. My girlfriend and I perfected it in school to forge notes from our mothers."

"Right-o." He drained the last of his coffee and banged his mug into the cup holder. "You miss your job at the University? I imagine the benefits were good." His tone was non-committal but he wouldn't meet my eyes.

My stomach lurched. During my long-ago first job interview with Jake, I'd glossed over my leave-taking from the university, referring only to philosophical differences about personnel and workplace issues. Of course, Bosco was digging for more.

"I don't miss it." With my back against the passenger door, I said, "My boss claimed I was insubordinate."

He shrugged and turned his hands palm up. So?

"She'd just spent fifty-seven thousand dollars renovating the executive offices and had the gall to demand that I trim our budget by reducing two staff to part-time and laying off another. I refused. She let it go for a while but she kept sniping, nagging, cajoling, then ordered me to do it. Bosco, those women were breadwinners with kids, for crying out loud. Excellent workers. I couldn't—wouldn't—jeopardize their employment. I had seniority and thought I was safe. What a joke. In the cafeteria one day, she cut me from the herd and read me her version of the riot act. It was hot, she was a bitch, my ex had been hassling me over division of matrimonial property. I snapped. Yelled some NSFW words. Told her how little she was respected, how cowardly she was taking money out of the mouths of children for designer office chairs, ugly art and glass-topped desks."

"Chill out, Woman. You're so flustered your freckles have disappeared."

"Sorry. It still chaps my ass. Anyway, as I wound down I realized the room was silent, like we were actors in a stage play. She poked me in the chest and said, 'You're finished here,' and swept out.

"Jake said you've taken judo."

"Actually, it was tai chi."

He shook his head. "I should have known. I bet you do yoga, too. And knit?"

"Yes, socks. But I prefer sewing."

"Not while we're working. What happened to the ex-Mr. Tedesco?"

"Geez, man," I snorted. "Ravi'd burst a blood vessel if he heard that. I kept my birth name. He hated that I'd always made more money. Luckily, he didn't ask for spousal support."

"You thought he might?"

"I did. He was angry enough. Let's change the subject. What about Jake?"

Bosco twisted around. "What about him?" His voice had taken on a cautious tone.

"I mean you and Jake were partners for a long time?"

"Oh. Yeah." Face slack, he let out a long sigh, crumpled up the sandwich wrapping and tossed it into the empty bakery box. He stared out the driver's side window but I had the feeling he wasn't seeing anything.

"What about that scar on his face?"

He didn't speak for a minute. "Not my story to tell. You ask him."

17

*B*osco and Jake were attending a Digital Forensics & Cyber Crime workshop at the Ontario Provincial Police Academy in Orillia for a couple days. Unless an emergency came up that no one else could handle, I'd have the time to myself.

I drove to the commuter parking lot, taking a circuitous route and scanning my surroundings with the regularity of a lighthouse beacon. The likelihood of party-boy Mitch being in my neighborhood or lurking around the platform for the 5:54 a.m. train from Otterton to Union Station was almost non-existent. Even so, I huddled in the lea of the station house roof and bolted for the train doors just as the second warning whistle blew.

Despite the early morning humidity making it hard to breathe, I was recovered enough to nod at the good-looking guy in the next quad of seats before snapping open my newspaper. And on the ball enough to insert myself in the midst of a surge of commuters headed for the northbound subway.

By the time I got to BB&F just after seven o'clock, a drum line was rehearsing in my head, my back was acting up and my ankle had swollen to the size of a grapefruit. Being paranoid was not good for my normally placid nature. My anxiety was fueled by the fact there'd been no messages from Mitch for a while. Was he lulling me into a false sense of security or was he running from the cops? I wanted not to care.

Fueled by pain pills, double espressos and fresh cinnamon rolls, I ploughed through my emails and cranked out three background check reports, leaving an electronic productivity trail should anyone care to check. Not wanting to risk public transit, I Uber'd to Bernards. Gavin, my point man when I wasn't on site, was also an early bird. We'd outlined a schedule of activities. Day by day, he filled the in-basket with useful documents. Even better, he was discreet. Six weeks of working side by side had convinced me the man was a keeper. I made a mental note to talk to Bosco about Gavin as a BB&F prospect.

My choice for number one finagler, Pepper Doane, had left yet another voice message asking to reschedule. He was avoiding me, which made me very curious but there wasn't much I could do until I had a better grip on who was what and how much leverage I could apply. From the interviews I'd done already, I knew the organization's front-line worker-bees operated reasonably well.

Obviously, senior managers were in another stratum. My plan was to show up with minimum notice and catch them off guard but this desultory approach to work was ridiculous. The brass plaque in the hallway leading to the locked doors of Bernards' executive office suite read, '8:15 to 4. Monday to Friday'. It was 8:45. Wednesday.

Leaning against the faux-stone wall, twisting mom's heavy gold ring and brooding about unsolved puzzles, I thumbed through email on my new giant-screen phone. At 8:57, a svelte blond swept by, keyed in her security code and flung open the doors. I waited until she settled into her chair behind the reception desk then crossed the plush carpet and read her name plate: Bailey Carter.

"Mr. Doane, please, Ms. Carter, when you have a moment."

She swiveled slowly in my direction. Every item of her outfit carried a designer logo. She slipped on a pair of hot-pink reading glasses and looked at me as if I'd appeared by magic.

"You scared me." She didn't look scared.

"We have an appointment at 9:15."

"He's not available," she said, shaking open the Toronto Sun. I draped a copy of Martin's letter of introduction over the top of the newspaper. She glanced at it then went back to the tabloid. "Actually, he's not usually in until ten o'clock. I have no idea why he'd tell you to be here earlier. Mr. Lambert and Ms. Fung are out as well." The other two managers-of-interest.

"All right then." I pulled up a chair and slapped my notepad on her desk. "You and I can have a chat while I wait."

Her false eyelashes fluttered like tiny hairy flags. "I don't know if I'm allowed," she said, fiddling with the lid of her coffee cup.

"Just a few questions. I don't bite. How long have you worked here?" I waited with my pen poised.

"Four years." She rolled her eyes then continued, "I interned while I was doing fashion marketing at college and figured working clerical was a good way to get noticed."

"What work do you do?"

"Answer phones, screen appointments, make travel arrangements, fill out expense accounts." She shuddered.

"Not much fun, eh?"

"I hate the frigging paperwork. I just want to put a pin in my eye sometimes."

"Do you get to travel?"

"As if! Mr. Lambert travels to Europe regularly–France, mostly, but that's where the designers are. Mr. Doane travels and entertains. A lot. Ms. Fung does the socialite stuff. My instructions are to smile, not give anyone any lip and do what I'm told." She examined her manicure. "It's better than telemarketing. I get to wear nice clothes and there're no smelly people." Smelly people? She caught my look. "Yeah. In first year, my major was social work but I found out I didn't much like the clientele."

"Do you think your colleagues here are essentially honest?"

"I've never had anything stolen from my purse or anything."

"We were taught in accounting school that there's fraud in most organizations," I said in a confidential tone. "You know, taking home office supplies, stuff like that."

Bailey's laugh reminded me of a seal pup barking. "In the fashion business, there's always people looking to score a freebie. I'm not complaining. Or snitchin'. Know what I'm sayin'?"

Oh my. Gangsta in Gucci.

"So they fit the expression 'tighter than a frog's ass and that's watertight?' " She snorted. I took that for a yes. "Has anyone asked you to do anything unethical?"

She brushed non-existent lint from her shoulder. "Depends on your definition. There's show tickets, ordering extra catering then bagging the leftovers, sneaking a designer sample off a rack to wear to a party then bringing it back reeking of who knows what."

"Uh huh. I've noticed some irregularities in expense accounts. What about employee discounts?"

She lowered her voice. "You're right about the travel and expense accounts. I mean, I fill out the forms all the time but I never ask questions. If someone wants to spend $400 on birthday flowers at Primo Verde, who am I to say they should have gone to Buds-R-Us? Half a dozen bottles of Vintages wine with dinner for a buyer? Ditto. Receipts from the same driver in Paris for eight cab trips in one day? It's not worth my career to be too interested."

"Anyone you know having financial difficulty?"

"You mean enough to steal? Hey, we're all in financial difficulty in this business." She glanced at her watch, punched a button on the telephone console and stood up. "I heard Gavin's working for you. He's been here forever. Ask him." She glanced at her computer screen. "Pilar Mancini, the Assistant Manager of Purchasing can meet you after lunch. She's honest as the day is long. A single mom with two kids. And what we talked about–that stays between us, right?"

I retreated to my out-of-the-way office to make notes. Gavin and I had covered the walls of the fishbowl with gridded flipchart paper and rainbowed those with Post-Its. I lost track of time making notes and re-arranging them. The phone rang five times before I remembered that Gavin had gone on an errand.

Bailey said, "Are you still interested in a tour of the Loading Dock?"

Damn skippy I was.

The Assistant Manager was a tall, pleasant-looking woman in a dark red knee-length dress. She ushered me into her office to a small seating area under a large print of Ken Danby's <u>At the Crease</u>. Interesting choice.

"I read the letter Mr. Bernard sent around a while ago. I wondered when you'd be coming by. How can I be of assistance?"

I gave her the official version of the audit project. She made tidy notes on a lined pad with a bejeweled pen.

"You want to know how the goods get from the factory in France or wherever to the sales floor?" She walked over to the closet beside the door and pulled out two lab coats. "It's chilly on the loading dock. I'm sure you'll find it interesting."

We emerged from the elevator into a concrete cavern the size of two high school gymnasiums. Pilar handed me a blue hard hat from a rack by the door. An array of full spectrum lights hanging from chains high above our heads cast a blaze of daylight. The loading dock was as noisy as an arena during the playoffs and crowded with lift-trucks shunting around like a drill team. Half a dozen open-doored containers attached to transport trucks were snugged between black rubber curtains to seal out the weather.

"Everything comes in by truck and gets unloaded in here."

We approached a bulky man wearing a red safety helmet and padded overalls. He was standing in a red-painted square by the edge of the platform, holding a clipboard in one hand and a long flat wand in the other.

"The Loading Bay Foreman. Foreperson." Pilar said.

"Acting Foreman," he said over his shoulder.

Another man, similarly clad but with a yellow hard hat sat nearby on a stool in front of a computer. They were both wearing on-the-ear headsets with microphones attached. The headset pulsed blue then red as they spoke into the mouthpieces. I watched a forklift drive into the belly of a truck container, snag a tall, shrink-wrapped wooden pallet of boxes and back up to the edge of the red square. The operator eyed us as he waited for the Acting Foreman to swipe his wand across a white label on the front of the pallet.

Pilar continued. "The label is affixed by the manufacturer shipping the goods."

She led me over to the computer monitor where text was raining from the top and filling the screen. Accordion sheets of paper chattered from a nearby dot-matrix printer into a box on the floor.

"Everything in that shipment is itemized in the barcode and is automatically entered into inventory when he scans it. See, this one contains lingerie in different sizes and colors from different designers, assembled by our supplier Maison Couture in Paris."

She spoke quickly for five minutes; my mind reeled from the details. Finally, I asked the computer operator for sample pages of the printout. He hit a combination of keys and handed the report over with a lopsided smile.

"Do you do manual counts?" I asked the guy with the clipboard.

He squinched up his eyes and stared down at me. "Nah, it's all itemized electronically. Why would we? That's what technology is for."

He turned back to the parade of forklifts and spoke into his mouthpiece. Pilar led me deeper into the warehouse. We stopped at the mouth of a narrow gangway between thick metal racks loaded with skids of pristine boxes piled two stories high. She pointed to the single railway track that ran down the center and curved around to the next aisle.

With a sideways look Pilar said, "Warehouse logistics are all automated."

"Are checks and double-checks in place for inventory control?"

She hesitated then muttered, "supposedly", changed her mind and said, "perhaps not."

"Really?" I started to ask a question then changed my mind. "I see."

On the way out, we paused in front of a wall of photographs under a Mission Statement reading: *Our staff are our most important resource. We aim to serve them and our customers with equal fervor.* Talk about shamming it too deep.

At the top left-hand side of the photo gallery was a studio shot of Martin. To the right and slightly underneath were the Board of Directors, the executives, the managers and their subordinates.

I pointed to a picture of a brunette with spiky hair, muddy eyes and pallid skin. "Berthi Giroux is the Loading Dock Foreman? Foreperson."

"Yes, but she's away."

"She reports to Mr. Doane?"

Eyebrows raised, she quirked her mouth in a crooked smile. "Yup, that she does."

Before I had a chance to ask what she meant, a metal door banged open and a lanky man in a cocoa pinstriped suit and mint green shirt loped over. Above a fashionable haze of two-day stubble, his cheeks looked like they'd been buffed with pumice.

He narrowed his dun-colored eyes then turned to the Acting Foreman.

"Thanks for the heads-up, Sam."

He grabbed my hand and gave Pilar a curt nod. She excused herself.

"Pepper Doane pleasedtameetcha."

Peter aka Pepper Doane, the VP of Purchasing and Inventory Management. Pepper reminded me more of paprika. He had lank reddish-blond hair that flopped over a high freckled forehead. He smelled of too much European aftershave and American cigarettes smoked down to the filter.

I jerked my hand from his too-tight grip. "You're a difficult man to track down."

"I'm honored," he said. A sheen of sweat glowed on the bridge of his flushed beak. "Don't get many legume enumerators checking out the common folk down here."

"Pardon?"

"Hehehe. Bean counters."

He pinched the elbow of my coat and said in a conspiratorial tone, "We haven't had any of your kind around here in a while."

I pulled my arm away. "Excuse me?"

"You know, good-lookin' pencil-pushers. No offence, eh?" He reattached his fingers to my forearm and tugged in the direction of the door. "Let's chat in my office upstairs. It's warmer."

"Perhaps later. You missed our appointment. Now I'm pressed for time."

Pepper worked his mouth like it was stuffed with Dubble-Bubble.

"Yeah, okay. We can use Berthi's office if you want a quickie. Interview, I mean." When I didn't react, he snapped, "Come with me."

Favoring my injured ankle, I followed him to a glass-walled office overlooking the loading area. He swiped his security card and waved me inside, half-blocking the entrance so I had to suck in my breath to avoid body contact as I slid by. The furniture was good quality. A pink hard hat hung from a peg on the coat stand above a bright yellow lab coat. On the credenza were vacation photos of beaches and mountains. The person I identified as Berthi was in both shots, hugging an angular woman with ice-cube eyes and short pale hair. They were dressed in rain gear in one photo and hiking shorts and tank tops in another.

He leaned his hips against the credenza, blocking the photos from view. "So, what can we do fer ya? This is sort of down-market for someone of your caliber, isn't it?"

That was three shots he'd taken at me in the space of ten minutes. I slipped into my bobble-head mode, ready to out-twit him.

"Mr. Bernard wants assurance the new electronic systems are working. I'd like to learn how goods are received, accounted for and distributed. What better place to start than at the top with you, Mr. Doane?"

He started blinking too fast. "Anything wrong?"

"Nope. Just trying to get the 'big picture' before I complete my report for the boss. You know how it is: you look around, find a little bit of this and that, then the job's done and everyone goes home happy."

I couldn't believe I made air quotes and simpered for the jerk.

"Yeah, I hear ya." His smile didn't reach his eyes. "Well, you look like a thorough kind of lady. Anything to help. Anything at all. We all want this company to be the best it can be. I've got a meeting I can cancel. We can go have a coffee somewheres. I'll walk you through a typical day at the dock of the loading bay. Hehe."

"Just a few quick questions for now." I pulled out my notebook.

He raised his lips into a toothy grimace and plied me with bullshit for half an hour while he avoided directly answering my questions. I had to listen attentively because he had the habit of running his words together. Pepper was a liar but not an accomplished one. He leaped to open the door when the Acting Foreman rapped a knuckle on the glass and made a come-along motion.

"Something's up. Gottago. Nicemeetingya."

"I can find my way out."

I turned on the recording feature of my phone and sauntered to my office through Goods Receiving, the Prep Room and Records, stopping to chat and ask questions. If Pepper had been as clever as he thought he'd never have left me alone to wander.

18

Gavin had left a DVD containing the records I'd requested from Finance and HR, along with a note reminding me he was taking his son to the orthodontist. I sighed. Another week at Bernards, another forest of trees killed for reports I refused to squint at on a computer screen. The case was progressing slowly but that gave me lots of opportunities to apply my inquiring mind to reams of boring data.

My interviews had made a lot of people fidget but when Gavin showed up to soothe frazzled nerves he usually came away with useful supplementary intelligence I hadn't known I needed. I'd accumulated a lot of relevant information and enough salacious gossip for a reality show. Apparently, the loading dock and inventory control monkey business had been going on for some time.

I did a quick circuit around the shop floor, noticing that despite Bernards high prices, their clientele didn't appear to have declined. Several of the sales clerks I'd interviewed early in the investigation nodded discretely. Although they weren't prolific enough with insider intel to be called informants, I'd received a few text messages that led me in directions that turned out to be productive.

I climbed the stairs to the mezzanine office and busied myself dictating the latest interview notes, then sorting through a fresh stack of credit card vouchers. I'd started filling in a fresh spreadsheet with details about clients, meetings, and expenditures when Gavin slipped in and pressed the door shut.

"Hey, how did the appointment go?"

"Someone is here to see you," he whispered.

"Here in purgatory? Who? And why are we whispering?"

"I think it's Berthi Giroux, the Loading Dock Foreman who's supposed to be out of town."

"Think?"

"Looks like her but something's...off."

"Show her in."

As soon as the woman stepped into my office, I understood what Gavin meant. She resembled the photograph in the rogues' gallery of Bernards' executives I'd pinned to my bulletin board but the hair was styled differently, the forehead narrower and the eyes a titch farther apart. She was dressed not in coveralls but in a fashionable dark suit.

Her handshake was cool and firm."Ms. Tedesco? Pleased to meet you." Her voice had a 1-900 quality, at odds with her severe demeanor.

"You've come to talk about the audit project?"

"Is that what you call it, an 'audit'?" Her tone implied that I was calling a dog a cat.

"Yes. I've been interviewing the senior managers." I walked her over to the round table and chairs in the far corner. Convinced that too much caffeine was affecting my judgment, I'd switched to hibiscus tea with honey. "Would you like some tea?"

"Yes."

"Your business out west went all right?"

"Out west?"

"I was told you were settling some matters relating to your parents' estate."

"That's my sister."

The woman spent her words like a miser's hoard.

"Who's your sister?"

"Berthi."

"I've been trying to meet with Berthi for weeks," I said, hiding my surprise. "Who are you?"

"I'm Yanka Giroux. The twin. She asked me to see you."

Well, well. I scribbled a quick diagram on my notepad—circles within circles. Even Gavin didn't know about Yanka. "What's been going on?"

Instead of responding, she drizzled sweetener to her cup and swirled the spoon around. She gazed about the office then examined the mug as if it were something special. I topped up my tea and decided to wait her out.

She set the cup aside and said, "She and I used to take turns doing the loading dock job."

"Why?"

"It was just easier." She shrugged. "It suited our purpose. No one figured it out because I was good enough to dupe the people who might have wanted to know. I did the same work at a company in Europe. Before I chose to leave."

Another piece of the puzzle snapped into place.

"Where is she now?"

"Having a baby."

"Whose?"

"Peter Doane."

"Pepper?" I opened and closed my mouth. "The Vice President?"

"Yes. The *salaud*."

Bernards seemed to have an awful lot of dirty bastards around.

"What about the photos of the two women in the Foreman's office?"

"My former girlfriend and me." Her tone turned bitter. "She dropped me for a rich man with a tiny prick and a big house."

I let that comment hang in the air. My mind was racing. "Do you know where Berthi is? I'd like to get in touch with her. Will you tell me?"

"Yes and no. The last months when Berthi got too big to hide the pregnancy, I stepped in." She angled her chair and pointed to the scraps of paper on the walls and cork boards. "You've made it too complicated."

"What do you mean?"

"Your investigation. Excuse me. 'Audit'. My sister was involved early on but only as a simple facilitator. Call it misplaced loyalty. She did not become rich from the scheme. On the contrary, she has been damaged. It's the men who win, always."

"Care to tell me who? How the scheme happened."

"No, madam. That is your job and not my place." She stood, picked up her purse and appeared to reconsider. "There are two pairs of men you should focus on. In Toronto and in France." With her hand on the doorknob she said, "Berthi won't be back and neither will I. Don't bother looking for us. Good day."

After Yanka left, Gavin rushed in. I repeated my conversation with her.

"The Giroux sisters are twins? Wait a minute." He rushed out.

I stared at the wall of multi-colored bits of evidence. I'd have to delete the pieces that didn't belong. Which were they? She said I'd make it too complicated but I didn't have the magic simplifying key. I was determined to find out just how dirty Pepper, father of Berthi's baby, was. If I couldn't out him as a fraudster maybe I could get him for workplace harassment or abuse of authority. After all, he was her boss.

Gavin returned waving a file folder. "Get a load of this.

Berthi's—and presumably Yanka's—previous employer was Maison Couture, Bernards' clothing supplier in France. It's in her personnel file. She never changed her next of kin."

"Okay, I'll bite. Peter Doane?"

"Pierre Giroux, President of...."

"Maison Couture. Hot damn, Gavin. Are we talking another sibling, a cousin or a spouse? Giroux is a fairly common name."

He was vibrating like a bow string. "I'm going to find out. This is bloody amazing. If Yanka hadn't shown up trying to clear her sister's name...."

"We might not have made that connection."

We high-fived over the desk.

"Hold on. I'll be right back." Gavin brought a tray holding two mugs of steaming coffee and two chocolate cupcakes. "From the bakery downstairs. Brain food."

"You know," I said, licking icing from my fingers, "I don't believe in coincidences, but guess who I met earlier today? Berthi's baby daddy. Peter Doane."

Gavin snorted. "He's the kind of guy who'd feed Styrofoam peanuts to park squirrels."

"Too unctuous, in my opinion. I figure him for a sleaze, just not a Mr. Big sleaze. I like Pepper for one of the guys making five-finger withdrawals from Martin's till. We'll have to dig deeper. The Berthi/Maison Couture/Pierre relationship intrigues me."

"Then you'll like Marius Lambert. You have an appointment with him next week. He sounds like he's Parisian French but he was born in Ste.-Agathe, Quebec. He's International Sales Manager. Always travelling, rubbing elbows with foreign buyers and running with the Grey Goose crowd. He's in a marriage of convenience."

"A roving eye?"

"I'd say, omnivorous."

"Interesting. One more question," I said. "I've talked to the administrative staff. They keep their heads down but they aren't happy. If this place is such a pit of misery why do they stay?"

He hummed, "Money, money, money, money," picked up the mugs and closed the door behind him.

I massaged my aching calf then dug into the accordion folders on my desk. They were stuffed with wads of expense claim forms and smudged chits for cabs and restaurants, flowers, and airfare for the senior managers. I made enlargements of their credit cards and the most outlandish purchases and tacked them to the cork board. How the hell had the auditors not caught these? Gavin was thorough; his marginal notes were cross-referenced in Excel spread sheets. According to Bosco, there's always a pattern.

Pepper Doane's purchases were eclectic: flowers from Fleurop-Interflora in Zurich, room service at hotels in Paris, tickets to FIFA soccer matches, an engraved titanium chain link bracelet for someone with the initials PG. By the time I finished compiling my list there were questionable items totaling almost $13,500, not monumental fraud by any means but a squirm-worthy amount.

Based on his Platinum card receipts, Marius Lambert was a bon vivant of pasha-like proportions. He favored first class and from the boarding stubs, it looked like he was a regular commuter to Charles De Gaulle airport. Kilos of goodies from boutique chocolate shops, custom made shirts from London tailors, men's brogues for 600 Euros, designer label home decorating items and two carbon and stainless-steel men's bracelets ringing in at three thousand Euros each. I got the impression he was setting up house with a special friend. Sprinkled among itineraries and flight receipts was a service charge for conversion of almost nine thousand Euro to Canadian currency. Big red question mark on that one, since Bernards didn't have any stores overseas.

The insistent throb in my ankle echoed through the tender

spot on my scalp. My torso ached like someone had run me through a mangle machine. I glanced at the wall clock—six-thirty. I shut down my computer, turned off the desk lamp and locked up my documents.

After being trapped with hundreds of pissed-off commuters on the delayed 19:10 train from Union Station and sweating through my nice clothes when the air conditioning on the upper level conked out before we coasted into the station at York University, I arrived at my doorway at nine eighteen to find a pair of earnest, white-shirted young men seated on my porch chairs, chatting. They jumped to their feet at my approach.

"Good evening," said the taller of the two. "How are you today?"

The 'no solicitations' sign on my front door might as well have been posted in Swahili. Maybe if I electrified the doorbell, unwanted callers would take it seriously. They weren't Mitch or his henchmen, but I was too damned weary to be polite.

"You boys selling magazine subscriptions or collecting bottles for your hockey team?"

"Uh, no ma'am. Have you found our Lord and Savior, Jesus Christ?"

Jesus Christ. Really? Ma'am? The way my life had snarled the last few weeks, all that interested me was a grilled pork chop and a Bombay gin with minimal tonic.

"I never lost him. Besides, I worship dangerous men, red meat, and alcohol. You fancy older women?"

They bolted.

19

*L*ate the next afternoon, I bucked the tide of homeward-bound humanity on my way north to BB&F, breathing through my mouth as I swung from a strap in the mosh pit that was the Queen Street East streetcar.

I sank into the ergonomic swivel chair behind my clean quiet desk in my clean quiet office. I unpacked my messenger bag before buzzing Jake on the intercom.

"I'm back."

"I heard. Wanna beer? Coffee?"

"Can't. There's a ton of urgent stuff piled up for me to read."

"Get done what you can. See you in a bit."

I lost track of time updating reports, skimming internal correspondence, running database searches and reveling in the list of projects I'd completed successfully. I was bloody productive.

Jake tapped on the connecting door and strolled in carrying a tray with two mugs and a plate of cookies. Luckily, his 'a bit' had lasted almost two hours, giving me time to shift the bulk of the In stack to the Out pile.

"Good timing," I said.

Dressed casually in black wool chinos, cordovan loafers and a botanical print shirt with the cuffs rolled up, the man made my mouth water. He'd had a haircut. I had a momentary vision of my fingers tracing that rim of paler skin. He paused beside my desk and raised his knee, exposing an expanse of grape-colored sock patterned with Minion cartoon characters. All I could think of was exploring the rest of the tanned naked skin on his long hairy legs. I shook that thought out of my head, pushed away from my desk and handed him a copy of my weekly briefing report.

"I have sock envy," I said and showed him my staid pink and blue Fair Isle design.

Like Jake, my coffee was tall and robust. I followed him to the couch.

"Everything's okay with you?" he said, flipping through the document. "You and Bosco getting along?"

"Sure. We've come to an understanding."

"He mentioned—things have changed." What Jake and Bosco meant was, I was changing. He set the report aside. "Good work. Time to discuss your next assignment."

"But, I'm nowhere near done with Bernards."

"Not a problem. We think you're ready. I've asked Seta to put together a package on the Global Mining Consortium."

All I could manage was, "Okay."

Six months ago I would have been chomping at the bit for a new project but now that Mitch was laying low, I'd come to relish the more measured pace to my life. I still stressed myself out and worked long hours, but when I stepped off the 18:45 train from Union Station and hopped into my rust-bucket, I wallowed in the peacefulness of being home.

"I'm the account lead but you'll case manage integrity testing and executive background checks. You've shown a knack for that."

Yes, I did have a knack. My puzzle-solving mojo was coming

back. Finally. A thrill of excitement zinged up the back of my neck at Jake's praise after all the mess I'd been in.

"They're a significant client and this is a significant new project. I'm confident the thing with Mitch Mehran was an anomaly. Metro has linked him to two other ghost employee scam creators, which elevates his antics to a criminal conspiracy."

"That's encouraging but neither Metro nor York Regional have been able to locate him."

"They will."

"I'm patient about some things, but this—not so much."

"You know 'as seen on TV' doesn't apply to real police work, Kenora. This stuff takes time."

He got to his feet and stretched. I stared at the broad muscles clearly defined under the taut shirt fabric and visualized slipping my fingers between the buttons. I must have made a sound because when he dropped his arms, he grinned then picked up the tray and sidled back to his office, leaving the connecting doors ajar. Nice bum. I knew he knew I was staring.

An hour later when I looked up from my computer screen he was leaning in the doorway with his arms crossed. I had no idea how long he'd been there. He said, "What are you thinking?"

I propped my chin on my upraised palm and let my eyes go unfocused.

That I couldn't remember the last time I'd shared an electric hug with a man I liked. That crying in the shower was a waste of energy. About warm hands drawing languid circles on the small of my back. Your mouth on me. Our hot sweaty limbs tangled together.

Shaking my head, I swallowed my longing and replied, "Work stuff mostly. My son emailed from Bolivia to say he's having the best time ever. Sump pumps. My dad's plans to construct a summer house in my back yard. Oh, and I have a meeting with Ginger Kobinski tomorrow."

He gave me an appraising look.

"What is it?"

"Do you have a little black dress?"

"Yes. Why?"

"I have an invitation to an industry event put on by the Canadian Association of Miners and Exporters. Tomorrow. Three Swedish reps from the Global Mining Consortium will be there. Sorry about the short notice, but it occurred to me it would be a good opportunity to meet and greet some of the movers and shakers."

My heart gave a lurch but I kept my voice steady. "What time?"

"Five o'clock. Europeans serve an excellent buffet and the best booze. How about you bring your duds to work? We'll leave from here."

I hadn't worn high heels in ages, but for Jake, I'd bear down and dress up.

* * *

As they say in police-speak, I attended York Regional Police Headquarters for my interview with Detective Ginger Kobinski.

The building, a tall glass and steel lozenge on a dead-end street in Aurora, glittered in the morning sunlight. I circled the visitors' parking lot half a dozen times before a motorcycle left and I slipped in, edging out a cube van with a police sticker on the back. A pleasant security guard signed me in, handed over a pale Visitor's tag, dialed a telephone number then waved me to a bank of plastic chairs to wait.

"Ms. Tedesco?"

I glanced up from my phone at the front of a pair of navy trousers circled by a leather belt holding a handcuff pouch and baton clip on one side and a holstered Glock semi-automatic on the other hip. I stood. She grinned and stuck out her hand. I was used to being one of the tallest women in a room but Ginger topped me by three or four inches. She had a complexion like creamed honey, a long graceful neck and thick auburn hair snugged into a high neat bun. She also looked familiar, but I couldn't place her.

"Detective Sergeant Ginger Kobinski. Thanks for coming in. Call me Ginger."

"Kenora Tedesco. I'm glad to be doing this."

"What is it?" She'd caught my covert glances.

"You...you remind me of my mother. Lovely. She wore her hair like that sometimes."

She blinked several times. "That's very nice."

Ginger punched her security code into the scramble pad and turned left through a frosted glass door to a long hallway lined with pale wooden doors. She ducked into the second one from the entrance. The space held a plain metal desk, computer monitor and three hard plastic chairs.

I stopped in the doorway. "Sort of basic, isn't it?"

"Yeah. Let's use the family room. It's wired up but a bit comfier." At the end of the hall she leaned in and said softly, "The video and audio recordings start rolling as soon as we cross the threshold. When we're done here, I'd like to talk to you about something else."

"All right."

She punched in another access code. Inside, we were immediately surrounded by a smothering silence that pressed like hands on the ears. She saw my look and said, "Soundproofing." Against loud screams, sobs, and cursing, I guessed.

The room had warm taupe walls, two small couches adorned with large boxes of tissues and a pair of armchairs. A jumble of toys was piled in the far corner under the black globe housing the microphone and video lens. She handed me a bottle of lukewarm water. I sat on the couch and sank into the upholstery.

"Is this supposed to replicate a soothing hug?"

"Actually, yeah. Take the other chair." She looked into the camera, stated her name and mine, the date and case number. "I've looked at Detective Mercer's notes and made some calls. I've got a few updates for you. Before I share them though, tell me about every assault or incident you've experienced during your time at Cheviot University, after your interview with Mitch and since you started working at Bernards."

Kobinski quirked an eyebrow and grinned when I opened my police notebook. I talked for forty minutes, interrupted by taking sips of water and answering her questions for clarification. When I was done she signed off, repeated the time and date for the record, closed her notebook, then ushered me to the main lobby.

"You've been very helpful. I'll keep in touch." As I was unclasping the visitor's tag, she tapped my elbow. "Do you have time for a coffee?"

Side by side, we walked in silence down a long, empty hall into a sunlit atrium. A media stage draped in blue cloth patterned with police crests sat along one wall. I picked out a small table in a corner by the opposite wall under a giant ficus plant and checked out the busy space while she waited for her order from the small snack bar.

""Detective Mercer said you fed him homemade cookies and good coffee," she said, positioning a chair so her back was to the room. "Best I can do is a store-bought muffin."

We chatted about knitting and photography then ran out of conversational steam. Ginger leaned forward on her elbows, dragging the coffee cup in small circles.

"How do you find working at Barclay's place?"

"Great. Interesting work, nice people."

Ginger's face was expressionless but there was something unfathomable going on behind her eyes.

"You work with Amber Donavon?"

That came out of left field. Cops I met usually asked me about the legendary Bosco or Jake.

"Sure. Amber's funny and very smart. After the stalking and identity theft thing blew up, she completed my threat assessment. I don't know her personally, though. How come?"

She frowned then shrugged and got to her feet. "Nothing, really." She wouldn't meet my gaze. What the hell was that about?

A fragment of conversation Bosco and Jake had at the end of my post-subway-shove debriefing wafted through my subconscious but disappeared before I could get a grip on it.

* * *

Jake parked under the portico of the International Hall. The valet who sprang to open the doors of Jake's silver Infiniti was kitted up like a Soviet-era general, complete with gold-braided shoulder boards and rows of fruit salad bars over his left breast. He bowed us along the red carpet to a black-suited functionary who checked our names then ushered us into the meeting room. Shoals of well-fed middle-aged men wearing tight European-cut suits milled around carrying drinks and glad-handing one another. Jake gestured with his chin to a short, florid man striding in our direction.

"I have to disappear for a while for a meeting. You'll be okay by yourself?"

"Sure."

Across the room, a pair of grey-haired men, one very tall and slender and the second thickset and of average height kept glancing in my direction, not hiding their scrutiny. I filled my plate at the buffet then circled the room schmoozing. I had just finished a conversation with the Consul-General of Mali when the shorter of the two grey watchers stepped abruptly into my path.

"Excuse me," he said with a brief bow from the waist. "I wanted to speak with you again." He had the low, strong voice of a man used to giving orders. "We chatted in line at the buffet," he added, pronouncing it 'boo-fate'. His name was Sanberg or Norberg. I didn't know what an English-speaking Swede sounded like but the accent was definitely European.

"Hello again, then."

He smiled, showing a gap between his front teeth. "I noticed your distinctive eyes. Like toasted moss." His eyes were watery blue above cheeks so smooth they must have been barber-shop shaved but his forehead was webbed with deep lines. A sailor, I thought.

"Thank you. Kenora Tedesco."

I handed him a business card. He slipped it into his pocket and didn't offer me his. I stuck out my hand. He shook it perfunctorily.

"You look familiar. And that ring you're wearing. May I?" Without waiting for an answer, he lifted my hand and thumbed the band around my finger, muttering, "Ah, yes. Cabochon blue sapphires set in red gold and platinum. Diamond beads on each shoulder."

I drew my hand away. "Excuse me?"

He flushed. "Pardon me, Madame. I have an interest in beautiful things. I could not resist."

"Mr. Nordstrom," said Jake from over my shoulder, "I see you've met my associate, Ms. Tedesco. She's working with me on your accounts."

Global Mining Consortium. I rapidly scanned my mental Rolodex. Nordstrom? Lars Nordstrom. Definitely Swedish. Jake's dark-suited bicep, warm against mine, steadied me. I scrutinized Nordstrom as they chatted, trying not to be obvious. With age his face had become fuller and his hair thinner but the eyes and chin were the same as one of the five young men in the photo Maggie had found in the old yearbook. One of the names someone had scrawled on the photograph like the one hanging in Martin's office.

Nordstrom turned to me, his expression that of a man satisfied with himself. "Charming. Very good. We will have much work for you." He said to Jake, "The Chairman expects Ms. Tedesco to spend time in our offices in Belgium. Soon."

"Of course." Jake and I replied in unison. We all laughed.

Nordstrom said, "Excellent." He reached for my hand again, angling it in Jake's direction. "I was admiring her ring. An heirloom, I presume? From...."

I tried to pull my fingers back but he tightened his grip. "My mother," I said.

"And where was your mother from, if I may ask?"

Was? I hadn't used the past tense. My pulse throbbed harder under his cool touch. Jake glanced at me then at Nordstrom. I raised my shoulder in a slight shrug.

"Quebec. Montreal."

"Ah, I see." He considered my face for a moment then turned abruptly and said to Jake. "Someone will contact you about arrangements for Ms. Tedesco's visit. Good day."

He turned on his heel and disappeared into the crowd.

"What was that about with your ring?" Jake said.

My cheeks burned but I held his gaze long enough to say, "I have no idea."

But I was damned well going to find out.

20

My weekend chores complete, I settled down to finish Elizabeth Gilbert's <u>The Signature of All Things</u> and find out what happened to Alma Whittaker. What an extraordinary life that woman had lived, compared to mine.

I hadn't meant to fall asleep but the combination of sinus medication and hot tea laid me out. I surfaced from a dream of being chased through Union Station by a snarling man in a gorilla outfit. He was wielding a brass school bell in one hand and a gigantic turkey leg in the other and whacking at me with them. I was thrashing frantically, stuck in a subway turnstile. No one paid attention to my screams. I jerked awake, unable to catch a breath. Maybe there'd been no fowl play but the combination of low barometric pressure and racing through the tropical sludge outdoors battening down loose furniture in advance of a severe thunderstorm hadn't improved my mood or the ache at the base of my neck.

Was it the rain pounding against the great room skylights that woke me? A bell pealed again, followed by a determined knock. The front door. Surely no one up to something bad would be out on a day like this. But wait, somebody with break and enter on their mind wouldn't be knocking. Struggling upright, I picked my ice pack and quilt off the floor then hopped from foot to foot to dispel my grogginess.

The monitor for the security camera was in the kitchen recharging. I'd have to identify the caller using old-school methods. Gripping the handle of an old hockey stick, I sidled to the curtained sidelights and peered out into the storm-induced dusk. The headlamps of a big silver truck squatting on the driveway winked off. A tall, well-dressed man with a backpack slung over one shoulder waited in the middle of the porch. He was holding a cloth liquor store bag in one hand and thumbing the screen of his phone with the other. The outline of that big body was familiar. Not Mitch. Jesus Christ. It was Jake. He rapped on the window with his knuckles.

"Anybody home?"

I snatched a look in the hall mirror. Of course, I had no makeup on. A vertical sleep-crease along my cheek made me look like I was sneering. And the *pièce de résistance* was the blooming prune-sized discoloration where the handle of a shovel I'd been trying to free from under a tree root had whacked my forehead.

"Just a minute."

At least I had on a clean white t-shirt and pressed jeans. Well, he hadn't given me any warning so he'd have to take what he could get. I moistened my lips, tucked in my shirt, fluffed up my hair and disarmed the security system. I had to brace my foot against the shove of wind as I swung the door open. Jake stepped inside. Rain glittered in his hair. The collar of a drop-spattered golf jacket framed his damp cheeks. Did the man have to look so good even when wet?

"Hey there." I coughed into my fist. My breath was okay. "This is a surprise."

"You said if ever I was in the neighborhood," he said with a lopsided smile.

The blood pooling in my groin caused my brain to stall. "Uh, sure. Come on in."

"I texted. When you didn't answer, I took a chance you might be home."

"I was dozing."

He handed me the clinking bag. I handed him a coat hanger. "Argentine wine," I said. "Yum."

Wine? Were his intentions honorable? I hoped they weren't.

"Highway 400 was closed so I took the back roads. They're worse than I remembered from the old days. Flooding in low-lying areas."

He shrugged out of his jacket, hung it up then brushed droplets of water from the hems of his pants.

"Those are great boots."

He arranged them on the mat. "Got them in Australia. What's with the hockey stick?"

"Bosco said I should always be prepared."

"What, for an impromptu face-off?"

"No, a sharp upward thrust to the groin of an intruder."

He grimaced. I was trying to be hostess-y and grown up but acting as awkward as a grade niner at a sock hop.

"You don't see argyles much anymore."

He looked down and wiggled his toes, heaving a deep sigh before he spoke. "They were the last pair my Mum knit. I was up at Holy Cross cemetery for a memorial service."

There was a catch in his voice. "I'm so sorry." I reached up to wipe moisture from his cheek then snatched my hand back.

"Are you comfortable with me being here?"

Depends on how he defined 'comfortable'. His nearness stimulated a long-dormant throb in a long-unused part of my anatomy. My body temperature was rising. I cleared my throat.

"I'll make coffee."

His fingers rested lightly on my shoulder. I caught a waft of expensive herbal soap. "What did you do to your face this time?"

"Attacked by a garden spade. No worries."

He followed while I turned on table lamps, asking questions about the art I'd finally gotten around to hanging, peering into the great room and asking where I'd sourced my light fixtures. I casually pressed the tips of my fingers against the pulse thundering in my neck. My goodness. Jake. In my kitchen. I distracted myself by setting out blue and white patterned cups and saucers. He turned over a saucer.

"Rörstrand? Mon Amie. Made in Sweden. Hmm."

"They were my mother's. I have no idea where she got them, but the flowers are lovely, aren't they?"

I showed him how to use the coffee machine. It was out of beans. I pointed him to the canister. He deftly refilled the hopper and brewed a pair of double espressos, chuckling when I told him about the tradesmen who only did renovations for cash and went by one name. They'd come highly recommended from my temp job boss, whom Maggie and I figured was washing profits from his illegal enterprise through a legitimate waste haulage firm. After the first week, I realized the guys were probably working the grey market but heck, they gave receipts and warrantied their work.

"Maybe you should have run background checks."

"Bosco said the same thing. But they showed up on time and I got deep discounts on building supplies. It's not like I was an accomplice."

"Plausible deniability?"

"You bet. Oh." I turned aside, dabbing at my chest with a soiled dish towel to create a smudge. "I need to change. Be right back."

I handed him the morning paper, zipped into my bathroom, spritzed my hair with conditioner and furiously brushed the curls into a stylish tousle. Stripping off my jeans, I tugged on black leggings, moisturized my feet and slipped into a pair of black ballet flats that didn't look like granny slippers. I slapped on foundation and eyeliner, brushed my brows and dabbed scented moisturizer on my arms and neck. I was back in the hallway in four minutes. Damn. I'd forgotten to change my t-shirt. I slipped into a black knit tank top then decided to shuck my sports bra in favor of a black and ivory lace push-up model. I pulled a turquoise striped shirt out of my closet and added a chunky silver necklace.

When I strolled casually into the kitchen, Jake was leaning by the patio door staring outside. The lightning piercing the evening sky reminded me of fireworks after the Calgary Stampede Grandstand Show. I paused to admire his muscular body, long legs and relaxed posture. Either he didn't feel awkward or he was very good at hiding it.

"I think the storm is getting worse."

He turned, his eyes widening when he caught sight of me. "Nice... deck."

I was smiling on the inside but put on a brisk tone. "I've done most of the gardening myself. My dad's going to build a summer house close to the water."

"What's cooking?"

Ask him to stay? Hell no. This wasn't a date. Then why did you change your clothes and your bra?

"Roast pork. I smoked it myself."

"You're a woman of many talents."

"I like keeping busy."

He gestured to the rain slashing against the darkened glass. "Maybe I'd better head out."

"Why don't you have dinner and see how it is later?"

He blinked a couple of times. "I wouldn't mind."

Wind gusts rattled pellets of hail against the windows. The electricity flickered and stayed off. The uninterrupted power supply bars around the house whined and the blue-white emergency lights flared.

"It happens a lot, unfortunately." I bustled around setting fresh tapers in holders. "I haven't invested in a generator yet."

The waves of heat surging up my limbs had nothing to do with the air conditioning being off or me standing beside the oven door. I wanted him to take me in his arms and make me forget the power outage but since the way to a man's heart was supposed to be through his stomach, I'd behave and keep my fantasies to myself. I dabbed at the back of my neck.

"We'll manage."

Jake carved and plated the roast, carried the serving platter to the table and poured the wine. He bowed his head and muttered a quick grace before meals. That impressed me even more than his visit to the Catholic cemetery service. I asked him about Nordstrom and his strange fascination with my ring but he didn't have any insights into what the man had really been after. We talked about our families, people at the office and some of the cases he'd worked on with Bosco. He had me laughing so hard my sides hurt. My eyes filled as he told me about his parents being t-boned by a drunk driver. I spoke about my mother until the words gridlocked in my throat.

When the power came on for good I turned off the overhead lights, leaving us in warm circles of candlelight. He declined when I offered to open the second bottle of wine. I kicked myself for being insensitive. He was an ex-cop and he had to drive home. Or did he?

"What is it?" He'd been watching me dice the last wedge of potato on my plate into tiny pieces.

I clattered my utensils down. As much as I wanted something else, something more, I knew it was a dumb idea to drink more and get reckless. Jake pushed back from the table and despite my protests, helped clear the table.

I made up my mind. "I have something to show you," I said.

He followed me to my office and stood close as I cranked open the window to relieve the stuffiness. The cool air smelled of wood sap and fried wiring. Shards of lightning shimmered behind the veil of clouds. His eyes scanned the back yard. I was acutely aware of his upper arm against mine.

"Look." He gripped my shoulder and turned me in the direction of his pointing finger. "On the north side of that stand of trees."

"Oh, crap." The top half of a towering old spruce was gone. One-third of the canopy of a gigantic Manitoba maple sprawled on the ground, its thinner limbs bobbing in the wind. "More money."

I closed the window. He didn't remove his hand. I leaned against his chest, trying to ignore the electricity building inside the room and concentrate on my breathing. We were jolted by a cannonade of thunder accompanied by brilliant lightning strikes.

"You got an arborist?"

"No. I may have to get a side hustle or double up my caseload. Or call my old boss, Vinnie, for a referral."

"Nah." Jake rummaged in his pants pocket for his phone. "Here, I'll send you someone who's done work for me at my cabin up north." My desktop computer pinged a 'message received' signal. "Done. Now, where were we?"

I was fantasizing about you taking me in your arms and kissing me until I got swoony and sweaty. Lord, I was forty-two years old and acting like a lovesick teenager. I reached for the photocopy of the picture with the five men standing by the exploration equipment.

"Look familiar?"

He frowned. "Sort of."

"It was with some mementos my mother left in an old yearbook. When I showed them to my dad, he went chalk white, cursed up a storm and tore the originals into confetti. I'd never heard him swear like that before."

"Maybe they brought back painful memories?"

"Perhaps, but I sense there's something else."

"It may be nothing but an old photo."

"No. Check out the two men on the right. The ones who look like roustabouts."

He slipped on his reading glasses. My eyes focused on the pulse dimpling his throat.

"Huh. The photo you showed me in Martin's office is the same as this one but cropped. The guy on the far right looks like.... Hey. Martin Bernard."

"Bingo. Turn it over. See? The men signed their names on the one I have. I suspect that's one reason the photo on his office wall was cropped. Back then he was Nattier Coubertin. The other guy was his brother. Martin called the men his gang. What was written on the back of this original—Our Gang—is in someone else's handwriting. Given the positioning and body language, I strongly doubt Martin/Nattier was the team leader."

"So what? Doesn't have to be a deeper meaning, Kenora."

I held out the family pictures. "See, on the back of the snapshot in the park it says M.L. Looks like the same guy who signed his name Markus Linden in the group shot, doesn't it? The second man from the left looks like a young Nordstrom and beside him is Nils Lindberg."

He tilted the photo to the light. "The GMC Chairman?"

"The same. I want to find out why they were in that place together and what went on."

Jake flipped his glasses onto his forehead and folded his arms. The warmth in his eyes cooled. "Hold on, Kenora. I can hear those gears turning in your head. No."

Even though I'd half expected his response my heart sank. "But Martin's right here, right now. A viable lead. If I could...."

"Don't go there. Martin Bernard, whoever he might once have been, is now our client," Jake said, pinning the photos to the bulletin board.

He pulled up a chair. We sat in the center of my office in a mist-grey silence with our hands in our laps, facing each other but not touching. A thunder-boomer rumbled nearby. We plunged into darkness until the emergency LED lights winked on.

"You're investigating a fraud in his company," he went on after a few minutes. "I'm talking conflict of interest."

"I know it looks that way but Jake, maybe he's my missing link."

"No, he's maybe one possible missing link."

"I know. That's why I want to question Martin. Gently. Respectfully."

As I spoke, Jake was shaking his head. "I said no."

"Fine."

He followed me back to the kitchen and watched silently as I brewed two mugs of coffee and set out a plate of pistachio shortbread cookies. I poured cream into a pitcher then returned it to the carton. My mind was wandering; we both took our coffee black. Instead of taking his place across the table, he dragged his chair next to mine. His large body radiated heat like a sunlamp. I leaned closer, figuring a hit of feminine wiles might have some effect.

"How about Nordstrom and Lindberg?"

"They're clients. If Martin is off limits. So are they. Do you understand?"

"But Jake?"

"Listen to me," he said, slashing the edge of his hand through the air. "No."

I'd had a plan. Now I'd have to rethink my strategy.

21

It bugged me that Jake was right. Damned ethics and integrity. Then again, he hadn't forbidden me from accidentally stumbling across information about Martin. In the cool lights and shadows my boss was all broad shoulders and chiseled features. There was more silver at his temples than I'd noticed in the daytime.

"What I can agree to is you using BB&Fs resources to further your general search. General. Not specific to our clients."

Jake wasn't giving off stress vibes but he wasn't loose and open, either. Eyes unfocused, he ate two cookies with an economy of motion. The lights flickered occasionally but the storm was dwindling to distant rumbles and the patter of rain against the windows. I sipped my coffee and looked everywhere but at him.

What are you thinking, Jake Barclay? Do you know I'm about to combust?

Time to change the subject. "Do you know what an 'enigmatologist' is?"

"Something to do with mysteries," he said. "No, wait. It was a clue in a crossword I did a while ago. A spy? A code cracker?"

"Best with Camembert. No, it's someone who solves puzzles using logic. When I was in high school I got addicted to crossword puzzles. I used to kick major ass at word games. My mind was a swamp of useless information. Still, winning Trivial Pursuit contests helped pay for my university textbooks. But I stopped."

Smiling shyly, he said, "I used to be master of Sudoku." I glimpsed the young man he must have been and wished I could have known him.

"God, never math. I sucked at math."

"How old were you when you gave up the games?"

"Twenty-one."

His intense gaze lit me up like a taper. "Why did enigma-whatever stop being fun?"

Too late, I realized his casual questioning had caught me in a gentle snare. I turned aside, shrugging as if the answer didn't matter. But I chose my words carefully.

"I buried my competitiveness."

"How come?"

I began playing with my shirt cuff, folding it into pleats then smoothing it flat. "I got married. My son, Anderson, was born. I went back to work. My daughter, Lilly, came along ten months later. Life got busy."

"Ah."

"Indeed."

We sat listening to each other breathe. I wanted to lay my head on his shoulder. The virile smell that was Jake's scent intoxicated me but I was still unsure. That made it easier to resist the competing urge to ask him to stay. I massaged the twinge of a budding migraine above my ear.

"Headache?" he said.

"Barometric pressure causes them." I didn't mention the physical and mental effects of raging estrogen.

"I used to get them the second night shift on hot days."

"It's not so bad. I had acupuncture six years ago and it mostly worked."

"Good." He picked up his used table napkin, folding it in half then into precise quarters before shifting the salt and pepper shakers across the tabletop like chess pieces. I'd never seen him so restless. "You've got your competitiveness back, I gather?"

"I'd say so."

"I agree."

"I need to take something before the pain gets worse."

His gaze was direct and serious. "I know something that'll help. If you want me to try."

He moved behind me and began to draw compact circles against my temples with the tips of his thick fingers. I dropped my chin to my chest and began to hum like I'd been plugged into a socket. My spine went soft. The pain receded.

Before I chickened out, I said, "How long have you been divorced?"

His hands stilled on my shoulders for a moment then he buried his nose in the curve of my neck and breathed deeply.

"You smell good. That's one of the first things I noticed about you—you don't wear stuff that makes some women smell like stale cupcakes."

His deflection wasn't going to work. "Answer the question."

"Is this one of those pivotal moments in our professional relationship?"

I twisted to look over my shoulder. His neutral expression was back. "You know a lot about me," I said. "I want to know more about you."

He retreated to the sink, rinsed our mugs then fussed with the coffee maker. "Let me ask you something first. Have you been dating since your divorce?"

How could I frame my answer so that I sounded like less of a loser?

"In a manner of speaking."

"Aha!"

"You know the joke 'my love life is like the Olympics'? As in, something exciting happens every four years. That's me. No serious dating."

"Me either."

"It's worse for females. A couple of gents I met for coffee dates gave tongue instead of shaking hands when we were introduced. There were balding studs who flashed pictures of their dogs/trucks/mothers/bass boats and thought I was a snooty bitch because I didn't treat them like the answer to a spinster's prayer. It's not funny."

"You get any beef-whistle photos?"

"No, no rampant schlongs. Stop laughing. Jake, this is the life of a middle-aged single woman. A couple of married dudes thought I'd be thrilled to be their fuck-buddy in between sales calls. Then there's the poor soul who didn't know whether he was gay or not but thought dating an older woman might help him decide. You?"

"No. There's been no one special," he murmured. "I wasn't laughing *at* you."

"I know."

My right leg had gone to sleep. When I uncrossed my knee, my foot slid to the floor with a thud. The corner of his mouth quirked upward.

"You're special, you know."

"Is that a good thing?"

He nodded then said, "Look, I agree you can make some low-level inquiries. But tread very carefully. I trust you not to go rushing into something that could blow up in our faces."

"I won't. I'll tell you or Bosco whenever I find anything and you can re-evaluate, okay?"

"Yes." He raised his arms above his head and stretched, then glanced at his watch. "Wine's worn off. It's late. I'd better get going."

"You know," I said slowly, "the roads could still be bad. I have a guest room. You could weather the storm here."

He shot me a quick glance, looked outside for a moment then said, "That's kind of you, but it's petering out. I think it would be better if I hit the road."

Better than what?

"I'll pack you some leftovers."

Jake donned his outdoor gear, aimed his key fob through the side window and pressed a button to start his truck.

"Drive safely," I said, although I wanted to whisper, *please stay with me.*

My mind was muddled with thoughts of 'it's too soon', 'office romances end up horribly for women', and 'maybe I'm not his type'. What if we did the deed and it was mediocre? If I was mediocre? *Not worth the risk.*

In the slice of headlight beam brightening the dim hallway, his eyes were glittering deep pools. He stood motionless, staring at my mouth. I reached up to smooth the crumpled collar of his windbreaker. He gripped my hands to his chest then pressed his lips against the hollow of my throat, rendering me breathless and overheated. Bright lights danced behind my eyes. When he fluttered the tip of his tongue over the pulse pounding beneath my flesh, my knees buckled. Gripping me around the waist with one thick forearm, he tipped back my head and kissed me lightly on the mouth, holding still until my lips opened to admit his probing tongue. He tasted delicious. Deliciously dangerous.

I fitted my body to his, peripherally aware beyond the kissing and murmurings and breathlessness that our respective parts matched comfortably. I slid my fingers under his jacket, drawing lines from the base of his spine to the nape of his neck. His flesh was firm and cool against the flame of mine. His hair was as soft as I'd imagined. He lifted his head and we slowly disengaged. Before I looked away, I swear I glimpsed the veil of heat shimmering between us. I took a shuddering inhale.

Holding his bicep for balance, I reached around his hip to turn the doorknob. In the rush of cooler air from outdoors, my glasses steamed up.

"Good night." He caressed my cheek and looked poised to say something else but he turned and loped to his truck.

He called at midnight when he got home and thanked me for dinner. I finished tidying up, had a cool shower then slipped my horny self between the cool sheets, sans BoB.

Being in Jake's arms and having him kiss me so tenderly was exactly what I needed but taking it further could be risky. There was a ring of truth to why he was in my neighborhood, but did he have expectations? I didn't think he was out for a quick tumble, but then what? Was he simply looking for friendship? No, Jake Barclay was not a simple anything kind of man.

All I knew was that I wasn't yet ready for the full Jake experience.

* * *

A week later, I was at the corner of Holland Street and Bradford Road belting out the words to Wilson Pickett's 634-5789 while waiting for the light to turn green when I caught a glimpse of a white SUV carving a quick U-turn then gunning up the inside lane behind me. The blinding roof lights dazzled my eyes. I eased my foot off the accelerator but had nowhere to go to get out of the way because I was already in the curb lane. I drifted toward the shoulder, figuring he'd swing around but instead the siren shrieked twice and the navy SUV with stealth markings snugged up to my rear bumper. What now?

With my gaze fixed on the rear-view mirror, I hit the four-way flashers, shifted into park and as they'd instructed at Police College, sat back with my hands on the steering wheel. The butt of a flashlight tapped the driver's side glass. I raised my left hand with my index finger extended and pressed the button to drop the window.

"Evening, ma'am. Do you know why we've stopped you?"

We? I looked to the right, shrinking back from the blue-white beam that lanced across my face. The hand gripping the flashlight belonged to a fresh-faced young woman with wide eyes under reddish bangs. I swung my gaze back to my questioner. His name tag read G. Pardlowe, South Simcoe Police.

"Uh. Good evening, Sergeant. No, I don't."

"License and registration?"

"Sure. They're in my backpack." The flashlight beam shifted to the passenger seat and stayed on my hands as I rummaged for my wallet. "What's this about?"

Instead of answering, he gave a quick nod and said something to his recruit. She walked to the front bumper, bent down and wrote in her notebook while he waited. They strolled back to the cruiser. Cars slowed to peer at what was going on. I sank lower in my seat. The red/blue/white strobe lights were making me dizzy. I tried to breathe into my belly but I was getting pissed and couldn't get my mind to focus on my third eye.

Should I call Bosco or Jake? Moving my hands out of sight to get my phone was probably a bad idea.

Ten minutes later, Sergeant Pardlowe leaned his forearm on the door frame. "The rear plate on your vehicle has no validation tag."

"Yes, it does. I put it on myself. The sticker is with my registration."

"That's not all. Plate's registered to a stolen truck that's been involved in a series of collisions. The front plate's legit. Do you have any idea about the discrepancy?"

Oh, I did.

"Let me see."

I gripped the door handle. Pardlowe took a step back and threw up his hand.

"Hold on, Ms. Tedesco." He pointed to the parking lot of a Royal Bank on the right. "Pull into that lot. We have to chat."

"Did you check CPIC for anything besides the stolen plate number? Do you have any idea what's been going on in my life?"

"What?"

Heat burned my ears. I squeezed my eyes shut and lowered my voice. "Sweet Jesus. Call Detective Sergeant Kobinski at York Regional SVU." I rhymed off her number.

"I'll do that. Pull over."

My hands were shaking so badly I had trouble navigating into the angled parking slot. The police vehicle drove behind, blocking me in. I felt like a felon. A sudden thought occurred to me, something I'd read about in an info bulletin at work.

"Sergeant Pardlowe," I called out. "Can I please take a look at that rear plate?"

He looked up from his notebook and scowled. "What for?"

"Humor me, okay?"

He stuck his arm out the window and made a sweeping motion. Pardlowe's recruit pulled open my car door and led the way to the rear bumper. I hunkered down for a closer look, then gestured for her to come closer and pointed.

"Notice when you have your light angled down, the plate's really shiny?"

She leaned over, poked at the blue letters with her thumb then called out, "Sarge. Come here a minute."

Pardlowe turned off the cruiser engine but left the door open. I ran my fingernail across the third letter and held it under the flashlight beam to show him the flakes of blue.

"Mitch, the guy who's stalking me—he could never have unscrewed the original plate because the bolts rusted long ago. It's some sort of overlay, like a decal. People use them to get out of paying tolls on highway 407."

I said a quick prayer to the goddess of read-everything-that-comes-across-your-desk. He unfolded a pocket knife and made a small slice in one corner of the fake plate.

"I'll be damned."

"Can I go now?"

"Come on back to the cruiser for a minute."

Detente was over. Things had been going too well. I should have known that bastard Mitch wouldn't go away without a final screw you.

"Did you speak with Ginger Kobinski?"

"Ginger, eh?" Pardlowe leaned around the driver's seat and held out the plastic folder with my documentation. "Yeah, but I want to hear your version."

22

Late one evening a week later, I turned off the lights in my office ready to go home but dithered for a few moments. Instead of leaving, I knocked on Jake's connecting door. When he didn't answer I let myself in. He was sitting in a pool of lamplight at his desk, staring at nothing. The corner of his lips lifted but it was more a grimace than a smile.

"I heard you on the phone with your ex."

He'd been yelling in fact, and the sound had carried.

"Sorry."

I plunked myself on the arm of the couch. "Were you the leaver or the leavee?"

He took his time shutting down his computers and sliding papers into his desk drawers then muttered, "You're not good at subtle."

"That's why I'm good at my job, right?"

My attempt at humor fell flat. He shrugged into his sports jacket and headed out the door. Well, if he wasn't ready to talk, he wasn't ready to talk. I locked his office and detoured to the kitchen to heat a slice of leftover pizza to tide me over on my commute home. The door to the rear parking lot slammed. Jake appeared, looking grim.

"Come."

I tossed the warmed-up slice into the recycling bin and hustled after him to my office. He stood by the far end of the work table with his head turned away. He spoke so softly, I had to move close to hear.

"I'd been at the FBI Academy in Virginia for three months. I got home a day ahead of schedule to find a strange sports car parked in the driveway. As soon as I let myself in I could hear two people having loud sex. The woman was my wife, Sara-Jane. I went out again and waited on the back deck."

"Were you homicidal?"

"Not really. Tired and dead inside. Relieved the farce was over. Sickened. I mean, doing another guy's wife in his own bed?"

"Who was it?"

"Lloyd Schoenberg. We were in the same recruit class at Aylmer. He lived down the street until he hit it big in the stock market, ditched his starter wife, quit the force and bought a fancy condo downtown. Sara-Jane played tennis with his new wife. Couple years before I went to Quantico, the White-Collar Crime Unit I led broke up a boiler-room operation. Lloyd was one of the principals. My testimony at trial helped put him away for twenty-two months. He was out in ten." He hammered a fist into the back of a side chair, knocking it over. "I ran into him later at a social event and almost puked when he came over and shook my hand. I knew he was laughing at me."

Jesus, I thought, how very Freudian. "You arrest him, he seduces your wife."

"There was no seduction. She knew he was a criminal but still she fucked him. Some twisted notion of revenge."

"Where is he now?"

"In the joint doing hard time."

"You have anything to do with that?"

"Indirectly."

"You mentioned revenge. What's that about?"

"I'm tired to death, Kenora. I'm done talking for now." From the look on his face I knew he meant it.

"All right. I'll see you tomorrow."

He waited until I stepped out the back door with my belongings then locked up. The whine of the security alarm made me want to turn back but what could I say? Certainly I was no expert at connubial bliss. My ex had been faithless, but at least he hadn't brought the woman into my house. Then again, I was playing hockey whenever I could and working sixty hour a week back then. How would I have known, unless she'd left her undies in the laundry hamper or I'd caught them *in flagrante*?

* * *

In the weeks following Jake's visit and his disclosure about his ex-wife it was as if he'd rebooted our budding personal relationship and forgotten to give me the password.

He was always pleasant and our banter was relaxed, but we were seldom alone. Even when we were our conversation never veered from the professional. There were no more late afternoon chats on the couch or invitations to business events. I couldn't even feel spurned because aside from the tentative necking in my hallway, there hadn't been any intimate interludes to cling to. I resigned myself to cordial handshakes and cool smiles across a boardroom table.

Damn it, what was going on? Had I forgotten so much about the mating game that I'd misread his signals? Was Jake playing coy for some unfathomable reason? Did he have a secret lover, had he sworn off women altogether or was he not attracted to me? There was no point in asking Bosco—he'd made talking about Jake a boundary issue I wasn't prepared to breach again.

23

Couples do relationship therapy or have make-up sex, men play contact sports or scarf down beer and wings. Maggie and I did drinks and tapas in a trendy Queen Street eatery owned by one of her clients. I primped for the first time in weeks, donning a lavender silk blouse, a flirty black and purple circle skirt and wedge sandals that tied with a bow around my ankles. Just because there was no man in my life didn't mean I couldn't dress up.

After several false starts, my friend and I were returning to a semblance of normal. For us, that meant talking fast and flinging our hands in the air as punctuation, laughing out loud, finishing each other's sentences and cutting up the more pretentious diners in our vicinity. My ex-husband—Madonna forgive him because I never could—would have scolded us for acting like wops. So? He wasn't there, we didn't talk about him, and we had a fantastic time.

"Your brother Bennett called me," Maggie said casually.

"Why?" I snapped my menu shut. She examined hers like it was an artifact.

"Said you've been hard to get hold of. Asked what was up with you and your father."

"Gianluca called me at work but I was in the middle of something," I said. "He asked the same thing."

"What's going on between you and Leo?"

"Jesus, you didn't say anything about the photos, did you?"

"No. What's to say?"

"Thank goodness. Listen, my sense is this thing goes beyond me being the mouthy daughter and somehow disappointing him. I think—I think my mother had an affair and I'm the result."

"What? Are you nuts? Your mother? Never."

" I know, I know. Sounds crazy. I'm going to keep digging."

She grimaced, opened her mouth to argue then acquiesced with an elaborate shrug. "As long as it doesn't come between us, I'm okay with that. I'll help if I can."

"There's something odd, I just know it. But I have to play it close to the vest. The only other person I've told is Jake."

Her eyebrows shot up but although she pursed her lips she made no comment. More than anything, she wanted me to finagle her an invitation to the Ontario Provincial Police firing range in Orillia.

A parade of plates of tasty *pintxos* and *bocadillos* came full and went empty, washed down with *tinto de verano*. By the time the wait staff started setting the tables for dinner we were stuffed, at ease and tipsy. I planned on staying at her condo overnight so neither of us had to worry about being a designated driver. I recounted my post-subway incident conversations with Bosco and Jake.

"Sounds more like Cold War disarmament talks to me. Lord, my butt cheeks have gone numb. Let's move, *chica*."

I paid the bill and detoured to the ladies' room while Maggie, who had a bladder like a wine barrel, window-shopped next door. My hand on the vestibule door, I smiled at Ms. Girl Scout chatting through the open window of an idling mustard SUV, gesturing over her fuchsia silk shoulder to the intersection. She rummaged in her handbag, pulling out a small pad and pen.

Half a dozen paces away, a man was approaching fast on her blind side. He was downtown condo village mod, clad in a studded blue-billed rapper cap, a European-cut denim suit and white-soled black leather designer kicks. Clutching a blue reptile-patterned briefcase in his right hand he circled behind Maggie and stopped by her hip, reaching awkwardly for the car door with his left hand. Whatever he said made her straighten and glance over her shoulder with a puzzled look. The glitter of gold fittings caught the sun as he raised his arm behind her back.

Suddenly, that bright flash registered. My boozy glow vanished in a heartbeat. A blue tooled leather briefcase. Mitch. Oh, shit.

I banged through the heavy door as if it were weightless, shrieking, "Mags look out, look out, run."

Unperturbed, she swung in my direction. Elbows up, I shoved through the gaggle blocking my path, wishing I had a hockey stick in my hands.

"*Cattivo ragazzo*. Run. It's Mitch." At that, she ducked into a point guard crouch and whirled away. Mitch grabbed for the hem of her jacket. Lunging for his arm, I yelled to the onlookers, "Call 9-1-1", hit him with an elbow to the ribs and snatched the briefcase, screaming, "You fucking bastard pervert."

Cursing in a foreign language, he scrabbled blindly for the car door handle.

"Hey, man," said a brown-skinned guy who stepped out of the clutch of bystanders, "I understand what you're saying."

"Fuck off," Mitch snapped. "Get away or I'll kick your ass."

The guy made an exaggerated grimace then gave him the finger. "You fuck off," was the retort.

Mitch swung his feral glare in my direction and lashed out

with his foot. I feinted left then powered up, driving the back of my Leatherman clad wrist into the soft flesh between Mitch's hip and his sternum, sending him sprawling.

"Your pants are ripped and your doughy ass is showing." Maggie's pointing finger was trembling but she wasn't ready to back down.

I gripped her elbow and jerked her to my side. "Let it go. This isn't a game."

Maggie and I were shaking so hard we had to lean against the restaurant window. My ears began to buzz as the adrenaline drained from my limbs. Growling and swearing, Mitch rolled upright like a prizefighter at the eight-count, snatched up the briefcase and launched himself inside the car door.

"Pussy," one of the bystanders called out. "You let a couple of middle-aged chicks take you."

Before I could protest the 'middle-aged chick' comment, the vehicle mounted the sidewalk and peeled away, leaving behind a ragged wedge of orange bumper.

"Write this down," I said over the babble of excited voices, calling out the vanity plate. BIGRYK.

"BIGRYK, small dick," Maggie said. Squeezing my arm like I was a stress ball, she was oblivious to the close-call-gone-wrong we'd escaped. "The Dynamic Duo strikes again. He was driving that ride like it was stolen."

"Probably was."

Her jaw dropped and she paled under her Mediterranean tan. "This is what you do for your job?"

"Sort of."

"Good grief, Kenny. This sure beats purging clients' closets. If only Sister Mary Frances could see us now." She sobered. "There's a cut on your cheek. And your sleeve is ripped."

The blouse I could repair, but I wasn't sure the greasy smudge at the cuff would come out. I gingerly probed the scrape, ending up with blood on my fingers.

"Are you going to get into trouble?"

"Jesus, I hope not." I examined my skinned knuckles. "The question is, did I use unreasonable force?"

"Unreasonable...what the hell? Girlfriend, you were amazing. I wanna be your sidekick."

The noise level dropped. We turned around. The chattering crowd parted. Two Metro bicycle unit officers in fluorescent yellow windbreakers and black cycling pants pushed their way through.

"Afternoon," said the female officer as they parked their bicycles in a V, hemming us in. "Constable Starch. My partner's Constable Chung." The stocky older cop nodded, adjusted his duty belt and drifted to the curb to check out the debris. She pulled out her notebook and jotted down our contact information. "Care to tell me what happened?"

"I'm gonna freak out," Maggie said, adopting a fearful expression as fake as her acrylic nails. "The guy behind the wheel of that shit-colored bucket tried to coax me inside."

"He lured her over by asking for directions," I added, trying to sound calm rather than jacked up. "The other guy—Mitch Mehran—has been stalking me for months. York Regional's SVU has an active investigation going on."

I ignored Maggie's hard stare. She wasn't happy that I'd withhold that nugget of detail from her. The case number rolled off my tongue. Starch's eyebrows rose to her blond bangs.

"He came up behind my friend and opened the door to push her inside." I glanced around and caught a few heads nodding. No way was I going to agree to no follow-up this time. "See, there were witnesses. Some of them took photos." Starch called Chung over. I offered a *coupe de grace* with two carefully selected key words. "It was an attempted abduction."

The officers exchanged a glance. Chung thumbed his shoulder mic, repeated the plate number, and asked for backup. Starch turned to the crowd and began gathering names. I turned away and fired off a text to Bosco, hoping that he wasn't offline or up to his elbows unpacking Ikea baby furniture parts.

Hell of a denouement to a lazy Saturday afternoon.

Damn, but I was pumped.

* * *

We were separated as soon as two backup cruisers arrived. Hopefully, Maggie would tell the truth without too much embellishment.

They let me tidy up at the station under the watchful eye of Constable Starch, after she'd searched through my belongings. In a pale green interview room smelling of fear, sweat and stale coffee, I nursed a cardboard cup of Tim Horton's mint tea and outlined my history with Mitch as the cameras rolled. Maybe I should put it on flashcards or a memory stick.

When I said, "I'm done", Starch snapped her notebook shut and left.

The click of the door locking did nothing to raise my spirits. I glanced at the video camera; the red light winked like an albino snake's eye. Starch returned fifteen minutes later with her sergeant, a bulky balding fellow with a fearsome tattoo of a dragon head peeking from under his short-sleeved dark shirt. Leaning by the door with his hairy arms crossed, he scowled and didn't introduce himself. I scowled back, but my heart wasn't in it. The fight-not-flight buzz had dissipated and my muscles had gone soft.

"Your version of events checks out," Starch said, handing me a sheaf of papers for signature. I signed, drained the cup, and stood. She handed me a plastic evidence bag with my personal effects, including the metal bracelet I'd hit Mitch with. "We're going to hold you for a while."

"What? I'm being detained?" I subsided into the hard plastic chair. "Why?"

The sergeant pushed away from the wall. "The guy you bashed called in a complaint. Said he required medical attention."

"That's rich. Mitch—who, by the way, is an embezzler and a confirmed stalker—called the police on me?"

"Go figure. Says it was unprovoked. Declined to come in for a chat. Wouldn't give me his contact info. Complained he was pissing blood." He smiled a Bosco-smile, reminiscent of a coyote contemplating a bunny.

"Serves him right. I gave his information to Constable Starch."

"The thing with Mehran's pretty messy, eh? We ran him on CPIC. The lad's a piece of work. I'm waiting to hear back from Detective Sergeant Kobinski."

"Why can't I leave?"

He flipped to the back of his notebook and read, "You are being held pending further investigation." Without looking up, he threw out his hand in a 'stop' motion. "Your detention is reasonably necessary given the totality of the circumstances. Do you understand?"

"Yes. But I'm not under arrest?" They shook their heads. That meant I had no immediate right to a lawyer. "What about my friend?"

"We told Ms. DiFrancescatti she could go," Starch said, "but she won't leave without you." She gave me a sympathetic smile. "I'll take you to one of the soft interview rooms. You can wait with her until the Super arrives."

I was suddenly hot with nerves. "Pardon me?"

'The Super'. That would be Jake. Detective Superintendent F. X. Barclay, retired. Shit. Would this latest incident count against me as the final major screw-up?

"Yeah. He'll be here soon," the sergeant grinned. "Big Dog'll be on a tear. I were you, I'd gird my loins."

'Big Dog'. My, my. I couldn't wait to hear the story behind that nickname. Oh, Lord. 'Gird my loins'?

"Do you have any Tylenol?"

* * *

Maggie and I perched on a scratchy beige couch in a dingy beige room, quietly comparing notes under the eye of a ceiling-mounted camera. A battered wooden table was bolted to the floor. The dog-eared magazines on the rack underneath were three years old and probably harbored more bacteria than a research lab. Buzzing fluorescent light tubes irritated overhead. A furred ventilation grate in the ceiling periodically puffed cooler air that smelled of old dust and lemon-scented bleach.

"God, I hope we don't contract Legionnaires' disease."

Maggie hooked a thumb at the tattered wall posters advertising social services and emergency shelters.

"This is a damned dismal place. Reeks of despair."

"I've figured out how Mitch knew where we'd be."

Maggie frowned. "How?"

"My old phones have been decommissioned but when I did his interview at the University, he knew your name, Lilly's and Anderson's."

"You told me that already."

"I think he got into your calendar and address book."

She jumped up and began to pace. "You're fucking kidding me. How come you didn't say anything?"

"I knew he was poking around in my personal information. Honestly, I didn't think he'd cast a wider net. He must have glommed on to your name in my favorites list when he hacked me the first time."

"Then what, he's been monitoring my accounts?" Her stare was ferocious but her voice was too quiet.

"I'm sorry, but probably yes. My devices are encrypted but yours aren't so he'd be able to read my messages in your email account. I was so focused on my own stuff I got pipe-sided. When you get your phone back, don't turn it on. Log on from home and change your passwords. I can have Buck and his team of techies look into it."

"Swell. I'll get a new one. I hope he doesn't mess around with my client lists."

"I think he was more intent on doing me personal harm. You'll have to alert your contacts about weird requests from your email address. I'm very sorry, Mags."

"Am I what's called collateral damage?"

"I apologize."

She huffed and stomped around until she ran out of steam and curled up on the sofa. We played 'what's that spot' but after an hour, our tempers were fraying, the warm soda water had gone flat and we'd tired of small talk. We looked up hopefully at a commotion in the hall. There was a burst of laughter. I was aware of the you're-in-trouble-now vein throbbing in my temple.

The door swung wide.

24

*J*ake strode in looking happy and dapper in black jeans and a blue striped pink shirt with the cuffs rolled up over his forearms. Constable Starch slipped in behind him. Her gaze slid from Jake's face to mine then settled on his. Her expression reminded me of someone meeting their favorite rock star.

"Ladies."

Maggie nudged me and muttered "tasty", without lowering her voice. Despite feeling all warm and flustered, I put on a serious expression and stood tall.

"Maggie, this is my boss, Jake Barclay."

She uncoiled from the couch and draped an arm over my shoulder. "So you're Mr. Barclay. I've heard a lot about you."

She emphasized 'a lot'. I threw her a cease-and-desist glare but she extended her hand to Jake like the royalty she was and deliberately didn't look my way.

"Jake," he murmured, giving her hand a brief shake. "I've heard interesting stories about you. You've been treated well?" he said, like we'd checked into a five-star hotel.

"I wouldn't say that," she replied in a cool tone. "We've been kept stewing for three hours because some creep attempted to snatch me off the street."

"Constable Starch grimaced. Jake's smile didn't waver.

"Procedure, Maggie. Kenora would have told you that."

"She did, but I'm not mollified."

Praying Maggie wouldn't make more of a scene I said to the assemblage, "Could you excuse Mr. Barclay and me for five minutes?"

I'd been mentally rehearsing what had to be said and it was now or never. Maggie gave me a cool look then stalked out. Starch followed and closed the door. I stepped just inside his personal space, taking shallow breaths so as not to inhale his mouth-watering aftershave and get distracted. Jake stuck his hands in his pockets and rocked from his heels to the balls of his feet.

"You have something to say?"

"Listen, Jake. This incident was not of my doing." I held up my index finger as he opened his mouth to speak. "But I understand it might be perceived as another example of me jeopardizing myself and the company although truly, it's not. However, as you will no doubt have heard, I took your advice and Bosco's and defended myself and my friend. If you consider me unfit to continue my employment, I can handle that. Just put me out of my misery quickly so I can get on with my life."

He raised one hand then shifted his eyes to remind me about the camera. "That's a dramatic pronouncement." Was his tone pissed-gentle or gentle-gentle?

"Well?" I drew out the word, ready for whatever he had to say.

He twisted his face as if his nose itched then stretched a crick out of his neck. I gazed at the wedge of hair visible through the open collar of his shirt. He set one booted foot on the coffee table and leaned close.

"Kenora, you did well. You're still part of our team."

My shoulders drooped with relief. "This Mitch thing is getting old."

"We told you he'd escalate. You're safe, which is the main thing. There's a hell of a lot more work for you to do."

Yeah, lots. Get Mitch off the street, make up with dad and my brothers. Oh, and do the job I got paid for.

"I appreciate that, Jake. I just wish I'd been able to punch him in the throat."

"You kidney-punched him. That worked. Hey, I just noticed. Your eyes spark when you're angry."

He chewed his bottom lip, started to say something else then reached back and twisted the door open. Maggie was alone in the hall. She flounced in, grabbed her purse, then stood so close he had to lean back and crane his neck to focus.

"Does my friend still have her job?"

His smile lit the room. "Why wouldn't she?"

"Oh, I've heard things."

Eyebrows raised, he swung in my direction. My knees were wobbly but I stood my ground. "Jake, why did the sergeant burn me and not ask who I wanted to call?"

"Gunner? We go back a long way. He was trying to be helpful. Bosco called him after you texted. May I give you ladies a ride somewhere?"

Maggie said sweetly, "It's gonna take a while to recuperate from the shock, Big Dog." Instead of slipping, Jake's smile widened. "We'll need a few drinks. And sustenance."

I hid my grin and busied myself folding the release papers Starch had handed me.

"No problem." He clapped his hands. "Let's blow this joint."

Hours later, we were still ensconced in Jake's preferred watering hole — a pricey mid-town venue decorated like an old-fashioned men's club. Maggie was glowing and in full countess mode. I was almost over being mortified. Buoyed by light conversation and laughter, we sipped cocktails at the bar, eased into dinner, several bottles of excellent wine and flaming desserts served by tuxedoed waiters. Jake was charming, sharing his attention between us, inadvertently warming parts of my anatomy that cried out for attention. When he stepped away to take a phone call from his daughter, I dragged Maggie to the washroom to beg off the sleepover we'd planned.

She gave me a knowing look and said in Italian, "Jake *è un uomo di prima classe.*"

"First class, yes, but…."

"That pot is obviously simmering."

We ended with coffee and brandy, an exchange of hugs and promises to get together again. Gripping our elbows lightly, Jake escorted us from the restaurant.

"Mr. Barclay." A tall man in a gleaming white shirt, navy tie and charcoal trousers tipped his chauffeur's cap and swung open the rear door of a pearl grey Town Car.

"Manny. Good to see you again."

Jake waved me in and followed, sitting in the middle with Maggie on his right. She was uncharacteristically quiet as the vehicle eased through the darkened streets of downtown Toronto. When we reached the entrance to Maggie's condo, she hopped out, said, "Go straight home, kids," and gave us a theatrical wink.

Jake slid his left arm around my shoulders and snugged me against his side. After the day I'd had, his touch was exactly what I needed. Our next stop was the commuter lot at the Oriole GO station where my car was parked. The driver glided into a slot behind an identical limousine then stepped away to speak to the occupants of the other vehicle. I reached for the door handle.

"Wait," Jake murmured, pulling me close and heating me up with a long kiss. "I called Manny 'cause we're—what do they call over-refreshed in romance novels?"

"Fuddled? Foxed." So, Bosco had told him about my reading habits.

"We're foxed." The vibration of his words against my cheek made me squirm. "I like that expression. Foxed. No driving tonight. I want you safe."

"Thank you."

His gaze was smoky in the dim interior. His rumbling voice lit the fuse of my desire. The hell with simmering. I knelt beside him on the bench seat then wrapped my arms around his neck. He smelled of soap and heated male. Outside ceased to exist.

Turning, he trailed kisses from my forehead to my throat, ending at my mouth. His tongue tickled the seam of my lips until I opened to him and tasted brandy and his want. I broke the contact and kissed his nape, across the soft stubble on his jaw and along the rims of his ears until we were both panting. My breasts ached for his touch. Hitching up the hem of my skirt, I swung one leg over his knees and lowered myself to his lap facing him, not caring that I was half exposed. Pressing his palms on the outside of my knees, he spread his own apart, opening me further. His grip was firm but his muscles trembled.

"Soft. So soft."

I drew in a big lungful of air. "Watch me." Whose hoarse voice was that?

His eyes were fixed on my fingers. I twisted open three buttons and spread his shirt front wide. The sight of the dark curly hair spanning his nipples and upper torso almost did me in. My clothes felt too tight. Despite the hum of the limo's air conditioning, I was misted with sweat. I licked the hollow of his throat, shuddering at that first spicy tang of his warm skin then pursed my mouth and blew cooler air against his burning flesh. I turned my attention back to his mouth, exploring the soft contours inside his lips, the cool sharpness of his teeth.

Chest heaving, he raised his hips so I could pull out the tails of his shirt, then he eased my body tight against his, against the pulsing heat of his erection. He stiffened when I trailed my fingers in figure-eight motions from side to side then down the furred arrow to his belly, then tongued his flat nipples until they were firm. I hummed, tugging them between my lips, matching my vibrating sucking to his rapid panting. He cried out and bucked, almost unseating me.

"Enough," he gasped, disengaging my fingers.

With a light rasp of his stubbled cheeks, he teased the tender flesh of my throat then eased the ruffled lapels of my shirt aside like he was unwrapping a gift. He paused a moment before dipping his head and pressing his lips to the bare skin between my collarbone and my pounding heart. His fingers mapped my ribs then the swell of my breasts. Moaning, he cradled them in his palms, squeezing gently but with an insistent touch, tattooing sensory prints into my flesh.

"More."

He obliged, grasping my nipples between thumb and forefinger and caressing them in hot, hypnotic rolls. My vision blurred. I pressed myself into his hands. He stroked until I burned then he shifted to cup my bottom with one hand and circle the other up my outer thigh to my hip, mmm-ing when he reached inside the hem of my panties. I leaned away, letting my head fall against the front headrest, silently urging him to delve deeper, to ease his fingers into the aching wetness between my thighs. His thumb skimmed the curls along my crease, firing voluptuous ripples from my head to my toes, but he ventured no further. I opened my eyes.

A sheen of sweat glistened on his forehead. His expression had gone blank. I stroked the hot ridge of his arousal. He went still. OhnohaveIgonetoofar? I lifted my hand. All of a sudden it was too silent: we were both holding our breath. His eyes were fixed on my face as he blinked—too fast.

"Something wrong?"

He murmured, "I'd forgotten—" then lifted his beautiful mouth in a shy smile, gripped the back of my hand and folded my fingers more tightly around his throbbing shaft, "how good....Yes, harder." His hoarse voice trailed off.

As his fevered gasps and pleasure-sounds mingled with my own and his touch grew hotter and more urgent on my skin, Jake's body scent shifted to something musky and more feral. Every time he called out my name, he turned each syllable into music. Stroking my nipples to swollen nubs with the flat of his thumbs, he detonated rockets of pleasure through my body. I was loud. I covered my lips with my fingers. No, we were loud.

"Jake, I...." There wasn't enough air for me to form a sentence.

He wrapped his arms around my shoulders, squeezing me tight against his chest. The contact between his skin and mine was incendiary. His low whisper resonated against my ear.

"What are we doing?"

The musky scent of arousal filled the space between us. The combination of our heavy breathing and the car's powerful air conditioning had fogged up the windows.

"If we don't move soon, my leg is going to cramp," I sighed against his cheek. "We're old enough to need a bed. This is like parking in Burgoyne Woods after a school dance."

Chuckling, he resettled me in his lap. "The feeling's similar, but different. Hotter."

"More intense."

"No one's waiting at home to take away our TV privileges."

I buttoned his shirt then rearranged his collar, glad he couldn't see the flush of mingled desire and self-consciousness on my face. No man had ever been so tenderly responsive. Of course I wanted more.

"Are you comfortable with this?" I said.

Instead of meeting my gaze he straightened my clothing. "More yes than no, but it scares me. The intensity. I never expected.... You?"

"Yes, a bit. But that was...."

We said 'very nice' in unison then fell silent. I hoisted myself off his lap. He picked up my hand and pressed his lips to the backs of my knuckles.

"Listen," he said, "It's late. There's two drivers in the other Town Car. Manny will take me home. His brother, Eddie, will drive you home. Their cousin will follow with your vehicle."

As if responding to a signal, Manny opened my door. I squeezed Jake's hand, planted a long, soft kiss on his lips then stepped into the sultry summer night, the full extent of his thoughtfulness squeezing me like a hug.

God, the man could kiss.

25

*J*ake was out of town for the next few days. That saved me from having to figure out how to act around him. Surprised that Maggie hadn't called to grill me about my post-dinner adventures, I called her. We talked about this and that, avoiding any direct reference to Jake until I'd started to say goodbye.

"He's a damned good-looking man, Kenny. But there's something sad and dark behind those sapphire blue eyes."

"I know. I mean, I know a little bit but he's not what you'd call an emoter. I like him. He's, um...."

"Are you planning on going to bed with him?"

"If he wants to."

"That's not what I asked."

"Yes."

"Then make it happen, my Friend. He looks at you like...like you're this delicate, sweet chocolate confection and he's reluctant to take a bite in case you shatter."

"Ah, I want to shatter in the orgasmic sense, that's for damned sure."

"Well, I think you'll have to break the ice. If the two of you can get over past betrayals, you'll set the sheets on fire."

After that little lecture I felt like *I* was on fire. I had to drape a wet hand towel around my throat to cool off before I headed out for another jaunt with my Partner.

* * *

After meandering the west end for an hour, we parked on a side street in The Junction. Bosco was still as a brick wall but it was a relaxed stillness, not the heightened state of awareness he'd displayed when we'd parked outside that derelict building on Ashby Avenue.

"You've recovered from your interesting weekend?" he said.

What the hell? Was he mind-reading my replay of the interlude in Manny's Town Car? No. Settle down, Kenora.

"Queen Street? Yeah. Thanks for talking me down from the ledge."

"That's what partners do."

"Bosco, I wasn't scared. You were right, being pissed off helped. As soon as I recognized what was happening, I jumped in."

"I hear you tuned Mitch up pretty good."

"That I did. Then Maggie and I had to cool our heels until Jake bailed us out."

"What did he have to say?"

"He wasn't mad, if that's what you're asking."

My mind kept skidding to thoughts of Jake's indigo eyes and the reactions his competent hands aroused in me. How would those fingers feel on my body next time? I bent over to retie my shoes and hide the blush rising up my cheeks.

Stretching an imaginary cramp from my shoulders, I said, "Bosco, have you worked with a female partner?"

"Not for any length of time." Eyes narrowed, he cocked his

head to one side. "In policing, there's always women around. Call-takers, other officers on platoon, witnesses, victims, criminals even."

"Don't take offence, okay? If you'd had one for real, would you guys have been expected to, um, hook up?"

"Not me. Some did. Do. It complicates things. Is your squeeze your cop partner, your fuck-bunny or a genuine romance? What do you do when they mess up–dress up and fess up or keep it to yourself? I've known lots of guys who think a relationship is successful if it lasts longer than milk."

"Sort of lazy, isn't it?"

He considered his answer. "I watched too many people flame out when relationships broke down. Couple of suicides, official discipline, serious domestic charges. Your ex is a type I'm familiar with. Sensitive as a sixteen-year old's foreskin. The less-civilized ones usually smack their women around."

"I told him once that if he ever laid a hand on me, I'd knife him while he slept."

"Damn, Kenora. That's some serious anger there."

"I thought of it more like proactive self-defense. When my son Anderson was seven, Ravi asked me if he was really his because of Andy's light-colored hair and hazel-blue eyes. I should have known then that the marriage was doomed."

The genetic origin of my son's fairness was an unanswered question, but I'd figure that out in time.

"Remind me never to piss you off!" We shared a chuckle, but there was little mirth.

"Work was my mistress. Until…."

"Until what?"

He shook himself and checked his watch. "Time for chow."

He opened the lunch hamper and handed me a rare roast beef sandwich. I popped two cans of pomegranate aloe vera juice. He wrinkled his nose.

"Try it. Only ninety calories."

He took a cautious mouthful. "Not bad. Pretty good, actually. The lumpy bits are strange."

"You have a knack, you know?"

"What do you mean?"

"Loosening people up. I couldn't ever talk to my ex-husband like this."

"Well, it's called building the foundation for our partnership."

"What about Jake?"

Bosco twisted around to look at me. "What about him?" His voice had taken on a cautious tone.

"I mean, you and Jake were partners for a long time."

"Oh. Yeah." He turned away. "Long time, Kenora. For most of our careers." He let out a long sigh. "Listen, I need you to get into the back seat on the driver's side. I'm expecting a guest to stop by."

Bosco said 'guest' the same way I'd say 'asshole'. He held my food as I climbed over the center console and settled in.

"Who?"

"Parag Musselman, aka Perry Messy, aka the human dandelion. He's one of my knows-everything regulars."

"Human dandelion?"

"He's a nuisance who spreads his seed indiscriminately."

I laughed so hard juice dribbled from my nose. I mopped my chin and the front of my shirt.

"I'm gonna make him an offer," Bosco continued.

"What...what if he turns it down?"

"Perry's a scrote. The only thing he's ever turned down is his collar." Bosco shifted in his seat. I busied myself gathering the food wrappings and stuffing them into a plastic bag. "Speaking of down, you've been sort of preoccupied lately. Anything going on?"

He had a way of peering into my innards that made me want to tell him everything. I wasn't ready for that. I met his gaze briefly then lost my nerve and reached for my notebook.

"The installers ran over part of the septic tank with a backhoe after it was installed. There's goo seeping into the back yard and I have to get the tank replaced." He winced. "Yeah. Gross. Maybe I'll sue Mitch and use the settlement cash for more renovations."

"Get right on that one. What else?"

"Nothing really."

I was getting better at keeping my face neutral. Either that or he was losing his ability to read my expressions. Bosco patted my arm and motioned with his chin.

"That's him."

Ambling through the circles of mustardy sunlight filtering through the trees was a slope-shouldered, abbreviated man wearing a satin club jacket zipped to the neck, wide-leg dark pants and just-off-the-shelf white runners. I thought, 'It's hot as hell outside. What the hell is he hiding?' He was scuffing along the sidewalk without a care in the world, puffing hands-free on the fattie clamped between his lips.

"One of the new age dwarfs." Bosco hooked his right leg over the gear shift and eased into the passenger side of the back seat without rocking the van. "Sleazy."

"What's he do?"

"Oh, a little bit of this and a little bit of that. I'm warning you, Parag comes on very suave but then the asshole elements float to the surface like shit. He's done business with Mitch so I'm gonna squeeze him like a teenage pimple." Bosco grabbed the door handle. Speaking quietly over his shoulder he said, "Now here's a lesson for you. Whenever you're walking by a line of parked cars, check to see if anyone is inside before you pass. Whether you see a head or not always, always walk as far away from the curb as you can."

"Why?"

"This is why!"

He whipped back the sliding door and bounded onto the walkway, planting himself directly in Parag/Perry's path.

"Fuck a duck!" Parag yelped, staggering backward.

He grabbed for his doobie with his left hand. He jammed the other into his jacket pocket. Bosco pushed close and pinioned the hand against Perry's chest. A half-opened razor knife clattered to the ground along with the marijuana cigar. Without taking his eyes off Parag, Bosco stepped back and bent to pick them up.

"Prohibited weapon and a weed porkie. Bad boy!"

Perry pressed two fingers against his nostrils and detonated a snot rocket near Bosco's boots. "Whew! Officer Poon, my man. You nearly scared the jizz outta me."

"Good thing that missed," Bosco snarled, pocketing the knife and slowly shredding the butt between his thumb and forefinger.

Perry moaned with dismay. "Why didn't you just call out or somefink?"

Bosco grasped Perry's left arm, turned it palm out and lifted the wrist halfway up his back. "Step into my office for a bit, won't you?"

He slammed the front passenger door shut and jogged around to the driver's side. Perry leaned around the seat, ogling dramatically. He smelled of weed and failure.

"A gracious good evening, Dusky Maiden." He exaggerated a shiver. "You won't be the first, but you may be the next."

"Cut the crap, Perry."

"Officer Poon," he turned to Bosco and made a circle with his thumb and forefinger, "your companion is so lovely I may just have to touch myself."

I suppressed a giggle. He pulled off his cap and revealed a scalp shaved hairless as a baby's bottom. Probably full of the same thing. Above a frowzy rust-brown beard, his complexion had the pallor of buttermilk, which was odd because he was South Asian.

"You dance? Ima mad DJ." He pointed to the gold embroidery on the wide flat bill of his hat: Bhangra Gangsta. "You know what I like in a woman? My…."

Bosco cuffed him on the shoulder. "Shut up. This is my partner. Be respectful."

"Oops." Perry put on a wheedling tone. "Whom of my acquaintances are you seeking, esteemed Sir?"

"Dudes named Sonny, Baljinder and Bhupal."

"Boo-paul?"

He fluttered his fingers over his mouth and hunched over with a fit of coughing. Bosco had told me Sonny Singh and Bhupal Naidu were genuinely dangerous guys of little consequence to any cases he was already running. His plan was to distract Perry from the main prize, Mitch.

"Rack that brain of yours Perry and gimme something useful."

"Sonny? There's lots of Sonnys in my community. Sonny Kumar, Sonny Ra, Gupta, Mehta, Shah, Khan." Perry's head bobbed in time to the names. "A veritable party."

"Quit showing off. What about the other dude?"

"Jennesaqua Bhupal."

"Oh yeah? That's not what I've been told."

"My memory, you know…."

Bosco crushed a handful of Perry's sleeve. "Want me to drive you to Sadie's where your buddies hang and walk you to the door like we're best friends?"

"What exactly're you looking for, Sir?"

"The technical free enterpriser. Where is he?"

"Now I remember! Baljinder, you said? Technical wiz. Meerkat. Meikle? No, Mehran. Passin' himself off as Mitch. Shamed of his roots, ya know?" Clapping his hands, he bounced in the seat like he'd just guessed what was behind door number two. "You'll keep this in confidence?"

"I may overlook that knife and your bad manners."

"Right. He lives out where the bus don't run. Saw him a couple weeks back. He's partnered with a couple dudes matching lonely men with willing companions for a small fee."

"Isn't that a euphemism for something else?" I said.

Parag turned around. Despite me being layered up, his eyes glommed onto my breasts as if they were glow-in-the-dark. "It's called capitalism, madam. Free enterprise." He put a finger to his chin like he was deep in thought. "Mitch is also a partner in an agricultural venture."

A grow op. Better and better.

"Where did you last run into 'em?"

"Cosy's Lounge."

Bosco said over his shoulder, "Cosy's offers beer, football and naked women." I smothered a cough then laughed out loud when he added, "Lap and face dancing, too."

"Mitch was getting a Monica. That chick was polishing his knob like it was brass. They were so tight even Moses couldn't have parted them."

His chuckle reminded me of a septic tank being pumped out. The man just couldn't tell a straight story. Bosco was being extraordinarily patient. Me, I'd have slapped Perry around to rearrange his thoughts faster.

"There was so much rump around the dance floor it looked like a cattle drive."

Perry was on a roll. My face hurt from holding back laughter. Bosco sighed. "Your story's thinner than prison soup, Perry. Gimme something useful."

The little man looked offended then resumed his narrative. Turns out that in addition to disrupting my life and illegal farming, Mitch was running an under-the-radar IT conglomerate.

"I'd stay away from him. Got fired from his job. Has a mad-on for the dame that did it."

That 'dame' would be moi.

"His live-in left him and took his old laptop and their kid with her. He's pissed cause she's at her mother's house on Georgina Island and he can't run her to ground. I hear the tax man's on his ass, too, and... he can't hide his ass...his assets fast enough." Howling and snorting, Perry doubled over.

Bosco held out his notebook folded open to a blank page. "Write down his coordinates."

"Okay, okay."

Perry let out a volley of damp farts, bent his head and laboriously printed out the information in small block letters. I wrenched down my window to catch some fresh air.

"If I find out you've screwed me over..."

"Nah, man. You can trust me. Contrary to urban legend, there's no honor among thieves. Mitch acts like the rest of us're beneath him, the arrogant SOB. Just 'cause he's got coin. But with all that's been going' down, he's seriously jumpy. Craves respect. That'll be his undoing, mark my words."

"You mentioned a girlfriend?" I said, "Mr. Musselman, what's her name?"

I held my breath while he pondered my question. Bosco's new cell phone rang. He looked at the display then reached across and shoved open the passenger side door.

"Bye, Perry. It's been a slice."

Perry turned to give me a wink, snatched up his hat, swung his legs out the door and hopped onto the sidewalk. "I hope our paths cross again, lovely lady partner of Officer Poon." Oh, they would for sure.

Bosco pulled the door shut and pressed the phone to his ear. He swiped his other hand across the passenger seat, examined his palm then nodded and gestured for me to return. I heard muffled rapid conversation from the caller and Bosco's repeated uh-huhs." "Will do." He grunted and drummed his nails on the steering wheel.

"Perry was helpful," I said in a cheery voice. "That went pretty well, didn't it?" Bosco's eyes slid across mine and settled on the dashboard. My stomach sank. "What's up?"

He took a deep breath then turned his ice-chip eyes on me. "Jake wants to see us."

Sweat prickled my armpits. "Um. What about?"

"He said 'right now'. Something about the threat assessment report."

"Ah, crap." Fucking hell. Not again. My stomach knotted. "Can we stop somewhere so I can go to the bathroom?"

"No." His fingers were clenched on the wheel. "Go at the office."

We didn't speak during the rest of the trip. Bosco stalked me back to my office, slammed the door and loomed over the front of my desk, lecturing. I had to pee so badly I could hardly think. When he finally wound down and stopped prowling like a hungry grizzly, I excused myself and bolted to the bathroom to relieve myself and lose my lunch. When I opened the door, he tossed me a roll of mints and told me to meet him in the boardroom forthwith. As in, don't waste any time to freshen up.

I tamped down my mortification, brushed my teeth, spritzed myself with cologne and layered on some MAC Rebel lipstick. A woman's gotta do what a woman's gotta do.

26

When I shuffled in Jake and Buck Tooey, the company IT specialist, were sitting on one side of the board room table chatting. Jake gave me a brief smile and pointed to the hot seat, directly across from them. Even with three feet of polished walnut between us it was too close for comfort. Bosco, seated two chairs away from me, tucked his arms across his chest and kept his chin down.

"I've seen more eye contact at a pickpockets' convention." I tried to sound jaunty but came off more like a bullied kid snitching to the principal. No one spoke. I tried again. "Except for the lack of bright lights, this looks like an interrogation set-up."

Frowning, Jake tossed his pen on the table. "Even you don't think that's funny, Kenora."

Chastened, I clasped my hands in my lap and made myself small.

"We'll start in a minute," Buck said, giving me a quick smile.

The door opened and in swept Amber Donavon, BB&Fs Threat Assessment Specialist. She had the reputation of being ruthlessly competent. Almost six feet tall, athletic and sporting a wild mane of curly auburn hair, Amber was so physically stunning I'd seen men lose the power of speech in her presence.

"Good afternoon, everyone."

She dropped an armload of file folders on the table and slid a half-inch thick report to Jake and Bosco. My name was on the front in big red letters. Jake flipped through then rhymed off my old cell phone number.

"Sound familiar?"

I mumbled yes.

"Where's the phone?"

"I, uh, recycled it at Best Buy."

"Why?"

My stomach turned over. "It was giving me trouble. I bought a new one."

"What you mean is that your accounts have been hacked and your identity compromised, right?" His voice was brusque.

Buck got busy rearranging two pencils and a notepad. Bosco was entranced by the back panel of his cell phone.

Amber's look was pitying. "You know you can't just recycle stuff or dump it in a bottom drawer, don't you?"

I was mortified but spoke quickly before I ran out of courage.

"I don't use that number anymore. Once I started getting strange email messages, I figured I'd been hacked so I changed providers. Mitch constructed the university payroll system so he had access to my information. I begged the university to shut down the old access points and change the passwords but their IT guy said it was too much trouble and I seemed to be the only one affected."

When Amber said, "Actually, it's not as bad as it could have been," I wanted to leap up and give her a hug. "The steps Kenora took mitigated the scope of damage. That text you got from Mitch a month ago was clearly a 264.1(1)." Seeing my puzzlement, she said, "Uttering threats is a Criminal Code

Offence." She added, "He also appears to be erotically obsessed with you. He used a term that may elevate it to hate motivated assault."

"You mean, the message that he'd 'fuck my Oreo ass up'", I said.

I didn't turn when Bosco snapped his pencil in two. Jake raised an eyebrow. "Yes. Moving right along."

"I've never encouraged him."

Buck blew out a breath. "Doesn't matter. The color of his sky is not the same as ours."

I wanted to laugh but sensed that wouldn't be a good idea. Amber distributed copies of the threat assessment report and a handout of her slide presentation. I took notes for a while but was overwhelmed by the charts and too much information about advanced persistent threats, penetration testing, social engineering, spear-phishing and reconnaissance worms.

"I alerted the university to the criminal intrusion," she concluded.

Buck added, "After he was fired, he was able to back-door the university's network and do more damage. He'd tried to delete system and data backup files but didn't have permission to do that from remote access. Maybe Mitch started out as a run-of-the-mill hacker-slug, but once Kenora exposed the thefts, it got personal. He spoofed her telephone number. If it's been reassigned, some poor schmuck's getting hefty invoices for data and long-distance calls."

"He got her contact information, signed her up for a bunch of forums and chat rooms and advertised her interest in farm animals and multiple partners." Amber's lips twitched. "You get any porn voice mails and unwanted deliveries of unusual products?"

"Damn right," Bosco grumbled. Jake held his hand palm up, in a settle down gesture.

"Not since I got a new number and moved out of town. A

few of my former neighbors said some weird people were lurking around our old house."

A smile played at the corners of Jake's mouth. My nervousness ebbed, although from the looks I was getting, I'd be receiving a yellow slip for detention hall and confined to the filing room until I made amends.

Amber snorted. "Can you believe some of those pervy guys left their real names and numbers? We've made copies of every message that was on your ISP's servers. You have any travel rewards points cards?"

"Yes, why?"

"It's a new wrinkle. Loyalty card security sucks. If Mitch has your credit card information, he might be able to shop your ID and passwords or use your date of birth info and social insurance number to fake a new login then siphon off your points."

I'd racked up thousands of points paying for my home renovation materials. If anything had been ripped off, I'd inflict damage on Mitch's myself. At least all of my new credit cards were chip-and-PIN.

"I'll give you the card numbers. I haven't checked lately. There's no end to this, is there?"

"There is. Mitch hit a dead end because only your old home address and a Shoppers Drug Mart post office box were on your personnel file at the University. Otherwise, he'd be waiting for you some night in your front yard. The incident at Lawrence subway was a shot across the bow. We've narrowed down the location he sent that threatening message from. Somewhere in Georgina. I passed my intel on to a guy I know at YRP." She slid a multi-page security checklist across the table. "Read this. Follow it to the letter."

I groaned. It would take me days to 'harden' myself as a target.

Buck said, "Have you sent Mitch any emails from here?"

"No, I've only spoken to him by phone. Why?"

Amber broke in. "He could try to harvest BB&Fs information using our mail server, then he'd hide behind a proxy or bounce box and forge email threads with compromising or embarrassing contents. We'd become his evil out-box with the world as his in-box."

"Good grief."

"We locked up our breach vulnerabilities when he tried the first few times," Jake said. "Give all your logins and passwords to Amber. And I mean all of them. She'll...take care of Mr. Mehran."

She gave me a wide smile. Oh, boy. "It's only a matter of time. Mitch is no Tyler Wrightson."

"Tyler who?"

"My hero. He wrote a book called Advanced Persistent Threat Hacking," said Amber. "We're going to reset all your passwords and security features here and for your personal equipment. Cut him off at the pass, electronically speaking."

I liked the sound of that.

"This Mitch guy is incredibly arrogant. He used his home computer to remotely access the university servers 'cause, as Kenora said, that access point hadn't been closed." Shaking his head, Buck pushed away from the table. "Guys like him are lazy and they're predictable. When YRP serves the warrant on his ISP, they'll be able to back-track his online activities."

"Detective Mercer hinted they were looking at him for a couple other things," I said.

"I'll give Mercer a call."

Jake shot Bosco a look. "I understand you and Bosco have done some offline research on Mr. Mehran."

"Yes, we did." Bosco cut his eyes at me then nodded.

"Our informant," I grinned at how good those words sounded, "said that Mitch's girlfriend took their kid and his old laptop when she decamped. Ayashe Trivet aka Ash-Leigh," I said to Amber, "was Mitch's accomplice when they lured me to a storage locker and tried to bake me out. I'm going to find her."

"No, Partner," Bosco said, getting to his feet, "We're gonna find her."

Jake gave me a direct, unreadable look. "I want you to wrap up the Bernards investigation."

"I'm going in tomorrow morning."

"Good. Get it rolling ASAP." The 'or else' went unsaid. "We're done."

Amber fussed around, stacking and reordering her papers until the men had departed. She said in a low voice, "Drop by my office. We can have a chat."

Relieved my public thrashing was over, I hustled to my desk and worked flat out for an hour. Bosco left for a meeting. Jake called goodbye to someone in the hallway then the rear door sneezed shut. I punched in Amber's extension.

"Can I ask you a technical question?"

"Come on down."

She was stretched out in her office chair with her booted feet propped on an open drawer. For a moment, her posture and facial expression reminded me of someone but I couldn't grasp the wisp of memory. On the desk were the remains of a falafel sandwich and a tall glass of what looked like carrot juice. Aside from the obligatory wall of framed degrees, awards and citations, the rest of Amber's office could have been a hospital surgical suite, it was so sparsely decorated.

"You look perturbed," she said.

"I want to 'penetration test' Mitch's ass but I need help to do it. I tried scrounging around the cell phone recycling bins at a couple of Staples stores trying to find a junker that still had enough juice in it for me to send him rude email messages."

"How'd that work out for ya?"

"The first time a store manager caught me. I said I needed my phone back because I'd forgotten to back up my contact list. He hustled me out the door and said that they were like the post office: once something was in their bins it was their property.

Another guy located an old Blackberry but when he asked for my username and password, I was busted."

She burst out laughing. "That-a-girl. What do you have in mind?"

"Cyber-revenge. Something along the lines of sauce for the gander. Throw him off his game."

"Feeling desperate?"

"No, just super pissed at his ramshackle stunts. I'm tired of being scared and looking over my shoulder. What the hell? He thinks he's so bloody smart but you've figured out he's not. I want to hit back. "

"I can help you with that." She twined her fingers together and pushed them palms out until her joints cracked. "We'll cling just inside the boundary lines of what's permissible. They don't call me Lady Ninja for nothing."

"Geez, is that your online persona?"

"Yup, among my peers it is. I'll help you find Ayashe, too." She jumped to her feet and cocked a finger at me. As Syndrome, my favorite villain says, "Let's. Get. Busy."

I followed her to a door I hadn't noticed in the far wall and stood to one side as she swiped a plastic card. She tapped a code into a keyless entry pad then pressed her thumb and pinky into a scanner. A wooden exterior door then a featureless metal panel whooshed into the wall to the left.

"Holy shit," I breathed, taking in the array of giant computer screens, glowing keyboards and processor units with flickering blue, orange and green lights. "It looks like a flight deck."

Amber's grin was huge. "Welcome to my domain."

She pointed to a deep leather chair on wheels. I sank into it, trying to comprehend what I was seeing.

"BB&F built this for you?"

"Yup. Listen, I've dug deeper into Mitch's background. He's not on the Deep Web, which sort of surprised me."

"Deep web? Is that like a Virtual Private Network?"

"No, my friend. VPNs are for pussies. This is not a work-around for getting American Netflix. Deep Web is an alternate Internet universe five hundred times larger than what's called the surface web. You know, the stuff you can access through commercial search engines."

"Do I want to know what's in there?"

"You should." She handed me a red folder. "Just don't puke on my floor."

I flipped through a dozen yellow printed sheets then slammed the folder shut. Bosco had trained me well: as sickened as I was, I wasn't nauseous. What I wanted to do was exact slow, painful revenge on the sickos inhabiting that netherworld.

"God, I'm so naive. I expected the porn but snuff, human trafficking, terrorism and big box drug operations?"

"And worse."

"Ninety-six percent of the web is hidden? How come I didn't know that?"

"Why would you? It's an anonymous paradise for illegal activity and criminal perversions you can't imagine. I don't visit often now, but when I worked in Sex Crimes and Crimes Against Children, that's where I spent a lot of my time." Amber's lips compressed to a thin line. "If you want to see...."

"God, no. You all right?"

She shook herself. "Yeah. Got counselling for PTSD but it never really leaves. Don't ever try to access Deep Web yourself through regular channels. You'll have CSIS, the RCMP, the NSA and the FBI knocking on your door in no time. You on Facebook?"

"Not anymore."

"Mitch is. He's got a page under Computers/Technology called Rocket Guru...."

I sputtered, "Give me a break."

"Right on, sister." She gave me a high-five. "Not a profile, so all we have to do is 'like' it to connect."

Curving her fingers like a pitcher preparing to throw a breaking ball, she sat in a spacecraft captain's chair before a large boomerang-shaped ergonomic keyboard with red letters and a joystick attached to the right-hand number pad.

"I thought Buck said I shouldn't engage? No communications."

She rolled her eyes. "Not as yourself." Yet another example of creative cop-terpretation. "Gimme some really rude Italian phrases. Gross insults."

"*Bastardo*," I offered. She shook her head. "*Pezzo di merda*—piece of shit. *Testa di cazzo*—shit head. *Rodomento de culo*—burned up the ass."

"Nah, they're too obvious or too long. If I was going to call you an asshole?"

"*La stronza.*"

"How does the name Venus Stronza sound?"

"Love it. I see big hair, tight clothing, too much eyeliner, fake nails and lots of cleavage."

"Sounds about right. Mitch'll love him some Venus."

"Until she starts kicking his ass." I realized I said that a lot. I just hoped I could carry out the kicking without losing anything or anyone important.

She opened up a web page for a playlist of 'Classics Go to War' and clicked the green arrow beside 'Ride of the Valkyries'. Lush sounds of instruments cascaded from hidden speakers, enveloping us in Wagner's rousing opera. I wanted to get up and march around waving my arms but watched in awe as Amber, humming along, opened email and social media sign-up pages and typed like her fingers were on fire.

"Okay, so you made me a profile. Now what?"

"We're gonna make Mitch your bitch."

27

Three days later I was back at Bernards, following Jake's injunction to wrap things up quickly. Gavin told me he'd had a phone conversation with Bosco after his background checks were completed, and they'd hit it off. He was just as eager as I was to pin the tail on the bad guys. Ginger called with a nothing to report status on Mitch. We chatted about inconsequentials for longer than normal. She was angling to ask me something unrelated to work but didn't. We quietly said our goodbyes and hung up. Life goes on, right?

 I rummaged in the bottom desk drawer and found a half-full bag of Swedish Daim candies. For forty minutes, I stood over the garbage pail unwrapping the crinkly red papers and letting the chocolate crunchies melt in my mouth while I contemplated the wall of multicolored Post-It notes and photocopies of expensed items. An idea poked at the edge of my consciousness like a tongue in a temporary filling. I called Gavin in, gave him a handful of candies and explained what I was trying to do.

 We stared at the wall, changed positions then stared some more. He rearranged the credit card chits into a horizontal line and stood a few paces away with his head tiled to one side. We turned our backs and stared over our shoulders, then straightened the rows vertically.

"Something about the card numbers," he said.

He was right. The last two digits of Berthi's credit card were 42, Pepper's ended in 43 and Marius' in 44.

"Let's compare our personal cards."

He copied the numbers on a blue square and pinned it beside the others. I let my eyes go unfocused, angling my head from one sheet of paper to another, scanning the wall of documents from top to bottom. We yelped and pointed to a cluster of receipts at the same time. He grabbed a yellow highlighter.

"The first two digits of our cards are 37, even though they were issued ten years apart. Theirs are 4 and 1. But why?"

I scrolled through my contact list and found the number I wanted. "I know how to get a definitive answer."

"What are you doing?"

"Putting my deception skills to work."

I tapped the hands-free button, dialed the customer service number on the back of my credit card then followed the disembodied press #1, press #3 directions until I finally got through to a human voice. A perky-toned woman answered: not the person I wanted to speak to. I disconnected and re-dialed. The next call was answered by a bored-sounding young man named Brody.

"Oh, hey, how are you today," I breathed in my best Valley Girl voice. "My name is Sam? Samantha. Brody—can I call you Bro? Oh, cool, ta. Listen, I'm calling from the Lingerie Boutique at Martin Bernards Fine Fashions? Yeah, I'm partial to French cuts, myself."

Shaking his head, Gavin set aside his iPad and smacked his palms against his cheeks <u>Home Alone</u> style.

I rolled my eyes and said, "Bro, I'm a lowly peon here and I don't want to ask my boss about this transaction. You sound like a nice guy. Um, can you help me, please?" He assured me that he could. "Oh, bonus." I lowered my voice and cupped the mouthpiece with one hand. "There's an older gentleman waiting at the counter. He's bought like almost $3,500 in merchandise and he's got this hot young woman hanging on his arm and, um, he gave me his Amex card to pay for the purchases but I'm not sure if it's authentic so I thought I'd better check. If he knows I'm doing this I could get into trouble but I want to be careful, right? He'd be more embarrassed if it got declined, right?"

Ten minutes and a few clarifying questions later I had the information I'd wanted.

"Well done, Boss."

I was in the middle of a Smurf dance around my desk when the phone rang. I hit speaker. It was Jake. Gavin rose to leave but I waved him back to his chair and picked up the receiver.

"Hey there. Gavin and I just had a breakthrough."

"Good, listen...."

"Don't you...."

"Tell me later. I've got a strong lead for you. Can you meet me at Desbiens Funeral Home at eight o'clock? It's a typical cop funeral with lots of so-so food and booze and people you won't know. I'd like for us to grab a bite after."

An outing with Jake. Yowza. What could I wear that was sexy but subdued?

"Okay, but can't you tell me now what the lead's about?"

Gavin's chair legs scraped the floor as he leaned forward, twisting his head from one side to another, sniffing. I mimed 'what' but he shook his head and pulled up the window blinds.

"Not right now." Jake rang off.

Gavin was snapping his head around like a dog on point. He sneezed. "Do you smell smoke?"

I picked up a wad of crumpled sandwich wrappings and sniffed. "Might be from the pulled pork sandwich I had for lunch." I dropped it into a plastic bag. A faint bong, bong, bong sounded in the distance. "What's that noise?"

I took a few deep breaths. It did smell—like burning cardboard. And gasoline. I pushed away from my desk and sprinted to the office door. The bonging was coming from a wall-mounted smoke alarm, augmented by a blinding flashing light. A paper recycling bin by the stairwell was alight, caved in on one side and leaking smoke. The layer of haze was only knee high and hadn't activated the overhead sprinklers. I called the security office. Gavin wrenched the extinguisher canister off the wall and smothered the flames under a blanket of chemical foam.

"Geez," he said, wiping his hands on his pants. "Geez."

The acrid odor of burnt paper and melted plastic hung in the air. I was relieved the lights hadn't gone out. Minnie, the Deputy Security Chief, huffed upstairs three minutes later.

"There's been four other fires in the last six months," she said, pulling out her smartphone and aiming the camera.

"Neither Gavin nor I were working on this audit back then. Maybe it's a fluke."

She scuffed the toe of her boot across the smoldering remains of the bin. "Doesn't feel like it. I'm going to review all the security tapes."

"I didn't expect expense reports to be so incendiary," I said. We burst into nervous laughter then sobered abruptly. "It's someone we know."

"Or who knows us," Gavin said. "We're closing in."

"But we don't know who or what we're closing in on."

He said ruefully, "Look at all the reports I've asked for from Finance, HR and IT. All the people you've questioned. This place leaks gossip."

Minnie hitched up her duty belt and pointed to the open file cabinet drawers and the mess of documents on Gavin's desk. "Somebody's after something. From now on everything—no matter how inconsequential it is—gets locked in the security cabinets. And be careful."

"Minnie, could one of your staff print me a report of security badge usage for the last month, month-and-a-half?" I glanced at Gavin. He nodded. "All entry points. I know it's a lot of work but…."

She rubbed her palms together. "My pleasure. It'll take a few days."

"You know it's not over," I said.

I was almost done packing up when Gavin raced in. He'd folded a tissue around his fingers and held aloft a wrinkled sheet of paper. "This was on my chair and the chair was wedged under my desk."

In 16-point Comic Sans font was typed: *Your getting warmier.*

"I guess we are."

I texted Minnie. She raced back up the stairs. "'Warmier'? You two are making my day."

She snapped photos of Gavin holding the note then bagged it as evidence. "Probably won't get anything useful but you never know. I called maintenance to fix this place up. Keep fighting the good fight."

She tugged her rucked-up protective vest closer to her waistline and gave us a mock salute.

* * *

*E*xcited about my latest adventure and the evening's promise, I hopped a cab back to the office to write up my report. It was seven o'clock by the time I finished. I did a quick sink-wash, freshened my makeup and slipped into one of the just-in-case outfits I kept in my closet. It was navy-blue sedate but with high heels, the flirty peplum jacket and fitted pencil skirt would highlight my bum and legs. It was drizzling, so I threw a light raincoat over my shoulders.

God, I hated funeral homes. I'd barely survived my mother's requiem mass. Why the hell was I at some stranger's wake? Jake. I stepped out of the taxi onto a sidewalk hectic with people dashing under the protective canopy over the front stairs.

Jake stood by the door looking grumpy but tasty in a navy pinstriped double-breasted suit, crisp ivory shirt, a blue tie patterned with FBI Academy crests and shiny black brogues. Before I could ask about his socks or say how weird this meeting-an-informant-at-a-funeral-home thing was, he said his contact hadn't shown up yet.

"Can I tell you about what happened at Bernards this afternoon?" I gave my trench coat to the coat room attendant and pocketed my claim ticket.

"Later, okay? Parlor Three."

The high-ceilinged space was crowded with men in sober suits and a handful of over-dressed women murmuring in low tones. With his warm hand resting lightly under my elbow, Jake introduced me to a middle-aged Asian couple from the Crown Attorney's office in Scarborough.

"I have to talk to some people. Shouldn't take long."

He headed toward a group of tall beefy men who were obviously cops. The blue perimeter opened and their conversation resumed. After a few minutes of small talk, my companions excused themselves. I wandered to the buffet in another room, staked out a spot in a corner and observed the ebb and flow of mourners as I nibbled the mediocre finger food.

I turned with a smile at the tap on my shoulder, thinking Jake had been true to his word.

It wasn't Jake.

28

"Well, well. Look what the wind blew in," my ex-husband said from behind an array of new ultra-white teeth. He brushed dry lips against my cheek, leaving behind the scent of cinnamon breath mints.

"Ravi," I said coolly, taking a step to one side and deliberately looking him up and down. Instead of us being eye-to-eye as we'd been for twenty-some years, he was an inch or two taller than I remembered. Good grief. He was wearing lifts in his shoes. I smothered a grin and straightened to my full height. "Well, well, indeed."

His hair, blacker than I remembered it, curled in tendrils over the high collar of his pale pink shirt. The European cut of his suit did nothing for the expanding swell at his waistline. His bride must have been ignoring his bitching about carbs.

"Been slimming? You're looking skinny."

"My stress levels are way down so no more emotional eating, Ravi. Oh, and Anderson said he hasn't heard from you."

The wattage of his smile dimmed. Boy, being snarky instead of sweet was a rush. I snagged a drink from a passing server.

"I've been busy." His gaze slid across my shoulder. "Ah, here she comes. You remember Chloris?"

I turned to watch the replacement wife teeter across the room.

Oh, I remembered Chloris very well. The too-tall hair, that blow-job-ready mouth, the overdone acquiescence—they were the same I'd noticed when she crashed my surprise fortieth birthday party. And that gathered-at-the-hip emerald frock she was wearing? Ouch. Maggie would say it was ten years too young on twenty pounds too heavy. I briefly chided myself for being uncharitable. After all, this was a funeral home, not a high school lunchroom.

She gripped Ravi's upper arm possessively. *He's all yours, honey.* Enough time had passed that I was more grateful than resentful of her role in upending my tidy suburban life. Chloris had been his Sunday night faith coach. Couch was more like it. He'd described her as 'a real woman who knew her place'. Whatever. Being dumped by Ravi had opened up a new life for me. Unexpected, but still good.

"How are you, Chloris?" I nodded, all smooth and gracious. I didn't extend my hand.

What a difference life with Ravi had wrought. Since our first and last encounter, the bird-witted woman had so much work done—teeth, face, boobs—she was barely this side of bionic.

"I'm okay, Kendra," she said in a voice so husky it could have pulled a sled. "Nice place, eh?"

Uh, no, chucklehead. There's a middle-aged man in a nice suit lying in a coffin in the next room.

We chatted about the weather, the cost of gasoline and the view from their new condo, looking everywhere but at each other. Even though I wasn't hungry for the finger food on my small plate, I nibbled a sausage roll then took a long sip of my too-sweet fruit punch.

My fashionable new shoes were pinching my toes. Where

was Jake? Had his informant shown up yet? I glanced around. No escape. I didn't know anyone else. If I went to the bathroom she might follow me and want to talk.

"Chafford, honey," said Chloris, "I'm going to get us some scotch and coke."

Scotch and coke? Is that what the faithful drank to get wild and crazy?

I cast my ex a skeptical gaze. "Good Lord. Chafford?"

He avoided my eyes. As long as I'd known him, he'd gone by the name Ravi. Chafford, his middle name, came from his Portuguese-British grandfather. He squeezed Chloris' arm and gave her a light push on the hip. I worked hard not to grin. *Go, girl. Fetch*!

As soon as she left, I said in a neutral voice, "You two make quite the couple."

"What are you doing here?"

"Business." That I won't ever tell you about.

"We saw you come in. I've seen that guy before. Really, Kenora? A date," he sneered, holding his hooked index fingers beside his head, "at a funeral home?"

I resisted the urge to whack him. "He's my boss."

"I heard you'd moved on from the library."

"I finished my Masters and got a fabulous new job. Did you remember to send Lilly a card for her birthday?"

"My daughter, my business." He screwed up his face. "A woman with too much education is a dangerous thing. You breaking the boss's balls yet?" he said with a tight smirk. My armor was still thin and his goading got to me, just as he intended.

"What did you say?" I hissed, leaning in close enough to smell the tropical-fruity aftershave I'd always hated.

"Oh, don't give me that surprised trout look. You heard me."

I took a deep breath then changed my mind about telling him to be on the lookout for strange mail forwarded from our old address. My days of appeasement and tongue-biting were over.

"Ravi," I said, sliding my plate hard against his shirtfront, drawing a schmear of grainy mustard across one lapel, his tie and part of his shirt, "you're a faithless *stronzino*. Yes, a conniving asshole." I smiled at his sour expression: Ravi had a prudish streak. "I don't have to put up with your bullshit anymore. Go find your poor dumb bride. And don't you ever use that pissy, judgmental tone again or I'll make a scene. *Vaffanculo*! Her, yourself, I don't give a shit. I'm done being bullied."

He shut his mouth with an audible click and stalked off. I huffed to the bathroom to run cold water over my wrists. By the time I returned, there was no sign of Ravi. The crowd was thinning. The groups of suits had departed. Probably off having a condolence toot in a back room somewhere. Still no Jake. The old Kenora would have hung around, waiting. The new me marched off to retrieve my coat and grab a cab.

Above a closed door in the hallway was a sign: If Cloakroom unattended, kindly retrieve your property. Management not responsible for loss.

Loss? Was I turning into a loser? Ravi seemed happy. Then again, he'd been happy with me for a while. A brief while. Had I ever been really happy? Thinking of Ravi's neck, I twisted the handle. I deserved better, dammit. Inside, a ghoulish light reflected off the red exit signs in the corners. I wrenched the locking knob. The high from my put-down of Ravi had dissipated. In a manner of speaking, Jake had stood me up. So much for hoping for something more. I wanted to break something or yell.

"God, what a night. What the hell am I doing here?"

I bumped my hip against the service counter, swore then retreated with my back against the door waiting for my eyes to adjust. It was broody quiet under the hum of ventilation sounds, an almost pleasant emptiness after the visitation parlor. I yelped when my cell phone vibrated. The ring tone was Paul Simon's 'Graceland'. Maggie's office number.

I fumbled in my palm-sized designer purse. "Hullo. What's up?"

"I've been thinking about something you said a while ago."

"Hello to you too, my friend."

"Yes, hello. I tried you at home and at the office. Where are you?"

"At a funeral home, waiting for Jake to show up."

She blew a raspberry. "Novel location for a date. You sure can pick 'em, can't you?"

"There's no picking involved. It's business, not a date. Give it up, Maggie. He's my boss, gone all cool and professional. And to add insult to injury, Ravi was here with his bride."

"Choir-loft coochie? My, my."

"Have you been drinking?"

Maggie was notorious for doing a drink and dial when she wanted the courage to take care of unfinished business.

"Sober as a judge. Remember the last conversation you had with Bernice?"

The air squeezed from my chest. "I apologized for.... Why are you bringing this up now?"

"And she said you'd never disappointed her." Maggie snapped, "Bernice never warmed to you marrying Ravi. You know that: I know that. What I wanted to tell you is that she once told me that marrying for respect and security weren't all they were cracked up to be."

"Was she talking about Ravi? Or Leo?"

"Probably your dad." She said in a softer tone, "Hon, none of this was your fault. Your dad will get over being angry. Everybody has secrets, including you. Stop beating yourself up looking for deeper meanings. You got a ride?"

"Jake was supposed to drive me. I'm a big girl. I'll find my own damn way home."

"Right. See you Saturday, okay? Gotta go."

The fruit punch had been much too sweet and my tongue hurt like I'd been bingeing on gumdrops. I dug my fingers into my scalp and clutched my skull.

"Why are things so bloody complicated? There'd better be a cab stand outside the entrance."

Shoulders hunched, I wandered around searching for my raincoat, growing increasingly pissed, sad and lonely. I located it on a rack below an exit sign. I jerked the coat from its hanger; half a dozen others tangled then clanged to the floor. I swore again and kicked viciously at a pair of forgotten toe rubbers, punting them three racks away. Someone coughed. I froze. The metal chain strap of my purse slid from my fingers.

"Who's there?"

I shut my eyes and held my breath. All I could hear was my pulse banging in my ears. Shit. I opened my eyes and turned slowly so as not to rustle the fabric of my clothing. The sound came again. The hairs rose on the back of my neck. I tried to make my tone deep and tough.

"Who's there? Show yourself."

"Me." A muffled voice drifted from the shadows. "Over here."

"Who's me?"

"Jake."

He was hunched on a tower of plastic chairs stacked against the far wall. The French cuffs of his shirt gleamed in the dim light, drawing me like a magnet.

"What are you doing?" I hissed.

"Meditating." He cradled his head between his hands. "Do you know how many veins there are in the human eyeball?"

"You scared me half to death."

"Shh. Please be quiet."

"Christ Almighty, don't you shush me."

He groaned. "I'm sorry."

"What's the hell's the matter with you?"

"Lana didn't show. It's been a lousy night. Tater was my friend for a long time. I'm...I'm not good with loss."

"It hasn't been fun-wow for me either, Jake. I hate being here. The only reason I came was you. You know, the day of my mother's visitation, I lay on the front seat of my car in the funeral home parking lot sobbing so hard I barfed?"

"Oh. Did you go inside?" He stretched out his arm. I swatted it away and pulled a crumpled hankie from my pocket.

"I drove to St. Lawrence Market and bought a cartload of daisies and yellow roses. Even though she said no flowers. What was she going to do, ground me?"

He gave a brief snort and raised his head as if it weighed a ton. I caught my breath. His eyes were red-rimmed and swollen. A bruise mottled his left cheek. He swayed to his feet, poked his thumbs under his eyes and burped. His knuckles looked like they'd been sanded with coarse grit.

"You've been fighting."

"Yeah. Someone said something then I said something. He took offence and we got into a dust-up." Teetering forward, he held his thumb and forefinger an inch from his nose and chuckled, "Just a little."

"Jesus. Where are your buddies now?"

He shrugged elaborately, tilting from side to side. "Our seconds took us to our respective corners."

I steadied him with my hand against the front of his suit jacket. His thick muscles shifted under my fingers. A wave of heat engulfed my annoyance, making me light-headed.

"Hold on there, Spike. Lean against that pillar."

I groped along the wall until I located a light switch. He was still immaculately turned out but there was a thin line of blood along the edge of his clenched jaw. His thick lashes were damp. I flicked the light off, throwing us back into shadow.

"That guy in there," he gestured with a floppy hand. "Peter

O'Sullivan. Tater. We were friends. Same recruit class." His lopsided grin tugged at my heart.

"Your face is bleeding," I said, handing him a tissue.

He sagged. I angled my shoulder against his chest while I dabbled at his cut. If he fell, there was no way I could get him up.

"Did you see that red-haired hat-rack by the casket?" he rasped, jerking the knot of his tie loose. "Tater's widow. She backhanded me when I said it didn't have to end the way it did. She said his death was partly my fault."

"I thought he had prostate cancer."

"He was more of a professional drunkard, eh. His best friends were called Jack and Johnny. He was always on the edge." Jake sniffed. "Said he wanted to fight the demons his own way."

"His choice, right?"

"Maybe. Maybe not. The Job can do it to you."

He levered away from the post, angling his chin toward my neck. I stepped out of reach. "Easy."

"You feel so good in my arms. That night after dinner on Queen Street...." My face flamed at the memory of his hungry mouth on my body. Of my hands touching him. Since then, thinking of him fueled my every late-night fantasy. "I respect you a lot, Kenora."

"That's good." What was the protocol for getting your drunken boss—whose bones you're hot to jump—out of a funeral home cloak room? "We'd better go."

Jake was trying to hold himself together: it wasn't working. He tilted back like one of those drinking bird toys then righted himself and dipped too far forward. Before I could sidestep, he wrapped his big hand around my bicep, lowered his head and brushed his lips against my temple. I didn't pull away.

"Sure. Tater had a vicious ex-wife. I know what that's like." He sniffed and, in a voice so softly slurred I had to lean in to hear, said, "But he also has...had a woman who loved him. He got by."

Right then, Jake reminded me of a kid who'd lost something irreplaceable. But oh, I was so torn. As many times as I replayed our encounter after Mitch tried to snatch Maggie from the restaurant, my second and third thoughts shrieked, *be cautious*. Perhaps the clumsy punches had been thrown by two grown men attempting to expiate their grief, but this guy was my boss and if I had any common sense, he should stay off limits.

He reached out a tentative finger and caressed my cheek. I sucked in a deep breath, intoxicated by the warm scents of expensive cigars, alcohol and Jake's body. I was overheating too, not because I was sweating booze but because of an insistent heavy throbbing in my groin that rattled my wits. How I yearned to relive the experience of his talented hands, his lush mouth, the flex of his thick muscles under my touch, the guttural tones of his smoldering passion. I wanted to stroke the knob of his wrist where it had been scraped raw—that seemed safe—but I kept my hands to myself and waited as he shifted from foot to foot. Then an inner good angel/bad angel argument distracted me for a moment.

Come on, we're both adults. The man's friend is dead.

Get him a nice card. Plant a tree.

We're in a funeral home, for chrissake.

That's your rationale?

It's not a public place.

Still is, even in here with the lights out.

What's the worst that could happen?

It'd be better if I was his friend.

Why is coming on to Mr. Tall, Wide and Handsome such a bad thing?

Could be a huge mistake.

He's too hammered to remember.

I'll remember.

As Jake hunched over in moody silence, I steered my mind away from thoughts of fishing off company docks by counting to ten, then to thirty. Uttering a long moan, he forced his body rigidly upright, pulled a crumpled handkerchief from his jacket pocket and blew his nose.

"The love of a good woman gets you by, you know? When even that wasn't enough, Tater killed himself."

He drew me close. I didn't resist but molded my body to his. He wouldn't remember. He eased his right hand under my suit jacket, caressing the base of my spine in a big circle, then tilting my chin and brushing his lips against mine as lightly as a shadow, then more insistently. I couldn't not respond. He had such a great mouth. Standing up to smooch was even better than necking in the back of a Town Car. His scent ignited something primitive buried deep inside. He pressed closer, enveloping me, lifting me onto my toes. I sank my fingers into his thick hair and deepened the kiss.

All right, I admitted to myself. I was ravenous. Slipping into addiction. Jake Barclay—all six foot four of intense, anguished, clever, lovable, scorching Jake Barclay—was my drug. His body was hot and large and firm. Drunk or not, Jake's back wasn't the only body part that was hot and large and firm. The censorious voice in my head went silent. Oh my, but he felt good. And so did I.

The door handle rattled. We jumped apart at the raised voices outside the locked cloak room and bent over with our hands on our knees, chests heaving like sprinters at the finish line.

"Crap," he muttered, scrubbing his hands over his flushed, haggard face.

"Time to go." The words rasped from my throat. My lips were hot and tingling but my body was a confusion of sensations. I tugged my clothing back into place then fiddled with the buttons on my coat until I caught my breath. "Give me your car keys."

He drew the backs of his fingers up and down my throat. Shivers caromed from my neck to my groin and back again, leaving me damp and weak-kneed.

"Will you come home with me?"

Did he mean it? His eyes were full of yearning and something dark. If we were going to get hot and heavy again, I wanted Jake to approach me with intention instead of hitting on me out of desperation.

"That wouldn't be wise," I said, reluctantly pulling away. "Jake, you're pissed."

"And you're pissed off."

"I'm also sober. What are you driving?"

He rolled his shoulders in an elaborate I'm-not-that-drunk shrug then dropped the key ring into my outstretched palm.

"Silver Infiniti. Parked around the corner."

We stepped through a fire door at the rear of the cloakroom into a deserted hallway by an exit to the street. I let him hold my arm on the way to the car. He slid into the passenger seat, fumbled with the seat belt then leaned his head back and fell deeply asleep.

He didn't snore. Bonus.

29

When I let myself into the back entrance early the next morning the lights were already on. Damn. I'd thought to slide unnoticed into my office because he'd be sleeping off his bender. Head turned away I called out good morning, intending to keep walking but no dice.

"We need to talk." Jake was sitting stiffly at the boardroom table sipping from a Scooby Doo coffee mug and staring in the direction of Canada AM playing on the wall-mounted television screen. "About last night."

I stepped through the doorway, juggling my messenger bag, a shoe box and an accordion folder of project research, wishing I were somewhere else. "It's not necessary."

His hair had been damp-combed and he'd shaved around the abrasion on his jaw leaving a shadowy scattering of beard. His pale green shirt was open at the throat. Aside from the smudges under Jake's eyes, the rough patch on his cheek and a discoloration in front of his ear, he didn't look too messed up.

"Please." He gestured for me to sit down. "It is. Hear me out."

For that, I needed coffee with something sugary and chocolate. So much for my pledge to start eating keto. "Give me a few moments to settle," I said and bolted down the hall. Settle. Right.

After I turned on my computers and stashed my paperwork, I unlocked my desk and pulled out the burner phone Amber had programmed for me. The blue incoming message notification light flashed with a cascade of texts.

Who the hell are you?

What do you mean dial back my ego-booking?

Dog, you spam-bombed my FB page. Your in deep shit now.

Our scheme to electronically bitch-slap Mitch was working. Yes! I opened my Wunderlist of prepared messages, copied them then logged into my fake WhatsApp account and fired back.

Heard Ayashe got tired of pumping air in your tires.

Your buddies still nickname you BJ like in school?

Heard everyone's droppin outta your loser party?

Not Mensa level ripostes but good enough. I turned off the phone and headed for the kitchen. The damn coffee bean holder on the espresso machine was empty and as I tried to hurry, I spilled half the bag onto the counter. In the board room, Jake took the mug of fresh coffee without his fingers touching mine then shoved back his chair, closed the door and began to pace. I sighed and blew across the surface of my drink before taking a sip. Why was it that cops had to be in motion when they were thinking hard or telling stories?

He puffed out a breath.

"The last six months, Tater was house-bound, wearing diapers and drinking roast-beef milkshakes while slowly losing his mind." He fumbled in his pocket then tossed a long silver tube onto the table. I caught it before it rolled off the edge. "Cohiba Toros. The doctor'd put him on medical marijuana—ironic, eh, a copper with a prescription for weed—but he hated the taste so we bought him a box. We'd break out the Stoli, smoke some cigars, tell war stories."

"He must have appreciated that." God, Kenora, how inane.

He manhandled a chair and sat close enough for me to feel the heat coming off his thighs. I considered rolling my chair a few inches away, not sure I wanted to be pulled into his gravitational orbit.

"Couple weeks ago, I told him about the photograph you showed me the night of the storm. The names of the five men. He called a few days later with a lead. Cop to the end," he said with a hard shake of his head. "Turns out his lady friend, Lana, knew someone with a name very similar. Not exact, but close enough."

"Lana?"

"Svetlana. Came to Canada as a temporary foreign worker. She said she couldn't face the visitation rigamarole. Or Tater's lawfully wedded wife."

"You mean she was an exotic dancer?"

"Yes, before she attended nursing school. Lana had some information about a woman who rents an apartment in a building Tater bought for their two boys." He caught my puzzled look. "His wives didn't want to have kids. Lana did. You know how complicated some cops make their lives." *And ex-cops.* All the more reason for me not getting involved. Jake's tone was low and sad. "Tater was such a vital guy. Seeing him in the box...." He reached into his shirt pocket and slid a square of folded paper across the table. "She emailed this. For you."

"Thanks." I looked at the paper but didn't pick it up.

"You know, I last saw Tater Saturday morning. Saturday night, he was dead."

"An unfortunate coincidence?"

"Turns out he'd filled a couple of the cigar tubes with heavy duty narcotic pain killers. He chose his time." He scowled. "Maybe I could have stopped him."

"How? He didn't ask for help."

Jake swiveled his head in my direction. "Not asking for help. Does that sound familiar?"

Well, that squelched my romantic flutters. "Why were you lurking in the cloak room?"

"The other coppers and I pounded back a lot of whiskey. Asshole called Omar Ralph from Vice and Drugs got in my face so I popped him in the mouth. Danny Calvin stepped in then Omar cuffed Danny so I had to clip him again to get his attention. Couple guys carried him out. All kinds of stuff was rattling around in my head. I had to get away before I did something stupid. Then you came in."

My cheeks burned. I fiddled with the note from Svetlana. "Did you know it was me or would any woman have done?"

His look was withering. "Give me a break. I wasn't comatose, just a bit tipsy."

"A bit. I'm ready with my report."

He stomped out of the boardroom and slammed his office door. Bathroom break or maybe some headache tablets? He returned a few minutes later and perched one hip against the table by my chair. My face was awfully close to the body-hugging shirt tucked behind the tooled leather belt of his trousers. I'd have to tilt my head back, stand up or continue the conversation with his belt buckle and try not to be distracted by what lay beneath.

"Of course I recognized you. You were on the phone. Then you stood there talking to yourself which, when you think of it, was kind of strange." Flustered and sweaty, I stood up and took a step back. Jake fixed his gaze on my mouth then smiled and said, "Your freckles also stand out when you're annoyed."

"I want to...uh, bring you up to speed on what's happened at Bernards."

"You have a distinctive low voice. You looked lovely. And lonely. I felt alone. No, I take that back. I'm not sure what I felt. I do apologize for startling you, Kenora."

I gestured to the bandage on his jaw. "You're going to have a nice bruise. Would you like to drop by for dinner on the weekend? I have lots of ice packs."

Why the hell did I say that? I kept my eyes on his, hoping he wouldn't know I was cringing inside.

He muttered, "I'm sorry if I—" It was the first time I'd seen him so discomposed.

"Did you know Bosco's going to be a daddy?"

"Are you serious? Audrey's pregnant?"

"Yup. Due in December. That's why he's been so moody."

"His new kid will be younger than his grandchild?"

He didn't ask why his old partner hadn't told him the news first. I knew he was glad for Bosco, but his smile reminded me of emptiness.

"I didn't mean to put you on the spot," I said.

"My life's still complicated, Kenora. I'm leery about making another mistake." Without thinking, I took another step back. "You know what it's like not to have any emotional fuel in the tank?"

My neck flushed hot but the rest of my body was glacier cold. "Yeah, I do. Like when my mom died. My second job interview when I thought you were going to say, 'thanks, but no thanks.' Getting suspended. Loose ends like Mitch and Bernards."

Suddenly, his eyes became wary. "What?"

I tucked my fists under my arms and flexed my fingers.

"Mistake?" I snapped, shaking my finger in his face. "Groping me in a dark cloakroom was a mistake. Our tryst in the back seat of the limo...."

"...was an interlude we both enjoyed," he said. "Does me being drawn to you make me nervous? Absolutely. What's really bothering you?"

'Drawn to me'? I shivered. So I wasn't repellent or boring?

"What must Manny think? We were in the car for a long time." My voice only quavered a little.

He frowned. "Why's that important? Manny and I've known each other a long time. Played squash and hockey together. Golf occasionally. His job is to drive, not ask questions. Stop worrying about what other people think."

"Just like that?"

"Just like that." He caught my wrist, and pulled me close, tipping my head back as if he was going to kiss me. I watched his mouth. "You know, your eyes are like roasted coffee beans, all bright and rich brown with a hint of forest green."

"I...uh." It was hard to think with him touching me but I had to finish. Pulling my hand free, I stepped out of his orbit. "Hear me out, okay? You and I are both over forty. Shitty things have happened. We've both done things we regret."

The warmth leeched from his expression. He said, "But rushing in won't…."

"If we let the bad stuff hobble us what's the point of getting up in the morning? When I screwed up those first two times at work, wasn't it you who gave me a lecture about choices? Change or leave? Adapt or wallow? I've changed since my divorce. Since I started working here. I'm done with wallowing, Jake. I'm on my own, but I'm not nervous anymore."

A group of men in loud conversation stopped outside the door, talked for a minute then moved on.

"Close call?" I made a face at Jake.

Wincing, he went still. "I also mentioned following the rules."

"I get that but we're not talking about work, are we? Some rules we can improvise." I folded my arms across my chest. Staring into his eyes, I said, "I don't want to be a complication. Or called a mistake."

He took a turn around the boardroom then stopped beside me and settled his hips on the table again. "You're not. I apologize."

Jake paused then hooked his arm around my waist. He drew

the tips of his fingers from my temple to my chin. Shivers raced down my back.

"Apology accepted."

He parted my lips with a heated kiss, dancing his tongue against mine and leaving me breathless. He gasped when I shoved my hand between the buttons over his belly and dug my fingers into his muscle.

"Kenora, I…."

Pulling myself from his embrace was the last thing I wanted to do, but I wasn't sure he'd locked the door. Getting caught in a clinch by my co-workers was a disaster I wasn't prepared to face. I withdrew my hand.

"I have to brief you. That's one of the rules. Have a seat. Please."

"We're okay, aren't we?" He reached for my hand. "Why so serious?"

"Someone tried to burn Gavin and me out of our office at Bernards yesterday."

He jerked upright. "No."

"I tried to tell you on before…before you and I got otherwise occupied." He had the grace to blush. "Bosco knows, though."

"Tell me." He pulled up a chair, not so close this time. When I finished speaking he held up his hand. "Minnie said there'd been other fires?"

"Yes. It's not just me that sets someone's annoyance aflame."

"You worried?"

"No. Gavin is usually there at the same time. Setting a trash can on fire is the act of a coward. I doubt they'd do anything physical." I gathered my papers, preparing to leave. "I told him to watch his back. I'll be careful."

The opening bars of the Dragnet theme song boomed from my phone.

"Bosco's ring tone." Jake rolled his eyes and motioned for me to answer. "He wants to have lunch at Sammy's Sangwich on Spadina Avenue. You're invited."

"You go. I've got a stack of files waiting." He snapped his notebook closed. "I've been thinking about the Martin Bernard angle. You said he reappeared in France in the late seventies but there's not much data on him in Canada until the early 90s? I'm going to ask my newspaper reporter buddies on the QT if they've heard the name in connection with activity not related to the store. I'll talk to some guys in Central Traffic–maybe they'll, you know, come across something when they're doing checks on outstanding tickets."

Yeah, or when they got bored. They might even tiptoe through CPIC records or go looking through old General Occurrence Reports. Technically, it wasn't me investigating our client, was it?

"Immigration won't be any help with personal information because it won't have been 50 years since he came into the country. If we don't know where he was born that's likely a dead end as well. Why don't you try the Land Registry Office? People tend use their legal names for a property purchase."

"The building housing the store? A house?"

"Yes. With more specifics, we'll know if there's anything worth pursuing."

"I like the sound of 'we'".

"Anything else?"

"Jake, I want to accept Nordstrom's invitation to the Globe-MinCo offices in Europe."

His eyes roamed the walls then fixed on my face. "After the Bernards investigation is locked up. That'll motivate you, won't it?"

"I guess."

"Listen. Some woman came up to me at the bar last night and introduced herself as Chloris Mandusar."

I threw back my head and laughed. "So, my ex-husband got

his replacement wife to change her name? How that must soothe his fragile ego."

He was trying to look serious but his eyes crinkled at the corners. "She asked if I was the guy you left him for."

I jumped to my feet. "That sanctimonious bitch. Left him for? That lying *pezzo di merda*. Jake, he left me for her."

"Calm down. I figured that out. Said you told me he'd told you he was leaving because he thought he was sexually ambiguous and couldn't live a lie any longer."

Jake's grin was wonderful to behold. I doubled over for a moment then wiped my streaming eyes.

"Oh my goodness, that is so evil. Thank you very much."

I mentally checked off item three on my list of must-haves: The man made me laugh.

30

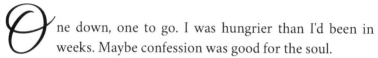ne down, one to go. I was hungrier than I'd been in weeks. Maybe confession was good for the soul.

After thirty minutes via subway then strap-hanging on the College and Spadina streetcars mouth-breathing too-hot body odors from under-dressed people wearing a cacophony of scent, I stumbled into Sammy's to meet my partner. We'd been occupied with other projects for a while but it seemed more like a trial separation. I'd missed him.

The rich deli smells of steamed meat and fryolator fumes made my mouth water. While waiting for my order of fries, green tea and a smoked meat on dark rye with hot mustard at the service counter, I checked my burner phone for messages. Nothing. I punched in two completely random phrases for Mitch: *Bros before hos* and *The farm called, your hair is ready*. Feeling empowered, I copied the messages to Amber.

Bosco was seated at a table by the washrooms with a trio of his street people. Despite the tropical temperatures outside, the two men and the woman had on matching army-surplus quilted jackets and Toronto Raptors ball caps, like members of an indigent street gang. They hunched over the table with their heads down and elbows splayed, scarfing down their free lunches. Industrial eating, my mother used to call it. I slid into the remaining red plastic chair. Bosco made introductions. His companions mumbled greetings around mouthfuls of latkes and chopped liver with fried onions.

"What's going on, Partner?"

From under the bills of their caps, our lunch companions' eyes darted from me to Bosco. Without a word, they hastily piled what was left of their food into Styrofoam containers, bobbed goodbyes and escaped out the back door.

"Something I said?"

"You spooked 'em. They know I used to be on the Job. Calling me partner brings back memories of interactions with the police they'd rather forget."

"You been holding court?"

"Perry was supposed to show up earlier, the douche. What a waste of time."

I was just as glad Perry hadn't made the rendezvous. He was a blabbermouth and I didn't want my mentor to know about last week's hurried conversation outside the washroom at Ernie's Eats on Roncesvalles Avenue. At least not until I could present him with my *fait accompli*.

Bosco was wearing a cream button-down shirt under a heather green summer sports jacket. His hair had been barbered to only one inch longer than respectable. He was clean-shaven and he'd ditched the skull-and-crossbones drop earrings. He tidied the towering contents of his sandwich, took a big bite and groaned with pleasure.

I said, "You look nice."

Blushing, he gestured with his sandwich. "I like your haircut. And the new specs – they complement that coppery tone in your complexion."

I wanted to crack a joke but one look at his earnest expression made me rethink being sarcastic. "Complement the what? I had no idea you even noticed."

"I've always noticed, you know. But maybe more so now because…." He squeezed out a cone of ketchup, dragged through a French fry then folded it into his mouth and chewed, "Audrey moving in has made me more aware of stuff like that."

I squeezed his hand, genuinely happy for my mentor but doubtful about my own chances with his old cop partner, Mr. Hot-then-Cool Boss.

"You sly dog. No wonder you've looked so contented."

He grinned. "Being loved for just yourself is really something, you know?" I sighed. "Maybe the right man for you isn't that far away in time or place. Karma–depend on the karma." I made a rude noise with my mouth and went back to chewing my sandwich. "Never mind me. How's the store project?"

"I've completed the interviews. There's some strange people running Bernards, let me tell you. Marius, the Assistant Purchasing Manager, kissed my hand then creeped me out when he added tongue. He's about 5'9", in his mid-forties and dresses like a runway model. Extensive man-scaping, longish dyed hair, tweezed brows and a mascot smile with lots of gleaming square teeth. When he cradled his coffee cup between his hands, I was reminded of a knuckle sandwich. Guy looks like he's lifted more weights than a prison lifer. He has a voice like a fourteen-year-old."

Choking, Bosco pounded his sternum with a fist. "Jesus."

I ate half my fries, smiling at him wiping tears from his eyes and trying not to laugh.

"The attempt to smoke us out was interesting." I reached into my pocket. "Someone left these notes under the corner of Gavin's desk blotter. The first one reads, 'Whose salad is Pepper tossing?' The second says, 'Marius is hot on storage.'"

Bosco held the notes up to the light then handed them back. "What do you think?"

"Computer generated. Regular stock paper. I have no conclusions but a lot of prospects. The other thing about Marius—he was wearing a fancy black carbon and stainless steel forever bracelet. As in, it's welded on."

"Some sort of club?"

"Don't know. Pepper Doane, the Mr. Smooth who's in charge of Inventory Control has one. He pretended to come on to me, but...."

"Sorta like a dog chasing cars?"

"Yup. He was spewing too much information without saying anything useful. Bamming, it's called. The Loading Dock Foreman, Berthi, is the one I wanted most to speak with but—get this—her twin sister dropped by to tell me Berthi had just delivered Pepper's kid and wasn't returning to work. The ladies used to double-team the Loading Dock job here and in Paris, mainly for the hell of it."

"Sounds like fun."

"Damn, this sandwich tastes good. Anyhow, Yanka, Berthi's twin, caught a glimpse of my progress chart on the wall. She said I was making things too complicated. Implied I should focus on the men. The kicker is that Maison Couture, Bernards' shipment aggregator in Paris codes all the inventory, not the original suppliers. Bernards relies on electronic inventory control. In fact, the receivers scoffed when I asked about manual counts. That's a risky gaping pit, in my opinion. Maybe I can't fly over and dig around myself, but I have a lead on someone working in Accounting at the French supplier."

"You said everyone's skittish?"

"Except for Gavin, the man I press-ganged into working with me. By the way, he's a gem. Fiercely loyal and works like a maniac. I wouldn't have got this far without his insider knowledge and all-round smartness." Bosco grunted. "You'll like him when you meet. He wasn't scared by the fire. There's some messy history I'm going to look into because I think it's related to the monkey business I'm uncovering. If there's nothing negative in his background, I'd highly recommend him as BB&F material."

"When we chatted about his background checks, I got a good impression."

"Here." I slid copies of a report across the table. "After that awful first interview—no, no, it was awful because I lost control even though my investigation was spot on. Anyhow, I opened a personal file on Mitch Baljinder Mehran. I tried to recall everything about him that wasn't captured already on tape or in other records. Something you said finally sank in: Know your opponents."

He shot me a sharp look. "Well, well, well."

"Yes, I was listening. I mined BB&Fs databases first then went to all the social media sites. Amber was a big help getting mew set up so I can't be tracked back. Ginger let a few more things slip than Mercer did. In between his cursing and threats, Mitch yelled, 'I got responsibilities'. He's a crook and yes, he's assaulted me and cyber-stalked me, but once I learned his story, I felt sorry for him."

"Give me a freakin' break, will ya." He rolled his eyes. "This another variation of the dead baby syndrome?"

"Once I discovered he had a child, I put myself in his shoes and took another tack. After I'd collected all I could on my own, I squeezed Perry."

"You what?"

I threw out my hands in a placating gesture. "He eventually dropped a nugget about Ayashe, Mitch's baby mama. She's the same young woman named Ash-Leigh who lured me to the storage locker. Once I got her phone number I texted her, explaining who I was and what I was doing, how Mitch was following the wrong path and how getting locked in affected me. Which, by the way was true, because I hate small, dark spaces. From when I was a kid."

Bosco muttered something unrepeatable.

"Anyway, she agreed to meet me. Bosco, she was so upset. Confused, guilty, worried about their little girl. Her pediatrician said the child's showing autistic tendencies and she's terrified. She and Mitch have been taking her for second and third opinions, more testing, intensive behavioral therapy, you name it. That stuff isn't covered by OHIP so they're constantly in need of money. That's one reason he started stealing. She's getting better, but in the last two years, they've spent over a hundred thousand dollars. Ash says she knew Mitch was tiring of the daddy gig."

"He stole a pisspot more, though."

"I know. Haven't figured that part out yet."

"Could be he was bankrolling other enterprises?"

"Um hmm. Ash was vaguely aware of Mitch's side-hustling but the child and the money for treatments were more important. One of Mitch's part-time squeezes let slip he was messing around. That was the final straw. He was away partying when Ash left with the baby, his stash of cash and an old laptop. I promised that I—I mean we—wouldn't do anything to interfere with her getting on with her life, in exchange for the computer. She had an idea there might be incriminating evidence on the hard drive—she's naive but no dummy—but she couldn't care less about him anymore. I delivered the laptop to Kobinski and Mercer. York's Technical Data Recovery people will have a field day, I'm sure."

Bosco wiped his fingers on a wad of napkins and high-fived me.

"Good job."

31

My tour with Bosco the next day was a welcome break from cudgeling my brain about what I was going to do about connecting all the evidentiary loose ends. He'd devised a fiendish new idea for training exercises that involved him dropping me off in unfamiliar neighborhoods to tune up my self-awareness skills. His idea of a bonus lesson included popping out of a doorway or hidey-hole as I strolled by. He'd scared a squeal out of me twice, but by the third time I clued in to his M.O. and learned to walk ready for ambush. The alternative was to carry my own defibrillator.

After my training was done, we parked on Nassau Street, a block from a yarn store I wanted to visit near Kensington Market.

"Nice neighborhood." I pointed to the transit shelter by the intersection.

The flying cartoon superhero-boy on an ad for an animated film had been defaced with a soul patch under his lip and a super-sized bulge in his size 6x tights.

A gangly thirty-something dude wearing camouflage gear and carrying a long board approached. He peered through the van windshield, did an about-face without breaking stride and was gone before I could raise my arm and wave. Bosco had said the whistle on Stoner McKay's train was real faint, but I had a soft spot for him. One day after I'd bought a McCafé combo and handed him the muffin, he'd asked if I'd consider dating a younger man. Since Jake was keeping himself at arm's length and even Mitch was leaving me alone, I took the lopsided compliment to heart.

My cell phone vibrated. Amber's caller ID popped up.

"I'm out of breath mints. Think I'll take a walk to the variety store while I take this call. I'll get lunch."

Without saying a word, Bosco unfolded the Globe and Mail and turned to the Business section. We'd come to a detente—I limited my bathroom breaks and regularly brought him fresh baked goods. He no longer bitched and moaned when I asked to make unplanned stops on his route. I hopped out and pressed the handset to my ear.

"Good job with the text messages," she said. "I want to replace the phone though, even if it's a burner. We're closing in, my friend."

I stopped in the middle of the sidewalk and stared at the crystal bright sky crowded with fat clouds, marveling at how far I'd come in the last eighteen months. Half an hour later, I hustled back to the van bearing a box of warm baklava, two falafel sandwiches with extra hot sauce and a pair of sour apple sodas. Bosco looked at me like I was an apparition.

"May the goddess of good Karma envelop you in her arms."

He grinned, tucking into his meal. When we were done, we cruised the west end for a couple hours, stopping to chat with Bosco's army of informants, picking up tidbits of this and that. We parked on a different side street close to Dufferin, but Bosco was antsy, drumming the steering wheel and grumbling to himself.

"Bosco, every outing with you is a learning experience but

nothing's happening. Let's go. I've got a ton of paperwork to finish."

He blew a loud raspberry. "Not today, Sunshine. There's someone I want to introduce you to."

My mentor had been in a weird mood since he'd picked me up at the office. He was alternately glum or keeping up a running commentary that had me laughing so hard I thought I'd choke.

He drove uptown to the Lucky Red Duck restaurant where I got to meet not just any someone but Audrey, the lady in his life. She was willowy, with light brown hair caught up in a high ponytail covered by a blinged-out hair net, large hazel eyes and a generous mouth in a sweet oval face. A dark waiter's apron bulged slightly over her belly. I envied the lingering look she gave Bosco.

After catching him in a hug, she gripped my hand between hers and said, "Bosco's told me so much about you."

"Really?"

I stared at him. He only had eyes for Audrey. She seated us at a corner table, poured green tea and hustled off to the service counter. His eyes were all soft and moist. As she walked about taking orders and processing credit card payments, he gazed at her like she was dessert.

"An amazing human being." His voice was wistful. "I think I've finally found a keeper." He tucked his paper napkin under his chin. "I'm going to ask her to marry me."

"Does she know that?"

"Uh uh." He fiddled with his tea cup.

"You're seriously in love."

A wave of crimson spread from his throat to his forehead. "And don't you go telegraphing it, either."

Audrey returned with three platters and a covered tureen. He pointed to the bowl.

"Buddha soup. Thirty ingredients. Good for the gonads."

I declined and nibbled spring rolls and mango salad. He downed his meal with gusto, lashing each serving with teaspoons of hot chili oil.

"So, Bosco," I said in a conversational tone, "if I wanted to find someone who might have disappeared a long time ago, would I follow the same process for a regular missing person?"

The spoon trailing squid parts and sea cucumber halted halfway to his lips.

"Sure. With some adjustments for the length of time and broken trail of evidence."

"I have a name. And I think he might have been involved with my mother when I was a baby. I'm not sure about the dates yet."

He narrowed his eyes. "Your mother? Let me think."

He lifted up his soup bowl, poured the contents down his throat and dabbed at his mouth with a napkin. When Audrey arrived to clear the table, he reached over and stroked her hip.

"Lindberg and Nordstrom from GlobeMinCo might have something to do with a man called Markus Linden, who's linked to Martin Bernard. I haven't had the chance to run the connections to ground. They were all in Peru at the same time searching for minerals."

He picked up one of my uneaten spring rolls and chewed thoughtfully.

"Technically, the work for GMC has nothing to do with family matters. You have no skin in their game. I wouldn't worry about it."

"Jake sort of told me not to get in too deep."

"Sort of?"

"I'm not you, Bosco. I don't have the history with Jake. I still feel like I'm on probation."

He grimaced. "You're not. We're past that."

"Well. Good. I don't like mysteries, especially when they involve me. My mother's gone and my stepfather refuses to talk about it. My brothers are pissed at me for upsetting him. Something happened between my dad, my mother and the Linden guy. I want to know what happened. That's why I asked you about Missing Persons."

Brows furrowed, he began to itemize with his fingers. "Find someone who knew them. Or who was there. Check passport usage. And renewals. Depending on the countries involved it could be harder or it could be easier."

"There's a few other things taking up my time." I held up four fingers. "The stalking and the identity theft, Bernards, the office fire and the tussle on Queen Street."

"That's what being a competent P.I. is about—multi-tasking. And from what we've been seeing lately, you're doing great. For a middle-aged newbie civilian."

"You're not serious about the middle-aged part, are you?"

"Nah." He aimed his spoon at me like a pointer. "You going to have time for BB&F work?"

"What do you mean?"

"I read the weekly reports on database logins. No problem with the volume of searches for company business. It's the others. The last few months, you've been relentless as a golden ager banging the progressive slot machine buttons at the casino. Martin Bernard, Lindstrom, South America. I'm curious."

"Sorry. Thing is, I haven't found anything useful. I'm hanging out at Bernards for the next few weeks. I want that sucker done."

He pursed his lips, school teacher style. "Try to keep the volume of personal searches to a dull roar, alright?"

I squeezed his hand. "Thank you. Partner. I know you know this is important."

Bosco hadn't asked if I'd already told Jake.

32

Mitch's radio silence was a relief and a worry. What was he cooking up for me? The rational P.I. part of me believed that, despite his taunts, I'd been able to insulate myself. He must know the police were hot on his trail because I'd sown that seed when I spoke with Perry, who'd looked alarmed then gleeful.

My dad was in Mexico again. Maggie agreed with me that rather than attending Spanish language classes, he might have a lady friend he was visiting. The thought didn't bother me as much as it might have a few months ago. Before I started investigating those mysterious photographs, I'd believed my mother had been the love of his life. Now, I wasn't so certain.

It was dark outside when I finished typing up my notes on the final re-interviews with Bernards' managers.

What a crop of likely felons. Pepper and Marius Lambert were on the road somewhere but when I braced Bailey, she said they weren't checking in regularly. Selecting the ones neck-deep in the inventory fraud conspiracy wouldn't be easy but Marius, Pepper and the French supplier were my top picks. Fueled by the eager disclosures of the folks I'd been interviewing, the list of their no-nos was getting longer every day. Gavin was on them like a hungry man on a burger. I didn't give a fig whether his enthusiasm was motivated by revenge or dedication to the cause. My suspicions that there had to be someone disaffected on the inside of the French operation had resulted in a name surfacing: Clément L'Eglise. We'd exchanged a few emails but he was jumpy as a crab in a vat of heated water.

Feet on the edge of the desk, I was relaxed in my chair, staring at the cluttered white boards crammed with charts and colored paper flags when a door slammed in the distance.

"Hello?" I hated how tentative my voice was. "Hey. Who goes there?"

The overhead lights dimmed then died. The sudden silence hummed against my eardrums. There was, thankfully, no smell of smoke.

Hands outstretched, I groped my way to the faint rim of brightness leaking through the blinds overlooking the sales floor. Pale pools of light spilled from the emergency fixtures onto displays of clothing. I shivered. From above, the mannequins looked like well-dressed aliens, all long contorted shadows, frozen outstretched arms and hidden faces. A series of thumps in the hallway was followed by dragging footsteps. I froze.

The pops and groans of the old building made it hard to identify the direction of sounds. Eyes accustomed to the gloom, I inched to my desk and pushed my chair out of the way with my knee. The wheels were loud on the plastic mat. Shit. I slipped on my backpack and fumbled around the bottom desk drawer for my heavy-duty flashlight. Arms spread like a parachute-jumper in free fall, I edged through the ghastly shadows cast by the bloody emergency lights in the hallway. The still air held a spicy-funky-foreign smell. Odd, but somewhat familiar.

"Hey!"

I dropped into a crouch as Bosco had taught me, pressing my

mouth against the fabric of my lapel to muffle my raspy breathing. Looking around was useless: I couldn't see a damned thing. On the positive side, the lurker was at the same disadvantage. Something flew by where my head had been and hit the wall by the door with a thud. I pressed my chin against my knees. A tendon popped in my heel. Screw this.

"Come on out, you goof!"

It was hard to sound authoritative with my head so close to the floor. I hefted the flashlight but didn't turn it on. It wouldn't be much protection if I put myself in the spotlight.

"I've called 9-1-1," I yelled over my shoulder.

A meaty thump of flesh against something solid was followed by a muffled curse and retreating footsteps. I shouted, "loser", half-stood up and began speed-crab-walking backward toward the exit light. I was groping for the flashlight's on switch when my foot jammed against a large hard shape.

Cursing and screaming, I pitched forward and smashed head first into a pile of metal.

* * *

"*Missus*, missus. Wake up now."

Fingers were gripping my right shoulder, bouncing it up and down. It was Albina, one of the night cleaning crew.

"Stop." My voice came out in a squeak.

I moaned, squinting against the glare. The buzzing hum of the fluorescent lights made my skull feel like I was wearing ear buds turned up full volume on a white noise soundtrack. A wet towel covered my forehead. I reached out a shaky arm and shoved it aside. I was laid out on the rug in the waiting area. I closed my eyes. I groaned and jiggled my knees—at least I wasn't paralyzed. What a stupid idea. I wanted to laugh but coughed instead.

"How you doing, Girl?" Minnie, the Deputy Security Director, lifted her hand from my shoulder and sat back on her haunches. "That's quite an egg you're growing there."

"What happened?"

Albina said, "You fall down. I was ina storeroom downstairs. A failure power happen. I hear big crash. When I come upstairs, you on the floor."

I remembered falling face down; now I was on my back.

"Did you turn me over?"

"No way," she said, holding her hands out at her sides.

I heaved myself onto one elbow. Damn. "Ow."

Shades of Lawrence subway. I pressed my fingers to my chest. Yes, I had a pulse. Wait. I was touching skin and not cloth. What the—?

I stared down in horror, cursing as pain shot from my scalp to my shoulder blades. The zipper of my pants had been pulled down, the buttons on my shirt were undone and my blue polka-dot bra was in full view. I wrenched my torso upwards shrieking, "what happened to my clothes?" and grabbed for the edges of my shirt front.

Woozy, I fell back and cracked my skull on the floor. Minnie laid a hand on my shoulder.

"Wait. Before you move and smear it, look at your abdomen."

I tried to bend my head ninety degrees but my neck felt like it was in a vice. It hurt to sit up. "What is it? I can't see anything."

"Someone draw to you stommy," Albina said, pointing to my mid-section. She clucked her tongue.

"I took photos. For later." Minnie held her cell phone close and waited until my eyes focused.

On my belly, someone has crudely drawn a narrow black oval under a thick wing of eyebrow. A sweeping curved line ended in a curlicue under the outside edge of the eye. A jagged circle around my navel - an iris – had been filled in with black scribbles. A red x had been slashed through the circle. Upside down, the rendering looked even more sinister.

"Jesus. What is that? An eye?"

"Cover the eye. Close the eye. No. Stop looking." Minnie nodded.

I fell back, out of breath again then lurched onto my left hip, scrubbing at my flesh with the hem of my shirt. "Get it off. Get it off."

"Ju use hand sanitizer," the cleaner ordered. "Here."

Albina handed me a tall plastic bottle. I pumped furiously and slapped at my belly. The gel was freezing but it quickly liquefied and oozed down the waist band of my pants into the crease of my thigh. I flopped another quarter turn and sat back on my heels, scrubbing blindly and blubbering and thinking, oh god, oh god, whoever did it came back after I knocked myself out.

"Is it coming off?"

Minnie leaned close and shook her head. I squirted on more sanitizer but couldn't see what I was doing. My breasts were in the way. Albina handed me a microfiber square. At least it was clean.

"Scrub with this," she said. "Not so hard. You skin turnin' red."

Nubbins of thought skittered through my mind. Someone had unzipped my pants. Taken the time to mark my body up. What else had they done? Did they feel me up when they opened my shirt? *Maybe. Probably.* Flashes of fury turned my vision red. How long was I out? *Not long. I'm going to be sick. No you're not.* They'd obviously used a flashlight to do their work. My flashlight? I stopped rubbing and looked around wildly. No. It had rolled against the leg of Gavin's desk. I began snuffling to slow the flow of tears.

"Here. Let me." Albina squatted, steadying herself with one

hand on the carpet. She tugged the cloth from my hand. "Is okay. Ju squiz, I clean."

She grunted as she swiped the cloth from left to right across my skin as if she was painting. Minnie steadied me with her knees against my back and her hands on my shoulders. The next blob of sanitizer burned. I yelped. I must have broken the skin. Minnie gave me a gentle shake.

"Did you see anything?" she said.

"No. Except stars when I hit my head."

Albina struggled to her feet and dropped the soiled cloth. I gingerly probed my scalp.

"You sure pees somebody uff. You dunno who?"

"Not yet," I muttered as I jerked up my zipper. "But I fucking well will soon." I recoiled at the clammy chill from my soaked underwear. "Then I will kick them to the curb."

"Let me help you up." Minnie grabbed me under the arms, hefted me to my feet then went to stand by the door with her fingers tucked into the armpits of her body armor vest. "When the main lights shut down in this sector, it triggers an alarm on my monitoring panel," she said. "All's I saw was a thick-set figure in dark clothes and a cap pulled down over his ears. I came running and yelling."

Although I ached like crazy, my limbs still worked. I leaned my bum against the edge of Gavin's desk and brushed myself off. I reached for the mirrored vase on his credenza and held it at waist height. The alcohol in the sanitizer had dissolved most of the ink. Rivulets of dark stains snaked from just under my bra to below my crotch. It looked like I'd soiled myself. Against the light brown of my midriff, the vague outline of the eye was still visible under a crisscross of red streaks. The scent of alcohol was choking. The scorching sting made me wince. I banged the vase on the desk.

"Minnie, could you take some more pictures?"

"Before and after," she said ruefully.

"Whoever planned this will regret it," I said, fumbling to button my blouse.

She pointed to the stairwell and the stepladder that had been jammed between the legs of Gavin's overturned chair and a side table.

"Good thing the obstacle course got in your way."

I felt like I was going to pass out. "If I'd been moving backward instead of forward, I'd have taken a header into the stairwell."

"Or worse. I think my calling out scared him off," Minnie said. "You were lucky."

All of a sudden, my body sagged like a half-empty balloon. Things had been going so well and now this. "I guess. Thanks."

"You want me to call somebody?"

"Not really." I said in a small voice, "Are you filing a report?"

I wasn't going to call 9-1-1—this was a major piss-off but not an emergency. Nothing was broken but my old rotator cuff injury ached like hell. Geez, I'd been hammered harder in a hockey scrimmage. I stood up straight.

Minnie sniffed and gave me a hard stare. "Not necessarily."

I glanced at Albina. She was off to one side with her back to us, swishing a feather duster along the top of the file cabinet. I gave Minnie a look.

"Listen. I'm already working with a detective in the Special Victims Unit about something else." Minnie's eyes flew open and her mouth rounded to an 'O'. "This can't be part of the something else, though."

Her lips snapped shut. "You've been charring a path through Bernards. You got a great bedside manner but you've made a few folks very nervous. They've had a good time until you two showed up. And Gavin don't fool me a bit. He's no softie."

That made me feel better. "Can we do an Air Drop? I'll send my SVU contact the photos you took. Can I come talk to you tomorrow?"

She eyed me for a moment then said, "Sure."

"Hold on." I rummaged through a couple of desk drawers and pulled out a crumpled white plastic bag. I snapped it open, draped the edges over the flashlight then picked it up and tucked the bundle into my backpack. "Might be evidence. Fingerprints."

Minnie nodded. I tilted my head in the cleaner's direction. "Will it be safe for Albina?" She turned at the sound of her name. "I don't care if the office is cleaned."

Minnie pursed her lips then checked her watch. "Albina, help me get this crap outta the way." She hooked her thumb at the ladder and pushed herself away from the wall. "I'll see you both out." Shaking her head, she patted me on the arm. "Alls I can say is, you must be getting close enough to some thing to spook somebody." Albina bobbed her head vigorously. "You have any pain pills?" Minnie said. "You may not feel it now but you will in a while."

"Good idea."

I'd been meaning to call in a refill of the prescription my dentist had given me when he'd pulled a wisdom tooth. I reached in my backpack for my wallet, called the automated pharmacy line and punched in the prescription number listed on my personal medication history sheet.

A genderless recorded voice intoned, 'We have no record of that item. Please call back during regular business hours." I called three more times and got the same answer.

"They say they have no record but that doesn't make sense. Look," I said, holding out the paper to Minnie, "the prescription's only six months old."

"There's an all-night Shoppers Drug Mart down the street. They can access your file."

I called and asked to speak to the on-duty pharmacist. A chipper-sounding woman took down my information and put me on hold. The last chorus of Sweet Caroline was playing by the time she came back.

"I'm sorry, ma'am," she said, sounding a lot less chipper. "Those patient records have been archived."

"Why? That's a mistake. I have two refills left."

She put me on hold again. When she returned, her voice was solemn.

"The notation is that the patient is deceased."

"But I'm not dead," I wailed.

33

Could that bastard Mitch have messed with my pharmacy records? Maybe. Nah, I was getting paranoid.

"No worries." I gave Minnie and Albina a fake smile. "I've got a bottle at the office."

Minnie called a cab and waited until I was safely inside before she re-locked the rear security doors.

It was almost midnight when I limped to the back door, tapped in my security code and pressed my eye to the iris scanner, disarmed the security system, reset it then hobbled to my office. Still shaking, I tapped in Detective Kobinski's number and got her voice mail. I left a detailed account of my evening and emailed her the photos Minnie had taken.

Being on my own wasn't as bad as it had been at first, but I couldn't face going home. Off balance and nauseous, I phoned Maggie but got voice mail. I fired off a misspelled text message, asking if I could crash at her place overnight. I got a reply in five minutes—she and Matteo were in Geneva. I threw the phone onto my desk and sobbed. How come she was never around when I needed her?

Once the dizziness passed, I kicked off my soiled pants and stared at the Egyptian-looking graffiti on my torso, furious that someone had touched me. Had looked at me. Without permission. A primal scream of rage blotted out the pain. I ran the taps until the water was almost too hot to endure, then lathered a facecloth and scrubbed the flesh from my breasts to my crotch raw. Still, I couldn't erase the last vestiges of the marks, even with antibiotic ointment.

I changed into a clean t-shirt and sweatpants, pulled a pillow and blankets from a drawer in the closet, closed the doors to my office and turned out the lights. I curled up on the couch, mentally rehearsed my debriefing with Jake and Bosco first thing in the morning then sank into a dreamless sleep.

Someone coughed. That was odd, because I was underwater. I pushed up my diving mask, spit the snorkel from my mouth and tipped my head toward the shimmery surface of the ocean and a warm mellow light. Was that coffee? Not underwater. I opened one eye and peered at my wristwatch. Six-thirty. I muttered a string of Italian obscenities then coughed, trying to dislodge the mesh scrubbing pad stuck in my throat. I pulled the blankets up to my chin and shifted deeper into a warm crevice smelling of cowhide and fabric softener.

"Good morning," said a familiar voice.

Kicking free of the covers entwined around my ankles, I peeled my cheek from the wedge between the seat cushions and the back of the couch. I rolled onto my back, releasing waves of hand sanitizer fumes.

"Ugh."

"What's going on?"

I jerked upright. "Ow. Oh." Jake was seated in the armchair opposite my improvised bed, holding a mug of steaming coffee. Good thing I hadn't passed gas. "What...what are you doing here?"

"This is my building. I live upstairs, remember?"

"It's so early." I shoved my hair back from my face and tried to look awake.

"Couldn't sleep. I do a walk around every morning. The alarm was on but your door was closed. Usually the cleaners leave it open. Plus, I get a text message alerting me whenever the security system is accessed after hours. You checked in at 23:19."

"Oh." My ability to speak in full sentences was on the floor with my discarded backpack. Thankfully, he wasn't looking at my face while he sipped his coffee and waited. I scrubbed the back of my hands against my cheeks. "Well, this is awkward."

"You're a mess."

For a fleeting second, I considered whipping up my t-shirt to show him what some asshole had done to my body. Since I wasn't wearing a bra, he'd also get a daylight gander at my boobs. Maybe touch them or check for bruises? Bad idea.

"Give me a few minutes, okay?"

His eyes shifted from my wrinkled t-shirt to the pile of folded clothing on the chair. "I'll give you ten."

Which skinny self-help talking head had said these were the best years of my life? What must Jake be thinking about finding me beaten up, conked out and probably snoring on the office furniture?

I groaned when I saw myself in the bathroom mirror. Minnie had been right—the laceration on the left side of my forehead had swelled into a mouse-sized lump. Raccoon rims of mascara ringed my eyelids. My hair looked like a nest abandoned by a creature seeking better real estate. I leaned in for a closer look. My right incisor felt loose and there was a jagged cut on the inside of my mouth. And when did all those frizzy pale strands show up at my temples? Henna or hair dye? Damn it, I was dying—of pain, mortification, anxiety and outrage. Pressing a hand towel against my mouth, I sank to my knees and burst into sobs.

Forget 'Fifty Ways to Lose Your Lover'. I was on Way Number Eight or Nine to jeopardizing my employment. Again.

When I let go of the door handle I'd grasped to crane myself upright, I caught another glimpse of my face. My bottom lip was swollen on one side, lifting my mouth into a weird smile. My eyeballs were mottled as the insides of an Alaska Pink apple. I stepped into the tiny seldom-used shower, scrubbed my scalp until it tingled then lathered a facecloth with lavender soap. I abraded my skin until it stung, but the marks were finally gone. I was grateful my hair was still short; there was conditioner but no hair dryer. Unfortunately, the foundation I dabbed on highlighted rather than hid the mess on my face.

Four minutes left. That whiff of scent at Bernards. Whose was it? I knew, but the name just wouldn't surface from the sludge of thoughts crowding my weary brain.

I pictured Jake sitting at his desk listening to the sounds of my ablutions and fantasizing about what I looked like naked. Yeah, right. Even my vivid imagination couldn't make that one come to life. I needed ice packs. A morning glory muffin dripping with butter. And lots of coffee.

Not ready to meet Jake looking like the victim of a car crash, I dressed in a fresh shirt and slacks with a glittery belt. I didn't look the part, but I pulled on a pair of Wonder Woman socks and slipped my feet into a pair of black loafers.

Jake had folded up the blankets and put the pillow away. A Minions mug of coffee and a dish holding a toasted everything bagel with butter and a side of cherry jam sat on a placemat on the coffee table.

"Thank you." I took a grateful sip. "I'm sorry if I was abrupt."

"You clean up nicely," he said with a slow smile. "What happened?"

I chewed a bagel half and wiped my fingers. "This?" I pointed to my forehead. "I was working late at Bernards. Someone with bad intentions hit the breaker and the lights went out. I was scouting who was lurking outside my office and tripped over a ladder."

He touched my sleeve with the tips of his fingers. "You okay?"

Without thinking, I rubbed the back of his hand. "Yes."

Jake and I jumped at the sharp rap on my office door. Bosco strode in.

"Good morning, peoples."

His eyes flicked in my direction. I nonchalantly withdrew my hand. He pulled up the other armchair and propped his green and red leather boots on the table. Lips compressed, he raised one eyebrow and tilted his chin up. I could almost hear the gears grinding in that labyrinthine brain.

"You two are making an early start. What's up?"

"Let me finish my breakfast," I said between bites. "I have some stuff to show you both. In the boardroom."

I recapped the events of the last few days. Jake sucked in his breath when I projected the photos of the office hallway, the tangle of debris and my defaced abdomen on the screen.

Bosco snapped, "What the fuck—? You hurt?"

"My pride more than anything. Minnie, the Deputy Director of Security, said that all she saw was the dark shape of a thickset man wearing a hat pulled low."

His face rigid, Bosco sat with his scarred fists balled on the table top. "Mitch?"

"No. He's tallish and not that chunky. Besides, the store was locked tight. No way he could get in. Few people know where I work. There's a locked door at the bottom of the stairwell that only staff with security passes can access."

"An insider, then," Jake said.

"Last night, after I stopped obsessing how I was going to get Mitch, I lay here on the couch counting my blessings. Sure, Bosco, you can be skeptical, but I did. I am... blessed."

I stood slowly then printed on the whiteboard: *Threatened. Trapped. Stalked. Shoved. Stolen. Smoked. Tripped.*

"A snapshot of the last year of my life."

"Why don't you sit down and take it easy?" Jake said.

I rested my shoulder against the wall. "Hear me out. Defacing my body constitutes assault, right?"

Jake nodded. I added *assaulted* and *declared dead* to the list.

"Until I came to work here, my life was totally unremarkable. Boring. Unchallenging. My mother, God rest her soul, used to say, 'Flame may melt wax but it fires clay and forges steel'. Yeah, I know. Corny. But they're called old wives' tales for a reason."

I paced the room twice then when a wave of wooziness hit, I sank into a chair at the foot of the table opposite Jake.

"Listen, until I hit my thirties I was so malleable anyone could mold me, make me change. And they tried, by god. They tried and succeeded. Being here is so different. Bosco, you helped me see how pissed off being threatened by Mitch should make me. Thing is, having my identity stolen was the last straw. I mean, how dare he? I was just doing my job."

I was gratified by his brief hand clap.

"Getting stuck in that locker, the stalking and Lawrence subway incidents were scary, but I survived. They helped me focus in fact, because I made dumb mistakes thinking I could handle everything by myself. Tried to fix things like I've always done. But you have to understand, that's what I've been doing all my life. It was my shrink who asked why I thought I was so perfect I could make things right. And he was right. I can't fix everything."

Bosco sat forward, ready to launch into speech. I held up one hand.

"Wait, please. Let me finish. You've both lectured me about trust and not second-guessing myself. That's why I was ready for Queen Street. If it wasn't for that damned ladder last night, I might have caught the guy at Bernards. I've realized I can strike back. And I did, with a little help from my friends. My days of melting under crisis are past. I am on fire."

Bosco ambled over, gently pulled me out of the chair and caught me in a light bro-hug. "You did good, Partner. Who do you think…?"

"I've talked to a lot of people at Bernards. I've got my suspicions but I'll get the facts to back them up. I'm just not sure yet whose buttons I might have pushed that hard."

Bosco was watching me with an impassive predator stare. "You're awfully cheerful about getting banged up."

"No, I'm motivated. You can be damned sure I'm going to get to the bottom of this crap."

Despite the craziness of the night before, I felt good. The two men looked at me then at each other. Jake said, "We've been wondering how long it would take."

"It?"

"Remember a while ago, I said, 'you've got this Kenora'? Now you know you have. I've been hoping you'd realize that."

Bosco turned to Jake with a big grin, "Didn't I tell you?"

"What?" I said. "Tell him what?"

They exchanged a secret smile. Bosco's phone rang. He fished it out of his pocket, peered at the screen then said to us, "Catch you in five," and left, pulling the door to the hallway closed.

"Obviously you're getting somewhere, " Jake said.

"Perhaps. But my father and brothers complain they don't know who I am anymore. That the old me is gone and my job has changed me into someone different."

"You're not the same woman. You said it yourself. It's not just your life that's different: you're different, too. What do you plan to do?" Jake said.

His smile was warm enough but his eyes, oh, his eyes. I knew what that smoky midnight blue heated gaze meant. When would our next time be? I turned away to wipe my list off the board, taking long enough for the blush toasting my throat and face to fade.

"I left Ginger a message last night and I'll speak with her this afternoon. I'll get my doctor to call Shoppers and confirm I'm not taking a dirt nap. I'm going back to Bernards so Gavin and I can crunch the expense reports again. That's where the snake in the grass is hiding."

"You'll work from here. Bernards has become too dangerous."

"But Jake, I can manage." I caught his gaze, hummed a few bars of the Rocky theme song then did a quick rope-a-dope shuffle. When he grinned, I sat down. "I'll only go in when Gavin's there. We're so close to being done."

Bosco returned, looking satisfied with himself. He said, glancing at Jake then at me, "They're getting bolder. It's smarter to disengage."

"Gavin will send whatever reports you need," Jake said with finality. "I'd rather you stayed away."

He pushed his chair back, sauntered to the end of the table, leaned over and pressed his lips to the side of my neck. I dropped my gaze but feathered my fingertips along his chin.

"Don't worry, we'll get him. Them."

Bosco cleared his throat then said, "Well, Pard." Jake straightened. I knew from the heat in my cheeks that my face was red. "In the meantime, I got an assignment I need my Partner's help with next week."

The ache I felt had nothing to do with my injuries.

34

Just as I finished loading my laptop and a wad of files into my backpack on Monday, there was a quick knuckle-rap on my office door. Bosco strode into wearing a black baseball cap, a navy shirt and matching pants over tooled black cowboy boots. The embroidered name on the left shirt pocket read 'Ernie'.

"Ernie? Good Lord, you look like a convict. And those aren't safety boots, my friend."

"Yeah, yeah. Jake and I had a quick chat. I appreciate that you talked to both of us and that you're working your plan, but I've got another idea. Meet you out back."

Seta knocked on the door jamb, threw Bosco a look then handed me a sealed white envelope. My name and 'Private and Confidential' had been printed untidily on the front. I stuffed the envelope into my jacket pocket and scooped up my stuff.

Frowning, Bosco held out his hand. "Let me see that."

I stood close as he peeled up the flap and spread the folded sheet of letter-sized paper open on my desk. The note looked like it had been composed using dull scissors and stained sections of an old newspaper.

'I know where you work, bitch. I know what you drive. Watch your back. It won't be long now. I have friends.'

I sagged against the desk. "It's Mitch. Which friends?' Is he going to sic a team of criminal crackpots on me?"

"Perry talked. I told that little shit to keep his gob shut."

"What do I do now? Because of me, he could end up in jail. His girlfriend already left. He's a loose screw on the lam."

"'Loose screw? On the lam'? Forsooth," Bosco said in a fake British accent. That made me giggle. "Stop hyperventilating." He patted my arm. "I'm going to give a guy I know a call. Lean on him. "

"Seta said someone dropped it off. The security cameras probably caught him."

Bosco turned the notepaper and envelope over. He held them up to the light. "You call Buck and get him to run the security video. I'll get Seta to send the paper to the lab weenies. Won't be much to find."

"What if he's following me around? He'll know where I live."

I'd been so cocky, thinking that my trail had gone cold. Now, as much as I tried to stoke my bravado, I wanted to be sick.

"Not likely. This just came today. I keep telling you, don't worry."

My hands were shaking. "But he's getting too close for comfort. I'm going to call Kobinski."

Bosco smiled a jackal smile. "One of us'll find him before he finds you next time."

"Next time?"

"Go on, get your stuff together. Get your shit together." In the van, Bosco handed me a bottle of cranberry juice. ""It has lots of vitamin C. Good for stress. We're going to Bernards."

"Bernards? How can you show up at Bernards?"

"Let's keep it simple. I've got a toolbox in the back. You know how people ignore someone in a uniform who looks like they belong? I'll wander up to your offices, knock in some nails or run the water in the sink. Open up the guts of the photocopier. Basically, I want to take some time to check the place out."

"You enjoy this, don't you?"

Bosco waggled his eyebrows and hummed a melody from The Sound of Music. "Old clothes and UC were my favorite things." Undercover. Of course he'd like play-acting.

I texted Gavin to let him know what was going on then followed in my car. Bosco drove to Bernards like he was responding to a Code two call. I couldn't keep up. He'd do a walkabout around the perimeter of the building then park in the municipal lot and text me to let him in the rear entrance. I didn't expect anyone to ask what I was doing. Except for my assailant with the ladder, no one had taken any unusual interest in my presence.

While we waited for Bosco, I made phone calls and reviewed my interview notes. Gavin wandered down the Finance to pick up the last batch of printouts. Even with what he'd lost through the thefts, Martin Bernard had more than enough blunt to cover the cost of printing. My money was on Marius as the ladder planter. He of the overly-friendly manner, muscle-bound insecurity and unusual cologne. And an all-access pass to the building.

No one was by the door when I let Bosco in twenty minutes later. He sauntered upstairs wearing a loaded tool belt and clanking like a bag of Christmas ornaments. Gavin locked the entrance to the stairwell. His excitement was palpable as Bosco motioned him over for a confab.

"Game on," Gavin said, fairly hopping around my office. He raced away when Bosco texted to ask for a tour of the less-traveled areas of the building. They were both still grinning an hour later when they returned. I'd hoped Bosco would run into Pepper Doane or Marius, but no luck.

"Give me a call later," Bosco said, clapping Gavin on the back and departing with a clatter. What was it about men and peril that got them jazzed up about chase games?

When I left for the day, Gavin was up to his nose in expense claims. My French connection had finally agreed to a Skype meeting on Sunday afternoon. I'd have to get Buck's people to set up the BB&F boardroom for the transmission and for recording our conversation. Things were really starting to move.

I wheeled my beater down Yonge Street to the office, aware that the thump-thump behind the rear passenger cabin probably meant the tire was going flat. Only on the bottom, Maggie would say.

There was nary a spot in the staff lot. I cruised the side streets and finally parked behind a painter's van one street over from the office. I'd only be there for an hour before I had to meet Bosco at Finch subway station. He was tracking a dentist alleged to have been administering more than painkillers to women under sedation in his chair. I was tapped to play decoy.

Jake was out but Seta brought me up to speed on that day's office news. She was assembling a file for my next case but wouldn't give any hints what it might be. Once I got through my emails, I scooped a stack of mail from my in-basket and a book-sized cardboard box sitting on the blotter, dumped everything into my backpack, tossed it into the back seat of my car then headed north.

The temperature dial on the dashboard read 32 degrees outside and 18 degrees inside. That was a lie. The gauge was broken. Traffic was mind-boggling. I drove north with the windows down at speeds slightly faster than walking, sweating like an asphalt tamper in the hot unconditioned air belching from the vents. Once the home renovation line of credit was cleared away, I'd start saving for new wheels.

Finch subway station at rush hour was an ugly place choked with ongoing construction, frenzied commuters, transit buses nosing in wherever they wanted and pedestrians jaywalking as if the streets belonged only to them. At the gate to the parking lot, I plunked in three coins and cruised for ten minutes before a truck pulled out halfway up the vast lot a few slots away from a light standard. Bosco was idling in the Kiss and Ride in a forest green sedan, a huge step up from the crapmobile. He looked very natty in a pale blue checked shirt with the cuffs rolled up.

I buckled myself in and tapped him on the arm until he turned in my direction. I'd been snacking on arugula salad, chocolate nut candy bars and cheap gummy candies so that I'd have a nice layer of gunk on my teeth. He turned away.

"That looks nasty enough."

"Maybe I should have worn a skirt if I want to entice him into something indiscreet."

"Not an issue. I gather from the Accountability Officer from the Association of Dentists that Dr. Dan's an opportunistic groper. Knowing you, if he pulls anything funny he'll be wearing his stones as a tie ornament."

"I don't have to let him put me to sleep, do I?"

"The first visit he'll only be sizing you up." He wheeled into a run-down strip mall west of Bathurst Street on Finch. "Literally."

"If he was gay would you volunteer?"

"Fuck no. That's the difference between involved and committed." He chuckled. "You know—"

"Yeah, the one about the chicken being involved in breakfast but the pig is committed. Old as dirt and just as appealing."

I fluffed up my hair, undid two buttons on my blouse and flipped up my collar preppie style. My phone beeped. Gavin had texted a copy of an email from the Loading Dock Foreperson saying she was back in town and wanted to see me ASAP. That was good news. Based on our research, she held the reins leading to a half a dozen suspicious horses.

Bosco reached under his seat again and handed me a pleated

pink scarf. "Tie this in your hair. I hear he likes the 50s housewife look. And could you look wide-eyed and lisp a bit?"

"Am I getting raise for this?"

"Just the pleasure of my company."

Bosco loitered in the waiting room with me, paging through a recent issue of Urban Cowboy. I didn't mind the prospect of getting groped as much as I did the wait. I alternated between mooning over an Elizabeth Boyle novel on my phone's Kindle app and checking messages.

I must have made a noise because Bosco dropped his magazine and said, "What? What happened?"

My mind was whirling and I had a pang of regret. I'd laughingly dubbed Parag Musselman 'Perry the Perv'. Never again would I disparage the strange little man. Perry had come through for me.

I fumbled the message app closed and said brightly, "Nothing, nothing. Just Maggie up to her old tricks."

He shot me a hot glare then snapped open a copy of <u>Boots & Belts</u>. Just as his patience was running out, the silent receptionist ushered me into a coffin-sized enclosure outfitted with an orange chair that looked more like a massage table. I felt like I was cheating on my regular dentist. A green-haired hygienist with a barbell through her nose completed my workup.

Doctor Dan appeared right after I spit into the basin and wiped the cleaning goop from my lips. He gave me the two-over. I gripped my shirt front under the paper bib to block him if he attempted a quick feel and so I wouldn't have to shake his hand. With a huge smile and without consulting my chart or peering into my mouth, he said I should return for a more thorough consultation in two weeks.

By the time Bosco and I paid the bill and left the office, it was almost dark. The evening was cloaked in an annoying swirling rain, too thin for an umbrella but heavy enough to dampen hair and clothing.

"I'll drop you at your vehicle," he said. "I'm gonna help Audrey make eggplant parmigiana for dinner tomorrow."

"Don't forget to use a handful of freshly grated Grano Padano."

"Yes, nonna."

He was so happy. I was happy for him. Third time was the charm. I wasn't prepared for that kind of trial-and-error.

The pay gate was up. The lot was half full. The piss-colored glow from the tall sodium vapor lights illuminated oily puddles, empty parking slots and windblown garbage. I pointed to my Altima in the distance and fumbled in my fanny pack for my key ring. Bosco gunned the engine. As he wheeled in a wide circle to the right, my keys slid from my lap to the floor. I gripped the center console for balance then bent and groped around blindly at my feet. My head banged against the glove box when Bosco jammed on the brakes.

"Hey."

He thrust the gear shift into neutral and parked nose to nose with my car. "What the fuck is that?"

He was glaring straight ahead, his hands gripping the steering wheel so hard his knuckles stood up like doorknobs. I followed his gaze and sucked in a huge breath. In the brilliant splash of light from the high beams, the vandalism was evident.

Scrawled on the windshield in grease pencil were the words: 'I told you Rosie. Watch out'.

I pounded the dashboard. "Mitch. How the hell did he find me?" I fumbled for the door handle. Bosco grabbed my arm.

"Wait. Check your surroundings." He killed the engine but left the headlights on. "Mitch, eh." His wolfish expression chilled my anger. I may have been fantasizing about kicking Mitch's butt and realigning his private parts; Bosco would actually do it. I pulled a waterproof running jacket out of my backpack's outer pouch. Bosco rolled his eyes. "Lime green?"

"It was on sale."

"You're gonna look like a caterpillar in that rig." He reached under the driver's seat, pulling out a six-cell matte black flashlight with a head the size of his fist. I lit up my four-cell replica. "Leave your other stuff." He pulled a folded square of dry-foam padding from the driver's side door pocket. "Let's do a walk around. Don't touch anything."

We slid out, pressed the car doors shut and peered around. No one in sight. No noise except the distant rumble of two articulated buses at the platform and passing vehicle wheels hissing on the wet pavement of a nearby street.

Heart thumping, I turned up my hood and followed as he circled the area then crisscrossed the empty spaces on each side. A sudden throb in my temples made me wince.

"Fucking Mitch," I said again.

Dozens of 2"x 4" white mailing labels—the kind that could only be removed with a blow torch or lashings of cheap olive oil—were plastered on the windows and the door panels. Bosco knelt on the foam padding and shone the flash under the trunk and by the hood. The misty rain morphed to a downpour. Water trickled between the hood and collar of my windbreaker, seeping down my shoulder blades. Knowing better than to complain, I stood off to one side.

"Anything?"

He stood up and brushed off the knees of his dark jeans. "No."

"Well, at least I can stop worrying about having to pay to fix the door dings."

Even as the words left my mouth, even before Bosco turned his flashlight beam onto my chest, I knew my whistling-past-the-graveyard attempt at sarcasm had been an inane fail.

He sighed and dropped the arm holding the light. "Are the doors locked?"

Nodding, I dropped the car keys into his palm. "I am so sick of this bullshit. When is it going to end?"

Instead of answering, he circled to the passenger side and pointed the flash at the back seat. "What's that?"

"File folders from work. A box with a book. Seta said it was between the screen door and the inside door when she opened the office this morning."

"You ordered a book delivered to work?"

"I didn't. Wouldn't. Wait a minute." I smacked my forehead. "My online account is linked to my home address. Besides, a real delivery guy would have handed the box to Seta...if it was legit."

"It wasn't legit." Bosco stared at me over the roof of the car.

"How could I be so stupid?" I wailed. Bosco shrugged.

"That's how he found you. Probably a simple tracking device in the box." He pulled out his phone and hit a few buttons. "You didn't open the package?"

"I picked up a pile of stuff from my desk and tossed it into the back seat before I met you. What're you doing?"

"Calling someone I know at 33 Division. The office is down the way."

My stomach clenched. "Geez."

"For sure. Ginger's on the harassment but this is different. Mitch has gone over the edge." He vibrated outrage. "Coming at you like that. Where you work. Where we work." He tilted the flashlight, illuminating the windshield. "'Look out' is a threat. And not the first. Come on." We speed-walked to Bosco's vehicle. "I need your license and registration."

He lined up my documents on the dashboard, killed the headlights and hit the door-lock button. That turned my guts to water. He pressed the phone to his ear.

"Good evening. Duty Officer, please." After a few beats, he said in a hearty voice, "Dingo my man. Bosco Poon." He chuckled ruefully. "Workin' harder now than when I wore the blue and gold, but lovin' every minute. Listen, I got something for you." In three minutes, he detailed the Mitch back story, described the vandalism to my vehicle and gave my vehicle information. I sat shivering in the dark trying to breathe quietly. "Yeah, a colleague. We've been working a P.I. case in the neighborhood for a couple hours." He listened some more then said, "Yeah, sure," and clicked off.

"Dingo said it's a slow night. He'll send a couple of Forensics Analysts in Training to have a look. He says he wants 'em to get their feet wet." His chuckle had an old-guy edge to it.

"Thanks, Bosco," I said in a small voice, pressing my arms tight across my chest. He patted my forearm. "Dingo?"

"Danny Dinsdale. Great guy. Long story. From FBI Academy days." I knew that was all the biographical information I was going to get for the time being. "They'll have your car towed to the evidence garage. Takes maybe a week for them to be done. I'll drive you home. Pick you up in the morning."

"Do you think it's safe for me to go home?"

"Ya. If he had your home address, he'd have been harassing you there long ago."

"Um, okay. I appreciate the ride. I have chocolate chip cookies."

"No thanks. Audrey has me eating clean. I don't know how much longer I can hold out without beer and inferno wings."

"Wait a minute." I rooted around in my wallet and held up a business card. "A service can take me home and pick me up. Save you the drive. Get you home to your Sweetie sooner."

"Manny's?"

"Yes." He needed no persuasion. "Listen, Partner. That text message that spooked me? It was your pal, Perry."

"Yeah? And?" Bosco said, wide-eyed.

A glow of satisfaction warmed my face. "I know how to find out where Mitch has been living."

35

*B*eing chauffeured to and from work was luxurious, but not having my own vehicle was a loss of independence I found hard to get used to.

Bosco assured me I was special. How many non-suspects had four detectives working on cases they were involved in? That didn't do much for my ego, though. What helped was the sense I was getting close to closing the Bernards investigation. Instead of being fixated on finding evidence, I was at the stage of having to analyze the wheelbarrow load of stuff I'd already collected.

I spent the next couple of days at my long work table with a fan of reports spread in front of me, trying not to fry my brains with thoughts of revenge or get side-tracked fantasizing about Jake working on the other side of our shared door. As I was packing up to leave Wednesday evening, he wandered in and pulled up a chair.

"I got a call from Mr. Nordstrom. Weekends and time zones don't mean anything to them."

"Uh huh."

"They're quite pleased with the quality of candidates you've vetted for them. Those were his words. He said they'd included a couple of ringers – people with fake credentials. You rejected them and your reports made it clear why."

"Didn't they trust me?"

"Don't get huffy. That's not unusual–testing the testers. What was more interesting is, he's formally invited you to spend three weeks in their office to get acquainted with their operations."

"In Sweden?"

"No, head office is in Brussels. For tax reasons."

"When?"

"In the spring. It'll be a great learning experience."

"How come they didn't ask you?"

"I've been there already. Plus, I'll have my daughter's wedding to get ready for, remember? What, you don't like the idea? Bosco's spent time in Germany and Italy doing the same thing. Three of the other investigators have gone on orientations. You're not doing anything new. Seta will make the arrangements when the time comes. What are you thinking?"

That I'm tired of not knowing if we're going to have a 'thing' or not, you and I. That I have no patience for a long, tantalizing courtship, if that's what the hell this hot then cool bullshit is about. How I'd love to spend three weeks of days and nights in Europe with you.

I shrugged, examining my nails then my palms. They were rough from gardening. If I wasn't going to get sweaty with Jake, then a hot wax treatment and a few sessions with Obi would have to do.

"Can I brief you and Bosco on Friday? It's about Bernards. An interesting side case that got resolved."

"Sure. Anything else?"

Instead of stepping off the metaphorical ledge and asking what he was doing on the weekend, I said, "Not really."

We sat in silence for a few minutes, listening to the crack and pop of the air ducts, then he uncrossed his legs and left.

* * *

"Methinks you need some Italian soul food," Bosco said the next morning as he lounged in my visitor's chair. "You're looking peaked. Plus, we need to celebrate."

"How come?"

"The woman I adore is having my child. You're getting into the groove, so I want to, you know," he said, making air brackets, "honor that."

"Such a nice guy."

"Yeah, I know. Got some business to do, too. Jake said I could take the Lexus. Let's go."

He took Avenue Road to the 401 west, then drove north on Highway 400 then east on Highway 7.

"Wow," I said. "We're doing the buffet at Ikea, big spender?"

"Smart ass."

He pulled into a spot in front of an auto detailing shop and Di Cecco Bakery. When he swung open the door, the scent of bread and home cooking drew me in. Almost every table was filled with guys straight out of an Italian men's club. The noise level from ringing cell phones, loud chatter and the clank of cutlery on thick china was ear-numbing. A thin, nervous-looking woman shuffling a wad of credit card receipts at the counter looked up. She threw down the papers and rushed up to Bosco with her arms open wide.

"Senor Bosco. Finally, you come to visit."

"It's been a long time, Alda." He introduced me.

She gave me a hug and said, "Tedesco. A good Italian name. Come. I cook for you."

I knew that meant no menu. By the end of the meal I'd have to unbutton the waistband of my pants so that I could struggle out of the chair. She tucked her hand into the crook of Bosco's arm and led us behind the gleaming food service counters.

"Sit, sit." She pulled two chairs away from one of four white-clothed tables tucked into an alcove in the open kitchen. She thrust her chin at me and said, "My son got in with a bad crowd after my husband died," making a rapid sign of the cross then touching her forefinger to her lips. "Paolo was in jeopardy but this policeman here, he talked sense into him. Got him to stop hanging out with those *caffone*." She pushed away Bosco's hand when he tried to wave her off.

I had a rough idea how Bosco would have talked sense into her son. Alda and Bosco flung themselves into a high-speed exchange in Italian with enough hand gestures and facial expressions for a theatrical. She caught my puzzlement and apologized.

"We're going too fast for you?" I nodded. "He opened his own business next door. The car place. He owns this whole plaza now," she said. "You have kids? Yeah, so you understand."

I asked for a glass of ice water. Alda pulled a chef's apron off a hook by the door and said, "You're not watching your diet, are you?"

She didn't wait for an answer. Even if I'd said yes it wouldn't have made one iota of difference. This was an Italian kitchen. I was half Italian, but Bosco? A thin waiter in a long apron slipped plates of antipasti in front of us.

"I should jog first. This reminds me of Sundays at my dad's cousin's table."

He tucked his napkin into the front of his shirt and laughed. "The *piatti*'ll just keep on comin', darlin'. Undo your belt and drink some more wine."

"I didn't know you were fluent in Italian."

"No biggie. My dad was Armed Forces, then he served with NATO. We were posted to northern Italy twice."

In the back of the kitchen, a metal door banged open then slammed shut, followed by a heated exchange of rapid Italian. A minute later a barrel on legs sporting a Hawaiian shirt over tan dress pants lumbered to our table. The man had a head shaped like an eggplant, short gelled hair, undersized features and oversized capped teeth.

Bosco gave him a tight nod. "Paulie. How you been?"

I flashed on one of my mother's oft-repeated expressions, 'he's got a face that only a mother could love'. It struck me that Paulie's would be a hard face to love even for a doting mother like Alda.

"Not too bad, not too bad. Ma said I should come pay my respects." His voice was as hard as his eyes. "Been keepin' my nose clean, workin' hard."

"Good, good. Makes your mama happy; keeps me happy."

"Heard you was looking for some guy. Mitch."

"Yeah."

"While back, he upgraded my inventory control systems, installed some new servers. He's was livin' at a farm off Keele Street just north of here but he's moved to Upper Buttplug or somewheres by Lake Simcoe. Brought one of his cars in for bodywork and detailing."

"What kind of car?" I tried to keep the excitement out of my voice.

He turned his back on me and answered Bosco. "Hemi orange. Told him he shoulda done it in Delft blue. Want me to buzz you when he's comin' by for the pick up?"

"Appreciate that, Paulie. The tax man's interested in him."

Paulie's swarthy skin paled. I couldn't help myself. "How come you're telling Bosco about Mitch?"

"You ride the short bus, Lady?" he snarled then stomped away, muttering in Italian. Unfortunately for my self-esteem, I understood what he said.

"I told you not to do that, didn't I?" Bosco smacked his palm against his forehead. "What he just did's called paying down the debt. He owes me. He owes Mehran nothing so it's no skin to give him up. Besides, for a guy in his line of work, someone who's wanted by RevCan is toxic." He sighed heavily. "If I was feeling more inquisitive or if Paulie hadn't been forthcoming, I'd call York Regional's Auto Theft guys in to have a look around his shop."

"With his mother next door, how much bad can he get into?"

Bosco swiped the last piece of focaccia bread through a puddle of olive oil and reduced balsamic vinegar.

"When people say, 'I know a guy' who can... whatever? Paulie's 'the guy'. He has no boundaries for whatever."

"Maybe I can get him to take care of Mitch?"

"That would be a final solution. But sure, I could ask."

I pushed away my plate of *calamari all'ortolano*. How many more chances would I get to be alone like this with Bosco? It was now or not for a long time.

"You know, Bosco, I have feelings for Jake."

As if he hadn't heard me, he kept forking his *carpaccio del Bosco* into his mouth and chewing appreciatively. He poured a glass of *Vietti 'Scarrone' Barbera d'Alba* 2003, took a long sip then carefully placed it beside his empty plate. He gave me a speculative look.

"My name isn't Abby and I'm not your girlfriend, so I won't be giving you advice or permission."

"I know it's probably not a good idea, him being the boss and all. But what do you think?"

"Kenora, Jake and I were partners for a lot of years."

"So that means you're not saying?"

"No, it means if you want to know something about him, ask him outright. I said that before. If he doesn't want to tell you, he'll say so."

"All right. It's just that.... You know I was married a long time. Burned by that *coglione infedeli*."

He smirked, "I know guys married and divorced three, four times during your tenure. But Jake, no. He was married. Made me glad when he wasn't any more. She was one fucked-up crazy woman."

"He's sort of a loner, isn't he?"

"I'd call it self-contained. That will change, when he's ready."

"When might that be?"

He shrugged. "He'll tell you the truth, so make sure you're prepared." I opened my mouth to speak but he forestalled me. "Can we change the subject? Finish our meal in peace?"

36

Today would be my day to shine. Bosco gave me a thumbs up. He and Jake lounged in their boardroom chairs with fresh mugs of coffee and a wedge of the chocolate zucchini cake I'd brought in. All was right with the world.

I held up my red lanyard with a white plastic photo-identification card attached and a blue rectangle the size of a package of gum.

"There's a radio transmitter in the access card to control access. I've got the tracking records and I've had a couple meetings with the head of security, a guy named John Phlashter."

"Oh, no." Jake guffawed, then wiped cake from his chin. "Medium build, moon face, jug ears?"

"Yes. Why?"

Bosco grinned. "He retired out of Metro a couple of years ago. Not the sharpest knife in the drawer. We used to call him Jumpy Jack Flash. When he was about five years in, he got into a scuffle with a druggie. Guy grabbed his Glock and figured out how to flip the safety and pull the trigger. Luckily for Jumpy, there wasn't a round in the chamber. He came back from stress leave a hard-core Christian. He'd pray over suspects, minister to the working boys and girls."

Did every ex-copper have such rich back stories?

"He's been helpful. The woman who does the heavy lifting is Minnie. Couple of weeks after I moved in, she started dropping by the upstairs office to brainstorm with Gavin and me. They had a problem with pilferage of men's suits. We're talking $2,500 to $5,500 a unit." I did an air-pump. "We solved it."

"How?" Bosco said.

"Surveillance video review, my good man." He snorted. I pressed my laptop and the projector blinked to life. "They have security cameras everywhere except the washrooms and change rooms.

It was an Eastern European gang of eight - teams of two men and a woman, usually. They'd change their appearance, go to different sales people, rotate among the store exits. They had a decoy, a blond with big...um...boobs. The guys would buy a coat or jacket that came in a garment bag. Then they'd do a 'switch and confuse' routine, boost a few more expensive items and put them in the bag with the legitimate purchase. Blondie would quietly pay for a scarf in the women's department."

Jake broke in. "What about the security tags?"

"Ah, I'm getting to that. One of her accomplices would steal an identical scarf and pass it off to her. The three of them would go through the exit at the same time. Of course they'd set off the alarm because thief number two and three were carrying stolen clothing hidden in plain sight in garment bags. Blondie would stumble into one of them just outside the security posts. When the security guy came to check things out she'd go into damsel-in-distress mode, fumble the package containing the stolen scarf from her bag and hand over the receipt. They'd assume the person ringing up the sale forgot to take off the security tag."

"Holy macaroni." Bosco shook his head in disgust.

"The security tags are worth about $500 a pop. Bernards

was losing a dozen of those a month, so that added up. Most of the goods were sold on line or from those open-Saturday-gone-by-Monday outlets. I helped Minnie write up the report for Metro. Along with the videos, it's pretty much a slam dunk."

Boy, had I come a long way from my first sweaty-palmed job interview with Jake Barclay. Bosco stretched out his hand and we did a fist-bump.

"I'm going to give this some thought," he said. "I'll text you. No. Let's meet day after tomorrow."

"Have you talked to Gavin lately?" I said.

"Why?"

"On your advice, I've been staying away from Bernards. He sends me the stuff I ask for but whenever I try to coordinate a visit, he's off doing something else. Feels like he's being evasive."

"Nah. You worry too much."

Maybe, but Bosco wouldn't look me in the eye. What the hell were they up to?

* * *

At the top of my in-basket was the daily news folder. I flipped through clippings about mortgage frauds, phishing scams and run-of-the-mill bad behavior. Underneath was a blue slipcase holding three pieces of the buff paper Seta used in the fax machine.

READ THIS had been scrawled on the transmittal sheet under the name and phone number of my contact in Paris. On the reports he'd obviously screen-printed from online newspapers, he'd underlined a few phrases.

<u>Unidentified Body Washed Ashore</u>

A body was pulled from the sea by a Sunday fisherman at Logaros beach south east of Paros. It was caught on the rocks and partially submerged.

"I thought it was an animal," Petros Kousas told this reporter. "When I saw the underwear and jewelry I knew it was a man."

The victim is a Caucasian male in his mid-forties. Police sources speculate that the man may have struck his head before toppling into the sea. The body has been transported to Athens for autopsy.

The second printout was much the same. I leaned back, popped a kink out of my spine then tossed the folder into my briefcase. *What am I missing?*

I re-read the clippings, did a Google search then fired off a text to Gavin. He called back in ten minutes. When I asked why he sounded so odd, he complained of laryngitis. My hand was still on the phone when it buzzed with a text from Amber.

* * *

Showtime.

There was only a slight tremor in my fingers as I saved the almost-final draft report on the Bernards investigation to Dropbox and BB&Fs server then shut down my computers.

Metro's forensics people were holding on to my car. As much as I enjoyed being treated like a celebrity, taking a limo for my commute had grown old fast. With Bosco's coaching and my sad-sack telephone story of woe, I'd browbeaten my insurance company into springing for a rental, but the damned thing was only slightly larger than a dog bed and there were no fancy features like automatic door locks or Apple Play. Sitting for more than an hour on that barely upholstered front seat turned my bum into pressed ham.

I put on my outerwear, turned off the interior office lights, slung my backpack over one shoulder, secured the back door then trudged down the steps checking email messages on my phone, loudly humming Kristina DeBarge's Goodbye and making sure to scuff my feet.

KENORA REINVENTED

The rental vehicle was parked down the lane between a rusted No Parking sign and a thicket of waist-high pylons marking a construction excavation covered loosely with plywood.

Humming louder, I kept my head down and meandered along. I knew the area well in daylight but this time of night was different. A nearby streetlight flickered like Morse code, giving the lime green trunk lid a psychedelic glow and setting misshapen shadows in motion. I looked up from my screen when something rattled nearby but kept walking. Probably a foraging raccoon. Or a clumsy bozo. Another sound, closer this time. Feet shuffling across uneven gravel. My pulse jolted.

Shifting my gaze from side to side, I held my breath, slipped the phone case strap over my wrist and stepped silently into the darker shadow of a lean-to attached to a slumping wood garage. From the stench, garbage and recycling bins were stored nearby.

A man-sized shadow crept into view down the lane. He was holding his hands ahead of his body like he was afraid of falling. The overhead light flickered to life. I caught a glimpse of his profile. My heart almost stopped.

Fingers hovering over the control buttons on my smart phone, I settled the backpack against my spine and shrank deeper into the gloom. My hip banged against a hard object. It toppled against another, setting off a noisy domino effect that sent a malodorous spew into the laneway.

He called, "come out, come out," as if we were in the middle of a game of hide-and-seek.

Maybe he was playing but I wasn't. Fucking Mitch. I was done with waiting to be victimized. This time, I was going to kick his ass but good.

Taking a step behind the stinking pile, I cried out in a frightened voice, "Is someone there? Don't hurt me." That was shamming it but I was counting on Mitch's ego to make him careless. "I'll give you my money."

He was chuckling as he moved toward the sound of my voice. Thank goodness he didn't have a flashlight. Stupid amateur. Two more steps.

"Please leave me alone."

As soon as the words left my lips, I scuttled silently to my right. Mitch lunged to where he thought I'd be. He lost his footing in a slimy puddle, windmilling his arms to keep from toppling backwards, cursing a blue streak when he dropped to one knee and caught the full aroma of whatever was seeping into his clothing. I leapt into the laneway. Crying out in simulated terror, I sprinted towards the car with the keys clutched between my fist.

"Oh no, not this time." He roared with rage, shoved upwards and lurched after me. "I got you cornered."

I pressed a combination of buttons on my phone then flung myself to solid ground at the far corner of the excavation, cowering and whimpering.

"Mitch? Is that you? Why are you doing this?"

He scrubbed his palms against his pant legs as he approached. "We're going for a ride, Rosie. Just you and me. You've been messin' in my business. That shit's over. Where's the keys?"

Pressing down on the 'record' button, I sidestepped closer to the loaner, snuffling for effect. "You can have the car."

"The keys, bitch. Quit stalling."

Acting flustered, I groped in my pockets. "Keys? Okay, okay."

Grinning, he took a few paces across the plywood. "Ima show you what you've been missing." Mumbling apologies, I edged further away. "Not so sure of yourself now, are you, Rosie? Ash told me you been twisting her arm."

Not true, but let him believe whatever made him happy. I glanced over his shoulder. A wedge of light cut through the shadows behind him then was gone. Two figures had emerged. Backs pressed to the rear walls of shadowy buildings lining the lane, they quickly closed the distance. My calf brushed the car bumper.

"Found them." I fumbled the ring of keys out of my jacket pocket, making sure to jangle them loudly. I straddled the rear quarter panel and the bumper, firming up my stance, swinging my arm from side to side like a stage hypnotist. "Here they are." Mitch's eyes followed my waving hand. "Fetch, asshole."

Mitch swung around in mid-step, automatically grabbing for the keys as they arced like a pop fly single, high and slightly off to one side. His leap propelled him near the edge of the slightly overlapping join between two pieces of plywood. The sole of his lead foot must have been wet because it scissored upwards while the other shot off to the side, sending him to the boards with a hard thump.

I reached into my jacket for a flashlight. Amber and Wolfette huffed up, each holding a high-powered LED lantern. Handcuffs glinted from their belts.

"You okay, Kenora?"

"Much better now."

In the unrelenting blue-white glare of our torches, Mitch thrashed about like a bug caught in pine gum, uttering threats, cursing that his new gear was ruined and whining for help. As we watched, the gap between the boards sagged wider. He scrabbled wildly in the air then belly-flopped into the hole with a splash.

"It's not that deep," I called out, not bothering to hide the glee in my voice, "but you won't be able to get out without a ladder. You fell into my trap."

Mitch's hollow voice cried, "Get me outta here."

I swept up a handful of gravel and tossed it into the hole. "Put a sock in it, Mitch."

"Police brutality. You're violating my Charter rights."

Wolfette made a moue of sympathy then said to no one in

particular, "If we were still in uniform we'd have to drag him out. Effect a rescue."

Amber grinned. "But we're not, so we won't."

"Hey." I leaned far enough over so he could see my face. "Who's gonna pump air in your tires now, Mitch?"

There was a moment of fraught silence, then a gasp followed by frantic splashing and an anguished roar.

"You? That was you sending me those messages? I can't fucking believe it." He jumped. One fist then the other poked briefly above the lip.

"Believe it." He let loose a torrent of cursing more energetic than imaginative.

I said to my colleagues, "I think we've just heard wailing and gnashing of teeth."

At the end of the lane, the blue-red-white strobes of a cruiser criss-crossed the darkness.

"Metro's here, Mitch. Save your energy," Amber said. "When they're done, York Regional has first dibs on your ass."

"Anyone else at the Big House?" I said, glancing over my shoulder, half-expecting a large masculine shape to materialize.

"Just us Mamacitas on night watch," Amber said. "Pipes is snoozing before his stakeout."

"Talk about a bad smell," Wolfette muttered, wrinkling her nose. "He thought he'd get away with it." We fist-bumped.

"After the threatening note and the number he did on my old car, we figured he'd try something desperate." I raised my voice. "Mitch, your ride is here."

The Metro cruiser braked beside my rental in a spray of gravel. Two burly men stepped out and tipped their hats to us.

"Ladies. Slow night?"

"The usual. Your passenger is in there," Wolfette said, hooking a thumb at the now-silent hole.

When the officers had pulled Mitch out and handcuffed him, I pressed a speed-dial button. "I'd better tell Bosco."

"Super's back tomorrow," Amber said in a singsong voice, slanting a glance at me. "Can't wait to tell him Ms. Intrepid bested the imbecile."

"Ms. Intrepid?" I said.

The two women high-fived each other and caught me in a hug. Amber said, "Yep, Girlfriend, you've earned your nickname. Have to live up to it, too."

We were doing a happy dance in the parking lot behind the office when my phone vibrated with two text messages.

The first, from Bosco, read: 'Fucking A. See you in the morning.'

I turned aside to read the second, from Jake: 'Kenora, good job. I'm so proud of you.'

37

The next big surprise was waiting for me in the boardroom when I arrived to deliver my briefing the following morning. I gasped when Gavin turned to face me. A livid scar dotted with suture marks snaked from the center of his forehead through his eyebrow to just below his right ear. His jaw was mottled yellow from a fading, shoe-shaped bruise.

"So that's why you've been avoiding me. What the hell happened?"

He looked stricken. I clasped his hand and glared accusingly at Bosco.

"He didn't want to worry you. Come on. Sit down. I got coffee."

Seta knocked on the door jamb and stuck her head in.

"Call for you, Kenora."

"Can it wait?"

"It's Detective Sergeant Kobinski. She said, right now."

I hadn't heard from Ginger for weeks. The episode in the lane would have given her a bucketload of evidence against my stalker. I turned to Jake.

"Put her through, Seta. We might as well all hear what she

has to say."

Seta must have warned Ginger she'd be on speaker phone because after we all said hello she switched to her cop voice, all cool and official-sounding.

"Hello, gentlemen. Ms. Intrepid." I winced. The cop grapevine worked faster than I expected. "I have good news for you, Kenora. We've collected Mitch from Metro. They'll follow up on the insurance fraud beef, but it's not as compelling as assault, threatening or criminal harassment. The information you ladies provided last night was icing on the cake. Hooking me up with Ayashe, Mitch's girlfriend—well, she was the glue that held the other pieces together."

I let out a whoop. "When? Where?"

"Vice and Drugs did a raid on what they believed was an illegal betting den in Pefferlaw. Turns out it was Mitch's hidey-hole, ops center and a bawdy house."

"They still call them 'bawdy houses'?" I said.

"Yup. They rounded up four guys and six women. Two are juveniles, so we're looking at human trafficking, too. Ugly business, that. Mitch was webmaster for all the operations."

"There's no way he can claim plausible deniability?" I said.

Ginger chuckled. "Nope. Remember when Steve Mercer said Mitch was 'in the wind'? Turns out we almost had him. He'd dropped by to collect his fee for services rendered and there was a dispute about payment terms, followed by a lot of yelling and banging around. A neighbor called 9-1-1 and mentioned there might be guns on the premises. ETF attended but before they were set up, Mitch caught the action on the surveillance cameras he'd installed at the front gate. He bolted to the jetty and rowed himself to the Government Dock.

His friends gave him up though and he was on the run until last night. The arresting officers ran the names, and Mitch's reports and wants popped up. I got the call because I'd authored an outstanding warrant for him."

"Great bad timing." I laughed from sheer relief. Jake and Bosco peppered her with questions.

"He's been remanded into custody. Since he skipped out on the CRA, there'll be no bail. Turns out he's also claustrophobic. You know how small the interview rooms are in 3 District? He freaked out when we left him for a while to contemplate his future. Started singing like a— like a canary. If he doesn't plead out, you'll have to testify at trial, Kenora." She paused, then said, "You okay?"

"Excellent. Amber Donavon and Wolfette—MaryAnn Spencer—responded when I hit the emergency beacon on my phone. Luckily, I wasn't far from the back door. Apparently, he's been stalking me here for a while. Thought I'd be easy pickings. Buck Tooey caught that when he reviewed BB&Fs perimeter surveillance tapes."

"Time to thin the herd," she said, and hung up.

"God," I said, "What a relief."

Jake leaned forward with his hands clasped on the table. "Not just a relief. It got finished because you planned a good takedown, Kenora."

I blinked back tears. Instead of answering, I said, "Bosco, next time you see Perry, go easy, okay?"

"Yeah, he told me after you did. Just in case, you know, something happened."

"The little weasel. He's not loyal to anyone, is he?"

"Nope."

Gavin had been sitting half-turned away from the table. I got up and pulled a chair beside him. He turned away. I tugged at his wrist then let go when he winced.

"What happened to your face?" He slowly rotated his chair. Although they'd faded, I could clearly see a thickened bump at the bridge of his nose and the diagonal cross-hatched scars above his eyebrow and at his hairline. "Shit. Someone beat you up."

"First time was about three weeks ago, just after the fire, in the passageway to the loading docks."

"Three weeks? Where the hell was I?"

Bosco gave me The Look. "In Halton, at the Advanced Interrogation course."

"I had a box of printouts in my hands," Gavin continued. "Wasn't paying attention. Someone shoved me from behind. I bashed my shoulder on the concrete wall but otherwise, I was okay."

"You told me you slipped stepping out of a hot tub." My eyes followed Gavin's as he glanced at his co-conspirators across the table. "Keeping secrets, gentlemen?" Jake shrugged.

"Didn't want to bother you. I hear you've already got a full plate."

"That's why you've been avoiding me." I rounded on Bosco, who was studiously avoiding my eyes. He must have been the one to drop a dime about Mitch's harassment because I certainly hadn't.

Gavin's grimace was lopsided, as if his lips were out of sync. "You wouldn't tell me, so I asked. Sorry." He took a cautious sip of his coffee. "The next time was three days after Bosco dropped by."

Bosco said, "He had the presence of mind to call me. I still had your security stuff so I let myself in to Bernards and limped him to Emerg at St. Mike's."

"The nurses recognized Mr. Poon from the old days so I didn't have to wait long. I'd been working late. Someone jumped me in the stairwell. Put the boots to me." He tilted his head to one side so I could see the lump under his chin. "Before my lights went out, I grabbed his leg and saw his shoes. I'm pretty sure it was Pepper. He favors poop-colored designer loafers with long square toes."

"What a chickenshit thing to do," I muttered. "Where's Pepper now?"

"Flown. I took a tour of his office the next night," Bosco said. "Cleaned out. Gavin and I went back on the weekend with a van and a couple of our colleagues. Took the liberty of packing up your offices. Left 'em clean as a baby's cheek. Tim, the Scenes of Crimes guy, videotaped your walls of evidence before we took them down. Gavin's put in his notice. He won't be going back and neither will you."

"Wait a minute." I pulled out the clipping and handed it to Jake. "This, and what I'm going to show you, are the final links. I was working on them last night before the Mitch thing. Get a load of this."

I handed out copies of my reports and set up my LCD projector and digital recorder.

"Obviously, what I took to be Martin blustering during our first meeting was real. Day after Bosco did his walkabout, Mr. Bernard appeared at our office door." Jake looked surprised. I poked Gavin's arm. "You almost had a coronary."

"Right. He never even walks the shop floor. I knew something was up."

"Martin was as oily-polite as ever. We tried to put him off, deflect the conversation, but he reminded us he was the client and stomped into my office. When he saw every wall covered in colored paper, the arrows we'd drawn linking clues, all the photocopies, he was shocked. Spent twenty minutes walking from one end to the other, reading everything. Then he plunked himself at my desk and was very insistent about being briefed."

Gavin sighed. "I tried to skim him through an overview, but...."

"The man asked specific questions about specific pieces of evidence we'd collected," I said. "We responded but resisted giving him more details. My point was that we weren't finished our investigation and premature disclosures might prejudice the outcomes. Lead to him jumping to unfounded conclusions."

Bosco leaned forward. "But they weren't unfounded."

"No. We knew by then who had done what and when, but not why. We know that now, too."

Gavin hobbled to the wall and leaned against it. "He's going to exact revenge on whoever's left or whoever he can get his hands on."

"If he hasn't already." I held up the newspaper clippings. "I suggest you ask Seta to invoice him ASAP, Jake. How close are you to Martin?"

"Martin? We're not close at all. Why?"

"Good. You'll see in a minute. Gavin, you start."

"Marius and Pepper were doing the equivalent of check-kiting, but with credit cards. They had two sets with different Bank Identification Numbers—the first 6 digits. One set was issued in Canada and one in France. The Air France Platinum card Pepper used doesn't have a PIN chip."

I said, "Do you know they call the chip *la puce*—flea? I called the call issuer and spoke to the Account Development Manager who, by the way, didn't bother to check my credentials."

Bosco grinned. "You're getting good at this aren't you?"

"I had a great teacher, Sir. What you're going to hear now is the man I tracked down at Maison Couture, in France. He sent a raft of incriminating documents. I recorded our Skype conversation but not the video." When Jake raised one eyebrow, I added, "He looked...bad. Broken. Barely holding it together. I decided that you not seeing him wouldn't make what he has to say any more or less believable."

A reedy man with delicate features, blue Harold Lloyd spectacles and thinning hair, Clément Léglise had been nervous as a cornered rabbit. From time to time, he'd taken out a handkerchief and wiped his eyes and I'd waited for him to compose himself. I pressed 'play' on my digital recorder.

A hesitant voice speaking heavily accented English said, "I heard from an acquaintance at Bernards in Canada about the stir your work has been causing. Someone tried to injure you with a ladder, no? And a fire?"

"That took me aback," I said. "I'd told no one aside from Minnie, you three and the police. The details could only have been shared by the person who bonked me over the head and defaced my belly."

"I am responsible for internal financial audits," Clement said. "A year ago, I became curious about regular large deposits between Crédit Assurance, Maison Couture's regular bank and a financial institution in India called The Protestant Prefect Bank of Kottayam. I found a pattern of odd transactions approved by Pierre Giroux."

"Odd? Why?" I sounded stern.

Clément had tilted his head and smiled. "Is it not odd that the Maison Couture's Directeur paid invoices for Amex purchases made in Europe by Pepper Doane and Marius Lambert? I would imagine that since they are executives of Bernards, they already would have expense accounts there, no? Are you aware that Berthi Giroux used to be Loading Dock Foreman in Paris and then the production assistant at Maison Couture's prêt-à-porter manufacturing facility in Thailand? She was Martin Bernard's protégé for a time."

"Yes, about the invoices. No, about Berthi in Thailand."

"She's Pierre's ex-wife, not his sister," Clément had said. "You see, Pierre is a homosexual. I heard she didn't want to play the beard in a front marriage."

"Being gay in the fashion business isn't news."

He barked out a laugh. "Don't I know that?"

"Were you aware Pepper Doane, the Vice President of Purchasing and Inventory was involved with Berthi?" I said.

"Sexually? Yes. She wanted a child, nothing more."

"I've discovered that Pepper and Marius are also partners in a logistics company that manages the shipments from Paris to Canada," I said. He'd nodded. "How does Marius Lambert fit in?"

"He and Pierre both were...involved."

"Involved?" I'd let the question hang, but he hadn't responded. "Aside from your professional interest, how are <u>you</u> involved, Clément?""

"Pierre and I were lovers. From when we were boarders at the Académie des Beaux-Arts. Before, during and after his marriage to Berthi."

My aha-light went off. Pierre's marriage of convenience to Berthi hadn't been important but when Marius entered the domestic picture, the equation changed. "And you want to unburden yourself?"

He'd stared intently into his computer camera. "As you can see, I am not robust. My ability to wreak physical havoc is limited. Even after I suspected what was going on, I protected Pierre at Maison Couture. Covered up his carelessness and excused his greed. He deceived me. Simply put, Madame, I am a vengeful *pédé*."

The deception followed the classic Greek tragedy meme. Clement had been in Bruges visiting his sick mother. Pierre, his ride from the airport, was a no-show.

"When was the last time he disappeared?"

"About two years ago, during Fashion Week. He developed a mad passion for some young African *pousse-crotte*. He came crawling back to me with intense contrition and a venereal disease."

"But you knew this time was different?"

"You know that feeling you get that no one is coming home?" I did indeed. "The houseplants we'd bought were all gone. There was a note to the *femme de ménage* saying that he did not need her services for several months. I searched the apartment. Inside a magazine by the bedsite table, I found receipts for two tickets from Paris to Athens, first class. For Pierre Giroux and Marius Lambert."

"You knew Marius?"

"Of course. The three of us sometimes had an aperitif when he was in Paris."

We sat listening to Clément's quiet weeping. He blew his nose and continued. "He was to visit the atelier two days after I first spoke with you. He did not appear. I was such a *tapette*. The matching bracelets should have given away their game."

"Bracelets?"

I switched off the recorder and held up a color photo of the titanium, black carbon and stainless steel forever bracelet I'd noticed on Marius' wrist the first time we met. "The newspaper reports refer to a designer bracelet."

Jake said, "That's pure gold."

"Sad. Clément couriered copies of bank statements, credit card invoices, waybill reconciliations, shipping records–the works. We're almost positive Pierre Giroux was the ringleader because he controlled inventory labelling and shipping documentation. Marius and Pepper were co-conspirators keeping the scam wheels greased at Bernards, with the help of a few low-level players on the Loading Dock. Have you heard from Martin? I've left messages with Eleanor but a veil of silence has descended."

Jake didn't look worried.

"It's not unusual," Bosco said, "when a client gets news he'd rather not have."

"My sense is, he suspected what was happening. After he saw what Gavin and I had collected, and even with the skimpy information we gave him, he drew his own conclusions."

"Yeah," Gavin said, "he couldn't ignore it. Like a bad boyfriend scenario, if you get my drift."

"Keeping with the bad boyfriend analogy." I held up the clipping. "I'm pretty sure the body is Marius. There must have been a falling out."

"Or," Gavin said, "Pierre was greedier than even Clément thought."

"Martin?" Jake said.

I shrugged. "He worked fast. Two days after Gavin and I spoke to him, there was an announcement about a new *directeur* to replace Pierre."

"Is that why Pepper tried to take me out?" Gavin looked horrified.

Bosco tsked, tsked. "Coulda been worse."

"That's not very comforting. I called Bernards' travel agent in Toronto, pretending I was from Martin's office." Bosco gave me a thumbs' up. "The agent confirmed that before he traveled to Greece, Marius had flown from Toronto to Thailand. Medical tourism.

That's a distinctive bracelet. Marius wore one as did Pierre, but Pierre hadn't travelled to Thailand for plastic surgery. The scars and residual suture marks on his face were partly healed from a surgical procedure.

The follow-up news report from the Greek authorities was that Marius had water in his lungs. Aside from being beaten up on the rocks, he'd suffered a blow to the base of the skull."

"He was deliberately bumped off." Bosco's tone was matter-of-fact.

Gavin said, "He had to know we were getting close so he bolted. If Kenora could find out Marius' itinerary, surely Martin could. Plus, he had the inside scoop on Pierre Giroux."

"Bosco," I said, "I need you to contact one of your police buddies in Interpol and see if you can get some identifying details about the body that washed up. Perhaps nudge them in the right direction?"

He jumped up and rubbed his hands together. "Guy I used to work with is an attaché with the Canadian Embassy in Athens."

Nothing like fresh quarry to get my partner on point.

"Two more things."

38

I clicked on a graphic of a much-enlarged photo of an oblong cartouche attached horizontally to a gold band.

"It's an Eye of Horus, a symbol of well-being and protection against evil. I figure it was Marius tried to trip me down the stairs. He drew the crude rendition on my belly in an attempt to scare me off. Minnie confirmed his security card was used that evening to access the doors to the mezzanine and to enter the unused service stairs to the back exit. Remember I said there was an odd smell before I tripped?"

Bosco snorted. "The combo of gym socks, flowers and stale beer?"

"It was his custom-blended French cologne."

"What about Pierre?"

"The Hellenic Police have classified him as a person of interest. I haven't heard anything about Pepper."

Bosco slapped his notebook shut and said, "That's good stuff."

"After we spoke, I arranged for Clément to visit a notary and be deposed. His statements were couriered to Seta, just in case. Should I send something to the authorities in Greece?"

Bosco exchanged a glance with Jake. "Let me follow up on that."

"The good guys didn't win, did we?"

"It's not about winning," Jake said, pushing back from the table. "Our job was to find out who was stealing from Bernards. You and Gavin did that. We can still try to schedule a final formal debrief with Martin, but the ball's in his court."

Gavin and I had both been attacked. We'd done a cart-load of research. Talk about ending with a whimper and not a bang. I slumped against the back of my chair, too disappointed to be angry.

"Crap. This is like trying to eat candy through a pane of glass."

He shrugged. "Happens. We've got new cases waiting. And you're going to spend time in Brussels with GMC."

"What about Pepper and Giroux? Can't we do something?"

"Like what?"

"I don't know. Call Interpol, brace Martin."

Gavin spoke up. "I expected the end result would be more satisfying."

"Listen, folks. We've done what we could for our client, which was to find the thieves," Jake said with finality. "The disappearances are out of our jurisdiction. Bosco will do his thing. In the meantime, finish your reports."

"No charges?" I persisted.

Bosco said, "This is small cheese. The thefts were internal. They're covered by insurance. The perpetrators have fled. Unless there's drugs or firearms involved, it'll be hard to stir up much interest here."

Gavin handed out another report. His right eye drooped but he soldiered on. I was bone tired. "We're almost done."

"Every couple of shipments there's a dummy bill of lading

with fake bar codes attached. Kenora mentioned no one does manual inventory counts? This con works because once the bill is swiped at the loading dock, it's as if the product was actually received. There may have been a full pallet of boxes, but a percentage of them were light-packed."

"'Light-packed'?"

"It's an old scam," Gavin said. "The outside of the box says forty-eight units but a lesser number is shipped and the space is stuffed with tissue paper."

Bosco eyed me appraisingly. I fiddled with the controls for my laptop and started a video recording the Loading Dock Foreman's ministrations with the code reader.

"Scanning bogus bar codes for electronic inventory works in their favor because there's no manual count to contradict their reports. The phantom goods never got to the sales floor, but the inflated invoice amounts were remitted to the supplier."

"How did you two figure that out?"

I piped up, "Shipping weights. Once Gavin rooted around the computer and charted weigh scale data and received goods weight, the pattern of variances was obvious. About one in every four shipments had been short-weighted."

"Why wouldn't the boxes get filled with heavier paper?"

"I don't think the bad guys cared," I said. "The major players controlled the supply chain. Even if the documentation was fake, the weight numbers didn't lie. Bernards was paying as if the full shipment had been received."

Jake frowned. "How come no one in charge noticed the discrepancy between sales, inventory and goods ordered?"

"Laziness. Criminal intent. A bit of both? The store's Divisions are compartmentalized. If sales were down, they blamed it on the economy or pilferage. No one did regular reconciliations."

"What next?"

"Complete the case file and send it to the authorities. I

touched base with my friend Jerry from Canada Revenue. He's checking into whether Bernards evaded paying duties and taxes on the full value of goods being imported. Of course, the conspirators didn't disclose their incomes."

Jake said, "Good work. Ask Jerry to notify Canada Border Services. They'll figure out who they're going after."

He stood and stretched. I stared at the line of dark fuzz above the waistband of his trouser as his polo shirt rode up. Bosco poked me on the arm, grinned and shook his head.

What Bosco didn't know what that Jake and I had a date. Partly work, but I considered it a date

39

My little black dress was actually a deep burgundy, elbow-length crepe wrap dress Maggie had picked up for me years before at Harrod's. It had always been too grand for faculty-staff parties at my old job. The pencil silhouette and semi-plunging neckline made me long for a jacket but I was still thin, I had nice breasts, the hem covered my knees and there were no unwanted bulges to make me self-conscious.

I'd fluffed my curls on top but brushed my hair smooth on the sides to show off the antique gold, enamel and pearl drop earrings my mother had left me. The pale strands at my temples showed too, but I didn't care because I looked fashionable and was damned happy.

When I sent Maggie-the-fashion-consultant a selfie of me in full makeup, tasteful jewelry and black suede Ferragamo pearl-heeled sandals, she'd called right away. She'd burst into tears, whispering, "It's about time someone treated you as you deserve."

When I stepped from my office into the hallway to meet Jake

at the front door, his eyes opened wide. He'd mimed a wolf-whistle and said, "Wow. I should have got you a corsage."

I took one look at him and wanted nothing but to take his clothes off.

He was dashing in a single-breasted charcoal and merlot wool and silk Ermenegildo Zegna suit over a pearl grey shirt and burgundy silk floral tie.

I knew those details because at Jake's invitation, I'd lounged in a plush arm chair in the Private Client Room at Harry Rosen one afternoon while he tried on sports jackets, trousers and shoes. We'd been as comfortable as if clothes-shopping was something we did all the time. He'd screwed up his face when I selected a pair of brown Berlin wingtip brogues. When I drooled over a pair of Boss Woven Leather Wingtip Derbies, he'd reluctantly agreed to step out of his comfort zone. My jaw had dropped when the sales associate totted up the bill and I heard the murmured total. Jake hadn't blinked.

Manny dropped us off at the National Club on Bay Street. The Rooftop Lounge was crammed with an assortment of folks in designer duds trying to look important and not doing that good a job of it. I'd stepped in puddles deeper than some of those people but that didn't matter. I was working the crowd with Jake, schmoozing prospective and long-term clients and having a great time sipping Prosecco and being admired.

We were lined up at the buffet table layering charcuterie, pickles and savory pastries onto tiny plates. I motioned with my chin in the direction of an ornamental palm across the room. A pale, square-faced woman leaned against the wall. I'd made her for a cop. Her restless eyes scanned the room but returned to us often enough to be noticed.

"Who's that giving us the stank-eye?"

Without asking who or where, Jake stabbed the cheese knife into a wedge of Roquefort and muttered, "Someone I used to work with in Anti-Rackets."

In case she could read lips, I turned my back to the room and faced him. "Some 'one'? Come on, give me some credit. The way that woman has been staring at you, if she was road tar, you'd be buried in a thick coat of black goo right now."

"Enough, okay. By the way, it's called 'eye-fucking'. Look and learn. It's a standard police technique."

I mouthed "eye-fucking."

"Yup." He tucked his warm fingers under my elbow and guided me to the bar. "What would you like to drink?"

"I'd like to know who she is."

"You just don't quit, do you?" He handed me his plate and asked for two glasses of South African red. "We may need to come back later." We cleared the clot of barflies, picked up cutlery and turned for the seating area. Ms. No-Name blocked our path. For a plus-sized lady she sure moved fast.

"Margie! Hey." Jake's greeting was as genuine as a corn dog. "How're you doing?"

Up close, her short haircut, like her too-tight suit, was expensive, but her makeup sat on her rough complexion like fat on cold soup stock. She leaned closer, edging me aside and pressing her forearm against Jake's.

"Same old, same old. Still living an elevator life." Her voice was so deep I wanted to toss in a penny and make a wish. "No highs, no lows. A few jerks every now and then."

She let out a volley of harsh laughter. For all the attention I was getting from her, I might as well have been a tablecloth. "How 'bout you?"

"Keeping well."

We edged around a group of people, trying to escape: she trailed along. Jake stopped at a café table for two. I cleared my throat. Her eyes, the color of pencil lead, bored into mine. Even though we were the same height her glare made me feel like I was short. What passed for a smile barely cracked her lips.

"And you would be?"

"Mr. Barclay's business associate." The expression, 'if looks could kill' flashed through my mind.

She made a rude noise with her mouth. "Really?"

Come on, bitch. That's the best you've got? I stood tall to show more cleavage and tried on a disdainful eye-fucking expression.

Jake put the glasses of wine down, rested his palm on my shoulder and said, "Kenora, Margery Benvenuto, a former work colleague."

Benvenuto–didn't that mean welcome in Italian? Not this time. Margie was as welcoming as barbed wire.

"So Marge, you two used to work together?"

Mottles of red arced up her neck and stained her cheeks. I nibbled a celery stick, brushed against Jake's arm, showed lots of teeth then tilted my head so that my earrings caught the light.

"Don't fuckin' call me Marge." She gave me a visual wedgie then turned at an angle to block me out with her shoulder. I knew that one–the blade stance. "Well, then. Good luck to ya, Bud."

"Thanks." He was glaring with that squinty-eyed volcanic expression he'd worn when he talked about his ex-wife.

An emotional tug-of-war animated the woman's features. "I still owe you, Big Guy." Her mouth pinched like a paper clip. She feinted a punch at his bicep. "If you'll excuse me, I'm off to gore myself at the buffet. Catch you some other time." She turned on her sensible-heeled pumps and slipped into the crowd.

"I'll be right back."

Jake wheeled away to the bar, returning with a bottle of wine and a tumbler filed with ice and dark liquor. He shrugged his suit jacket onto the back of his chair, sat down and began to alternately drink then eat as he greeted passing clients, standing up to make conversation or introduce me to new ones. When the pace slowed he sat, stretched out his long legs and stared speculatively at me. He stroked the back of my hand with one elegant thick finger.

"That frock is very flattering."

Frock? Flames wafted up from my groin. I shifted in my seat, trying to find a spot that wasn't throbbing.

"Thank you. It's nice to get dressed up."

"I've been thinking about what's under there."

I drained the wine in my glass. He refilled it. I played with my food for a few minutes.

"What was that about with Margie? Her bitterness was positively viral. I feel like I need a cleansing."

"Never mind Margie. She likes to decant her bile in public places."

"Jesus."

"No, Lucifer. Exorcism is the only thing that'll fix her. One of the few women I've ever called the 'c' word. To her face."

"You must have done something really bad for her to act like that."

He tossed his fork onto the plate and swiped the napkin across his mouth. "No. I didn't do anything, that's why she's acting like that. She wanted: I didn't want. It was a long time ago but she's always carried a grudge for longer than it takes to treat herpes."

"Really?"

"Yes, really. Now maybe you'll take the hint when I don't want to tell you something. The bottom line is, I preferred women. For Margie, I was supposed to be some sort of trial run to the other side. Please close your mouth. Half eaten food is not attractive."

He stalked off and came back with a plate of shrimp and chicken satay, more cheese, a side of grapes and a bottle of red wine.

"Wait, wait. She wanted you to have sex with her but…but what?"

"Forget it." He went back to forking wild rice pilaf into his mouth. I polished off the cheese and fruit.

"Well, well. You've certainly had some interesting experiences with women, haven't you? God, I'm beginning to feel boringly normal."

He stood up abruptly. "I'm going for dessert. Want some?"

"Sure. Bring an assortment. Please."

40

"*L*et's walk. I need to burn off some energy."

Jake was silent as we strolled from the Convention Centre through the nearly empty hallways underneath Union Station past the sports displays and giveaway cars to the Air Canada Centre lobby. He didn't lope along as usual but slowed so that I could keep up in my high heels and not look like a dope. It was starting to drizzle as we jay-walked across Bay Street to the parking lot where Manny was waiting. He greeted us warmly and opened the car doors.

I sank back, resting my forehead against the cool of the passenger side rear window as I listened to the muted hiss of the big car's wheels on the wet pavement.

"I've had too much wine."

"That you did." Jake tugged my hand into his lap and played with my fingers. His lap was very warm.

"You kept pouring and pouring."

"You kept drinking and drinking."

"My head's starting to throb. I think Marge put a curse on me."

He pulled me close. "You need coffee."

"I'm all Tim'd out."

"I'll make you an espresso. With a chaser of Fernet-Branca."

"You stock Italian digestif? I'm impressed. Can I have a double?"

"Anything you want."

He fiddled with the audio controls. A velvet-voiced Radio-Canada announcer introduced a Brahms concerto. A swell of strings filled the car. After a few more minutes staring at the hypnotizing swipe of the wipers across sparkling raindrops, I closed my eyes and surrendered to how good I felt.

"Rise and shine, wino."

Jake was shaking my shoulder. My eyes ached from the inside. We were stopped by the back steps of the office. Manny stood by my door with a gazebo-sized umbrella. The path from the lot— finally paved—glistened under the amber security lights.

"Where are we going?"

"I promised you coffee. My place."

My first week on the job Seta, our Office Administrator, mentioned in passing that Jake didn't have far to commute to work. She went on to explain that when the side-by-side robber-baron mansions Jake purchased were being renovated, he'd made the top floor of the main building his residence. Everyone at work knew where he lived but Bosco was the only one who'd been through the locked door that was almost invisible within the carved wooden paneling in the hallway.

The cool damp air cut the edges of fog from my brain. Jake and Manny were having a quiet conversation. I swung my legs to the ground and straightened with a groan. My left foot had cramped. The Town Car disappeared down the lane with a wink of tail lights.

"What day is it?" I leaned on Jake's arm as we climbed the steps to the rear entrance.

"Friday. Almost Saturday. Worried someone might see us?"

"A bit."

He locked the metal door to the main floor of the office and reset the alarm, walked six steps to a recessed keypad to disarm a second security system and unlocked the door leading to his living quarters. He guided me up a wide flight of stairs carpeted with an antique runner. At the top, he punched in another series of numbers then pushed open a carved wooden frieze door he said had graced an old Spanish church.

I dropped my clutch purse on an upholstered bench near the door and looked around. A pair of silver candlestick lamps glowed on a wooden sideboard, flanked by a vase of exotic blooms. An intricately patterned ruby-toned Persian carpet covered the plank floor. The unadorned walls shone like fresh butter. The smoky tones of Oleta Adams and a tenor sax floated in the air.

"Lovely." I untied the suede bow on one shoe, kicked it off and reached for the other.

"Leave them on. It's okay." He stroked my wrist, leaving an electric trail. "I believe beautiful things should be treated well, but gently used."

He knelt to replace my shoe, slipping a warm palm under my heel as he guided my toes under the instep strap. Goosebumps stippled my forearms. He rose with a smooth motion to face me.

"What?"

"In the light, the raindrops in your hair sparkle like jewels," he said.

He ruffled the curls at my temples then leaned in to nibble my bottom lip. He tasted of whisky and crème brûlée. Just when I was feeling too breathless to stand, he stepped away then clasped me under the elbows.

"Come with me."

He ushered me down the passageway to a large kitchen straight out of *House & Homes* magazine. I sank into a saddle-seat stool in front of the breakfast bar, tugging the narrow hem of my skirt over my knees. Jake pulled out his cuff-links and tossed them into a pottery bowl on the counter, folded over his cuffs and rolled the sleeves up to his elbows. Staring at those meaty wrists and arms made my pulse speed up. My head felt heavy. I leaned my elbows on the counter and rested my face between my palms.

He pushed buttons on a commercial coffee machine tucked into a corner and organized a pair of cups and saucers on the granite counter top.

"I had no idea you had barista skills."

"I'm a man of many talents."

I'll bet you are, Jake Barclay, I thought. "I'm intrigued."

He regaled me with the story of how he'd acquired the property at an estate sale. "Swear to god," he said, "the house hadn't been touched in forty years. And the cat-piss smell! The offer to purchase was signed on the hood of my unmarked cruiser."

"Sounds like quite an adventure."

"It was," he said, handing me my coffee and leaning his hip against the edge of the island. Unconsciously, he scratched a spot on his left side. For a guy his age he was taut in all the proper places. "I like adventure."

Oh, boy. A pang of longing clogged my throat. I quickly swallowed the rest of my coffee. Jake was busy loading up a serving tray with cheese and biscuits and a bottle of brandy. I snuck a quick look at my watch, wondering what I should do next. Jake made the decision for me.

He picked up the tray and gestured with his finger to the far side of the room. "Want to have a quick bite?"

"I do. Thanks." He meant food. Only food.

I plunked myself in the middle of a deep coral love seat with my knees primly together and my feet planted on the floor. He hooked the toe of his shoe around the leg of a leather ottoman and sat across from me. It was almost hypnotic watching him pouring and arranging. Was there anything he wasn't good at?

He held out a cracker topped with a thick ooze of Riopelle cheese. I closed my eyes and sighed at the creamy richness on my tongue.

He patted the space beside his thigh.

"Want to put your feet up?" A long muscle in my calf spasmed as he loosened my shoes and slipped them off. He lightly caressed the quivering until it subsided. "Don't be nervous. Nothing will happen that you don't want." He handed me a crystal snifter half-filled with amber liquid. "Calvados. Did you know Napoleon's soldiers used it as an antiseptic and anesthetic?"

I inhaled then took a cautious sip. "Good grief, but this is amazing." The elixir slid down my throat, adding fuel to my smoldering inner fire.

"Dessert?" he said with a shy smile. I knew that I was what he wanted for dessert. There was no denying it—he was certainly what I wanted.

"How come the snifters have a thumbprint on one side?" I dropped my gaze from his mouth to his hands. "And your initials?"

"My daughter bought them as a retirement gift."

"Ah. Detective. Thumb print. I get it."

He cupped his right hand around the arch of my foot. "You have a run in your stocking."

Taking care not to spill my drink I straightened and craned my neck to see. "Ah, nuts. I got them on sale at Bernards. Can you imagine, the full price was $37.00?"

HIs fingers trailed upwards, setting off tremors in my belly. "There's another one halfway up your shin."

Our eyes met. I said slowly, "Guess I'll have to take them off."

He blinked a few times, nodded then pointed me to the powder room in the front hall. I snatched up my purse then pressed my back against the bathroom door and composed myself. The wine buzz was gone: I was definitely *compos mentis*.

I knew I wouldn't be turning away from whatever might come. I smiled at myself in the mirror. From *whoever* might come.

The ruined pantyhose I tossed into a brass waste basket. It took me three minutes to rinse my mouth, swab under my arms and between my legs with a mini towel I'd stashed in my bag then slather scented moisturizer on my neck, arms and legs. When I returned, Jake was seated on the ottoman with his loafers off, displaying maroon socks festooned with tumbling ice cubes. I sat opposite him. He lifted my feet onto his lap and began stroking from my ankles to the hem of my dress.

"That feels nice."

He lifted his hand. "Nice?"

"Okay then, soothing." I wasn't going to say arousing. Yet.

"Soothing wasn't what I had in mind." He circled my ankle with his thumb and forefinger. "What's this bumpy ridge on the inside of your calf?"

"My brothers and I were playing in an abandoned barn. I jumped from the hay loft and and got slashed by a barrel hoop."

"Ouch." With him rubbing and sending high voltage currents through my body, it was hard to focus. "Your skin is so soft."

I glanced at the empty glass in my lap. Where did the brandy go?

He said, "I can take that if you'd like."

"What *do* you like, Jake?"

The darkness was in his eyes, but without shadows this time. He draped one hand over my knee. The light pressure of his long circling fingers rocked me, and I imagined them skimming across my flesh, tantalizing me into finally letting myself go.

"Dark chocolate, good wine, sun-dried sheets. You."

"Oh my." I wasn't nervous but I wanted to be certain. I started to repeat what he'd said at my house. "I think it would be better if I..."

"What are you afraid of?" he said, lifting his hands. My skin chilled. I wanted that heat back. I needed the heat.

"Nothing. Lots of things."

"Me?"

"No."

"You sound surprised."

"This isn't something I expected."

"Define 'this'."

"Being here. With you again. The boss."

"I'm not your boss, Kenora. Especially now. You feel harassed?" He was serious.

"No."

"Will you be honest with me?"

"Yes."

"And I with you. The rest, we'll muddle through." He lifted my feet from the ottoman, picked up the tray and carried it to the kitchen. I followed and leaned against the island, clutching the cool stone counter top.

"What are you afraid of, Jake?"

Some 'thing' shimmered through the three feet of granite and dimly lit air separating us. He leaned against the refrigerator door and folded his arms.

"As you noted, I haven't had much luck with women."

"There aren't many of us like your ex-wife and Margie, you know."

"My left brain knows that but I don't want to mess up again."

"Who does? It hurts like hell." I snorted. "Been there, done that, cried me a river. You said you've learned from past experiences. Could be time for things to change."

"A guy my age has baggage."

"Some folks have hatboxes; some have hockey bags. I've got scars too, Jake."

"Haven't we all?"

I pulled aside the neckline of my dress, pointing to a puckered ridge near the swell of my right breast and an untidy dark line that started just below my clavicle. "Real scars. Not just from childhood accidents."

He stretched out his index finger, stopping short of contact. "Does that make you self-conscious?"

I took a couple of deep breaths then reached for his left hand and pressed it against my chest. His heat against my flesh felt right.

"I've had a couple of lumps removed." I caught his look. "Not cancerous, but it made me rethink a lot of things. Then my mother died. I promised myself I wouldn't do anything more in my life that made me feel like my skin was too tight."

"Is it tight now?"

"No."

He drew small circles with the tips of his fingers. "You are so warm." He smelled of what I had come to know as Jake; an intoxicating blend of powerful man, starched cotton, crushed garden herbs and citrus soap.

"Actually, I'm hot."

His fingertips outlined my breasts. "How does this make you feel?"

"Loose," I said, drawing out the sound. "I mean relaxed."

"That's good. The loose part, I mean."

I slid my arms around his waist and pressed my head to his shoulder. My hands barely overlapped the valley of his spine. A rush of thoughts ordered into clear impressions: how strong the thud of his heart was, how comfortably my forehead fitted between his jaw and his throat, how precisely his hands tucked into the hollow of my back as he traced the swell of my buttocks.

I murmured into his shirt. "What happens now?"

"This." He lifted my chin and lowered his mouth to mine. Sparkles danced behind my eyes.

Much later, when we'd talk about that rainy evening, we'd agree that the kiss lasted a long time and that our lips were trembling; that my knees buckled and he had to back up against the island, squeezing me against the length of his body until our breathing synchronized; that without a word, we finally untangled from the embrace and sauntered hip bumping against hip, to his bedroom.

I stopped in the doorway. An Art Deco lamp cast a pool of jeweled light over the night table and expanse of bed. Music drizzled gently from overhead speakers. A silver vase crammed with fresh lavender sweetened the air. Sheer curtains billowed gently in the breeze from the open window.

"Come." The comforting pressure of his elbow against mine propelled me across the thick pale carpet.

He sat me on the edge of the bed, wrenched off his tie and knelt to one side of my legs. I unbuttoned his shirt, drawing my palms from his neck to his waist, pressing my lips where my fingers had been, aware of the tremor in his muscles as he held himself still.

"May I?"

He reached around, eased the zipper down the back of my dress, slid it to my hips then sat back on his heels. I rose and shrugged it to the floor, leaving myself clad only in my lace push-up bra and sensible French-cut lace panties. Still kneeling, he traced the puckery scars above my knees. The room was warm but gooseflesh sprouted on my arms.

"Arthroscopy?"

"Yes. Basketball, volleyball and hockey. Every game I play is a contact sport."

"I'm intrigued." He grinned. "And hopeful." Nodding, I stroked his cheek.

He pressed a kiss to the tender flesh on the inside of my left thigh then stripped off his shirt and flipped back the duvet. He repositioned himself between my knees, pressing gently with his elbows until I stopped resisting and let them fall open. This time when he took my mouth there was a potent urgency to his explorations. I clutched his biceps, conscious of the play of hard muscle under my fingers. He pulled himself away, thrust his arms out at his sides and rested on his haunches. Tipping forward, I steadied myself with one hand on his chest and burrowed my nose into the crease of his arm, sucking in lungsful of aroused, sweaty Jake until I was dizzy and had to sit up. He was watching me. And smiling.

It had been a very long time since I'd undressed a grown man but I hadn't forgotten how. I unzipped his fly, unbuckled his belt and yanked it free of its loops, just as I had in my fantasy.

He rose to let his trousers fall to the floor. "Tada."

I cracked up. "The socks and leopard-skin patterned briefs are really something. All you need is a black rectangle over your eyes."

He smothered my laughter with a flurry of urgent kisses.

"Next time," I said, "you won't need a whip and a chair."

He looked surprised. Then chuckling, he stripped off his socks and stretched out on his stomach beside me, leaning on his elbows. Not worrying about what he might think, I stared assessingly.

Jake was even more splendid in lamplight—the broad expanse of his thick muscles, the sleek grey-brown hair framing his nipples and arrowing down his muscular belly rendered me flushed and breathless. There was no doubt he was aroused, and comfortable with it. His tanned wideness was interrupted by a brace of light colored scars under his arms and a puckered hole under his right rib cage. The thought that someone had tried to kill him made me cringe.

"And this time?"

I took a deep breath then turned my back. He sat up and unhooked my bra using both hands, not bothering with a showy two-finger flick of the hooks. When I didn't move, he nudged my shoulders and shifted me around.

"I know I'm not supposed to compare a woman to food, but...."

"Go ahead," I said. "I want to know. Now is not the time for political correctness."

"Your skin reminds me of butterscotch." His voice was hoarse. My mouth watered. With trembling fingers, then the tip of his tongue, Jake traced the scars on my chest, stimulating every nerve, evaporating the last of my nervousness. I couldn't take in enough oxygen. "Warm and pliant and smooth. That day in the elevator...." He buried his face against my neck. His breath shivered the hair at my nape. "My foundation shifted."

I cupped my palms under his chin and pressed a lingering kiss to his mouth. "Mine did too."

I raised my hips and shimmied out of my panties. He tossed his briefs away. My mind emptied of everything but what was happening in the moment. Gasping and murmuring, we busied ourselves exploring each other's flesh.

"God, you are so beautiful," he murmured.

"I thought you were beautiful, the first time I saw you."

He drove his fingers into my curls, smoothing his thumbs over my temples then tipping my chin to expose my throat. He licked a sizzling path to my mouth then across the swells of my breasts. Dipping his head, he caught first one nipple then the other between taut lips, tugging them firm and leaving me scalded. A thought intruded for a nano-second. The man wasn't trying to tune my erogenous zones like I was an antique radio. I felt bold and curious.

"Do you mind if I watch you?" I said when I was able to catch my breath. Never had I been able to talk like this with a man in bed. Or out of bed.

His laugh was rumbling and suggestive. "My pleasure. And, I hope, yours."

The charged stroke of his tongue trailing the dark line bisecting my belly to the folds between my thighs set me on fire.

His probing fingers were electrifying. He glanced up; his eyes were wide with desire. The air filled with the rich aroma of our arousal. I desired him. I needed no time to second-guess being naked in Jake's arms, in his bedroom. I'd never felt as aflame and sexy as I was with him.

"Do you understand how much I want to make love with you?" The husky, hesitant voice belonged to a Jake I didn't yet know.

"I want you, too. Badly."

He grinned like a conquering warrior. "Excellent."

He tightened his grip around my shoulders, pressing until we tumbled side by side to the cool sheets. We rolled and he covered my body with his from knee to navel, sparking my nerves until I was light-headed from the hard, hot weight of him.

I pushed my palm against his chest. "Jake. Wait."

"What?"

His tumescence in full view, he sat back on his heels and languidly drew his fingertips across my belly. As much as I ached to tangle my fingers in his dark triangle and stroke him witless, I aimed my gaze on his throat.

"What about...ah, protection?"

"You mean a condom?" He eased into a seated position with his legs crossed. "A prophylactic?"

"Y-yes."

"Geez. I might have some." He sounded stricken. "Wait here."

With an easy, long-legged stride, he disappeared into the bathroom. He had a magnificent bum. I heard the whine of his electric toothbrush. The toilet flushed and water ran in the sink. He returned, squinting as he rotated a small box from side to side.

"The damned print is damned tiny." I sat up and handed him his reading glasses. His voice barely above a whisper, he said, "The best before date was eight months ago."

"Pardon?" *Merda. Porca troia.* Crap. "You're kidding me." Frowning, he flung the box into the wastebasket. "Expired."

I didn't know whether to laugh or cry. He massaged the bridge of his nose with his thumb and forefinger.

"Who was the last man you were with, Kenora?"

I hugged my knees to my chest, not bothering to cover myself. "My ex-husband."

"How long ago?"

I squirmed. "Three years, four months and twenty-nine days." Jake's expression began to clear. "Before he started to sample at the fool-around buffet."

"Since then?"

"Born again virgin."

He blew out a long breath. "I haven't been with a woman in at least that long."

"Unlike the condoms, you haven't passed your best before date, have you?" I said.

"I sure as hell hope not." He tossed the glasses beside the lamp and sat on the bed. "You healthy?" I pressed my body against his broad back and began rubbing his temples. He leaned against my hands with a deep sigh.

"Yes."

"Me too." He shifted position and wrapped his arms around me.

"Then I guess we're okay."

"When did you get that tattoo?" He stroked the pair of rune symbols on my side, halfway between my armpit and my hip.

"Maggie and I got inked during a boozy weekend in Vegas." I held up eight fingers. "It means strength, power, danger, wildness, potential, health, healing and virility."

"Guess I have my work cut out for me. And this scar on your belly?" He traced the line above my public hair with his index finger, launching a sunburst of sensations.

"A hysterectomy when I was forty."

"Looks like a smile."

"I'll remember that."

"Listen," he said diffidently, "there's no rush, if...."

I curled my fingers into his chest hair and tugged. "Like hell there's not."

He growled, raised my hand to his mouth and licked a sinuous trail from the base of my thumb to the inside of my elbow. I focused on breathing as he kissed a meandering path from my collarbone to my breasts.

"Come here, you."

Jake's intoxicating scent tripped my on switch, rocketing pleasure deep in my core. Pressing gently, he tipped us over. We were joined breast to knee. His erection was hot and firm against my swollen cleft.

His long, strong body was as hard as mine was molten. I writhed deliberately. He moaned and tried to shift aside. I mirrored Jake's movements, raising my hips as I stroked his back. I gripped his buttocks. He stilled and raised his head. We stared into each other's eyes for a long moment. Then slowly, oh so slowly, he slid inside my heat.

For the next few hours we didn't say much of anything while we journeyed to the edge of just enough.

ABOUT THE AUTHOR

Hyacinthe, an award-winning short-story writer, is a founding member and Past President of the Writers' Community of York Region. She's a member of Sisters in Crime, Crime Writers of Canada, Romance Writers of America and the Alliance of Independent Authors.

Her work has been published in Herotica 7, Whispered Words and Allucinor, The Elements of Romance anthologies. She is the author of newspaper and magazine articles, the *Kenora & Jake* series, poetry, non-fiction and two blogs.

Check out Hyacinthe's writing at:
https://writeinplainsight.com
and
https://hyacinthemillerbooks.com

ALSO BY HYACINTHE M. MILLER

Coming Soon

The Fifth Man, Book 2 of the *Kenora & Jake* Series

She's finished paying the no-name guys who renovated her house. Her new career as a private investigator is going well and she's adapting to the rules. Her second-chance romance with Jake Barclay makes her happy but she's still cautious.

Life is back on an even keel. Or so Kenora thinks.

When her best friend Maggie drops off two boxes of documents stashed by Kenora's mother before she died, her life is upended. Again.

The incendiary secrets those boxes hold send Kenora on an international quest to investigate the truth about who she really is. Her life will be changed in ways she could not have imagined.

I'd appreciate you leaving a review on the site where you bought my book. Reviews are important to writers and help new readers find new novels like Kenora Reinvented. *Share your thoughts with me via my website, on social media, with your friends, book club and book bloggers. Thanks.*

Made in the USA
Monee, IL
06 December 2019